Short Story Collections by Joyce Carol Oates

The Frenzy: Stories

Flint Kill Creek: Stories of Mystery and Suspense

Zero-Sum: Stories

Extenuating Circumstances: Stories of Crime and Suspense

The (Other) You

The Ruins of Contracoeur and Other Presences

Night, Neon: Tales of Mystery and Suspense

Night-Gaunts and Other Tales of Suspense

Beautiful Days: Stories

DIS MEM BER and Other Stories of Mystery and Suspense

The Doll-Master and Other Tales of Terror

Lovely, Dark, Deep: Stories

High Crime Area: Tales of Darkness and Dread

Black Dahlia & White Rose: Stories

The Corn Maiden and Other Nightmares

Give Me Your Heart: Tales of Mystery and Suspense

Sourland: Stories

Dear Husband: Stories

Wild Nights!: Stories About the Last Days of Poe, Dickinson, Twain, James, and Hemingway

The Museum of Dr. Moses: Tales of Mystery and Suspense

High Lonesome: New and Selected Stories 1966–2006

The Female of the Species: Tales of Mystery and Suspense

I Am No One You Know: Stories

Faithless: Tales of Transgression

The Collector of Hearts: New Tales of the Grotesque

Will You Always Love Me? and Other Stories

Demon and Other Tales

Haunted: Tales of the Grotesque

Where Are You Going, Where Have You Been?: Selected Early Stories

Where Is Here?: Stories

Heat and Other Stories

Oates in Exile

The Assignation: Stories

Raven's Wing: Stories

Wild Saturday

Last Days: Stories

A Sentimental Education: Stories

All the Good People I've Left Behind

Night-Side: Eighteen Tales

The Poisoned Kiss and Other Stories from the Portuguese

The Seduction & Other Stories

Where Are You Going, Where Have You Been?: Stories of Young America

The Goddess and Other Women

The Hungry Ghosts: Seven Allusive Comedies

Marriages and Infidelities: Short Stories

The Wheel of Love and Other Stories

Upon the Sweeping Flood and Other Stories

By the North Gate

THE FRENZY

THE FRENZY

Stories

JOYCE CAROL OATES

HOGARTH
London/New York

Hogarth
An imprint of Random House
A division of Penguin Random House LLC
1745 Broadway, New York, NY 10019
randomhousebooks.com
penguinrandomhouse.com

LIBRARY OF CONGRESS CATALOGING-IN-PUBLICATION DATA
Names: Oates, Joyce Carol, author
Title: The frenzy : stories / by Joyce Carol Oates.
Description: London ; New York : Hogarth, 2026.
Identifiers: LCCN 2025037743 (print) | LCCN 2025037744 (ebook) |
ISBN 9780593978115 hardcover | ISBN 9780593978139 ebook
Subjects: LCGFT: Short stories | Fiction | Short stories
Classification: LCC PS3565.A8 F74 2026 (print) | LCC PS3565.A8 (ebook)
LC record available at https://lccn.loc.gov/2025037743
LC ebook record available at https://lccn.loc.gov/2025037744

Printed in the United States of America on acid-free paper

1st Printing

First Edition

BOOK TEAM: Production editor: Loren Noveck • Managing editor: Rebecca Berlant • Production manager: Jane Haas Sankner • Copy editor: Aja Pollock • Proofreaders: David Goehring, Su-Yee Lin, and Caitlin Van Dusen

Book design by Debbie Glasserman

The authorized representative in the EU for product safety and compliance is Penguin Random House Ireland, Morrison Chambers, 32 Nassau Street, Dublin D02 YH68, Ireland. https://eu-contact.penguin.ie

To Warren Frazier

CONTENTS

1.

THE FRENZY

Is the irrevocable, unforgivable act behind him, or ahead?

Early afternoon driving south on the Ocean Highway with the girl beside him. Passing Point Pleasant, New Jersey. Passing exits for Toms River. Something haphazard in his driving today which is unlike him.

Wind from the Atlantic rocking the Subaru Forester so he feels a thrill of, what is it, a tug like a tug of wills, invisible hands on the wheel which is *his wheel* so his reaction is to correct against the intrusion like the subterranean pull of sleep when he wakes in the morning in the dark before dawn stunned and exhausted by dreams.

Still, he is feeling reckless. *Young.*

"Is something wrong?"—the girl asks sharply.

How like this girl—(*this girl* to him, though she has a name)—to register the nuance of a moment, a half-moment when he'd (almost) lost control of the car.

Affably he tells her no, not a thing is wrong. Just *wind.*

Resenting the question, one of the girl's rude-child questions. Not that he will indicate resentment, his manner with the girl is more bemused, placating.

Leaving the Garden State Parkway for the Ocean Highway she'd asked if they could *please not talk* for just a while?—the view is so special, she doesn't want to be distracted.

The coastal view *is* special. Wintry Atlantic churning, frothing, glittering like a gigantic skin shaking itself, great galleon-clouds passing overhead torn and tattered by winds.

Still he's feeling rebuffed. Rebuked. *Please don't spoil things by talking.*

Wanting to protest: *she* has set things back into motion, not him. Calling him the night before, clandestine call at twelve-twenty A.M. when she'd known that he would be awake and his wife would be asleep because this is an intimacy he has shared with *the girl* to allow her to know how admirably she differs from *the wife.*

At the time she'd called he had (in fact) been lying in bed. Beside his (sleeping, oblivious) wife. Lying in bed and thinking of her, *the girl,* the *teenaged mistress,* what he would do with this girl or to this girl if they were alone together in some neutral space, an impersonal and unnamed space, a very private place, high-ceilinged luxury hotel room without windows or even a door; a floating kind of place, an off-shore kind of place, *soundproof.*

Making his way barefoot and unerring through the familiar dark of the bedroom to an adjacent room where his cell phone was charging like a heart detached from its body.

Hand shaking?—no, his hand *was not shaking.*

In the bedroom his wife slept unknowing.

In their rooms his teenaged children slept unknowing.

That giddy-drunken sensation of giving in, sinking, as if boneless, will-less, to which he was becoming addicted.

And now, next day, next afternoon driving south on the Ocean Highway along the Jersey coast with *the girl* beside him. Thrilled, exhilarated. Some kind of miracle. Never have predicted, for each time they'd said goodbye it has seemed to him the final time, the (sensible) (final) time.

But no, think again. For here he is, and Brianna is beside him. In that fraught period before Christmas when his life is about to shatter and re-organize itself.

In his elated state driving at just above the speed limit. Keeping to the right lane, letting others pass. Enormous trucks, impatient SUVs. No hurry about the drive, they will arrive at Cape May well before dusk.

He, so often impatient on the turnpike. Not impatient now.

As if, the girl beside him, he has all that he requires. So long as they are alone together, and she is in his custody, so to speak. *His* vehicle.

Through swaths of bright blinding sunshine punctuated by flitting shadows of storm clouds.

Brianna has been sitting forward in the passenger's seat, taking pictures with her iPhone. Marveling at the view. The boulder-strewn shore, wind-buffeted ocean waves. Light shivering and rippling to the horizon dissolved in mist. It is not, to Cassidy, an extraordinary ocean view but it *is* the Atlantic Ocean, a welcome change from the thunderous Jersey Turnpike and numbingly banal small cities, suburbs strewn out beside it.

Brianna's concentration appears to be genuine, unforced. He envies her this childlike enthusiasm, so different from her frequently sulky, peevish mood.

Teenaged mistress! What else can you expect.

In fact, Brianna is (nearly) twenty years old.

Her birthday is next month, January. Zodiac sign Capricorn (she'd told Cassidy).

Should a year's difference matter? If/when his wife discovers the liaison, if/when he decides to reveal it to her, an affair with a *twenty-year-old* seems slightly less reprehensible than an affair with a *teenager.*

In fact, a *teenager* known to the family, daughter of friends in Fair Hills.

Cassidy winces, considering. Feels like a thorn or thistle in his throat, isn't sure if he needs to cough, or to laugh.

Bastard, what the hell are you doing? Why's it feel so good?

Waves glittering to the horizon, pewter-colored, hypnotic. Cassidy is reminded of how he'd once purchased a ticket for a chartered boat out of Provincetown, taking passengers on a five-hour excursion out into the Atlantic. Fifteen miles from land? Fifteen *knots*?

Open ocean, immense sky, rocking boat, no sight of land. Mild sensation of panic.

After three hours the guide summoned passengers to hurry to the railing, the *Provincetown Princess* was cutting through a *plankton path:* a wide swath of ocean stretching out of sight where fish were feeding, thousands of fish, millions of fish, writhing silvery bodies in the dark water, savagely feeding, frenzied activity of a kind that Cassidy had never seen before, that left him appalled and shaken.

It was explained to observers that a concentration of plankton had drawn swarms of small fish to the area, in the millions; the concentration of small fish attracted larger fish, which devoured the smaller fish; and these predators attracted larger predators, to devour them. The popular term was *feeding frenzy.*

Along with other passengers Cassidy stared transfixed by the horror of it, repelled, yet unable to look away.

Feeling the first twinges of nausea. Mild at first, then not so mild.

Spread out before him was a region of unfathomable appetite: foaming, churning, flashing, quicksilver with the eel-like bodies of fish, a thrashing as of sheer boundless energy itself, to infinity. Life devouring life. Living creatures devouring themselves. The guide prattled on, reciting prepared words. *Are there sharks?*—children were asking. Passengers crowded at the railing, taking photographs. For always there must be the *taking of photographs,* to render any brutal scene merely aesthetic, entertaining.

An abrupt loathing of the ocean itself swept over Cassidy, the very sight, smell. What beauty there was in the ocean was a matter of distance, fairy lights twinkling on heavy, heaving water, not-seeing the *feeding frenzy* beneath the surface.

Is not all beauty a matter of distance, Cassidy thought. Resolutely not-seeing what is beneath the surface.

The ceaselessly rolling, jolting boat had been sickening to him too. Arrythmic, asymmetrical, unstoppable. That the heaving was *unstoppable* and that of his own volition he'd condemned himself to five hours of this misery further disgusted him.

Soon then Cassidy broke away from the railing. In a windowless lavatory below deck, sick to his stomach.

Heave out your guts. Flush toilet.

He'd been alone on the chartered boat, not yet married. Not yet with Charlotte whom he would marry within two years. No woman at his side to lay a hand on his arm, to comfort and distract.

I am here, I will not abandon you in your hour of need but yes of course!—you can abandon me.

Cassidy has an impulse to tell the girl beside him about the horror of the *feeding frenzy*—he likes to tell her about incidents out of his past, accounts he has embellished over a period of years, new to her and, if new to her, new to Cassidy as well.

Except: she'd pleaded with him, *Please let's not talk for a while, OK?*

Also, the *feeding frenzy* happened long ago, before Brianna was even born. Could be embarrassing to bring it up.

Next exit, Barnegat Light. Cassidy feels a pang of nostalgia. No children in this vehicle, no plans to exit, climb the winding steps to the top of the old lighthouse, peer at the ocean through mounted binoculars. Gulls and terns circling the balcony as if expecting to be fed.

If this were one of the family drives of years ago except of course *it is not.*

Does Cassidy miss being a daddy?—a daddy to small children? The overseer of so much emotion, a puppet-master whose arms can grow weary.

Cassidy half-expects Brianna to suggest exiting for the lighthouse, it's the sort of tourist attraction that might appeal to her, an occasion for girlish enthusiasm; great views of the ocean from the top of the lighthouse, pictures to take on her iPhone. But to Cassidy's surprise Brianna isn't absorbed by the view any longer but is peering at the phone in her hand, her shoulder turned from him as a child might do, hiding the little screen from adult scrutiny.

Scrolling through emails. Or Instagram, TikTok.

"Have you been taking some beautiful pictures?"—can't resist, innocently inquiring.

"Y-Yes! Yes. I have."

Smiling at Cassidy sidelong, quick flash of very dark eyes, almost shy.

Quicksilver as darting fish, churning scintillant in roiling water.

"Great. You can show me, later."

His own cell phone he'd switched off that morning before Varick Street. Wanting to be, for the next forty-eight hours or so, *off the grid.*

Cruel to refer to Brianna Rinzler as Cassidy's *teenaged mistress* since Brianna is (nearly) twenty years old and mature for her age; and she is Cassidy's *mistress* only intermittently, and unreliably.

Also, *mistress* is a comical word. Outdated, quaint.

Ten days before Christmas feels like an ultimatum. Not sure why.

Each time they've been together—five, six times—seven?—has seemed to be some sort of test, not yet resolved. Whatever is to be proven remains unproven.

He isn't desperate, yet. He doesn't intend to push the girl. He has leased the condo overlooking the East River but she has known this for a week at least, no need to dwell upon it. Knowing from experience that that is exactly what you don't do with them—*dwell upon a subject, push.*

His own daughters. Other men's daughters.

Not sure where they will end up today. Brianna doesn't like to make plans, shrinks from *premeditation.* Planning to have sex, for instance: *gross.* Planning an outing together, slipping away on a weekday, spontaneous, brazen—*cool.*

A child of upper-middle-class suburban privilege, not unlike Cassidy himself, accustomed to others taking charge, protecting her. Looking out for her as you'd look out for a blind person boldly stumbling with a cane, crossing a street. Out of husbandly/fatherly caution he'd made a reservation at the most highly rated inn in Cape May just in case.

Passing exits for Ocean City, Sea Isle City, toll bridge at Corson's Inlet, Seven Mile Beach. Coastal marshes, shore birds. Warbler migration in spring and fall, monarch butterfly migration in the fall . . . It has been years since Cassidy has driven this far south in New Jersey, years since he's hiked along the shore at Cape May Point State Park.

Amazing to think that he'd picked Brianna up in the late morning at a loft on Varick where (she says) she is staying with friends, having moved out of her parents' house in Fair Hills, New Jersey. He'd pulled up at the curb, she'd run out to him, to his vehicle, uncombed streaked-blond hair, unzipped jacket, tossed her neon-pink backpack (an eyesore: Cassidy winces at the sight) into the rear, and climbed into the Subaru half-falling beside him, turning her face to him startling in beauty, in trust, trust of *him.* Turning her face to be kissed, confident in being kissed, and kissed really hard, so she'd laughed, in mild protest.

"Hey. I've been missing you."

"I've missed *you.*"

He hadn't been angry with her then, isn't angry with her now.

That's the surprise of it, every time: how you forgive them.

He'd liked it, he'd liked the intimacy, the girl's breath smelled of sleep, just slightly stale, no time for mouthwash, toothpaste in her haste to see him.

Anywhere—out of the city! Cape May? Jersey coast?

So it's winter, what the hell.

Always a jolt when he sees the girl with the streaked-blond hair, futile to dwell upon how he distrusts her. For the fatal fact is, he's crazy about her.

Has to accept it. The obfuscation between them, on Brianna's part. Squid ink released in the water to blind, confound predators.

Final exit: Cape May. One of the first hotels they pass on Beach Avenue is the Cape May Heritage House, at which Cassidy has made a reservation. He tells Brianna he'd like to check into a hotel now, this hotel is said to be the best in Cape May, she can wait in the Subaru while he runs inside, he'll be just five minutes; but Brianna is impatient to get to the ocean, to the beach, as soon as possible. She doesn't give a damn where they stay, she says. It's three-twenty P.M. and the sun will be setting in an hour and she wants to get out of the damn car and *walk, run.*

Her skin is luminous-pale with indignation. Her inky-dark eyes are all-pupil. Pointless to argue with Brianna in this mood, Cassidy doesn't dare touch her as he'd like to: grip her shoulders and shake her hard, wipe that petulant look off her face.

Saying in his most reasonable voice they'll have time in the morning to walk on the beach, yes? All day tomorrow?

All day *tomorrow*? Brianna regards Cassidy as a child might regard an adult suggesting something so ridiculous, so hurtfully stupid, she cannot find words to oppose him but is struck dumb, mouth quavering.

Brianna zips up her bulky quilted jacket, pulls a crimson angora cap down over her forehead. Stamps her feet in Italian leather boots, a little horsey ready to gallop.

Telling Cassidy to just please let her out, if he doesn't want to walk right now. He can check into the inn by himself, she'll meet up with him later.

Jesus *no.*

Cassidy is panicked. What the hell is Brianna thinking?—running along the beach without him? All this way, fucking Cape May in December, she's suggesting getting out of the vehicle *without him*?

Stunning to realize, she's just a kid. She *is* a teenager. Impulsive, not thinking ahead, not thinking of anyone except herself. *Jesus.*

Silent on most of the drive as if she'd forgotten Cassidy's very existence, totally immersed in her damned phone—(Cassidy suspects Brianna of texting with unknown parties constantly, compulsively)—Brianna surprises him now with her sudden animation, as if a switch has been pulled.

Haphazardly Cassidy has been driving though the near-deserted historic district of Cape May. Desperate to interest the *teenaged mistress* in stately old Victorian-era architecture. Hotels, inns, charmingly quaint bed-and-breakfasts. Old Washington Inn, the Chalfonte Hotel. Our Lady Star of the Sea Catholic Church. Former gambling casino refashioned as an arcade. In the 1890s Cape May had a brief fashionable notoriety: horse-racing, yachting, gambling. A more genteel version of Atlantic City.

Intrigued, Brianna is taking pictures again through the passenger's window.

Cassidy remarks it's *off-season* here but also *off-century.*

Like a *time-warp,* Brianna says. She loves these old-time places!

But there are few people visible in the historic district, little traffic. Not all the specialty shops and boutiques are open. Some hotels are obviously closed not just for the season but permanently. Against the moldering stucco wall of the grand old Atlantic Hotel, folded-up café umbrellas like upright corpses.

Darkened restaurants, a tavern with a red neon sign lamely advertising *Molson's.* Sand-swept crumbling sidewalks below the boardwalk.

Folly to have come here, Cassidy thinks.

Over the water the sky is glazed with an Arctic pallor. Massive snow clouds like battalions are about to smother the light. The last thing Cassidy wants to do is hike along the edge of the ocean, he's dying for a drink in a cozy bar, still it's a relief at least to have stirred some emotion, some *feeling* in Brianna.

Easily bored: adolescents. Notoriously.

"Come *on,*" Brianna says, poking Cassidy. Suddenly playful, forgiving.

". . . trapped in this car for *hours.* Jesus!"

Brianna is roused to childlike elation. The sulky mouth is beautiful again, smiling. Eyes glistening. She's all elbows, knees, uncoiling legs. Cassidy recalls his daughters, his son, when they were small children, sudden explosive energy. When they still adored their daddy, never doubted or distrusted their daddy.

Before Cassidy can properly park the Subaru beside one of the sand-swept walkways Brianna scrambles out. Winding a long crimson scarf around her neck. Tugging on matching mittens. In the knee-high leather boots she resembles a springy colt yearning to run wild along the beach while daddy-Cassidy is left behind to lock up the stodgy vehicle.

He will punish her, Cassidy thinks calmly. That will be his reward, once they are alone in the room he'd reserved in the Cape May Heritage House.

Laughing and waving at the long-legged girl in the crimson cap, hurrying to catch up with her.

In love! This is how we behave when we are in love.

Hiking at the water's edge. The wind is colder than Cassidy has anticipated, razor-sharp, making his eyes water. Beside him the girl is exclaiming in excitement about the beauty of the ocean, the "unspoiled" beach, funny little birds—*sandpipers?*—pecking in the hard-packed sand. She seizes Cassidy's gloved hand in her mittened hand and tugs him along, swinging their arms, forcing an antic mood in a way Charlotte would never have done even in her youth.

. . . heedless in love, crazy for love. See us.

Except for an elderly gentleman walking his dog some distance away, both taking mincing steps, the beach and the boardwalk are deserted. No one to observe the lovers, no one to envy the middle-aged man with the much-younger girl taking a romantic (if windy) walk along the beach at Cape May in December.

Folly, Cassidy thinks, slightly out of breath, gripping the mittened hand hard—*fate.*

Badly he would like to ask Brianna why she hadn't answered his calls for five days. Why she shrinks from acknowledging that since he has acquired a condo in Manhattan there is no reason for her to continue to stay with friends in a drafty loft when she might move in with him.

But Cassidy knows: at the first sound of reproach, at the first demand, Brianna will flee. Any hint of *stern daddy.* Can't risk it.

In their most intimate moments Cassidy has felt the tension in the girl's slender body, nerves strung tight as wires. Brianna seems to swing between two moods: intense enthusiasm, intense repugnance. It's Cassidy's fancy (admiring, awed) that Brianna thinks with her entire body, strained, finely trembling. Her skin is always slightly feverish, a few degrees above normal, unlike his own which feels lukewarm to him, only half-alive. Or maybe it's the effect of pills, little white pills Brianna carries loose in her pockets, amphetamines, opioids, antidepressants, traded and bartered among her friends as casually as in another era children shared sticks of spearmint gum.

Brianna has dropped his hand, pulled away from him. Venturing so close to the spattering surf that her tight-fitting jeans are dappled with wet.

Despite his discomfort Cassidy likes it that Brianna Rinzler has led him to a place, a specific place, to which he'd never have gone except in response to a whim of hers. He likes it that he is doing something out of character, that would astonish his wife, his children, his friends, his business associates, could they know.

Astonish, dismay. The realization that they'd never known him.

Also, Cassidy likes it that Brianna is nearly as tall as he, in the Italian boots he'd purchased for her. In stocking-feet, and barefoot, she will be much shorter.

And when they are both sitting, or when they are lying down together, and the girl is naked, soft-skinned as a mollusk out of its shell, Cassidy looms over her.

Cassidy lowers his head against the wind and the freezing ocean spray. Hurrying to keep up.

Trotting along the beach at Cape May, in December! Forty-six years old. In the company of the *teenaged mistress.* In L.L.Bean fleece-lined suede jacket, corduroy trousers. His male vanity is such, he is even hatless. Freezing yet uncomplaining. Short of breath yet invigorated. His pulses ring with an animal excitement indistinguishable from dread, panic: a flood of adrenaline, as if his life were at risk.

Brianna would be furious to know that Cassidy thinks of her, even half-seriously, as his *teenaged mistress.* Sexist-asshole thing to say, shitty, stupid. She'd slap his face. Hit him with clenched fists. Tell him to *fuck off, go to hell.*

As it is, Brianna sometimes jokes uneasily about the age difference between them. Yet, she'd pursued *him.* That has to be acknowledged.

Cassidy catches up with Brianna, slides an arm around her shoulders to rein her in. His prancing little horsey! Kisses her mouth but the gesture is awkward, clumsy; their teeth strike together, Brianna winces. Her lips are luxuriantly cold, icy-cold, a pleasurable shock against Cassidy's skin.

"Hey—I love you," he says, as she turns away, "but you know that"—but the surf is too noisy, Brianna seems not to hear.

Last time they'd been together Brianna asked him not to talk *like that.* Hinting that she should move in with him now that he has acquired a condo with a "fantastic" fifteenth-floor view of the East River—*No, please.*

Still, Cassidy isn't discouraged. Following after Brianna.

Beside Brianna. He will wear the impetuous girl down, he is sure.

At this moment the cloud bank shifts and the waning sun glares, broken on the waves, eerily beautiful, blinding.

What scares me, how people disappear.

Turns out, there are friends of Brianna's who have *disappeared.*

A boy named Colin from her high school in Fair Hills, six weeks after he'd started classes at Stanford he'd gone hiking in the Santa Cruz Mountains and never returned. His parents flew out to Palo Alto, stayed for months, police looked for him, there were posters everywhere, search teams, but—he'd just *disappeared.* And a girl in Brianna's residence at Bard, she'd *disappeared* in New York City, or anyway she'd taken the train into the city for some purpose unknown to her suitemates and never returned.

One of Brianna's own relatives, when she'd been a little girl. (Male) cousin of her mother's said to have *disappeared* in Tangier.

How serious Brianna is, pressing into Cassidy's arms! So fascinated by her, often Cassidy scarcely hears what she is saying.

Confiding in Cassidy, in a small hushed voice, in the deep of night in Cassidy's arms, how there was this boy she knew, in fact she'd been staying with him earlier in the semester after she'd dropped out of Bard and came to New York where (it turned out) he was dealing drugs, mainly pot but coke too when he could get hold of it, he'd been at Bard but transferred to NYU, but he'd dropped out of NYU too (which Brianna hadn't known, exactly) and was living over on Avenue A. He'd (evidently) made some enemies which was a serious mistake, whoever they were they broke into his place when no one was there and trashed it and next time (this was after Brianna moved out, to Varick Street, it was a scene she couldn't handle) they killed him. Just—killed him.

Stabbed him to death, like thirty-seven stab wounds. Torso, neck. Groin.

The body was in the apartment for three days, only because someone in the building noticed the smell were police called. *It was, like, an actual—murder. Like something on TV.*

In a slow wondering voice Brianna spoke as if she doubted the authenticity or even the plausibility of what she was herself saying and presenting to Cassidy as an adult with the power to interpret.

What she couldn't forgive was what she'd done, she said—left her friend who'd once been her closest friend without telling him, didn't leave a note, didn't text, no explanation, she'd just *fled.*

Shivering in Cassidy's arms, tears wetting her cheeks, naked, so vulnerable, he kissed her and assured her she'd had no choice, had to save her own life, she'd done the right thing by leaving, otherwise she might have been killed herself. Comforting her, rocking her to sleep like a young child.

Happiest hour of Cassidy's adult life.

When had he fallen in love with his friends' daughter?—this is Cassidy's secret, too precious to be shared with anyone except Brianna, who is embarrassed to be told about it.

Four years before, at a Christmas concert at the Fair Hills school, which Cassidy and his wife attended, in fact with the Rinzlers. Both their daughters were in the girls' chorus.

Did she remember the Palestrina she sang, Cassidy has asked Brianna. The "Exultate Deo"?—did she remember the Vivaldi psalm?

Brianna frowned, remembering. Trying to remember.

So long ago, she'd been, like, *sixteen.*

Maybe it hadn't been *in love,* exactly. Though certainly a sensation of falling.

Slow-paced candlelight procession down the center aisle of the auditorium and onto the stage and Cassidy found himself staring at a girl he hadn't quite recognized as Brianna Rinzler at first, heartbreaking face, utterly lovely, couldn't look away even when he realized belatedly who the girl was. A clutching sensation in his chest, a wave of vertigo, of a kind he hadn't felt in memory.

The candlelight procession was one of the features of the annual winter concert. For weeks Veronica and her friends had excitedly discussed what they would wear. Two by two the choruses filed in from the rear of the auditorium to the stage, girls in high-necked white silk blouses and long wine-colored velvet skirts, boys in dark suits, ties. Slow solemn Christmas music accompanied them, as in church. Cassidy and Charlotte sat with the Rinzlers who were longtime acquaintances though not close friends, the couples made it a point to see one another several times a year.

Cassidy craned his neck, waiting for Veronica to appear: his daughter was a plump-cheeked earnest girl with close-set brown eyes, limp brown hair, a manner shyly appealing, like Charlotte's; Cassidy loved his daughter, fourteen at the time, and feared for her, for all that was to come, for *almost-pretty* could be a harsh fate. There was something hypnotic in the way the candlelight procession continued, girl after girl and boy after boy, accompanied by the musicians; just a few of the candlelit faces, like the face of Brianna Rinzler, warranted a second glance, attention other than the obligatory attention of parents for their children. Almost, Cassidy had forgotten Veronica by the time she appeared, she and her boy-companion passed nearly unnoticed as Cassidy found himself staring at other faces, at the Rinzlers' daughter, he might have sworn he'd never seen before.

But you never exclaim to them: God! How you've *grown.*

Brianna seems scarcely to recall the winter concert. She has forgotten the choral pieces they'd sung, girls' chorus hadn't been a high-school activity to which she'd devoted much serious time, vaguely she recalls the ceremonial procession, the fluttering candle flames, the white silk blouse she'd worn and the senior boy with whom she'd been paired. Of the blurred sea of rapt adult faces, her parents' among them, and the faces of their friends the Cassidys, Brianna remembers nothing at all.

What Cassidy recalls of his Fair Hills life is its *routine.* The comfort of *routine.*

How many years, decades. His wife, children. His friends, acquaintances, neighbors who'd formed a circle of sorts, unless a net, to secure him; define and confine him. Endless round of dinner parties, cocktail parties, receptions. Holiday season beginning after Thanksgiving and not ending until the last open house on New Year's Day . . . After the Christmas concert he'd been stunned realizing how *boring.*

His wife's family, his family. "Relatives"—none of them chosen.

The entire texture of that life, its willed imposture. Not that it died quickly, it did not. Like the carefully tended grass of a suburban lawn that gradually thins with time, is invaded by crabgrass, a slow diminishing, death.

Three years after the winter concert Cassidy had more or less forgotten the Rinzlers' oldest daughter. Hadn't seen her in the interim, never thought of her, she wasn't a friend of Veronica's. Vaguely he'd recall hearing his wife remark that their friends were having difficulties with their oldest daughter, she'd dropped out of the expensive liberal arts school they'd sent her to, possibly drugs were involved, she was living in New York and estranged from her family . . . In Penn Station where Cassidy was about to board a train to Fair Hills, Brianna Rinzler had approached him, boldly, flirtatiously, in retrospect Cassidy would understand that Brianna was high, radiantly high, her skin luminous with heat and her glassy eyes glistening. She'd been with a tall pasty-skinned boy with features as striking as her own, might've been a male model, photographed for Calvin Klein or by Mapplethorpe. Both Brianna Rinzler and this boy were wearing striking clothing, designer clothing, taffy-colored leather, heather-colored suede, falling loose and open from their thin shoulders; in the congested area where passengers were waiting they stood basking in the glamour of youth, as if in a magic space just for them.

"Hiiiiya!—d'you remember me, Mr. Cassidy?—it's Brianna, Brianna Rinzler, d'you remember me? I was, like, two years ahead of your daughter in school, I've forgotten her name, at Fair Hills High, you and Mrs. Cassidy know my parents, I guess—d'you remember, Mr. Cassidy?"

After the first shock passed, yes. He did remember.

———

Are you in love with someone else?—calmly Charlotte asked Cassidy, her eyes grave and wounded, her voice steady. *We can talk about it, if you are. If you think you are.*

He'd avoided answering Charlotte. Unprepared, hadn't the words, just yet. Easier to suggest that Charlotte was imagining things. Or, she'd been hearing things, unfounded rumors, she's possibly misinterpreted.

Soon after, Charlotte had a minor accident with her car.

Pavement slick with freezing rain, she'd skidded into the rear of another vehicle. Terribly shaken, bursting into tears but wasn't injured. Thank God, Cassidy thought.

If Charlotte had been injured, if seriously—if she'd *died.* He could not bear it, the burden of guilt.

But the incident had awakened in Cassidy the understanding that his marriage was *impermanent,* expendable. A marriage can melt like wedding cake in the rain—of course.

One day, he would confide in Brianna, he'd come to realize that his life has been an impersonation of someone whom he didn't know, didn't respect.

Brianna had been in a giddy mood, pushing up against Cassidy, laughing, stumbling, holding out her iPhone to take a *selfie* of the two of them, disheveled and flush-faced.

Just for us, she'd assured him. Just private.

He'd wanted to tell Brianna more of his discovery, that had split his life in two asymmetrical parts. He was sure that the girl would be impressed, if he could explain clearly enough. Much of this phase of Cassidy's life had to do with explaining himself, his motives and insights—*epiphanies.* How he'd gradually lost his ability to impersonate himself, the way you lose a skill like piano playing, or swimming, playing chess. Like suffocation, not enough air, the skill dies.

Brianna was finding it hard to keep her exquisite face from crinkling like an ugly doll's face into wild laughter.

Standing on (bare) tiptoes, kissing the middle-aged daddy-lover on the mouth wetly, unabashedly.

Rarely did Brianna call Cassidy by his first name, as if it didn't matter that he had a name, a very common name, somehow it wasn't *his name.* But sometimes in the right mood she'd whisper in his ear *Big Bear.*

Absurdly flattering, his face goes hot with blood, recalling.

Confiding in Cassidy, in turn, a frequent complaint of hers, if only people would let her alone! Not try to manipulate her.

Sometimes Brianna slips, says *you people.* As if Cassidy were *you people.*

When Brianna speaks of manipulative persons she is sometimes referring to her parents, or to one or another professor (at Bard, from which Brianna has taken leave for a semester), or to mysterious persons who remain unnamed, unknown to Cassidy. These are persons who are trying to *blackmail her emotionally, put pressure on her. Coerce, push. Fuck with her head.*

There is a therapist, or there was a therapist who'd seriously *fucked with her head.* Friends she'd thought were trustworthy, who'd betrayed her.

It's titillating to Cassidy when Brianna speaks of her parents. As if in complaining of them, a Fair Hills couple whom Cassidy has known for years, Brianna is acknowledging that he, her lover, is not in the stifling category *parent, middle-aged* to which the Rinzlers belong.

He'd made his decision to move out of the house in Fair Hills in which he'd lived (happily enough, in fact—that was the baffling truth) for nearly twenty years. Not (yet) prepared to tell Charlotte, that would come in time.

The ideal situation would be Charlotte putting the onus on *him.* Asking Cassidy to move out.

Why are you doing this to us—Charlotte asked. *Why do you want to destroy what we have created.*

Cassidy winced at *us, we.* For Charlotte had no idea, none of this related to her.

Grateful for his wife's restraint and dignity! Those very qualities in Charlotte that made her so reasonable, reliable, dully predictable, he valued now, in leaving her. That Charlotte is so *fair-minded,* she can be relied upon not to rouse the children against him. For he could not bear being considered *selfish, cruel*—*a bad daddy.*

Cassidy did not, in fact, consider himself selfish or cruel or a *bad daddy.* He has become a truth-teller, he has not spared himself in his condemnation of his marriage of so many years.

But why?—help me understand. I am just trying to understand, Matthew.

Hearing himself speak. Words to placate Charlotte, for the time being.

The condo has been leased, Brianna knows but not yet Charlotte. He is still living in Fair Hills, officially. Just last night, sleeping beside the wife. Explaining to her, not-explaining to her, carefully chosen words, Cassidy's normal voice that is affable, consoling, circuitous, non-confrontational. Couldn't trust himself to speak otherwise. He hadn't the script. No way to confess to his wife of so many years that his secret sorrow has been gathering like phlegm in his throat, he wants only to spit it out.

All this while, Brianna has been collecting things on the hard-packed sand of the beach at Cape May.

What sort of things?—anything that seems to catch her eye, anything droll or strange, for instance a piece of driftwood resembling a human arm; a child's sneaker washed clean and pale by the surf; a mollusk shell marked with hundreds of tiny stipples like spines. Brianna takes a picture of the shell on the beach, then holds it in her hand, staring as if at a talisman.

Cassidy, who would like nothing better than to hike back to the Subaru, drive to the hotel, and have a drink, asks Brianna if she'd like him to carry these things for her?—they should be heading back to town . . .

It is nearing four-thirty P.M., the sun is slanting toward the horizon in the west. The Atlantic wind has become increasingly cold but Brianna seems scarcely to notice. She hands her worthless little treasures to Cassidy then turns away to find more. There is something antic, coltish, too willful in her behavior but Cassidy supposes it's genuine.

They have hiked a mile or more from the historic district of Cape May. The beach has become rougher, shabbier. The sand is eroded into curious little ditches, there is litter underfoot, mummified remains of dead fish. They are beyond the boardwalk but a flight of wooden steps leads to the crest of a weedy hill, about twelve feet in height.

A wet pungent odor of rot reminds Cassidy of the plankton field off Provincetown. That frenzied feeding, the savagery and pointlessness of appetite; eel-like silvery flashes of fish, water foaming, churning, children on board the *Provincetown Princess* crying excitedly, is it sharks?—*is it sharks?*

As if the only creatures that devour are *sharks*.

"Brianna? Shall we head back?"

But Brianna is trotting off in search of new treasure, taking pictures with her phone, sending pictures, continuously and compulsively recording whatever strikes her eye, whatever distraction, waves, surf, her own wetted boots, twisted clots of seaweed, broken glass, Cassidy himself (he knows, she has been taking pictures of him since they came to the beach, playfully, mischievously, though he doesn't want her to, lifts his hand to shield his face, it has become a kind of joke between them, not a joke that Cassidy finds funny), even as he is thinking ahead to their evening—to the night—a room in the Cape May Heritage House furnished with *period antiques*—after a candlelight dinner in the *historic dining room*—a nightcap in their room, from the mini-bar—utter privacy, secrecy. Brianna has a way of semi-collapsing on a bed, giddy-drunk, giddy-high, only just laughs at whatever her middle-aged lover does to her of which she's (sort of) aware, unprotesting—*thinks it's funny, no big deal.*

Why do you want to destroy what we've built?—Charlotte has asked as if the question might evoke a reasonable answer.

Brianna's slender twisty eel-like body, thrust of pelvic bones, shiny eyes rolling back in her head in passion or in a simulacrum of passion . . . Once, he'd grabbed her hard around her narrow hips and she'd snorted in surprised laughter, kicking him, as a child might kick, tugging at his hair, clawing his cheeks, playing rough, puppy-rough, unexpectedly strong for a girl so underweight, saliva glistening on her chin like a tusk. She'd been high, radiantly high, her skin dry and burning to the touch, an artery pulsing in her throat he'd had to kiss, hard.

Cassidy tells Brianna not to climb those steps: the wood looks rotted.

Brianna ignores him because she has glimpsed something in the weeds at the top of the hill—looks like a broken doll.

Monkey-quick Brianna climbs the wobbly steps, snatches up the doll as Cassidy stares after her. Jesus! If she should fall, if she should injure herself . . . Is he responsible? Would such an accident be reported, find its way into a newspaper?

Brianna waves the bit of rubbish in the air, looks like a raggedy doll.

Cassidy is prepared to catch Brianna if she falls climbing back down the wobbly steps but when one of the steps collapses beneath her weight she falls heavily, grunting to the ground, Cassidy isn't strong enough to catch her in his arms, cursing, vexed with himself and with her. God damn! She can't have hurt herself, Cassidy thinks, stooping to help her up, she's whimpering, tears glistening on her cheeks, dead weight at first, uncooperative. Has she twisted her ankle, has she sprained something? Why the hell hadn't she listened to him, Cassidy demands. Worried that, if he stoops to lift her, he might throw out his God-damned back and suffer for days, weeks.

Brianna is whimpering petulantly, groping about for her cell phone which is somewhere beneath the rotted steps, she pushes Cassidy's hand away, Cassidy is furious with her suddenly and snatches up the damned phone and tosses it into the ocean, cursing as Brianna has never heard him curse before.

In that instant Brianna is stunned into silence: eyes widened, mouth drooping open, *she cannot believe what Cassidy has done*.

Her iPhone, lost in slovenly slapping waves. Freezing-stinging waves, spray wetting their faces. *Cannot believe what has happened to her phone . . .*

Cassidy yanks the stricken girl to her feet. Gives her a hard shake to stop her whimpering. Tells her he will buy another God-damned phone for her in the morning, they are going back to town now, to the hotel. For the night.

Brianna paws at Cassidy, she is desperate to retrieve her phone, Cassidy curses her, saying the fucking phone is *gone,* it's in the water, the water is too cold for her to wade into, too cold for him, fuck it by now the phone is ruined, soaked and ruined, just *fuck it.*

Brianna is sobbing, limping as Cassidy walks her roughly back to the Subaru. His blood is up, he feels no remorse for what he has done. Telling Brianna, promising her he will buy a new iPhone for her in the morning, an updated model, newest model, don't worry the information on her phone is saved somewhere, in the Cloud, whatever the Cloud is. He's sure. Brianna continues to sob in a state beyond surprise, like one in shock; broken, defeated.

He has triumphed, as he'd hoped. Expected. Eventually.

Demanding of her, driving to the hotel on Beach Avenue, why hadn't she answered his calls?—twenty or more calls, over five days? What the hell was she thinking? *Was* she thinking? And calling him late last night when his wife might have overheard, what was that about?

In the passenger's seat of the Subaru, Brianna is stiff with something like fear, guilt. Cassidy is fully in control now. The headstrong girl has become docile, unresisting. She has seen what Cassidy did with her iPhone, she has felt the strong impress of his hands on her, her resistance has melted away like a tissue dropped in water.

Only just murmuring in response to his questions *Don't know* and later, in the hotel room shrinking from his angry face, pleading, *Sorry, so sorry.*

———

In the morning Cassidy heaves himself from the king-sized bed. He is naked, prickly-skinned, and smelling of his body. Bodies.

Shaky on his feet. Mild thrill of disgust. Regards the still-sleeping girl in rumpled bedclothes on the farther side of the absurdly vast bed, sickly-pale face not very attractive now, matted streaked-blond hair, her eyelids quiver as if she is trying to wake up but cannot. Her soft mouth is agape, she is still stunned. On one of her bare shoulders, a thumb-sized bruise, which Cassidy sees with something like satisfaction, though also tenderness.

Recalling, how the girl had stared at him the night before, in fear of him. Once they were alone together. Fear that is a kind of awe, reverence.

Knowing, accepting, that she deserved whatever Cassidy would do to her. This submissiveness in the *teenaged mistress,* Cassidy has found addictive, like a narcotic. He'd loved it, Brianna's eyes glassy in submission, pupils dilated. Soft pale skin, submissive. His quick hard hands. The authority in such hands. For all this he will forgive her. He will reward her, he will purchase for her the very newest iPhone model, the cost is nothing to him.

In the beautifully white-gleaming bathroom, luxury bathroom, eager to shower the body-odors from himself. For it *is* disgusting to him, in a way.

Though, can't resist smiling into the steamy mirror.

"Big Bear."

She hadn't resisted, stumbling into the room the night before. This, the *Monarch Suite.* He'd helped her to the bed, pushed her onto the enormous bed, feebly she'd pushed his hands away even as she continued to apologize *Sorry, I am so sorry don't hurt me.*

Maybe she'd sprained the ankle. Or strained a tendon. She'd been desperate searching through the neon-pink backpack, pills wrapped in a Kleenex, *painkillers* she called them which she needed badly, swallowed dry. Neither of them was in a mood for the *historic dining room* where you were expected to dress, men with jackets, no blue jeans or sports clothes for women, fuck it. He'd ended up practically feeding her the pricey room service dinner, she'd kept falling asleep. Cried thinly, soft mouth quivering. She hadn't resisted Cassidy, she never resisted Cassidy, like a Raggedy Ann doll obliging and to a degree even cooperating if only she could keep her eyes open which she could not. He'd tugged off the damned tight-fitting Italian leather boots. Tugged off the damned tight-fitting jeans. She'd pushed away his hands like a large baby as he'd adored her, declaring he would love her, he would take care of her, when they returned to the city he'd help her with her things, move out of the loft on Varick, move in with him. *You know you love me. You know that.*

Later this morning he will purchase a new iPhone for her. Probably there's a mall somewhere near Cape May. People lose their cell phones all the time, can't be a serious problem to replace. Maybe then lunch, then a visit to the lighthouse. Historic museum(s). Another night at the Cape May Heritage House, he's reserved for two nights.

So simple. You make a decision, you act. Why hadn't he realized earlier in his life.

What's called *love.* A decision you make.

If only Brianna would remain the way she is now, has been since the accident on the beach. Docile, meek, submissive, grateful for him. Grateful that he forgives her.

If only this, permanently. The two of them. Like this.

Taking his time, in no hurry in the luxuriant white-tiled bathroom now fragrant-smelling. Shining chrome shower-head, all surfaces gleaming-clean. Cassidy shampoos his thinning hair, covers his body in white-soapy lather, rough-caresses his body, going to fat at the waist, potbelly covered in hairs, legs spread for balance. Taking care he shaves his jaws with his safety razor, now is not the time to rush, risk cutting himself. Rubs body lotion onto his hands, chest. Prides himself in the grizzled chest-hair, thick hairs on his arms, genitals drooping between his legs just visible beyond the swell of his belly. Beard so heavy, he should shave twice a day. *Testosterone.*

Regarding himself sidelong in the large steamy mirror, squinting, head cocked, half-consciously Cassidy has learned how best to observe himself, *you do not want to look too directly.*

Leaving the bathroom he calls to the girl in the bed, *Good morning!*—white terrycloth bath towel wrapped around his thick waist, in an elevated mood calling to her, taking note that it's eight forty-one A.M. by the digital clock on the bedside table nearest him but there's no answer, standing flat-footed astonished seeing that the vast king-sized bed appears to be empty, only soiled sheets like white snakes entangled.

"Brianna? Where—"

On the floor there's a pillow, one of the large ornamental pillows he'd kicked off the bed the previous night.

Slow-blinking stunned seeing that Brianna is *gone.* Unless in the closet . . .

Not in the closet, he checks, foolishly. And nothing on the wooden hangers, nothing on the shelves inside the closet, or on the floor.

His clothes, his things—not in the closet, and not on the chair where he'd tossed them, nor are the girl's clothes here, no quilted jacket, no Italian leather boots, no damp shoes, the neon-pink backpack is gone, even a mirror against a farther wall appears vacant as Cassidy stares trying to comprehend.

"Brianna? Hey, Jesus!—c'mon . . ."

His breath is coming quickly. He is feeling light-headed, weak. Telling himself—this is not happening, of course Brianna is in the room somewhere, playing a prank on Big Bear, she'd slipped into the bathroom without his noticing and so Cassidy re-enters the bathroom smelling of fragrant steam, inspects the shower stall with the soap-spattered glass doors, no one here, nothing. On the bathroom floor, sodden towels he'd let drop, kicked to the side for the housekeeper.

Returning to the room, glancing quickly about: his things he'd left on the bedside table, on his side of the bed, where are they?—wallet, cell phone, keys.

Not on the floor, nothing on the floor except the pillow.

Not even his socks, underwear. The girl's jeans he'd tugged off her limp lower body, her underwear, he'd let fall to the floor, no sign.

Her pullover cashmere sweater with the soiled neck, his L.L.Bean suede jacket, corduroy trousers, water-stained shoes—where?

On a table, the filth-stiffened, raggedy doll Brianna had found on the beach. This, she'd left for Cassidy.

Just the white terrycloth towel wrapped around Cassidy's waist. Naked beneath, he's barefoot, shivering now, his teeth chatter with cold and a sudden hard throbbing in his head.

Numbly checking the closet again as if he has forgotten that he has checked the closet and found nothing. Pulls out bureau drawers, nothing even to rattle in the drawers, no cell phone, no key to the Subaru, the girl has dared to take the Subaru key, she has taken his wallet, his cell phone, his clothes, his shoes, she has stolen his Subaru Forester and left him alone in the Cape May Heritage House, *naked.*

Rapidly Cassidy's mind works, thoughts rush at him like missiles, it is not possible that Brianna Rinzler has abandoned Cassidy in Cape May, New Jersey, it is not possible that Brianna can drive the Subaru back to the city, has the girl that capacity, that sense of purpose, will she abandon his vehicle on a wide deserted street on the West Side, Meatpacking District, warehouse district, hiking back to the Varick Street loft, what will he do abandoned in New Jersey, *what can he do*?

Paralyzed, numbed. Such thoughts fly at him. Yet, his mind is blank, thoughts slip past like water through a sieve, hands outheld to receive water, spilling through fingers.

How did the girl deceive him!—deeply asleep as if comatose, drugged; helpless as a mollusk out of its shell. Oblivious of him (he'd thought) as he stood over her gloating and protective, tenderhearted.

"No. Can't be. She wouldn't."

She'd waited until he was in the shower, rapidly then slipping from bed and throwing on clothes, haphazardly gathering his clothes, even his shoes, his wallet, keys, cell phone she'd pushed into the neon-pink backpack and zipped up, no time to put on the leather boots, she'd have to carry the boots as she would carry his suede jacket, thrusting her arms into the sleeves of the quilted jacket breathless and charged with adrenaline as if fleeing for her life leaving the room and shutting the door behind her within how many minutes, seconds.

Door clicking shut behind her, locking. In the bathroom he'd heard nothing.

Cassidy checks the bathroom again: nothing. Another time, the closet. Drops to his (bare) knees, peers beneath the bed but the king-sized bed is mounted on a solid wooden platform, no space beneath the bed, nothing to see.

Exhausted now, light-headed. Pulses beat in his head, Cassidy is numb with fear of a stroke, the pressure of his blood is mounting. Sitting heavy, leaden on the edge of the bed. Trying to think, to comprehend: what must be done next.

Stares at the digital clock for several seconds without registering the time: eight forty-eight A.M.

At last there comes a sharp-knuckled rapping at the door, in this instant Cassidy is flooded with relief, Brianna has returned, of course Brianna has returned, she has taken mercy on him, he is halfway on his feet to open the door except the voice is unfamiliar, a woman's voice expedient and charmless—"Housekeeping."

THE FEAR

Of the two she wasn't Juliet, she was Janette.

Asked if they were twins they'd learned to smile but say *no.* Juliet always said *no.* Janette wasn't so sure, Janette only shook her head *no,* she was shy around adults always leaning over to bring their huge faces too close.

"Oh—you two are *not twins*?"

Juliet knew, they were *not twins.* In fact they were not even sisters but something called *cousins.*

Janette understood, sort of. *Not sisters: cousins.*

Girl-cousins born to sisters who'd married in the same year. And had their first babies within a year of each other: Juliet, then Janette.

Strange to Janette, that Juliet was eleven months older than she was. Which meant that for just one month (August) Janette was the same age as Juliet; but soon then, overnight, it was Juliet's birthday and Juliet became *one year older.*

Janette could not comprehend this, exactly. Thumb in mouth, stricken with (silly) shyness, not quite a mirror-image of Juliet if you looked closely. (Not so pretty?)

As Juliet's hair was curlier, and Juliet's eyes were brighter, and Juliet was potty-trained before Janette was, and smarter, and taller, with a way of pushing herself ahead of Janette that made it look as if Janette was lagging behind on purpose, timid and clumsy.

Was that fair?—Janette wondered. Was that *right*?

Janette was *not jealous* of her cousin. Janette wanted to *be* her cousin.

Weekends, visiting the grandparents in Charlevoix. Staying overnight in the big old white-painted brick house on the cliff overlooking the lake. So many rooms a child couldn't count them: Juliet and Janette sharing a pink-floral children's room, twin beds with white headboards embossed with satin lambs and piglets and between the beds an eighteen-inch Mother Goose lamp that, if either girl was frightened of the dark, could be left on its dimmest light through the night.

(Janette's secret: it was the Mother Goose lamp that frightened her! No one else seemed to notice the mean look in Mother Goose's eyes or the sharp beak that threatened to peck if you got too near.)

Recalling their childhood in the white-painted brick house which hadn't been entirely happy the girl-cousins' mothers were determined that neither of their daughters should be favored over the other. If Juliet was given a new doll for her birthday, Janette was given a new doll too, not an identical doll, for *identical* was to be avoided, but a doll of the same approximate quality and cost from the same store. If Janette was given a new coat, Juliet would have a new coat, too. New shoes, new clothes, new coloring books, new picture-books.

Childhood should be precious, the sisters believed. Children should not be forced to compete with each other for attention, for love. No!

Especially, the preschool years. The happiest years. For all too soon, by early adolescence, rivalries would be impossible to prevent, the sisters knew well.

Still, when Janette saw Juliet with her new doll Bonnie, it took her breath away that Bonnie was much nicer than her doll Betsy: nicer face, nicer hair, nicer clothes. Though Janette's new coat came from the same children's department in Neiman Marcus yet it seemed to Janette that the coat was not nearly as special as Juliet's coat, as Juliet's pebble-blue eyes were becoming so much more striking than Janette's pebble-gray eyes.

A child's lifetime thinking, *Why is this, this is not fair,* for Janette was only ever herself, waking in the twin bed that was hers and not Juliet's in the grandparents' house, no matter how she calculated, opening her eyes she was always Janette, she was never Juliet, who'd learned to walk earlier than Janette had learned to walk, and who'd learned to talk first, and to read first, and to add and subtract numbers first, and began Montessori school first.

Until finally it was no longer asked of the little girl-cousins—*Are you two twins?*

But here was the first shock of Janette's life: her sixth birthday.

Instead of a birthday party at the grandparents' house with all of the relatives, and Juliet sitting close beside her whispering and giggling, and helping Janette blow out the candles on the big chocolate cake, and piles of glittery-wrapped presents, and everyone singing *Happy birthday, dear Janette,* there was just—*nothing.*

Well, not exactly *nothing*. A birthday cake at home, a few presents, all from Mommy and Daddy.

No party at the grandparents' house. No Juliet.

Janette wanted to cry, it was unfair!—for just a little while she'd caught up with Juliet, and no one cared not even Juliet.

And when the phone rang just as Mommy was cutting the birthday cake for Janette, Mommy let the knife fall onto the tablecloth and hurried to another room to take the call speaking in a lowered voice that Janette could not hear.

Yes, there were presents for Janette. It *was* her birthday.

But Janette was hurt, that Juliet was not with her. Always the girl-cousins were together for their birthdays. Always, seated beside each other at the big table at the grandparents' house with all of the relatives gathered.

It could not be Juliet's fault, Janette thought. It had to be Aunt Leslie's fault for Juliet could hardly drive to Janette's house by herself. Or maybe it was Granma and Granpa's fault for not having the birthday party as they always did.

When Mommy returned to the table where Daddy was slicing pieces of birthday cake Janette saw how Mommy's face looked as if the skin was drawn tight and all the blood had drained away beneath, and Janette was furious with Mommy for ruining her birthday, that should have been a special day; and had to be cajoled into eating chocolate cake though chocolate cake was her favorite cake; and the cake was dry in her mouth and made her cough, she was missing Juliet so much, and she was angry with Juliet, too; and Aunt Leslie, and Uncle Stan, and all the adults for it seemed to Janette obvious that the adults had come between her and Juliet, and were ruining Janette's special time of being her cousin's age and not a year younger.

But later, at bedtime, Mommy hugged Janette and said in a whisper, in her ear, that Juliet had wanted to come to Janette's birthday party but *something bad* had happened to Juliet that prevented it.

Something bad. Janette was very frightened, hearing these words which were unlike any words that any adult had ever told her. So frightened, she did not dare ask Mommy what *something bad* was.

Mommy held Janette shivering in her arms.

"Don't worry, honey. It will never, ever happen to *you.*"

Next weekend was Easter. And when Janette was taken to visit her grandparents the first thing she saw was that Juliet was not there.

Not waiting for her just inside the door, or upstairs in the pink-floral room they would share.

Nor were Aunt Leslie and Uncle Stan waiting. Almost no one was in the drafty high-ceilinged house except Granma and Granpa who hugged Janette harder than usual, and made her feel uncomfortable, and were looking older, and sad and quiet; and without Juliet to play with Janette was soon restless and bored and wanting to go home.

Janette asked where Juliet was but the answer was vague, evasive. Juliet was *away.*

But soon, Juliet would *return.*

Nor would anyone explain what the *bad thing* was. Janette did not want to ask more questions for fear of what the answer would be.

Alone together the adults talked. Murmuring voices behind shut doors but no laughter where usually there was laughter amid a clatter of glasses, bottles.

By herself Janette played with Betsy. Hid away in the floral-pink bedroom with the twin beds where she'd never been without Juliet so it seemed to her that Juliet *was* there, in the corner of her eye.

But when she turned around, there was no one.

So strange, where there'd always been Juliet, there was *no one.*

Where if there'd been Betsy, there'd be Bonnie.

This was scary. This was a *bad thing.* For if Juliet (who was everyone's favorite) could disappear, Janette (who was no one's favorite) could disappear.

But where do you *go,* Janette wondered. When you are *gone.*

From the earliest time she could remember Janette had wanted to sleep in the bed that was Juliet's which was farthest from the door. This was a nicer bed than the other (twin) bed which was "hers." (But Janette had never chosen this bed, had she?) But now that she could sleep in either bed she did not wish to sleep in either bed. Nor even lie on top of Juliet's bed and kick at the bedclothes to rumple them.

A mean thought came to Janette, she could crawl inside the bedclothes of this bed and make herself pee; and the pee, which was nasty, and smelly, and something to be ashamed of, would be blamed on Juliet, and not *her.*

Oh, who did this?—the adults would cry, crinkling their noses.

Did Juliet do this?—Granma would be shocked.

But no, Janette could not crawl into Juliet's bed and make herself *pee* for the pee would get onto her, soil her clothes, and she would smell of it, and the adults would know exactly who had peed in the bed, and blame *her.*

Without Juliet she was hating the floral-pink room. In the corners of her eyes she saw things moving but if she dared to look, there were only shadows there.

Without Juliet everything was so *slow,* and so *boring.*

Wanting badly to be taken home. Not stay overnight in the

(hateful) room by herself. For there was the Mother Goose lamp with the mean goose-eyes fixed on her.

For the goose-eyes knew: the *bad thing* that had happened to Juliet was a secret which made Juliet important while there was nothing secret and nothing important about Janette.

"Janette?—honey? What on earth has happened to your doll?"

Mommy stood in the doorway, she must have pushed open the door without knocking. And now Mommy was looking surprised, and frowning.

Janette saw on the carpet Betsy's head where it had rolled to a stop. Betsy's head must have loosened and fallen from Betsy's body somehow without Janette noticing, now the head was lying there with its glassy eyes opened wide and silly mouth gaping.

"Did *you* do this, Janette? To your own doll?"

Frowning Mommy picked up the doll-head and tried to fit it onto the doll-body but it would not fit, which made Janette snort with laughter.

"Really! Is this *funny*?" Mommy was indignant, hurt.

Even funnier, the way Mommy stalked out of the room leaving Betsy in two pieces on the carpet so that laughter bubbled and roiled inside Janette like something wild trying to escape.

Soon after Easter there was "news." And now, it seemed that the adults were willing to tell Janette what the secret was.

The *bad thing* that had been growing in Juliet's jaw had been removed! And soon now there would be a second "surgery" on Juliet's left eye where the *bad thing* had spread.

These terrible words, Janette scarcely heard. *Growing, surgery, bad thing, spread.*

Terrible words! *Jaw, left eye.*

Instead of asking questions as her parents expected, Janette did not ask any questions at all. Her face was stiff as a doll's face, her eyes were glassy with boredom. Particularly Janette resented that Mommy was making such a fuss having hurried from a phone conversation in another room to squat before her breathlessly in that annoying way that adults often do, when they want to pretend to be no taller than you, but still they are much stronger than you, and can grip you in their arms to hold you still, and bring their huge faces close to yours, and their huge teary eyes, so that you can't look away but are trapped and can't breathe.

Ewing's sarcoma, it was called.

A special kind of *cancer,* it was.

Now Daddy was saying these terrible words and leaning over Janette, too. So it was something important, if Daddy too was involved, and not just Mommy who was always so emotional. Still, Janette did not have to listen if she didn't want to. No one could force her to hear those words—*Ewing's sarcoma, cancer.* There was a derisive roaring in Janette's ears, her face had become very hot.

It just seemed silly, a *bad thing* could grow in Juliet's jaw and spread to her eye—Janette jammed her knuckles against her mouth, to stop from giggling.

The adults were disappointed in her, Janette knew. But what did they want of *her*!—if the *bad thing* was anyone's fault it was Juliet's fault not *hers.*

Daddy's face was flushed, and Daddy's breath came hard. Already as a small child Janette understood that adults do not like you so much when you behave in a way they don't expect even if it is a way truthful to you.

Still it seemed funny to Janette, something to make her laugh, that a *bad thing* could grow in someone's face. Only grass, trees, flowers, weeds *grew* like that. Trying to understand made her head hurt, like something wrong-sized was being forced into her head, which was scary to Janette, as if a *bad thing* had taken seed in her own head.

Daddy was asking if Janette had any questions?—but Janette did not have any questions.

Mommy was saying it was a “terrible shock” to them all but the doctors were “very optimistic” and Juliet was being a “very brave little girl.”

After the second surgery, after a few days, when Juliet was home from Children’s Hospital, they would take Janette to visit her. That was a promise.

Children’s Hospital! The two words did not belong together, Janette shuddered to hear.

A sensation of cold washed over her, making her shiver. And then, she could not stop shivering and her silly teeth chattered.

In a bright voice Mommy was saying they would take gifts for Juliet. A new stuffed animal, for Juliet had to spend time in her room, in bed; and flowers, and cookies, Mommy would bake chocolate chip cookies, which were Janette’s favorite cookies, which Juliet liked, too.

Janette could not push out of Mommy’s arms for Mommy would prevent her. And Daddy was hovering above her, too.

Her only escape was shutting her eyes. For she was very tired, the strain of not-hearing ugly words was exhausting to one so young, like not-laughing out loud.

Like switching on TV she was in another place. Something was chasing her, and her feet were sinking in mud, and all around her strange shapes were “growing” out of the mud, but she could not wake up to escape from these unless she opened her eyes but she could not open her eyes for they were stuck together.

. . . quite a shock for her, the poor child!

. . . upstairs to bed? Sweetie?

And there was Daddy hoisting Janette aloft with a soft little grunt in Daddy's strong arms as if she was a baby again and nothing bad could happen to *her.* Not ever.

But something was wrong: a plan to visit Juliet at home was arranged, anticipated, then canceled.

And another time, a week later: a visit arranged, anticipated, canceled.

Infection, ER admission, follow-up surgery.

Radiation, chemotherapy.

No idea what these ugly words meant but Janette understood that they were hurtful for they took place in Children's Hospital.

Whatever such treatments were, they would never happen to *her.*

At first Janette was excited at the prospect of seeing her little girl-cousin after so many weeks but gradually as visits were planned, and canceled, she began to wonder if the adults ever told the truth about Juliet.

Was this some sort of game they were playing? *She* did not care!

For now Janette was in school. Not preschool but first grade. Juliet was not in school, Juliet was being kept at home until she was "stronger." Behind shut doors Janette's mother often spoke on the phone with Aunt Leslie but her voice was kept low, Janette could not eavesdrop and did not wish to eavesdrop.

Though sometimes even through closed doors she could hear her mother sobbing.

Janette hated this! Hated silly Mommy who *sobbed like a baby.*

Adults were not supposed to cry. You did not want to hear

an adult cry, you would press your hands over your ears to keep from hearing.

Also, it was not-right that Mommy cried over Juliet, and not Janette.

Janette was Mommy's little girl, not Juliet.

Sometimes, it was just funny. Have to laugh. An adult woman crying, such a silly sound.

Granma, too. Tears caught in the wrinkles in Granma's soft white skin when they went to visit. *Silly.*

Janette would listen on the stairs, at Granma's house. After dinner, at night when she was supposed to be in bed in the floral-pink room she'd come to hate.

At such (secret) times Janette's thumb sought her mouth. Though thumb-sucking was forbidden. Though Janette was (now) seven years old.

No one to see, no one to know, greedily sucking her thumb. Until the thumb came away extra soft, white, and puckered.

(If no one saw it did not count: sucking your thumb was not real if no adult knew.)

Relatives at Granma's house, their voices uplifted, sharp.

What! Are you sure—Ewing's sarcoma? A child?

Never heard of such a thing.

Isn't that—AIDS?

Must be genetic . . .

That air of reproach, blame. Even a child could detect it.

Something that her aunt and uncle had done, maybe. Some kind of punishment they deserved.

It was on the stairs one night that Janette learned from the adults' conversation that her cousin's hair had *fallen out.*

Why this had happened, Janette had no idea. She felt a thrill of panic, then relief, such a terrible thing could not happen to *her.*

You had to wonder if Juliet was being punished. It was Juliet who'd broken the head off Janette's doll, and Juliet had peed in her bed, like a baby. Juliet had spilled chocolate ice cream on a sofa in Granma's house and giggled and wasn't sorry, she'd put a pillow over the spot to hide it and no one had ever known.

Except Janette had known. But no adult had known.

Just heartbreaking! That beautiful curly hair.

How do you explain to the child . . .

They say she doesn't cry so much, anymore.

Soft fine curly chestnut-red hair Juliet had had, it was hard for Janette to believe that this hair had "fallen out." Her own hair was losing its red glints, gradually turning brown, not so curly any longer.

Janette's hair, not so special. Like her face which was plain. It seemed wrong, a mistake, that Juliet was being punished instead of Janette.

The adults were saying that the hair would "grow back"—eventually. That was the promise. In the meantime, Juliet wore little knitted caps on her (bald) head to keep warm.

Little knitted caps on her (bald) head so that people would not stare at her curiously and other children would not laugh.

Bald head. These words made Janette squirm with embarrassment, she wished her mother would not say such words out loud.

And showing what she'd been knitting to whoever came into the house!—Janette wanted to scream at her mother, in resentment.

For Mommy was knitting a little wool cap for Juliet, in fuzzy multicolored yarn. Out of nowhere knitting needles flashed and clicked, balls of yarn rolled underfoot.

Janette did not like it, Mommy insisted upon fitting the cap on Janette's head as she was knitting it, and if Daddy was home, Mommy called Daddy to look.

Often Mommy made a mistake in the knitting, and had to unravel rows of knitting that had gone wrong.

Knit, purl. Knit, purl. Janette watched the knitting needles flash and click, hypnotized.

Mommy said, Would you like to learn, honey? I can teach you.

No! Janette did not want to learn anything so silly and sad. Just for something to put on a *bald head.* No.

At last after weeks Mommy finished the knitted-rainbow cap which looked unexpectedly pretty. A final time it was fitted on Janette's head. It was just slightly loose, for Mommy had stretched the wool with her inexpert knitting but the colors were soft and pretty. Janette peered at herself squinty-eyed in a mirror and for the first time wished that the cap was hers. She felt how unfair it was, Mommy had never spent so much time on her; Mommy had never knitted a woolen cap for *her.*

Before Juliet became sick she and Juliet were given the same things. Neither was favored over the other. But now, Mommy and Aunt Leslie were always thinking of Juliet and never of Janette.

In a hurt little voice Janette asked if Aunt Leslie would be knitting a cap for her?—but Mommy pretended not to hear.

When Janette said certain things Mommy often did not hear.

Uncle Stan had moved away from his family, it was revealed. When Daddy heard, Daddy cursed—*That bastard!*

Janette's mother visited Juliet in the hospital and later in the new place that her aunt Leslie had rented but Janette was not invited to come with her mother nor was Janette encouraged to ask questions about these visits.

Mommy might say that Juliet was doing very well, doctors thought.

Or, Mommy might say—*Those damn doctors! Juliet is in intensive care again, a new infection.*

———

Like a ghost in sunshine Juliet began to fade.

Almost, Janette couldn't remember how her mother and her aunt Leslie had brought her and Juliet together two or three times a week, together in strollers they'd been pushed by their mothers, they'd spent hours at each other's houses as well as at the grandparents' house but now Juliet was beginning to be forgotten, even the name "Juliet" was not so often uttered in Janette's household.

For Janette had made friends in school. Their faces, their names, began to crowd out "Juliet" as a weak radio signal is crowded out by stronger radio signals.

Sometimes, Janette went to a friend's house after school, to play. Sometimes, a friend came to Janette's house after school.

Janette never told any of her friends about Juliet. There was so much to talk about!—continual chatter.

If Mommy had news of Juliet a certain tense expression came into her face which Janette learned to detect, sometimes Janette slipped away before Mommy could tell her; and if Janette had a question to ask about Juliet, if a certain expression—stiff, still—came into Mommy's face, or into Daddy's face, Janette quickly changed her mind and did not ask.

A child learns young: Calculate what the look in the adult face will be. Most urgently, the adult male face.

What you want is a smile, approving eyes. Bask in such approval which is love.

By the age of eight, Juliet had undergone *twelve surgeries.*

By the age of ten, Juliet had undergone *fifteen surgeries.*

And now, Juliet would be undergoing *reconstructive surgery.*

Such family news began to be discussed more openly in Janette's presence. For *reconstruction* was considered to be "good news"—"hopeful."

Rebuilding the face.
Once the scans are clean.
Unless it comes back—again . . .
Jesus! Their insurance won't begin to cover it.

And then one day after so long, Mommy took Janette to visit Juliet!—a surprise for Janette, who was cautioned not to show "shock" in her face.

For it seemed that Aunt Leslie and Juliet were living in a rented duplex, a brick rowhouse at the edge of the park, only two miles away.

"Juliet is looking so much better than in the past. But the surgery isn't perfect, you know."

Janette swallowed hard. What was she supposed to *know*?

". . . she has suffered a great deal. But she's been so brave. You will have to be prepared, honey. Just act like nothing is wrong, OK?"

Janette nodded, frightened and resentful. *OK.*

Instead of being taken to visit with one of her school friends Janette was taken to visit her cousin Juliet. This was *unfair.*

The reunion was meant to be casual, low-key. Mommy and Janette were just "dropping by" Aunt Leslie's house, and would not be staying long. It was explained to Janette that Juliet had almost no visitors for there was a danger of infection and (of course) Juliet hadn't been going to school, and was said to "tire quickly"; but the strange thing was, Janette was so anxious about the visit, and so distracted by the brick rowhouse in which her aunt and Juliet were living which was much smaller than their old house, and which she'd never seen before, she did not seem to recognize Juliet when she saw her right there in the living room: a stunted-looking child of some age younger than Janette, with a pasty-pale face that looked as if it had partly melted like wax, then hardened again, but not evenly; the left eyelid drooping, the eye unnaturally shiny, unfocused, like a doll's eye.

A face that might have been broken into two asymmetrical halves, then forced together again, like broken crockery.

Something mismatched about the lower jaw. And the nose, one nostril much narrower than the other, hardly more than a slit.

And on the head, that seemed unnaturally small, like a shrunken head, the fuzzy rainbow cap that Mommy had knitted.

Though Janette understood *this is Juliet* yet something in her brain balked and resisted *this is not Juliet!*—even as the adult sisters were looking anxiously at her, and the stunted little girl with the melted-away face was looking too, trying to smile.

Trying to speak to Janette, her chin quivering—*Hi! J-Janette . . .*

There came a jeering voice into Janette's ears *No no no* for this child, this freaky little thing, was shorter than Janette, and Juliet had been taller than Janette, everyone would know that.

And Juliet had not looked like *that.* Everyone knew.

Janette's eyes were rapidly blinking. Shrinking from the little stunted thing in loose-fitting denim pants and a too-bright yellow T-shirt, exactly as she'd been told she should not. Her upper lip curled away from her gum in the way that a dog's lip curls when it snarls but she was too shocked to speak, to make any sound at all.

Waves of dread, fear came over her, leaving her trembling, cold.

Aunt Leslie was moving to Janette, as if to hug her.

"Janette! Come here, honey . . ."

And Mommy was urging: "Say hello to Juliet, Janette! You haven't seen each other in *so long*."

The women's eyes grabbing at her. And the glassy disfigured eyes of the stunted child, fixed upon her so *eagerly*.

Badly Janette wanted to run away. Badly Janette wanted to hide her own face, shut her eyes.

But then, no. Janette steeled herself.

The mouth of the stunted little child twitched in a shy smile, to encourage. It came over Janette that the stunted child was feeling sorry for *her*.

Saying what sounded like *It's OK*.

Meaning: Juliet understood, Janette did not want to look at her.

But no, Janette would *try*. Stammering words, and smiling. Still her eyes were frightened. A pulse like a giant worm beat hard in her head.

It's OK, you don't have to.

Oh but I—I—

Eyes snatching at Mommy, for help. And Mommy was nodding urgently, pushing Janette gently forward.

A buzzing sound like wasps. But Janette was determined, she would be OK.

They were given bowls of chocolate ripple ice cream by Aunt Leslie. And Mommy had brought fresh-baked oatmeal cookies. On a sofa Janette sat awkwardly, feet dangling. The stunted little girl-cousin in the bright yellow T-shirt sat in a chair of some soft fabric that was child-sized, pulled close to Janette's dangling legs.

Juliet was having trouble eating for her mouth was twisted. Melted ice cream ran down her chin, which Aunt Leslie wiped with a tissue. Still the glassy eye remained fixed on Janette, which made her feel uncomfortable.

Spoon in hand, trying to eat ice cream that hurt her mouth,

so cold. Slowly chewing a cookie, hard to swallow since her mouth was so dry.

Mommy was urging Janette to tell Juliet about school for Juliet was going to be starting soon, in Janette's very school.

She'd had "tutoring" at home. And Aunt Leslie had tried "homeschooling." But Juliet would not be in Janette's grade: Juliet would only be in third grade, at the age of ten.

Third grade! Janette was in fourth grade. She felt a stab of hope that maybe she would not see Juliet, ever.

"You like school, Janette, don't you?—you like your teachers . . ."

Janette nodded, *yes.* But could not think of a thing to say.

"Who was your teacher last year, in third grade? Juliet will probably have her, too—Miss King—Klinger—"

Nodding *yes.* Squirming in misery, even chocolate ripple ice cream couldn't distract her from those glassy staring eyes only a few feet away from her, both knowing and forgiving.

Soon then, visits to the grandparents' house resumed. Not so often as before the surgeries, and neither girl had to stay overnight, but there was Juliet (one weekend following a visit to the ER, in a wheelchair), and there was Janette always expected to spend time with Juliet, and sit beside her at the long oak table.

Wanting to cry, Janette so resented it.

Not fair. Not fair to *her.* Everyone knew that Juliet *smelled.*

An odor like copper pennies held in the hand, wafting from Juliet's skin.

Or, worse, like something sickish sweetly rotting.

It was explained to Janette that the smell, if there was a smell, was just antiseptic from nurses changing the "port" in Juliet's chest (Janette *did not want to know* what a "port" was), or maybe it was the aftermath of chemotherapy (Janette *did not want to know* what "chemotherapy" was).

"The least you can do, sit with Juliet for a while. You know she tires easily, she'll be going home early."

"Oh, all right!"—Janette could have wept, this was so unfair.

Thinking—*I hate you, and I hate her.*

Unable to eat much. Sulky, sullen. Trying not to look too closely at Juliet only a few inches away. Only just nodding and murmuring to Juliet as Juliet tried to talk to her.

Trying not to inhale, to smell the chemical odor wafting from her cousin's clammy-looking skin. Trying not to become nauseated.

For days afterward Janette would complain to her mother: the sickish smell had gotten into her own hair, food smelled funny, she couldn't *eat.*

Resentful, and ashamed. For she knew that she was being cruel, and selfish, and hateful, and truly she did not hate Juliet, *she did not.*

Her mother looked at her with an expression of—what? Not dismay, not disgust, but pity.

"Oh, Janette. *You* have the life that has been taken from Juliet."

Janette crept away, abashed. How unfair was *this*!—Janette would never forgive her mother for saying such a thing.

Cosmetic reconstruction was a process that seemed never to end.

For always there were further surgeries for Juliet to undergo: skin grafts, bone grafts.

By seventh grade Janette's girl-cousin had a wan pale

delicate face that might have been mistaken for a "normal" face if you didn't look too closely.

But of course children look too closely. It's in the nature of (cruel) children, particularly middle-school boys, to *look too closely.*

No matter that Juliet's hair had mostly grown back: thin, fine, but a beautiful chestnut-red, springy with curls. And Juliet's mother bought her beautiful clothes, bright colors, soft textures. Still you could see that there was something wrong with Juliet's face, something asymmetrical, broken. And that look of being hunted in her face, almost a look of guilt.

I know, I am scary to see. I am sorry!

Glisten of fear in the "good" right eye, skin like something melted and coagulated.

Juliet's body was frail, undersized. She would not experience "puberty" as other girls did, it was explained to Janette in vague terms just clinical enough to make her cringe with embarrassment, mortification.

(Though in a way Janette envied her cousin: *not* to have cramps in the lower abdomen every few weeks, *not* to leak blackish vile-smelling blood from between the thighs . . .)

(*Not* to have to worry, ever, about becoming pregnant, having to have a baby. Whatever the ugly words meant—*knocked-up.*)

Juliet's medical condition, and the unpredictable nature of the condition, was known to school authorities, teachers. She had to be absent from school often for her white blood count was erratic; she required "infusions" for anemia.

Her (mismatched) eyes were enormous in her face. Very quiet, watchful, with that small smile of apology, or regret.

Freak-face—the boys called after Juliet.

Laughing, jeering. Taunting. Following her at school, if no adults were near. Following her after school. And if she turned her small pale face toward them, shrinking back in exaggerated horror.

Not all boys, only just some boys.

Not all days, only just some days.

Janette kept her distance. Knowing that Juliet's distress would be her distress if she came too near.

Winter afternoon. On the ground, hard-crusted snow.

Sharp cold like wires shoved up the nostrils and into the brain.

Is that Juliet walking ahead? On her way after school to the public library downtown?

Rare for Janette to see her cousin after school. Rare, Juliet walking alone on the street, for her mother usually drives her to school and picks her up after school.

Concerned about her health: Juliet picks up colds easily, becomes exhausted easily. Prone to respiratory ailments not related, it is claimed, to the cancer.

Now, the cousins are sixteen and fifteen. Both are sophomores at the high school, Juliet has been promoted ahead one year. But they don't often encounter each other since they are in different homerooms and have different schedules.

Poor Juliet!—wearing one of those silly-sad knitted caps (again). Which makes her head look shrunken. Which she doesn't remove in school. For the cancer has returned, now in something called lymph nodes. *She has weekly chemotherapy, Janette has heard. All her beautiful chestnut-red hair has fallen out (again).*

Such a shame! Such bad luck.

Janette has been hearing these exclamations for years, from her parents, relatives.

There is a weariness even of sorrow, grief. Like a muscle that has been pulled too often, and has lost its elasticity. Especially, the pain of another can become dulled.

Janette too is headed for the public library, to research a social studies project. She has meant to telephone her cousin, to ask what Juliet's project is, and how Juliet has been, for the cousins are in contact now, to a degree, though not often at school.

And Janette is older now, not so childish.

It has turned out that Juliet is a good student after all. Though her test grades are erratic, like her white blood count.

If her medications make her drowsy, she struggles to be average. At other times she is a reliable A student, she will have done homework assignments, studied diligently for tests and quizzes.

Janette's grades are B's except in math for which she has no aptitude, her teacher has told her bluntly. She has heard that Juliet has an A- in this subject, geometry, which she finds difficult to believe.

It's the mothers of the girl-cousins who carry tales back and forth between them. Sister-mothers who speak on the phone every day as if their lives matter so very much, even more now that their parents have passed away, the big old white-brick house has been sold, and all weekend visits to the lake have ceased forever.

At least, Janette thinks, with satisfaction, the damned Mother Goose lamp has been thrown away.

The pink-floral bedroom, she will never have to sleep in again. And Bonnie, Juliet's doll, she will never have to examine again, to see how superior a doll it is to Betsy, her stupid doll.

Though she feels guilty when her mother asks if she sees Juliet at school. For Aunt Leslie complains that Juliet has a hard time, kids can be so damned cruel. Janette explains to her mother in a contrite voice that she doesn't run into Juliet often at school for they aren't in the same homeroom and have only one class together—social studies. And yes, for sure, when Janette sees Juliet she always says hello and is extra-nice to her cousin . . .

Janette points out that Juliet was elected secretary in her homeroom so the kids are not all cruel. She *has never been elected to any office at school!*

Janette's mother acknowledges yes, that was nice of the students in Juliet's homeroom, that was kind of them, but why can't Janette sit with Juliet at lunch, Leslie is always complaining that Juliet doesn't have anyone to sit with in the cafeteria; but Janette protests there is a table near the entrance of the cafeteria reserved for students with special needs, a teacher sits with them in case they need assistance. She *wouldn't have been welcome if she'd tried to sit with Juliet, at that table.*

(Of course, this isn't true. A ridiculous lie, Janette wonders how her mother could believe it. And Juliet could sit with Janette and Janette's friends at any table in the cafeteria, if Janette invited her.)

Problem is, no one wants to see Juliet—her face. Even if you feel sorry for her, and like her, that face is, well—depressing.

Guys want to laugh, mostly. Girls, too. You do not want *to be depressed.*

If (for instance) a guy is (sort of) interested in you, and Juliet is with you, and he glances at Juliet, and . . .

These objections, tumbling through Janette's brain in the bright cold winter air like cheap colored plastic balls.

A half-block behind her cousin Janette can see how pedestrians stare at Juliet as they approach her, and pass her. Even adult women, who should know better.

Not that Juliet's face is luridly disfigured, it is not. After so many surgeries it is not a terrifying face, not a freak-face. And yet, it is more frightening than these because it might seem to the casual eye "normal"—until you look more closely and see the mismatched patches of skin, the asymmetrical jawline, the glassy-dead eye with its drooping lid.

Like looking into a mirror. Seeing in your own (familiar) face something profoundly unfamiliar, unexpected. Unfathomable.

For there is something in the human brain that fears, dreads, shrinks from deformity. From even the mildest deformity, which the eye can detect.

As a predator's eye is conditioned to detect the slightest motion, to recognize prey, so the human eye detects something not-right to signal to the brain.

Fear, disgust. Dread of difference. Disfigurement. Panic, hysteria.

A wish to deface the other: de-face.

So strangers, sighting the diminutive figure of Juliet on the street, looking much younger than sixteen, neither clearly female or male, very thin, in boxy jacket, loose-fitting slacks, knitted cap pulled low over her forehead, knowing nothing of her except that there is something not-right about her face, not knowing, not caring that she is sixteen years old, a cancer survivor (so far), a survivor of twenty-two facial surgeries (so far), a lover of animals, and a beloved daughter, react as if she were a threat, even an adversary to be shunned.

Middle-school boys are the worst. High-school boys, sometimes as cruel.

If they are in a group, not singly. If there are several of them they stare openly, mercilessly. Egging one another on, lips curling in disdain, sexual derision.

Hey! Gorgeous!—*crude monkey-laughter, wolf-whistling.*

Worse than the cancer, Juliet has said bitterly, how people stare at her in public, the things they say.

Janette wants to run to Juliet, to walk beside her. Wants to slip her arm through Juliet's arm. She will scream at the next crude louts who confront Juliet—Leave her alone! Leave my cousin alone. There is nothing wrong with her, it's *you.*

She will hug Juliet. You are beautiful—they are ugly. Pay no attention to them. I love you.

Janette's heart beats hard in indignation, anticipation. But she finds her steps slowing as she approaches the library. There are more pedestrians on the walkway here, more teenagers. Bravely Juliet continues, unwavering. If adolescent louts gape and stare at her, and mutter jeering words in her wake, Juliet ignores them. She is a frail girl but she has had years of practical, stoic poise, resignation. Her stitched-together face is a masterwork of impassive irony.

Janette watches as she climbs the stone steps to the library, pushes open the door, and steps inside, a quick glance back over her shoulder.

And the mocking boys left behind, forgotten.

And Janette, at the foot of the steps. Calculating how long she should wait before following her cousin into the library.

Heart beating in shame, guilt. For she suspects that Juliet has seen her.

Still, Janette remains irresolute on the sidewalk. Doesn't follow her cousin into the library. Not just yet.

"Oh, Janette, have you heard? Terrible news . . ."

Her mother burst into tears. Immediately, Janette knew.

Knew, and wanted to hurriedly break the phone connection.

". . . poor Juliet, she . . ."

Seven weeks into the fall term at Michigan State where Janette was living in a freshman residence, with two suitemates. While in Ann Arbor sixty miles away Juliet was a freshman at the University of Michigan, living alone in off-campus housing.

Juliet had been taking difficult courses in a pre-med sequence: biology, chemistry, statistics, computer science. Her early grades were high B's, an A-. But she'd begun to miss classes after a few weeks, her mother would learn. Discovered by a custodian in a locked bathroom in her room, comatose after an overdose of drugs, no idea how long she'd been there, alone.

Painkillers, sleeping pills: massive overdose. She never regained consciousness but died in the emergency room of University Hospital.

Ironically, at the time of her death Juliet was said to be cancer-free. Her last scan, six months before, had been clear. Her white blood count was stable. Her mother would claim she'd been excited about the university, "challenged" by her courses, "making new friends." She'd had her twenty-seventh surgery at the start of summer, cosmetic reconstruction of her jawbone and cheekbone. Her face she'd learned to "make up" with care, using special cosmetics. Her hair, thin, but wanly curly, still chestnut-red, she wore in a way to disguise the scar-stitches in her skin at her hairline.

Juliet had requested permission to live in off-campus housing, she had not wanted to endure the stress and commotion of a co-ed residence hall. She had not wanted to have a meal ticket for a cafeteria, she'd preferred to prepare her own food, for she had many dietary restrictions. She had not wanted roommates, to spare strangers her medical dramas, the protocols of her special needs. She'd wanted privacy, she could not bear pity.

She'd been "going out" with a young man, her mother

claimed. Janette, who had not (yet) had a boyfriend in East Lansing, was skeptical about this but said nothing of course.

She'd "seemed happy" over the phone. A visit home was planned at Thanksgiving.

Why would Juliet take her own life?—why *now*? This question had no answer yet would be asked relentlessly, pitilessly.

Janette dared not ask her mother if Juliet had left a suicide note behind. If the word *suicide* had even been uttered. If a coroner had ruled suicide, or accident.

Accidental death by overdose. That seemed likely, that would be the story that accrued to the premature death of a cancer survivor at the age of nineteen.

At the start of the fall term the girl-cousins had exchanged emails. They'd spoken on the phone briefly, once or twice; Juliet was the one to initiate both emails and calls. Juliet had expressed a guarded sort of enthusiasm for Ann Arbor where she knew virtually no one, she'd been excited about her courses, she'd confided in Janette that she was feeling "kind of lonely, sometimes."

Janette hadn't confided in Juliet. How anxious she felt about sorority rush, how uncertain about her courses, how lonely she, too, was feeling on the enormous windswept East Lansing campus where, like Juliet at Ann Arbor, she knew virtually no one; and anyone whom she did know, from high school, wasn't much interested in knowing Janette.

Why didn't I keep in touch with Juliet.

What is wrong with me!

God, what is wrong with me . . .

There would be a funeral in two days, Janette must return home.

Quickly assuring her mother of course, of course she would be there. Of course!

(Feeling a wave of despair, resentment. She would be missing events that weekend, crucial events, an open house at

Kappa Gamma Phi, which she was hoping to pledge, and there was a boy named Kevin, or Colin, who sat just behind her in her economics lecture, who'd suggested they might "get together" on Saturday night . . .)

Not telling her mother that Juliet had left a phone message for her two weeks ago Janette hadn't gotten around to answering.

Not wanting to admit to her mother that that was the last time she'd heard her cousin's voice.

Janette? Just would like to talk with you. I'm going through kind of a hard time . . .

Are you OK? Hope so!

Love you.

She'd meant to call Juliet, definitely. But somehow, she had not.

Recalling her mother saying to her as a child, in reproach—*You have the life that has been taken from Juliet . . .*

What a strange thing for a mother to say to a daughter!

How could it be *true,* it could not be.

The words made no sense. Her mother had spoken impulsively, recklessly. As if accusing Janette of being, simply—Janette, and not Juliet.

Abruptly breaking off the call with her mother, needing to escape. Sorry that she will seem rude. Sorry that she will upset her mother even more. Sorry that she can't bear to hear her mother crying again, all of them crying again.

"For her. Not for *me.*"

Chill overcast sky, late October, a smell of dank wet leaves.

She has rushed out of the residence hall without a jacket or coat!—people are looking at her, quizzically.

Needing to escape! Needing to breathe.

Trying not to cry. Enough crying! Her face is contorted with the effort, her mouth hurts like a fish's mouth, from which the hook has been roughly torn.

On the walkway swerving to avoid colliding with strangers. Her eyes are downcast, she dares not see faces. Her heart is pounding. There is something wrong with her coordination—her balance. Is she drunk? Drugged? That distraught-looking girl? Without a jacket or a coat, in forty-five-degree weather?

Eyes snag upon her like thorns. Shyly lifting her gaze she sees the concern in faces. And something more than concern.

She sees Kevin, or Colin, in a khaki jacket on the sidewalk ahead, he stares at her coldly and without recognition.

Usually she inspects herself carefully before leaving the privacy of her room. Usually she checks her makeup, her lipstick. Without makeup she is a plain earnest girl, without lipstick she appears lipless, unsexed. Her body is sturdy as a winter squash, her legs are dense with muscle. She finds herself at the edge of campus. Crossing Sixth Street, a flurry of horns in her wake. Hurrying past fast-food restaurants, clothing stores. No one else is running on Sixth Street, Janette is making a spectacle of herself. If she were a jogger she would be dressed differently. If she were a jogger she would know better than to run on the sidewalk annoying pedestrians.

In a bookstore window she sees a wraith-like face on a sturdy body, shadowy hollows for eyes like the eyes of a skull. Her jaws are clenched, unnatural. Her jawline is angular as an elbow. A child clutching his mother's hand stares at her, frightened.

Worse than the cancer, such stares.

Go away, go to hell! What do you know of me.

Her heartbeat is elevated, painful. Her breath comes in jolts and jags. She is desperate to escape being *seen.*

Panting, staggering, she makes her way to the university arboretum. On chill damp days the arboretum is near-deserted.

Still there are joggers in spandex stretch pants, proper running shoes, who glance at her startled. Strangers who regard the surprise of panting clammy-faced Janette with carefully neutral expressions.

Nowhere to go. Can't return to the residence, not yet. Heedless she'd run outside without a jacket or a coat or her cell phone, she can't call her mother, or Juliet.

Calling to explain. To apologize. *Not too late, just a touch on the phone screen—Juliet's number. She will!*

Juliet? Hi . . .

Gravel underfoot like crushed ice. An ache in her left side, badly out of breath. Run until your heart fails. Run until your heart bursts. In a lagoon in which desiccated lily pads float, festooned with broken rushes and cattails, there is murky rippling water. The face reflected there is rippled as if pockmarked, skull-eyed.

The oddly disjointed jaw, miniature fish-mouth gaping and panting.

"Mommy, look!"—a small child is staring at Janette, a few feet away.

"Shh!"—the young mother whispers, frowning.

Janette recoils, walks quickly away. She is abashed, wounded.

Cold air has stiffened her face, that fits her like a plaster mask. Her groping fingers discover that it is frozen, disfigured, as if a savage expression were stitched into the skin.

THE BICYCLE ACCIDENT

1.

Evie's accident with the bike, they would call it. Or, if reproach was intended, a hint that Evie had no one but herself to blame for almost getting killed on the Cayuga Street bridge, and for the summer of misery that followed, *Evie's accident with her bike.*

Was it a subtle distinction?—*the bike, her bike.*

Growing up in the family was like that, all of the children would recall. The household atmosphere was hearty and cheery like an indoor gym court, bright-lit, no shadows, sounds bouncing off the polished hardwood floor and off the high ceiling, nowhere to hide.

Nothing that seemed, to the children, not freighted with meaning.

Arlette, the children's mother, took care never to allude to the accident on the bridge in that way. She never blamed Evie.

She'd never have blamed any of the children in such circumstances, she'd been so grateful that her daughter was *alive.*

Before the accident, and *after.* Almost it would come to seem to Arlette, it had been her own knee that had been shattered on the Cayuga Street bridge, and her own skull cracked.

She tried to keep in mind, now that she was a mother, and a very responsible mother, that to children the world of adults is essentially non-negotiable. You have to listen to adults. Literally, you have to *look up* to adults. They lie to you when it's convenient for them, you won't discover until years later; if they tell the truth it's because truth gives them an advantage. They make excuses for themselves but blame you for what isn't always your fault, except you lack the capacity to explain. They can make you cry—but you hadn't better make them cry, they will never forgive you.

To think that you almost died, Evie—on that bridge! And we didn't even know where the hell you were.

How could you—sneak away like that, without telling me . . .

That had been the hurtful thing. *Without telling me.*

But none of this she'd allowed Evie to know. She wasn't that kind of mother.

Early that morning Arlette had enlisted Evie to help her prepare food for the outdoor reception she'd planned, to celebrate a niece's engagement. Mother and daughter working as a team in the kitchen. In the backyard, the boys helping their father set up rental tents, tables, and folding chairs.

Forty-eight guests! For weeks Arlette had been anticipating this day. On the kitchen wall calendar June 23 was circled in red marker pen like an exploding nebula.

Of the forty-eight guests at least one-third were Cassie's fiancé's relatives and friends, strangers to her. Arlette planned to prepare the food herself, she refused to hire a caterer or pre-order food.

And now, rain was forecast for late afternoon. A prospect of huddling beneath dripping tents instead of spreading over the lawn where banks of bridal wreath and crimson peonies were blossoming.

It had been a season of summer squalls, rainstorms. By mid-morning the sky was pale and featureless, no rain clouds in sight, still you couldn't take a chance less than twenty miles from Lake Ontario.

In Strykersville they'd all grown up beneath that sky. Storm clouds could take shape within minutes, above the massive lake. Thunder in the distance like a sound of rolling barrels, lightning, quick pelting rain, walls of rain yet within an hour a sudden break in the darkened sky, rays of sun shining through as if it were the most natural thing in the world—sunlight, and not storm.

Since she'd first set the date for her niece's reception, Arlette had had difficulty sleeping. Frequently she woke from dreams of food, guests, weather. Kevin laughed at her, she'd become so fixated on food. Like foaming waterfalls entire menus rose and fell in her brain. Appetizers, entrées, desserts were roiling fevers in her blood.

A summer buffet meant cold things: Platters of fresh-sliced turkey breast, Virginia ham, roast beef. German potato salad, cole slaw. Sweet corn. Deviled eggs. Tomatoes. A green salad of romaine lettuce, Boston lettuce, fresh basil. Everything fresh-prepared, nothing acquired readymade from a food store or the farmer's market. The sourdough bread Arlette would bake that very morning, anyone who entered the house would smell the mouthwatering aroma. A fruit platter, artfully arranged: pineapple chunks, melon balls, pitted black cherries, strawberries, blueberries, raspberries. Banana cream pie, angel's food cake with chocolate chiffon frosting, several flavors of ice cream.

Arlette was disappointed that Kevin had agreed to let their

well-to-do older friend Rob Nash provide the more costly drinks—wine (white, red), whiskey, vodka, gin.

Cassie, the niece, was deeply moved that Arlette was hosting the party for her and her fiancé. Yet saying, weakly: "You know, you don't need to do this for us, Aunt Arlette. A catered reception would be so much easier. No fuss."

It wasn't *fuss,* Arlette protested, hurt. Since Cassie's mother had passed away three years before, it seemed to Arlette the least she could do for the family. For her sister.

Kevin thought that a caterer was pretentious—"putting on airs." Nothing so riled up Kevin as "putting on airs." Still, forty-eight guests were many more people than they'd ever had at a backyard barbecue.

At least, he wasn't going to try to barbecue for the guests. Arlette insisted upon providing everything, a cold buffet.

Kevin took pride in the three-acre property at the edge of Strykersville. Bi-level ranch, redwood façade, white aluminum siding, shingled roof. Mowed the lawn himself on a tractor-mower, built the redwood deck with the help of a carpenter-friend. Varsity football and baseball, Strykersville High; courses in business administration at Chautauqua Community College. He was a part-owner of Ace Hardware at the mall. Shaking hands with customers six days a week, convivial, good-hearted. A businessman's reputation is his capital.

Nothing *pretentious* about Kevin Hansen. With a chainsaw he kept the trees and shrubs on his property trimmed, from the deck you had a scenic view of farmland behind the ranch house, rolling foothills of the Chautauqua Mountains.

Whistle while you work, guys!—in the backyard Kevin ordered the boys around in his funny-Daddy voice.

In the kitchen Arlette put Evie in charge of appetizers. Deviled eggs were the challenge. Time-consuming, and not so easy. Why her mother couldn't just buy deviled eggs at the

Safeway, Evie had no idea. All this work. Her work. To prove—what? To save money?

Evie was thirteen years old, no longer a young child flattered when Arlette cooed at her, calling her *Mommy's little helper.* No longer grateful for her mother's praise. She'd resented being wakened so early on a Saturday. She resented her brothers out in back with their father, laughing and shouting.

With Daddy, there was always some kind of *horsing around* as Arlette called it disapprovingly.

With Mom, there was nothing like that. No loud laughing, no fun. You had to take care not to seem impertinent—"mouthy."

By late morning Evie had begun to grow fatigued, restless. Cramped quarters in the kitchen working at the Formica-topped counter beside Arlette who was edgy, irritable. Evie begged to be allowed to ride her bicycle to the end of the cul-de-sac and back, just five minutes.

"Not right now. We don't have time to waste."

So envious!—Roy and Billy got to ride with Daddy to the mall, to pick up supplies. They were away forty minutes at least. (Stopping at the Dairy Queen for cones, Evie just *knew.*) Her father liked to pretend that Evie was *Daddy's little girl* but really, he preferred her brothers who were eleven and eight. The way he played with them rough and growling with laughter was nothing like the way he'd played with Evie, treating her like a doll that might break in his hands.

It was unfair, unjust. Evie was captive with her bossy mother in the kitchen stuck with the task of preparing three dozen deviled eggs which had to be done in stages: one dozen eggs at a time. Bringing the eggs to a slow boil in a pan, making sure they didn't crack. Cooling the eggs in cold water, in the sink. Removing the shells, which required precision and skill, and patience, which Evie didn't have, so the task took twice as long and was messy, bits of eggshell stuck to the rubbery egg whites Evie had to pick off singly, with her nails. *So many eggs! So boring! She just hated kitchen work!*

But that was just the preliminary step. Now came carefully scooping out the hardboiled yolks, one by one. Mashing the yolks in a bowl with a fork, mixing in mayonnaise, lemon juice, vinegar, paprika, red pepper, salt. Then, spooning the mixture back into the egg whites taking care not to ruin them while (Evie was bitterly thinking) at the Safeway you could purchase deviled eggs on a large plastic circular platter with shallow indentations for the eggs so that they wouldn't slip and slide onto the floor.

"You're doing a messy job with those eggs, Evie! Pay attention! We don't have time to waste, it's almost noon."

Evie lifted a plate precipitously, two eggs slithered to the floor.

"Oh *damn.*"

Half-sobbing under her breath but of course Arlette heard.

"Watch your mouth, young lady. Finish up those eggs and put them in the refrigerator with waxed paper over them."

The things you hear yourself uttering!—*Watch your mouth, young lady.* And your daughter staring at you like she hates you.

Problem was, her role in all this was *mother.* Someone had to be *mother,* Arlette was it.

Kevin was one of those exasperating fathers, if the kids were dogs he was the parent to let them run off-leash secure in the knowledge that the mother would discipline them as Arlette bathed, clothed, fed the younger children, responsible for keeping all three of them not only alive but presentable in the sharp-assessing eyes of others.

By *others* meaning family, in-laws. Relatives. Neighbors,

friends and acquaintances with whom you'd gone to school, whose scrutiny you cannot ever elude.

"Excuse me, Arlette honey—d'you mind?"

Rob Nash entered the kitchen needing to use the bathroom in the hall. Any space Rob Nash entered, he took up all the oxygen. Big ruddy face, big beaming smile, faded Rolling Stones T-shirt strained tight over his torso round as a drum. A wink for Arlette and a waggish thumbs-up for the thirteen-year-old Evie—plain, pale face, hips narrow as a boy's.

One of those friends of Evie's parents who'd say to her, half-chiding, reproachful, as if she'd played a prank on them: "Hey, sweetie! You've *grown.*"

Expecting you to explain, somehow. Apologize?

Just stammer and blush like an idiot. Resist the urge to run away.

Rob Nash had arrived mid-morning in his Land Rover to help Kevin and the boys set up for the reception, Arlette had been hearing his braying laughter out back. You couldn't help but smile, Rob Nash was on the premises. Rob was a great joker, a teller of tales, brazen in exaggeration, kind, generous. True, he was bossy; but funny-bossy. Rob was one to *make much of you,* if he singled you out for attention.

Arlette had a suspicion that Rob had talked Kevin into allowing him to provide not only drinks for the reception but the rented tents, tables, and chairs—if not, Rob had surely arranged for Kevin to rent the equipment at a discount.

Rob Nash liked to boast that he knew everyone in Strykersville. When it came to favors he was the *most owed.*

Often Rob joked mysteriously, laying a forefinger beside his nose. Rob's nose was broad and flattened as if the cartilage had been broken and had only part-mended. His cheeks were stippled with broken capillaries close beneath the skin. You were made to think that you were in on the joke while others were excluded but in fact you weren't really in on the joke, had no idea what the joke was, but Rob Nash was inviting you to pretend you did because he liked you.

Because you are a favorite of his. Rob Nash's inner circle. Because you are special.

Rob Nash had been her father's friend initially. He'd been a lawyer, businessman, philanthropist. (Not that *philanthropist* was a word casually employed. *Generous, gives away money* was the more likely expression.) At one time he'd been an amateur actor, the high point of his acting career had been the role of the Stage Manager in Thornton Wilder's *Our Town* when Arlette had been in middle school. She recalled seeing him moving about the stage as a spotlight moved with him—not a handsome man exactly but with the assurance of a handsome man, a ringing voice that could drop to a husky whisper. He'd had hair then, thick-tufted leonine hair, going gray at the temples.

As Rob Nash aged, his body had thickened. He wasn't so tall as he'd once been. He dressed to catch the eye—plaid blazers, floral neckties, seersucker suits in summer; his casual clothes were T-shirts, jeans, khakis. His eyes were a pale bemused blue. He had a habit of sagely stroking his chin as if stroking a beard. His speech was liberally sprinkled with profanities and obscenities when he was in the company of men; in the company of women, he took care to speak courteously. Kevin was shrewd enough never to discuss politics with Rob Nash and of course, Arlette would never have discussed politics with any of the men. Invariably Rob had the *inside story* on local and state politicians. He knew *where the bodies were buried.* Some of the stories were shocking, scandalous. You didn't know whether to believe him. In the midst of a story Rob would break off, laughing: "You believe this bullshit? I was just testing you."

Rob had been married twice, divorced twice. Arlette had a

vague memory of the wives—both pale-blond women, "stylish." No children. Often Rob expressed disappointment, no children. Life disappointed him. Women disappointed him. But he didn't dwell upon the past, he was a *progressive.* What you'd call a *progressive-conservative.*

It was generally known that Rob Nash had drawn up his will more than once. He had intense friendships, he demanded loyalty. He'd disinherited relatives who had disappointed him. Kevin knew: you took great care what you said to Rob Nash even when he seemed to be inviting frank talk, intimate exchanges. Rob frequently hinted that Kevin, Arlette, and their children would be "remembered" in his will. It was said of Rob that he was a devoted friend but he could be an even more devoted enemy. You did not ever want to *cross* Rob Nash.

Arlette thought this was unfair. All sorts of nonsense was said about prominent personalities in Strykersville. She'd never had the slightest feeling of unease around Rob. He *was* like an uncle to her, she'd basked in his attention as a girl. He had given her gifts—cashmere sweater sets, charm bracelets, a $100 gift certificate at Strykersville's leading clothing store for women. When she'd graduated from high school he'd hosted a party for her at the Chautauqua Country Club.

It was true, Rob had a way of praising girls and women that could be insulting, dwelling upon their physical appearances, but he rarely spoke in that way of Arlette. Once, he'd said, *Your children are beautiful, Arlette. But that's no surprise, they're your children.*

Arlette had tried to joke that Kevin had had something to do with the children, too. Rob Nash had recoiled with a look of distaste. *No!*

What that could possibly mean, Arlette had no idea. You laughed at Rob Nash's jokes, or what might have been jokes.

As a young married couple Arlette and Kevin seemed to

have inherited Rob Nash as a kind of uncle, the kind that gives gifts, sometimes expensive gifts, but insists upon no gifts in return—"I can afford it, kids. You can't. No problem." Rob had lent Kevin money for a down payment on Kevin's Ford Ranger pickup, he'd helped out with the Hansens' property taxes from time to time. How much he'd invested in Ace Hardware Arlette didn't know, but he'd certainly invested something.

Couldn't ask Kevin, that would provoke a frown between Kevin's eyebrows sharp as the mark of a knife blade in bread dough.

Rob Nash lingered in the kitchen talking and laughing with Arlette as she stood at the Formica-topped counter preparing potato salad. Rob was a shameless gossip, offering Arlette tidbits of information about mutual acquaintances, to which Arlette would respond, drawing in her breath: "Oh, Rob! That is *not true.*" (Of course, Evie was to overhear all this as well.) Rob had been drinking ale in the backyard, he and Kevin both. The men were most at ease with each other when they were drinking. Rob's face was looking windburnt, pleasantly flushed. The much-faded Rolling Stones T-shirt had worked up on his torso, baring a patch of waxy-white, slack, and shiny midriff.

At the farther end of the counter Evie was hoping that her mother's talkative friend wouldn't take notice of her. If Rob Nash addressed her at all it would be teasing, which she dreaded. She'd been urged to call this friend of her parents' *Uncle Rob* but never had, not once.

As a young child she'd been a daydreamer in school, in church, in any situation in which adults were in charge and you were held captive. Recalling how once she hadn't been able to avoid overhearing a conversation between Rob Nash and her parents outside on the deck, how Rob Nash was boasting he planned to help out with her college tuition someday, for instance if Evie wanted to attend a private university like Syracuse or Cornell—*You both know, you can count on me, right?*

Evie watched in disgust as her mother lifted a spoonful of potato salad to Rob Nash's gaping mouth. Was her mother *flirting* with big-bellied Rob Nash?

"Fan-tas-tic, Arlette"—Rob smacked his lips.

Breaking off then a piece of Virginia ham in his fingers, chewing and pronouncing it also "fan-tas-tic."

Evie looked away, shuddering. *Gross!*

As if Rob Nash had been reading her mind there he stood looming above her laughing at her discomfort. Inspecting the platter of deviled eggs. Evie dreaded him scooping up an entire egg and devouring it but instead, as if more intimately, Rob drew his forefinger in a circle inside the bowl Evie had used to prepare the mixture, tasting it and declaring it *"délicieuse."*

"Arlette, you've got a terrific little helper here."

Evie was vastly relieved when Rob Nash left the kitchen. But within a few minutes there came Rob back to the door, bringing his large beaming face close to the screen, startling both Evie and Arlette with his ebullient voice—"Hey! Sorry to interrupt again. Arlette, your husband is sending me for ice, he's freaking out that the 7-Eleven will run out if we wait much longer. Evie, you coming with me?"

Quickly Evie shook her head *no.* She didn't dislike Rob Nash but wasn't comfortable around adults. Even adults of whom she was fond. Nothing to say to them but they talked at you non-stop, like you were a deaf-mute. Even Daddy, sometimes when they were alone—nothing to say to each other really.

"Yes, go with Rob, you can help him with the ice. Keep him company. You've been whining to have a break, *go on.*"

Arlette spoke pleasantly. Not at all bossy.

Evie laughed uneasily. Muttering *guess not.*

"Don't be ridiculous, Evie. Go with Uncle Rob. He's been working hard helping your father, out there in the sun."

Evie rolled her eyes, only Arlette could see. Why was Mom doing this!

Siding with Rob Nash. For always adults will side with each other. Rarely will adults fail to side with each other.

Briskly Arlette said: "I'll finish up here. You've left quite a mess. Go on with Rob, be useful for a change."

Grinning Rob Nash was holding the screen door open. Evie had no choice but to slip through, beneath the man's brawny forearm.

It gave her a shivery sensation, to feel the top of her head, her hair, lightly brush against his arm.

So Evie rode off with Rob Nash in his sporty Land Rover, to the 7-Eleven in town. They would be gone nearly an hour but Arlette took little notice since she was on the phone with her niece Cassie, not an urgent call but a time-consuming call; shortly after, the phone rang again and it was a friend explaining why she couldn't come to the party, had to cancel, sorry for the last-minute notice as Arlette felt her heart pound with dread—*What if more guests cancel? Don't show up?* She had made herself so vulnerable.

By this time Kevin had succeeded in erecting the party tents. The backyard was looking crowded but festive. Arlette was feeling encouraged.

Most of the food preparation was done. The refrigerator was crammed.

Time for the hostess to hurry upstairs, shower. Change into a halter-top summer dress, white cotton percale with splotches of red poppies, belted waist. Blow-drying her (dark-blond, fading-but-still-glamorous) hair which felt like luxury to her, sensuous, comforting as a disembodied caress. In the mirror, frowning as she rubbed moisturizer into her (just slightly dry) skin, creamy-beige makeup, powder. No mascara to highlight her eyes, not in daylight. But poppy-red lipstick giving life to her mouth.

When Arlette returned to the kitchen she saw the Land Rover rolling into the driveway. There was Rob Nash unloading two massive bags of ice cubes from the rear of the vehicle—one of these he left outside with Kevin, the other he brought slung over his shoulder into the kitchen to shove into the freezer.

Straggling behind Rob Nash was Evie, both arms crossed against her chest carrying a grocery bag with bottles rattling inside: tonic water, seltzer, six-pack of Coke. These were purchases Rob Nash had made on the spur of the moment—"Just so you don't run out. Better too much than too little, right?"

"Rob, thanks! What do we owe you for this?"—Arlette felt she had to ask, out of politeness.

Rob Nash laughed, dismissing her question with an airy wave of his hand.

"It's on the house, of course. It's on 'Uncle Rob.'"

He was going home now to "spruce up"—Rob said; he'd be back soon for the gala event.

Hard to be a bachelor living alone in Strykersville, Arlette thought, with a twinge of sympathy, pity. Such a *family* kind of town.

Arlette had the uneasy idea that Rob intended to give Cassie and her fiancé some sort of engagement present, possibly a check. And if a check, a large check. No one else would have presents for the couple, not for an engagement. Rob Nash had always to *amplify* things, that was his way.

Why some people thought that Rob Nash was a terrific person, and why some couldn't stand him.

There stood Evie with the grocery bag still clasped across her flat chest. Her hair was disheveled, her pale blue eyes puffy-damp, narrowed.

Arlette told her to put the bag down, please! Go upstairs, take a shower, put on something nice for a change, not those same old denim shorts.

"And be sure to shampoo your hair, and use conditioner so it won't frizz like dandelion fuzz. And don't take forever, we're running late."

Evie let the bag fall rattling onto the kitchen counter. Stony-faced pushing past her mother without a word.

"And don't run on the stairs!"—even as the girl lunged upward on the stairs heavy-footed as an adult.

Arlette felt a stab of dismay—*her* daughter.

Never would she have confessed to anyone, certainly not to Kevin, that she envied her women friends whose daughters were attractive, charming—fun to be around. At least two of them startlingly beautiful, at Evie's age.

It was a damned hard world, for a girl who wasn't attractive. Regardless what people said. Feminists meaning to be optimistic, encouraging. Of course it would help that Evie was bright, at least at school, but the fact was, no one would glance twice at Evie, if there were other girls in the vicinity.

Arlette knew. Arlette knew all too well. She'd barely qualified as *pretty,* in high school and beyond. Determined to make the most of what she'd been born with, at least.

Try to explain to your children, they wouldn't have been born except for you. Desperation coursing in your veins, to find someone to love you well enough to marry you.

That was the challenge.

Arlette located the boys, herded them upstairs to see that their faces and hands were properly washed, get them into clean clothes. Billy with a dirty face, looking like a ferret!

Roy was old enough to take care of himself but couldn't be trusted.

Never finished, taking care of children. Treadmill. Infinity of details. Like opening a kitchen drawer, seeing a swarm of tiny black ants, quickly shoving the drawer shut again. Can't face it just now. No.

Downstairs the first guests were arriving: cousins who'd volunteered to help with the reception.

You're looking terrific, Arlette!

You're *looking terrific!*

Damn!—the phone again. Arlette drew a deep breath, steeled herself for another apology but it was only one of Kevin's annoying relatives asking what time the reception began.

(Where was Evie? Still upstairs? Arlette shouted up the stairs for her, she was needed in the kitchen.)

Cassie arrived with the fiancé. Nervous laughter, hearty handshakes. The fiancé was taller than Arlette remembered, better-looking. Cassie had done something with her hair, a kind of weird pink rinse that wasn't becoming. Arlette felt a rush of emotion—*engagement, wedding, marriage. Love.*

All this behind her now. Just slightly spoiled, rank as a container of milk in the refrigerator beginning to sour.

Still, you are grateful. Arlette *was.*

Other relatives arrived. As if a dam had burst, a sudden swarm of people.

Was it going to rain? Thunder, lightning? What if there wasn't enough food? Enough to drink? Rob Nash would help in an emergency, Arlette could rely upon him to drive her into town to the food store . . . Thank God Kevin was herding people out of the crowded kitchen, onto the deck.

Outside, loud rock music. Kevin's speakers, on the terrace. Tuned to a local rock station which wouldn't have been Arlette's choice.

Greeting guests. Quick hugs. Lipstick smeared on cheeks. In her sandals with a medium heel Arlette was stumbling, carrying platters outside.

Stylish shoes, sexy, not practical. Wanting to show off her shapely legs, almost-slender ankles. Recalling how when she'd been pregnant each time her ankles had swollen. Her belly, but also her face. Puffy-eyed, short of breath. With his stiff vacant smile Kevin had managed to avoid looking at her, touching her.

In a while she'd kick off the shoes. After a drink or two, why not? Barefoot. That was sexy, too. She wasn't yet forty years old. She was the hostess, her toenails were polished bright poppy-red.

Cassie had waylaid Arlette in the kitchen. Speaking in a lowered voice, Arlette couldn't follow. More guests arriving. Someone in a Jeep parking on the lawn beside the driveway, if Kevin saw he'd freak out.

Cassie seemed to be concerned about something. The pupils of her eyes looked dilated, her complexion was blotched beneath heavy makeup. Her hair was frizzy as an Afro, or nearly: brassy-blond-pink rinse. It had long been one of Arlette's wishes, that her (deceased) sister's daughter would connect with her; yet now, amid this commotion, Arlette found herself laughing nervously, shrinking from intimacy. Could Cassie help her carry out the appetizers?

Bowls of nuts. Fresh-cut vegetables, creamy-dill dip. Evie's deviled eggs quivering on a platter.

In a snug-fitting blue-striped seersucker jacket and white cord trousers Rob Nash reappeared rubbing his hands together in anticipation.

Drinks? Plenty of drinks. Tubs filled with ice, cold drinks.

A party is like a stream, Arlette was remembering. You are anxious at the start but soon the fast-moving current carries you away. You begin to relax. You have a drink—white wine with an Italian label, provided by Rob Nash. You have a second drink. Soon you are laughing with the others.

Of course what other purpose is there to a party?—laughter.

Party-buzz, hilarity. Even with an overcast sky, ominous rumbling of thunder in the distance.

Kevin the husband: military-style crewcut, muscled shoulders, polo shirt, and khaki shorts, happily handing out ice-cold cans of beer, ale, soda.

It might have been a half-hour, forty minutes. Arlette was summoned inside the kitchen, to the phone.

"Oh hell, who is it?"

One of the older women relatives, calling to her through the screen: "I think—they're saying—the hospital?"

"The—*what*?"

Arlette hurried stumbling into the house. Blindly seizing the receiver.

"Yes? This is the Hansens' residence, who is this?"

In this way, so abruptly their lives cut in two. As if with a meat cleaver.

Loud rock music, uplifted voices and laughter, a buzzing in the mother's ears as she hears herself asking in disbelief, "What? What are you saying? *What?*"

2.

Evie wasn't upstairs, and Evie wasn't in the backyard. Evie was in the ER at Strykersville General Hospital.

She'd had an accident, riding her bicycle across the Cayuga Street bridge two miles from home.

Witnesses reported that the thirteen-year-old had been pedaling her bicycle rapidly—recklessly—on the pedestrian walkway where warning signs were prominently posted: *Bicycles Must Be Walked Not Ridden Across the Bridge.*

The Cayuga Street bridge was a two-lane iron-girder bridge of another era. Vans and SUVs had to maneuver carefully to pass each other on it; larger vehicles were banned altogether.

The ramp leading up from the roadway was steep, the floor of the bridge was open-mesh grating. If you looked down through the grating you could see the river moving swiftly beneath in a way to dazzle the eye and benumb the brain.

Halfway across the bridge the bicyclist had to swerve to avoid colliding with a pedestrian, a young mother pushing a toddler in a stroller. There were screams from both the young mother and the cyclist whose sneakered foot slipped from the right-hand pedal of the bicycle in such a way that her bare leg was dragged down below the pedal, trapped between the underside of the pedal and the open-mesh grating against which her knee and leg were being scraped raw as the bicycle hurtled inexorably forward. Head-first she was pitched over the handlebars and fell entangled with the bicycle, hard. In the adjacent lane vehicles were braking, sounding their horns. For it looked as though the young bicyclist might tumble into the lane of traffic.

A woman passenger in a passing car screamed from the car window. And the cyclist herself was heard whimpering as she lay in a tangle of bicycle wreckage, the full length of her right leg trapped beneath the pedal exposing tendons, ghastly white bone amid a gushing of blood.

Fallen hard, sprawled with arms outstretched as if from a great height, thrown with force. Her head was bleeding badly from a three-inch gash in her scalp, it would be discovered that her skull was fractured. Her upper front teeth had been knocked from her ravaged gums. Her useless right leg was not only massively lacerated but broken below the knee, her right knee shattered. The sneaker was wrenched from her right foot, white cotton sock torn and bloodied. The mangled bicycle would be left behind on the pedestrian walkway, nearly unrecognizable as a bicycle.

In the ambulance the stricken girl was unable to speak, to identify herself. Her mouth filled with blood from the broken teeth and had to be suctioned repeatedly, to prevent her drowning in her own blood. She passed in and out of consciousness as a creature fleeing for its life passes in and out of splotches of sunshine and cloud-shadows. An oxygen mask was pressed over her mouth and nose, alternating with the suction device. In mute anguish her broken fingernails clawed at a wall of solid rock that appeared before her in stark oneiric vividness, frantic to claw, grasp, in an effort to climb the blank rock to haul herself up impossibly.

Medical workers could discover no ID in the pockets of the girl's torn and blood-splattered clothing. It was believed that they might lose their patient before arriving at the ER on West Avenue but somehow that did not happen, her young heart faltered but rallied, continued to beat.

After forty minutes in the ER the patient appeared to be stabilized. The oxygen mask was tentatively removed. Numbness surrounded the patient like an opaque fog. Embedded in a pain so massive she could not feel it, like one buoyed aloft by a dark sea so massive it cannot be seen.

In a faint voice the patient provided her name, address—*Eavanne Hansen, 1664 Post Road.*

A call was made to the Hansen residence, her mother spoke with the hospital dispatcher, both parents came at once to the hospital where their daughter was undergoing an fMRI scan.

Following which, emergency surgery to reduce swelling in her brain.

Later, the parents would recall the vigil at the hospital, through the night. Well into the next day. Dazed, lethargic. Disbelieving. Utter shock: that their daughter hadn't been safely at home, as they'd assumed, or would have assumed if they'd been questioned, but miles away, fighting for her life.

The particular shock of such a revelation, amid the festivity of a backyard party.

Never would Arlette forget the disbelief with which she'd learned, from a stranger, over the telephone, that her daughter was elsewhere. When she would have sworn, *she was absolutely certain,* that she knew where Evie was.

What—are you saying? What?

These words echoing in her head, for days afterward. Weeks, months, and eventually years.

As they'd parked crookedly at the curb outside the ER, in a zone clearly marked *No Parking.*

Forgotten as if it had never been: the reception for Cassie and her fiancé.

An event obsessively planned for weeks, deleted from consciousness abruptly as a light switched off.

So abruptly had the Hansens left their guests back at the house, only a few (who'd happened to be in the kitchen at the time of the call) knew where they'd gone.

When Rob Nash heard the news, incomplete as it was, like a ship's captain he calmly assumed responsibility for the situation. Briskly informing guests that there'd been a "family emergency"—Evie had had a "bicycle accident"—suggesting that they go home and refrain from calling the Hansens until (maybe) the next morning.

Rob Nash, in charge. Not jovial but stark cold sober as he was rarely seen. Now that his broad smile had faded, the laugh lines at the corners of his eyes looked like minute white stitches in the skin.

The boys' grandparents were at the reception, they would take care of Roy and Billy who were looking terrified at their parents' rapid departure with not a word to them.

At the hospital Arlette and Kevin were telling themselves—*All that matters is, our daughter is alive.*

Weeks, months to follow—*All that matters is, our daughter is alive.*

Hesitant to ask doctors if there would be a *full recovery.* Better not to ask, just yet.

Shattered knee, requiring surgery; broken femur, skull fracture. Bleeding in the brain.

Arlette wept in gratitude, her daughter was *alive.* For the time being, that would be enough.

Some sort of bicycle accident, Rob Nash would say. Shrug of his shoulders, a gesture signaling that whatever it was that had happened on the Cayuga Street bridge, precipitated by the daughter, it was essentially a small matter, foolish, juvenile. *Blown up out of all proportion. Fluke.*

Soon to become one of Rob Nash's tales, told about town. For Rob Nash was something of a first-hand witness, the Hansens' closest family friend.

In the telling Rob would not speak of Evie by name. Giving the impression of not knowing her name.

Kids riding their bicycles in traffic, not watching where they're going. Over the Cayuga Street bridge! Supposed to get off and walk their bikes over the bridge but they don't. That age, think they will live forever. (Hell, we thought we would live forever, didn't we?) You hear their music, that's in their heads twenty-four hours a day. No wonder they can't think straight.

But you run over one of them, you will be the one that's arrested. Spend the rest of your life in prison.

Well—maybe not. Maybe not in prison. But feeling guilty, for sure. Spend the rest of your life feeling guilty.

Rob Nash, flush with drink, laying a forefinger beside his big-pored nose, intoning with a grave shake of his head as if passing judgment on an entire generation.

Wouldn't think a bike accident, a kid on a bike, could be so serious, ruin everybody's life but of course if they're not wearing a safety hat, helmet—what d'you call it—which she was not, that girl—Kevin Hansen's girl . . . Whose fault is that?

For eighteen days Evie was a patient in the Strykersville hospital. These were bleary, blurry days of which she would have little recollection afterward.

Initially in the intensive care unit, where her condition was *critical.* Moved then to the general hospital and from there to the rehab clinic adjacent to the hospital where she was first an in-patient wincing with pain when the opioid haze protecting her wore thin then an out-patient (wheelchair, crutches, walker, finally a single crutch) driven to the clinic usually by her mother through the remainder of the interminable summer and well into the fall when everyone she knew of school age returned to *normal life.*

When not at the rehab clinic she was in a dental clinic in Rochester, sixty miles away, undergoing surgery to repair her injured mouth and, in time, being fitted for a partial plate replacing the five upper front teeth literally knocked from her mouth; to these sessions as well, Arlette drove Evie.

For of course, Kevin could not take so much time off from the hardware store. That went unquestioned.

"Smile, Eavanne! Wide smile! Try like you mean it!"—the jolly portly dentist encouraged his patient so forcefully, Arlette found herself grinning a wide clown smile in her daughter's place.

At home, a rented hospital bed had been brought into the TV room, which awkward space became Evie's quarters for the next several months; and those months were a succession of doctors' appointments, blood tests, X-rays, and CAT scans, fMRIs monitoring the damage to the part of her brain known as the frontal lobe, where the fracture had been most severe.

In her weakened state Evie was susceptible to infections, sudden fevers. Often she was prescribed antibiotics. Medication for pain, for sleep. Medication to counter the gastric distress of other medication. By slow degrees her right leg and knee were healing but Evie had a morbid fear of easing her weight onto that side of her body, rebreaking the broken bones.

"I can't. I can't. Just *can't*."

Arlette said gently, "Of course you *can*."

For weeks Evie was almost wholly dependent upon her mother. Big weepy baby. Could not make her way to the bathroom unassisted—(that was humiliating!). Could not prepare her own food, deal with such practicalities as bathing herself, shampooing her hair. Changing the soiled bedclothes two or even three times a week.

Waking in the night not knowing where the hell she was. Night itself confused with day amid the prevailing opioid numbness like cotton batting through which flashes of pain penetrated like flashes of lightning in a clear sky.

Pain-flashes that left her grasping, in pure visceral shock. They could come at any time, you could never predict.

"Mom! *Mom!*"—heard herself crying, calling like a helpless child. For indeed she was a helpless child, in thrall to her captors.

Arlette came at once. Even in the night, hastily, anxiously.

There was a kind of power in this, that Evie could summon her mother by raising her voice. Evie could disturb the entire household if she called out loudly enough, in a voice tremulous with terror.

When Arlette asked Evie why was she so frightened when she was safe here at home Evie answered in a hushed voice: "But I am not safe here. We are not safe anywhere. They didn't tell you—I died in the ambulance. They were afraid of being sued, probably. I saw my actual soul, like smoke. It came out of my mouth just like smoke. I am not attached to my earthly body. *You* should know, Mom. You were there."

So calmly Evie spoke, Arlette was stunned, perplexed.

She would never repeat Evie's bizarre words. She would soon forget Evie's bizarre words.

The days of Evie's convalescence were less fearful than the nights. But still Evie felt displaced, obscurely cheated, in the TV room where furniture had been rearranged, sofa pushed against a wall. Made to feel like an intruder. Annoyed when her brothers wanted to watch their stupid TV programs but lonely-feeling when she was by herself; she could hear others elsewhere in the house, oblivious of her. There were friends—girls, in her grade at school—who wanted to visit but Evie shook her head mutely *No!*

And no relatives, after the first week or two. Hating the pity in their eyes, and whatever banal utterances issued from their mouths—*No thank you!*

Rob Nash came to see the bedridden girl, bringing a bouquet of flowers for Arlette and a box of Godiva chocolates for Evie. But Evie refused to see him.

(Previously, Rob had tried to visit Evie in the hospital, but Evie had insisted *no.*)

Arlette had no choice but to send Rob away abashed, furious. Protesting to Evie that she was being rude—"You know, your Uncle Rob is concerned for you."

"Is he!"—Evie's eyelids were half-shut, she refused to look at Arlette.

Evie sucked at one of the Godiva chocolates and spat it out into her hand.

"Evie! What is wrong with you?"

Evie laughed, muttering something inaudible.

"What? What did you say?"

Evie shook her head mutely. Pushed away the gaudy Godiva candy box, winced as if her head ached. Since the skull fracture she'd become hypersensitive to light, a migraine headache could come over her like a suddenly overcast sky.

Quickly Arlette had to lower the shades or Evie would begin to scream at her.

Wondering uneasily what would happen if Rob Nash became disenchanted with the Hansen family. What losses they would all suffer, of which they might not even be aware.

Through the autumn Arlette was the liaison between Evie and school, bringing Evie's homework assignments to her teacher Ms. Deluca and returning the marked papers. Evie hated how homework took twice as long for her as in the past. Her vision swam, her eyes ached. She much preferred drawing in a sketchbook Arlette bought for her with a fancy marble-swirl cover in dark reds suggesting the interior of a body.

Evie overheard Arlette speaking on the phone in the kitchen to a friend or relative declaring how she'd always wanted to be a nurse when she was a girl, now she was her daughter's nurse—"and loving it."

Evie could detect no irony, no suggestion of complaint, rather more a bright buoyant boastfulness in her mother's voice, that made her resent her mother's very cheerfulness, optimism. "Yes, Evie is expected to recover fully," Arlette said often, as if dispelling doubt at the other end of the telephone, "and return to school in a month or two. Hey, it isn't easy, rehab. 'Physical therapy.' It *hurts.*"

Unable to bear it Evie shouted at her mother: "No! You don't know! *I* hurt."

Still it happened, daughter and mother were becoming very close. Wet dreary leaf-strewn autumn days alone in the house together. When Evie finished her homework, Arlette allowed her to watch TV in the afternoon, might even join

Evie for a while before the boys returned home and the TV was (hastily) turned off.

Roy and Billy had become shy with their sister who seemed to like them less than she had before *the accident.* Where once she'd been protective of them now she was impatient, sarcastic. Roy resented the adult attention deflected onto Evie. Especially, he resented Arlette's attention. Saying to Evie in an undertone, so that their mother couldn't hear, "I bet you could walk if you wanted to," and Evie said coldly, words of a kind she had never before uttered in his hearing, "You ugly little rat, *die.*"

Roy was shocked. At eleven he said things he didn't mean, that flew into his head, that no one took seriously. Evie had retaliated as another eleven-year-old boy might have retaliated. He wasn't prepared for such a response—*Ugly little rat, die.*

Roy would never feel comfortable with his sister again. He would never trust her again not to say something awful to him under her breath.

Eventually, with Arlette's assistance, Evie made her way into the sunroom at the side of the house which was glassed-in and heated. This attractive room, Kevin had added to the house with the assistance of his carpenter-friend. Propped up against pillows on a rattan sofa Evie drew in her sketchbook for long hours, drowsy from medications. If she lifted her eyes she had a view of skeletal trees, open fields, and in the distance the foothills of the Chautauqua Mountains. She and Arlette worked on jigsaw puzzles set on a low table beside the sofa. These were large, intricate puzzles depicting American landscapes painted by nineteenth-century artists Frederic Church, Albert Bierstadt, Thomas Cole. Dreamlike vistas, rivers, skies that could take many hours to complete. There was fascination in the jigsaw puzzle–solving but also a sense of entrapment, for once begun, a jigsaw puzzle could not be abandoned. Out of mischief, unless it was pure meanness, Evie hid away crucial puzzle pieces so that Arlette searched in vain for them—"Oh, Christ! Where is it!"

During these long quiet hours when the boys were at school and Kevin was at the mall Arlette confided in Evie as she would not have, otherwise. Saying how, when she was Evie's age, she must not have been happy with herself. "There was this game I played in secret: whoever was the next person I saw, whoever came around a corner, I would 'change places' with them. This was, like, a wish I could make."

Evie was perplexed, disapproving. "You mean you'd rather have been any old person instead of yourself? A homeless person, someone in a wheelchair, someone with cystic fibrosis . . ."

"Well, it was childish. I was a child . . ."

"What you were was spoiled, ignorant. Trading places with just *anyone.* That is so—that is such a—*betrayal.*"

"I agree. But mostly it was—childish. I didn't think I was at all pretty, or that anyone would like me."

"It was *stupid.*"

"All right, Evie. You've made your point."

Betrayal. What an odd word for Evie to utter. A fancy word, Arlette knew exactly what Evie meant by it but would never have thought of it herself.

Whoever the child Evie had been before the accident, however annoying at times, this judgmental young person was quite different. No longer a child yet not mature. Her face in repose was naturally peevish, petulant. Her skin was sallow, her eyes without luster. Hair had grown back thinly over the jagged scar in her skull, Evie fretted that it would never grow back entirely. Other kids would notice and jeer at her, she'd have to wear a cap indoors.

Three times a week Arlette took Evie for therapy at the rehab clinic. The change in her daughter here was amazing to

Arlette. She tried not to be jealous of the (woman) physical therapist whom Evie clearly admired, respected. No slouching at rehab, no muttered asides or sighs. Evie obeyed this young woman's instructions as she would never have obeyed her mother. She was willing to undergo pain for this young woman as she would never have for her mother.

"Oh!—oh, God!"—wincing with pain, tears running down her cheeks. Staggering to get her balance.

At which the therapist paused to commend her, to praise her. Touching her lightly on the shoulder.

"Good, Evie. Now let's try it again."

It was noted, Evie was *making progress. Regaining muscle strength, coordination.*

Evie's fear was that she would never again walk like a "normal" person. People can detect a limp, the human brain is poised to notice the smallest deviances from "normal."

Arlette looked through Evie's sketchbook. Surprising to her, that her daughter seemed to have some genuine talent for drawing with pencils, charcoal sticks, and colored chalks. If she concentrated too hard, the drawings were stiff; if she worked swiftly, almost carelessly, the drawings were more lifelike, inspired.

"Sweetie, what's this?"

A wrecked bicycle, that seemed to be also a twisted, deformed scrawny girl-figure with a (toothless) mouth open and distended in a silent scream.

A flower opened wide, petals covered in tiny dots—ants?

A grotesque fat hog, sinking in mud, with a face that looked almost human—*Rob Nash?*

Evie was watching Arlette's face, with a curious smile. Arlette turned pages numbly. Most of the drawings, she saw to her relief, were of trees, clouds, landscapes. Ordinary scenes, objects. Kevin in profile, in charcoal. Arlette seen at a distance, through the doorway and in the kitchen, turned away, an anonymous female figure with a conspicuously small head.

You want to say: Some good will come of this. There is always some good to come even of tragedy.

Was this true? Arlette wanted to think so. In the past, Evie had never remained in one place long enough to accomplish much. She'd been restless, jumpy. Reminding Arlette of one of those long-legged leaping spiders. It was all she could do to stay still enough to finish her homework. Never would she have so concentrated on drawing. Never with such evident pleasure, immersed in a drawing for long minutes, scarcely glancing up.

Of course, Arlette understood, this was not a *tragedy.* All that really mattered was, their daughter was alive.

Everyone assured them, Evie was making great progress. Evie's doctors assured them. Evie was young, resilient. The (slightly crooked, grayish, not very attractive) front teeth knocked from her jaw had been replaced by flawless, unblemished teeth. Her young bones would heal—were healing. The head fracture would heal. If there was some damage to the brain, likely that would heal. The human body is wonderfully self-healing. At least, the young human body.

Tragedy would be a broken neck or spine, a more severely cracked skull. Paralysis for life. Comatose. What's called a *vegetative state.*

Of course, Arlette would have been her daughter's caretaker, as she was now. That would be her place, her role. *That* would have been the tragedy.

We never knew what talent Evie had. She never knew. Until she was thirteen, the accident with the bicycle . . . Arlette imagined a joint interview: Daughter, mother. On local TV news. National news. Close-ups of Evie's chalk drawings, portraits. Paintings. Such pride in her daughter, Arlette shaking her head in awe, gratitude. *Eavanne Hansen, of Strykersville, New York.*

But often, as if to spite her mother, Evie seemed indifferent to the drawings. Some of those that Arlette most admired, Evie tore out, crumpled.

"It's just something a million other people can do, Mom. It isn't special."

"Well. You are special."

"Am I!"

Arlette tried not to be hurt by Evie's rudeness. Reasoning that her daughter was testing her patience, her love. When Evie tried this with her father, Kevin might speak sharply to her, or walk out of the room.

See? I can just walk away from you. You'd have to hobble after me.

As others in the family were estranged from Evie, and tended to avoid her, Arlette remained close, loyal. Often when they were alone together mother and daughter fell into a doze, Arlette in one of the rattan chairs, Evie on the sofa.

Arlette found herself trying to entertain Evie, summoning back old memories, out of the past.

"It was an accident, how I met your father. I was twenty years old . . ."

This would have led into a fond remembrance but Evie interrupted Arlette with an uplifted hand.

"You don't mean my 'father,' Mom. You met a man, a stranger, and he would turn out to be my 'father.' You didn't meet *my father,* that's a stupid way of speaking."

Arlette couldn't remember her daughter being so pitiless in judgment of her, in the past. So unforgiving. Arlette had never spoken like this to her own mother—her mother would have slapped her face.

Still, Arlette recounted to Evie the story of how she and Kevin had met, not exactly on a blind date, but in a way blindly, by chance brought together by mutual friends. It was a story that Arlette had told others, but it did not seem so interesting now. In a TV scene, mother and daughter would "bond" over such tender confidences; in real life, Evie made no attempt to disguise her boredom, rapidly sketching in her sketch-pad as her mother spoke.

Arlette recalled how much of childhood is pretending to be interested in the remarks of adults. No one was allowed to register boredom, let alone disdain.

"In this YA novel I read, everybody is adopted. The society works out better, nothing is left to chance." Evie laughed, as if genuinely amused.

"Well—you're *not adopted.*"

"And if I was, you probably wouldn't tell me. You and Dad—you'd keep it a secret."

"Adopted children can be loved as well as biological children . . ."

"So did you win the lottery, or did you lose?"

"What do you mean?"

"Did you *want* a daughter? If you knew who I would be, would you have wanted *me*?"

"Of—of course . . ."

"If you went to an orphanage, and there were other girls, would you have chosen *me*?"

"Evie, this is unpleasant. What are you getting at? You know—you are loved . . ."

"Any baby you'd brought home, you'd have loved. So what?"

"I did want a daughter. In fact."

"Did Dad?"

"Yes! He did." But Arlette spoke uncertainly, she wasn't at all sure. And why did it matter, what either of them had imagined they'd wanted? The family they had created was the family they had created.

"A female is her body, that's the problem. A man is his brain and what he can make of it but a female is just—she *is*. People look at her and make a judgment in one second."

Evie spoke flatly, with finality. Arlette stood up and went away, all but limping, as if she'd been wounded, to another part of the house.

Each time Rob Nash dropped by, Evie refused to see him. When the hospital bed had been returned to the rental agency, and Evie was back in her old room, if she heard Rob Nash's voice she never came to join the family; if he was invited to stay for dinner, Evie stayed in her room with an excuse of homework.

Fortunately, Rob Nash ceased asking after Evie. He turned his attention to Roy and Billy, who laughed at his jokes.

Carefully Arlette said to Evie, "You don't seem to like Rob any longer, Evie. Is there any reason?"

Evie laughed harshly. "You should know."

"What do you mean—'You should know'?"

"'*You* should know.' That's what I mean."

"I don't know what you're talking about, Evie. Really."

"Really!"—Evie laughed, then began coughing. Walking away, gracelessly, favoring her right leg.

3.

In time, Evie did return to a kind of *normal*. Returning to school in January as she'd long yearned to do but during the long misery of her convalescence something had gone wrong, her friends had lost interest in Evie Hansen, or she'd lost interest in them. Her absence from their lives had been abrupt, willful; her refusal to allow them to visit her. They could not think of it as other than hostile. They were too young and silly for Evie, or, in another way, physically, Evie was too young for them, underdeveloped, a stunted creature.

She'd lost the pace. She'd stumbled and fallen behind. Limping, her damned knee. Sobbing, cursing.

This was new: *cursing.* Arlette was shocked to hear her daughter muttering under her breath such words as *hell, God damn, shit, bullshit, fuck, fuck-all.* Her daughter!

Trying to take consolation from the fact that friends of hers with high-school-aged kids were reporting the same behavior. The boys were worse than the girls—of course—but the girls too were acquiring *dirty mouths.*

It starts with high school. Overnight!

Video games, social media were to blame. Cell phones. Internet.

(Though Arlette noticed that Evie rarely cursed when Kevin was within earshot.)

In tenth grade one of Evie's friends from middle school seemed to reappear in her life—Thalia James. Arlette had not glimpsed Thalia in two years or more. Arlette was more thrilled than Evie when Thalia invited Evie to a sleep-over birthday party. Evie shrugged: "I'll go, OK. It's no big deal. But I'm not going to bring any damn present."

"Of course you're going to bring Thalia a present!" Arlette said. "We'll pick it out together, at the mall."

"It's OK, Mom. No big deal."

"You can't show up at a birthday party without a present. You will not."

Arlette spoke excitedly. As if her very reputation as a mother were at risk. Evie had to laugh at her mother, though possibly she was touched as well: Mom seemed to care *so much.*

At the mall, shopping for a present for Thalia James, who would be fifteen. Nothing too fancy but nothing too cheap, either. "Too bad we can't find something at Ace Hardware, we could get a discount," Evie said; and Arlette said, as if Evie had been serious, "Well—I was thinking that, too. But there'd be nothing there for Thalia."

After the marathon shop Arlette was exhausted, swaying on her feet when she and Evie arrived home, after myriad disagreements finally agreeing on a purple suede handbag with a shoulder strap, that had cost twice as much as she'd expected to pay. Evie conceded: "It's OK. It's kind of cool. Thanks, Mom."

Arlette waited for Evie to ask for a new handbag for herself since her old handbag, really just a tote bag, was worn threadbare; but Evie seemed not to think of it.

When Arlette happened to encounter Thalia's mother not long after the sleep-over, Michelle James seemed not to know anything about it. Sleep-over? Birthday party? At her house? Was Arlette thinking of someone else? So far as Michelle James knew, Thalia and Evie hadn't seen each other for a long time.

"After Evie's accident on the bicycle. On the bridge. Last summer? Or was it the summer before last?"

Arlette was stunned. Arlette could not think of a reply.

Fleeing home, stricken. In a kind of disgrace.

Evie lied. Lied to me. Stayed away overnight.

With whom?

Realizing, later—*Kevin will kill me if he finds out*.

It was her fault, had to be the mother's fault. She had failed to be vigilant. She had failed to be suspicious. She had failed to ask the right questions. She had not driven Evie to the James house, someone else had picked Evie up outside in the driveway. Nor had she picked up Evie the next day: someone had brought Evie home, late afternoon, a Saturday.

Betraying us. Betraying me . . .

By the time Arlette dared to confront Evie with the *sleep-over* it was too late. Arlette had surrendered her authority, her righteous anger. Evie did not seem surprised to be discovered, however belatedly. At once she backed away evasive, defensive, it would do no good to interrogate her. Evie claimed that she'd told Arlette that the sleep-over had been canceled, she'd gone to the movies with other friends that night, girls whom Arlette didn't know, nor did Arlette know their mothers—"No big deal, Mom."

"But where did you spend the night? That's what I'm asking."

Evie shrugged, daring to walk away. Stalking off to her room as if she'd been insulted. Exaggerating her limp, as if to aggravate her mother.

My fucking right knee as Evie called it.

From that point onward Arlette knew that she could not trust her daughter. She dared not tell Kevin of her disagreements with Evie, which were constant. She dared not quarrel with Evie, the consequences were immediate and extreme, like daring to stick her finger into an electrical outlet.

For suddenly everything had become *No big deal, Mom!*

How heartbreaking it was, the two had been so close!—the long winter of Evie's convalescence, when Evie had been so weak, so much in pain, susceptible to infections, wincing when she'd tried to walk. Leaning desperately onto Arlette, as if Arlette were a crutch. Arlette *had been a crutch*!

Her daughter's caretaker, and her daughter's companion. All of the relatives had taken notice—had been impressed. As a mother you are always performing for other mothers, who know exactly when you fail as a mother, especially the women in your family, sharp-eyed, alert to shortcomings. Arlette's older sister, dead now for several years, would have been particularly impressed—no one could have predicted that Arlette would turn out to be *such a wonderful mother.*

"And now, she's punishing me. Why is she punishing *me*!"

The convalescence had become confused, in a part of Arlette's mind, with Evie's early childhood. The unspeakable intimacy of mother, infant: the startling tug at the breast. Arlette had been a terrified young mother unsure of herself. Unsure of her ability to keep an actual, living baby *alive.*

Such sweetness. Love for the lost child flooded Arlette, her eyes filled with tears of longing.

But infants don't remain infants. Invalids don't remain invalids. Eventually a crutch is cast aside. No one wants to recall a damned *crutch.*

In high school Evie's grades were erratic, unpredictable. Her enthusiasms, like her hatreds, came in surges, and faded. She rarely spoke of her teachers except in derision. She had lost, it seemed, her ability to skim pages of homework, to assimilate what was essential. In the long lethargy of her convalescence, waiting for broken bones to heal, she'd become *disabled. Disengaged* from her very self, Arlette was thinking.

But she loved the sketch-pad that Arlette had purchased for her. When the pages ran out, Arlette purchased another. In this sketch-pad Evie drew penguin-like figures with broken feet and gaping toothless mouths, lurching about like drunken persons. Tirelessly she drew humanoid figures, clownish, missing parts of their bodies. Her self-portraits were crude, cruel—she gave herself a pimply, blemished face with staring blank eyes.

She began to stay after school, involved with the school newspaper. Her talent was for cartoons, caricatures. Proudly she showed her family a feature in the school paper titled *Evie-Eye*—"See, you're meant to think of the 'Evil Eye.'"

No one knew what the "Evil Eye" was. Evie had to explain.

A Mediterranean superstition? Middle East? Muslim?

"The joke is, the 'Evil Eye' is a superstitious omen, to ward off evil spirits. But see, in my cartoons, *I am the evil spirit!* That's the joke."

Roy and Billy were impressed with their sister's comic

strip in the newspaper. Amazing to them, that Evie's childish doodles had been *printed.*

Kevin frowned at the comic strip. Clearly didn't know what to think but wasn't sure that he approved.

Arlette stared, smiling. For a mother must always smile.

"Gosh, honey—this is so *professional*!"

Her daughter had an undeniable talent for caricature—which meant cruelty, with a comic twist. Or, comedy with a cruel twist. Were these caricatures of actual people at the high school, Arlette wondered. Classmates of Evie's? School stars? Teachers? Or were they only just generic humanoid figures, foolish, self-important, vain, obese or skeletal-thin, with spindly legs, bumpy breasts, stalk-like necks? One of the females—fat lips, jowly cheeks, insipid little smile—seemed to resemble Arlette herself.

And there was the loathsome hog, with an ugly snout face, features so cleverly arranged that they suggested, to those who knew Rob Nash, unmistakably *Rob Nash.*

Though Kevin didn't seem to recognize his old friend. Staring at the hog-caricature, trying to see how it might be innocently funny.

"Is this, who?—the school principal?"

Nor did Roy and Billy recognize Uncle Rob.

Only Arlette. Who would have winced except she knew that Evie was watching her face, closely.

"This is wonderful, Evie! Like a comic strip in the newspaper. Your teachers must be so impressed . . ."

Evie laughed, delighted.

"More likely, they're afraid who's next."

Months later, news came that Rob Nash had *passed away,* of lung cancer.

It had been known in Strykersville that Rob Nash had been ill for some time, undergoing chemotherapy.

Arlette and Kevin had visited Rob in the hospital several times. Heartbreaking, how Rob Nash had changed!

His face had thinned, like a balloon that has lost air, resiliency. There was little joking, banter, which had been Rob's way of relating. "Y'know, kids?—I am tired. Ti-red."

Squinting at Arlette and Kevin as if he didn't exactly remember them, the youngish-middle-aged couple who'd brought, to his flower-festooned hospital room, a potted African violet wrapped in tinfoil.

From somewhere, relatives of Rob Nash had appeared overnight, taking up much of the space in Rob's hospital room, and then in his hospice room. As Strykersville friends of Rob Nash observed cynically—*Vultures coming home to roost.*

But would Rob Nash alter his will for these strangers? Or was it too late? Neither Kevin nor Arlette spoke of it: *the will.*

The promise that Rob Nash would *remember them in his will.*

(Unless it hadn't been a promise, exactly? A possibility?)

When Arlette told Evie that Rob Nash had *passed away,* Evie had little reaction.

"Who?"

"What do you mean, 'who'? You know who Rob Nash is. Was."

Arlette felt such dismay, sorrow, exasperation with Evie—seeing the peevish expression in her daughter's face she burst into tears.

"The poor man! Poor Rob! He was such a loving friend . . ."

Meanly Evie laughed. Arlette was sure she could hear her daughter mutter under her breath *Fat fucking hog, die.*

It was an emotional time for Arlette. Really, she'd loved Rob Nash—as Rob Nash had loved *her.*

No one would look at Arlette again in quite that way. That—special way of his . . .

Beginning when he'd been her father's friend, that long ago. Long before Kevin and long before motherhood.

Kevin was grieving, too. In his stiff, silent way, that suggested a deep unease as well as loss.

(Where Rob Nash's money had gone, how much his estate was worth at the time of his death—no one seemed to know.)

(Maybe Rob Nash hadn't had as much money as people had thought? As he'd led people to think? That began to be the word around town.)

With the excuse of emptying Evie's wastebasket, changing the badly soiled sheets on Evie's bed—(as Evie failed to do while insisting that she could keep her room clean by herself)—Arlette discovered, in a drawer in Evie's desk, some very ugly—obscene—Japanese comic books.

Could not believe what I was seeing. Schoolgirls in school uniforms doing disgusting things to old Japanese men!

Arlette wondered, were these actual Japanese publications, or some sort of vicious anti-Japanese propaganda? Not wanting to examine the comics too closely.

Graphic novels, picture-books. YA novels with lurid covers.

Bitch Planet. Queer Appetites. The Sailor Who Fell from Grace with the Sea—elaborately illustrated, as if for children.

Arlette hurriedly dropped the book. What on earth had she *seen*?

Elsewhere in the room Arlette discovered pages torn from Evie's sketch-pad of naked cartoon-figures: girls, women, adolescent boys. Some were kissing and touching one another inappropriately and others were fighting with knives or swords or undergoing horrific tortures. Beheadings, dissections. Breasts hacked off, intestines dragged out of abdomens. Most ghastly: a fetus torn from a woman's belly.

A smug-smiling fattish woman with Arlette's face—*Momster.*

Arlette was shocked, sickened. It was clear to her, Evie had fallen under the spell of someone at the high school. Her homeroom teacher? An unmarried woman with hair trimmed so short, it was practically a crewcut?—Geary? Greary? Evie had mentioned this homeroom teacher several times, not mockingly, as she tended to speak of her other teachers, but rather admiringly.

Without speaking to Evie—(who would never tell her the truth, and would only just try to prevent her)—Arlette drove to the high school. Classes were still in session, it was just mid-afternoon.

In the assistant principal's office Arlette spoke forcefully, angrily. She'd brought Evie's drawings with her, as evidence. A lesbian teacher, on the Strykersville faculty! Corrupting children! Her daughter had survived a traumatic accident just two years before, at the age of thirteen, she wasn't fully recovered, she was impressionable, naïve—just the sort of child to be *groomed* by a perverted adult.

Soon then, Arlette was speaking with the principal as well. Others on the staff were summoned, finally Isabel Greary who professed utter astonishment at Arlette's charges and claimed scarcely to know Eavanne Hansen but declined to acknowledge that she was, or was not, a "lesbian."

By this time Arlette was sincerely upset. The sound of her own voice, high-pitched, quavering with indignation, roused her to further excitement; the more calmly the others spoke, the more Ms. Greary claimed not to know what Arlette was talking about, the more upset Arlette became. She threatened to "go to the media." She threatened to call the police, to call a lawyer. At the same time she didn't want her daughter to be personally involved—"Evie is too sensitive. She had a skull fracture, she almost died. I just need to know that she's protected here at school. We need to know—her father and me."

Though involving Kevin was the last thing Arlette wanted. Any kind of fuss, that might have a public aspect to it, anything that might "get into the newspapers" and be "bad for business"—Kevin would not have wished.

Following this incident Evie was transferred to another tenth-grade homeroom. Isabel Greary was not fired, to Arlette's disappointment, nor even suspended from teaching, but allowed to complete the school term, then transferred to another school in the district.

Of course, Evie soon learned what had happened. Evie was humiliated, furious. She refused to speak with Arlette, even to remain for very long in a room with her. She accused her mother of ruining her life—"My life that had already been ruined. By *her.*"

Evie began skipping classes. Skipping school altogether. She stayed away overnight, over an entire weekend. She was spending time with a new friend, a girl who'd graduated from Strykersville High several years before and was now working at the Target store at the mall.

Sending text messages to Arlette:

I'm OK—I am not going to hurt myself. YOU have done that.

I am happy here with J. D. I am not COARSED.

You can't bring me back in chains, I will return when I am ready.

I love you all OK—but this is MY OWN LIFE needing to be saved.

4.

Very little they could do: *parents of a "runaway."*

Pleading with Strykersville police that their fifteen-year-old daughter was a minor, had medical issues, (possibly) mental issues following a bicycle accident she'd had two years before, from which she had never fully recovered. She was "highly impressionable"—"easily coerced"—"needing therapy"—staying with an "unauthorized person" who was not a relative, not a friend of the family, possibly she was in danger, possibly there were drugs involved . . .

Police officers listened patiently but never did a thing. *Runaway* was not a top priority in Strykersville, as *abduction, kidnapping* would have been.

A female police officer spoke with Arlette patiently and sympathetically but advised against trying to bring her daughter home forcibly—"That never works out, ma'am. If they want to be somewhere else, they will go somewhere else. You can't keep them prisoner."

"But Evie is *fifteen*!" Arlette protested.

"*Fifteen* isn't *five,* ma'am."

In fact, Evie was just turning sixteen. Arlette had to concede, sixteen wasn't exactly a child.

It was pointed out that Evie had voluntarily left home, and there was no reason to think that she wouldn't return home. Most "runaways" did, fairly soon. There was no evidence that she was being kept against her will. She was attending school, in fact. Not every day, but frequently. If she were charged as a "runaway" that might involve her being detained for several days in the county house of detention and would probably involve sessions for her parents in family court . . .

Arlette shuddered at the prospect. Kevin would never forgive her, if this *got into the papers.*

"You won't help us until our daughter is hurt," Arlette said.

"Ma'am, it sounds like your daughter is already 'hurt'—some kind of accident, you said?"

Indeed, Evie did return home. But soon then, Evie stayed away overnight, and Evie went away for weekends. Evie was with "J. D."—or with "Carroll"—"Ernie"—"Smithie." When Evie was home she barricaded herself in her room. She'd cultivated a sidelong smile—a smile of cutting indifference. Arlette was stricken to the heart. Unnerving how, if you smile at another person and that person does not smile back, you feel annihilated, as if your mirror reflection has vanished. You are made to feel invisible.

Was this a symptom of Asperger's, in Evie?—an inability to register social cues?

Had Evie's brain been injured in a way that hadn't shown in the MRI?

But Evie was well aware of "social cues," Arlette thought. She just refused to acknowledge them.

Like playing a game with no intention of following the rules. Laughing at fools who followed the rules.

Like hiding a jigsaw puzzle piece. Making it impossible for the jigsaw puzzle to ever be completed.

Like inquiring of her father, as if innocently, "How are things at 'Ace Hardware,' Dad?"—as if the name of the store were quaint, amusing.

Sometimes Evie ate meals with the family, sometimes not. Rarely did she help Arlette prepare a meal, or clean up afterward. It did no good to be exasperated with her—arousing *exasperation* might have been the point of Evie's behavior.

If you don't want me here, just tell me.

I am only temporarily here, anyway.

At seventeen she dropped out of school to live with new friends in Rochester, and then in Niagara Falls, of whom Arlette and Kevin had never heard. In Niagara Falls she worked in a farmer's market, sending photos of herself in oversized bib overalls, grinning with her perfect-plastic teeth. One of the photos was of Evie with a giant, deformed pumpkin which had been carved for Hallowe'en with an exaggerated gap-toothed grin.

Having a great time. Working in the earth. Erning $$$.

When Arlette called the number she had for Evie, to invite her home for Thanksgiving, she was told that Evie had left, driving to Illinois with a friend with plans to work on an organic farm. Evie was "in the wind"—she'd wanted them to know. But she would "check back in" with them, when she could.

It was months before they heard from her again. Then, just a hurried call.

"I told you, there's nothing to worry about. No big deal. I'm going to hang up if you start crying, Mom! *I will not be emotionally blackmailed.*"

A postcard from Denver, Rocky Mountains in Day-Glo colors, a hastily scrawled note barely decipherable except for *Be Well! Love you, E.*

Postcards from El Paso, Albuquerque, Los Angeles. Shasta, California, with Mount Shasta in Day-Glo colors.

Vaguely it was believed in Strykersville that Evie Hansen had "gone off to college" somewhere distant. As in time Billy went to the state university at Plattsburgh, at the Canadian border, to study computer science.

Roy enlisted in the US Army, was away for several years before returning to work at Ace Hardware until Kevin retired early for health reasons, and Roy took over the store.

5.

Because I died once, I am not afraid to die again.

Because Death is all around us & in the air we breathe.

Because Death is in the soil, I love to sink my hands into the soil. I love to "dirty" my face.

In the ambulance I saw my soul fly out of my mouth like smoke. I never told anyone.

In the ambulance they made me breathe, & my soul returned to me, but it was not the same.

When you came to see me in the hospital it was too late. Because I had died then, & was not your daughter.

The cord had been broken, you never understood.

What you believe to be Family is just accident. There is no meaning in accident.

The Spider Web is easily broken.

The envelope from Evie, postmarked Traverse City, Michigan, was covered in bright Day-Glo colors. Inside was a thick swath of handwritten pages.

Arlette wiped at her eyes as she read the letter, passing the pages to Kevin, who was having difficulty reading with his bifocals. The handwriting was slanted, urgent, in purple ink. Arlette could not have identified the handwriting, that might have been a stranger's. She could hear nothing of Evie's voice in the shrill speech of the letter.

It had been—how many years since they'd last seen their daughter? Evie would be in her late thirties now: Arlette had a difficult time imagining any age for her at all.

Kevin said irritably, "Can you *read* this? Chicken-scrawling."

"D'you want me to read it aloud?"

"Don't bother."

"Kevin!"

"Oh, all right. Go ahead."

Arlette read slowly, with difficulty. It seemed to her that Evie was talking to herself, fretting and quarreling with herself. In the margins of the letter were small cartoon-faces, grotesque figures.

Arlette wondered if Evie was correct, family was just *accident.* There'd never been any connection between any of them, and Evie, thrown violently from her bicycle at the age of thirteen, was the only one to perceive this.

"She isn't herself, Kevin. Whoever wrote this, it isn't Evie."

"Who is it then? Christ!"

Kevin spoke in disgust, knocking the pages from Arlette's fingers, to flutter and fall to the floor.

6.

Three weeks after Kevin died, and his obituary appeared in the *Strykersville Gazette,* a call came to Arlette from Evie, living now in Bolton Landing, in the Adirondacks—approximately three hundred miles east of Strykersville.

Kevin had been just sixty-three when he'd died, of a sudden heart attack; Arlette was just sixty-one. Not old! Not old at all.

Hearing her daughter's voice Arlette's first thought came in a rush of hope—*She will come home now. She will live with me now.*

In an agitated voice Evie was demanding to know when exactly Kevin had died. Had there been any warning? When was the funeral? Where was he buried? Where were Roy and Billy—had they come to the funeral? In the background was a muffled cacophony of voices as if Evie were making the call in a large room or hall.

From what Arlette could gather Evie was in communication with someone in Strykersville, who kept her posted on the latest hometown news.

"D'you still live in the same house, Mom? How will I know where you live?"

"Of course I live in the same house."

"I don't remember the name of the road. I don't remember the number."

"You must remember—Post Road! One-six-six-four."

"'One-six-six-four' . . ."

"Evie, are you all right? What is all the noise there?"

"It's the same tacky little 'ranch house,' right? With the aluminum siding?"

"Are you—are you in Strykersville?"

"Look out the window, Mom."

Arlette hurried to a living room window, facing the road. She could see nothing out of the ordinary.

"Are you here? In Strykersville? Evie?"

"Maybe I'm driving around the block. Maybe I'm 'stalking' you, Mom."

Arlette ran outside, into a wintry November wind.

"Evie? Hello?"—Arlette cried into the phone receiver, which had lost its connection so far from the house.

At the roadway Arlette stood shivering convulsively, looking first in one direction, then in the other. Her heart was beating rapidly with hope—*My daughter! My daughter.*

No idea what sort of vehicle Evie might be driving. When Arlette tried to envision Evie she could imagine only the photo taken at the organic farm in Rochester, many years ago—Evie in slovenly bib overalls grinning into the camera with her mock-perfect teeth, stooped over a gigantic and misshapen pumpkin as if over a fallen adversary.

As Arlette ventured farther out into the road an approaching station wagon slowed to a halt.

"Hello? Is it—Arlette? Mrs. Hansen? Is something wrong?"

Arlette recognized a neighbor. In her excitement she couldn't have said the woman's name.

"I think—my daughter is back. Evie. She's somewhere close by . . ."

"Your daughter? The one who went away to college?"

"Yes. Evie—'Eavanne.'"

Arlette stood in the middle of the road, disheveled and confused. Her eyes brimmed with tears from the cold wind. In a kindly voice the neighbor was asking her if she wanted to be driven anywhere? If she had an idea where Evie was?

Distractedly Arlette shook her head, *no.* Adding, to be polite: "No thank you! She's probably on her way. I'll just wait for her."

"You could wait inside the house, Mrs. Hansen. She'll know where to find you."

"Yes. That's so."

"It's kind of cold this morning. Maybe you should wait inside. Unless you want me to drive you somewhere . . ."

"No! That isn't necessary."

Arlette turned away, as if she were going back inside the house. The neighbor waved to her, driving away; but Arlette remained at the end of the driveway, in the whipping November wind.

Feeling absurdly gratified, that this was how Evie was described locally—*the one who went away to college.*

7.

Health issues! Let's not go into (morbid) details.

At Pheasant Ridge where Arlette went to live after the house on Post Road was sold there was altogether too much conversation about *health issues.* Damned if she would participate, she had better things to talk about.

Most residents of Pheasant Ridge were widows. Most residents had known one another in their former lives, some as long ago as high school, elementary school. Regrouping now, those who remained. Those who'd survived *marriage, children.*

No self-pity! *She* wasn't one of those who fretted, wept, moaned that their children/grandchildren failed to visit them as often as they'd have liked.

Though Arlette was beset by *health issues* of her own: osteoporosis hollowing out her bones, bronchitis that left her breathless and weak, an upper row of abscessed teeth needing to be removed and replaced by expensive dentures (not covered by insurance), glaucoma controlled by nightly eye drops, alarming memory lapses like cuts in an aged, defective film.

With old friends bravely regrouping, widows, a divorcée or two, reclaiming old alliances. Those who couldn't resist boasting about grandchildren gravitated together while others, like Arlette, with no grandchildren (yet) to boast of, preferred one another's company.

Gin rummy, book club, square dancing—graceless, bouncy, joyful all-female laughter and panting. Three mornings a week, swimming (slowly) in the turquoise-tinted pool that smelled eye-smartingly of chlorine.

Arlette did have visitors: relatives. Her niece Cassie came to visit every few weeks.

Fondly recalling "that barbecue you and Uncle Kevin gave for us—that was so kind of you . . ."

It hadn't been a barbecue, just a cold buffet, lavish as Arlette could make it, with drinks supplied by Rob Nash; but Arlette was grateful for the memory and did not correct her niece.

"And poor Evie had that accident on the bridge, on her bicycle. That was a close call!"

For a moment Arlette couldn't comprehend what the words meant: *close call.*

Realizing then, that Evie hadn't died. *That* was the close call, for which she and Kevin had been so grateful at the time.

"Evie called me, you know. After Kevin died."

"Yes, you told me, Aunt Arlette. That was nice of her."

"She was coming to visit but—something happened . . . She had to postpone."

Too embarrassed to tell her niece that Evie seemed to have forgotten where she lived. Couldn't remember the name "Post Road"—after so many years.

And one afternoon, in fact on the eve of Arlette's seventieth birthday, Evie came to visit her at Pheasant Ridge, unannounced.

"Mom, hey. It's—me. 'Evie.'"

In the doorway of Arlette's room abashed, squinting, an individual with a weathered face, pale blue eyes, slouching shoulders, of no evident age except not young: head shaved and stubbly, glaring piercings in her face. She wore much-laundered jeans, corroded white along the seams. A synthetic snakeskin jacket. Lace-up boots. The perfect-plastic teeth looked less white, shiny. Lines bracketed the thin-lipped mouth that ventured a hesitant smile.

Arlette stared, astonished. Arlette burst into tears: her daughter!

"Evie, come in! Come in! Give me a hug, come *here.*"

Arlette tried to stand, grew dizzy, and fell back into the chintz easy chair that was soft and boneless, fitted to the contours of her body. Evie, embarrassed, came to her, limping just perceptibly, breathing hard as if she'd been running. Her breath smelled ashy, stale.

Evie explained that she'd happened to hear that Arlette was in this place—that had never existed when she'd been living in Strykersville—"All there was here, on this road, was fields and trees past the high school . . ."

Evie spoke awkwardly, like one not accustomed to speech. She stared at Arlette, staring and blinking, as if seeing something that frightened her, and so provoked her to smile inanely and chatter as if she didn't know what she was saying.

Arlette reached out to take Evie's hand—clasped it tightly.

What a cold, thin hand! Knobby knuckles, and a glimpse of something smeared like blueberries, at her right wrist. A tattoo?

"So good to see you, Evie! What a—a lovely surprise! Please—can you stay? We can have dinner together . . ."

Evie muttered something inaudible, apologetic. Shrugging her shoulders in the old way, that Arlette recalled with a pang of regret.

What was she doing now? Well, she was *between gigs.*

She'd been working on an organic farm in Bolton Landing but there'd been a "meltdown," half the staff had walked out. Probably she was going to stay with her friends in Michigan, if she could pin them down on dates.

Right now, she was taking a road trip, a "break."

In Bolton Landing she'd had time to devote to her art. Her cartoon-art. Proudly Evie drew out of her backpack what appeared to be an unusually thick comic book, titled *Bitch-Storm-Warnings,* a collection of women's cartoons in which work by "E. Hansen" was included.

She'd acquired a national reputation finally, Evie said. She posted her cartoons online regularly, she had subscribers. She'd been teaching at Adirondack Community College—"The Art of the Cartoon."

"Have you! Teaching! Your father would be so impressed . . ."

"Yeah, well. That's OK." Evie swiped at her nose.

After a few minutes Evie fell suddenly silent, as if she'd run out of news. She was sitting on a chair now facing Arlette, her back to the door, that was just slightly ajar. Arlette tried to think of more questions to ask, things to tell Evie; her manner was animated, enthusiastic. She didn't want to appear anxious. As long as she kept talking, Evie wouldn't leave—would she?

Asking Evie for the second or third time if she'd like to stay for dinner in the dining room. Early dinner, five P.M. (It was just three-forty P.M., now.)

Evie replied evasively—*Yeah, maybe. OK.*

Evie asked after Roy, and Billy, and Cassie, and other relatives, several of whom had passed away without Evie knowing.

Asking then, as if she'd only now thought of it, whether Arlette and Kevin had ever inherited anything from that friend of theirs—"You wanted us to call him *Uncle Rob*?"

"Rob Nash."

Arlette had not spoken the name aloud in many years.

But hadn't Rob Nash passed away, before Evie had left home? Wouldn't Evie already know the answer to her question? Arlette couldn't remember, exactly.

She felt a stab of loss. Recalled loss, and chagrin. The loss of a dear friend, and the loss of the bequest Kevin had believed they were to receive from Rob Nash.

But when the will was read, Arlette and Kevin had not even been present. No one had notified them. Families close in upon themselves when there is a death. Especially, Arlette had come to know, the death of someone with a sizable estate.

Still, Rob Nash must have canceled a debt of Kevin's, a loan he'd made to Ace Hardware.

Kevin had always intended to repay Rob Nash the loan but when Rob died, no one contacted Kevin about the thirty thousand dollars, or whatever he'd owed; apparently there wasn't a record of it in Rob Nash's accounts.

Kevin hadn't shared much with Arlette. He'd have been embarrassed for his wife to know that Ace Hardware had required a loan.

Evasively Arlette told Evie *no,* she didn't think so. She didn't think there had been any inheritance from Rob Nash, that she could recall.

"It was a long time ago. I'm not even sure where Rob is buried . . ."

Arlette spoke earnestly, apologetically. Conversational subjects seemed to shift away from her, as if she were reaching for a balloon that eluded her. She could see it, she could see what she meant to do, and what she meant to say, but lost concentration.

"So it was all for nothing."

Evie spoke not accusingly but with a sense of wonder.

"What was—'nothing'? I can't hear you so well, Evie."

"I said—'It was all for nothing, then.' That's what I said."

Tears welled in Evie's pale eyes, of sorrow, or anger, or bafflement, Arlette could not have said. On Evie's knobby right wrist, a smudged tattoo of a bird with wide-flung wings and a sharp beak in profile.

Arlette wasn't sure what the subject was. What Evie had been asking. She had to be careful not to agree so readily.

At Pheasant Ridge, the predilection was to nod *yes, yes* like a yo-yo, Arlette had noticed. It was a sort of creeping malady. As soon as you moved in. A number of the residents were stone deaf but eager to please. Which resulted in misunderstandings.

The subject seemed to be inheritances, wills. Arlette told Evie that Roy was managing the hardware store, he'd taken over from Kevin. Still at the mall, same place. Kevin had wanted to expand but they never had. Billy had some sort of computer-consultant job in Albany. Billy was what's called a *computer-whiz.* He hadn't gotten married, but Roy had. But Roy was *separated.* No children.

Evie shrugged, hearing news of her brothers. Her leathery face betrayed no more emotion than if she'd been hearing news over the radio.

"Your father left me his 'estate'—the house, you know, and the land, and some part of the hardware store, and the rest of it to Roy. I think that's what it was. He'd left something for Billy too—not much. There wasn't—isn't—much. I don't remember the details. You know, your dad didn't want to worry me with 'money matters.' We didn't know where you were, Evie . . ."

Arlette spoke slowly as if groping her way. Evie shrugged, her face darkening. If she was hurt, or angry, Arlette couldn't judge; her vision wasn't so good any longer, like her hearing.

The fact was, Kevin hadn't spoken of Evie in years before he died. After his first stroke he'd seemed to forget that they had a daughter. Before that, he'd been furious with her—the *disrespect,* he called it.

He'd never troubled to correct anyone who spoke of Evie "going away to college." Some in Strykersville had the idea that Evie Hansen had some kind of wasting disease like MS, and was in a hospital somewhere; but mostly, no one spoke of her any longer.

In the awkward silence Arlette heard herself say guiltily, "There is some money, Evie. I set it aside for you. In my bank account. I knew that you would come back—I knew it. It isn't much, I'm afraid. I'm using more of it than I had expected, in this place. There's all kinds of hidden charges, 'fees.' But I could—I could make out a check . . ."

"Could you, Mom! That would be very generous."

Evie was looking embarrassed. Swiping at her nose with the back of her hand like an uncomfortable child.

Arlette gave instructions to Evie to look for her checkbook which was—where?—in a drawer . . . It took a while for Evie to locate the drawer, and the checkbook inside, from the Strykersville branch of the Bank of America.

Evie brought the checkbook to Arlette, and a ballpoint pen from out of her backpack, and Arlette fretted over a blank check, uncertain how much to give to her daughter. She could afford to give Evie five hundred dollars—or was it five thousand? Fifteen thousand? She smiled, Kevin used to tease her about being confused by *zeros.*

Evie said, "I can fill in the number, Mom. You just have to sign the check."

Pressing the palm of her hand against the edge of the table to prevent trembling, Arlette signed the check—*Arlette B. Hansen.*

Since Kevin had passed away, how lonely this was! She was *Mrs. Hansen* but there was no *Mr. Hansen.*

"Thanks, Mom! Gosh! You are very generous. I remember how people said you were—generous. God bless you."

Evie's face was flushed now, she'd become elated, animated. She ripped the check out of the book, folded it neatly, and slipped it into a pocket of the snakeskin jacket.

Arlette too was moved. *God bless you*—if sincere, or some sort of Evie-mockery, Arlette wasn't going to fret over it.

Someone had advised her, once: maybe it had been Rob Nash. *Don't look closely into the motives of the people in your life.*

He'd laughed, then. Rob Nash's gut-laugh, that had been so infectious.

Sitting together, with her daughter, as dusk deepens outside the window. Neither makes a move to turn on a light, as if a spell would be broken.

As years ago they'd gazed out the window of the TV room where Evie's hospital bed had been positioned, into the distance of foothills, deciduous woods to the horizon. Here, there is a parking lot, but beyond the parking lot an uncultivated field, hills stretching out of sight to the Chautauqua Mountains miles away.

Overcast sky like slept-in bedclothes. Comfortable, soft-laundered. Are they waiting for dinner, Arlette and her visitor? The summons to dinner at five P.M.?

In her elated state Evie is humming, sketch-pad on her knees as she rapidly draws a likeness of Arlette in the chintz easy chair, in a chenille bathrobe loose about her thin arms and chest. Arlette seems to have grown sleepy from the intense conversation, to which she isn't accustomed. Arlette's mouth has become slack, spittle gleams in the corners of her lips. She'd have rubbed pale coral lipstick onto her lips if she'd known that a visitor was coming but she'd had no warning.

As her pencil moves swiftly Evie observes her subject closely. Soft-creased white skin, not an elderly skin, Arlette does not seem *elderly* but soft-boned, tentative, smaller than Evie recalls. For there'd been a time when Arlette was taller than Evie, of course—Evie had been *Mommy's little helper in the kitchen.*

Little helper, no choice but to help *Mommy.* Do as Mommy instructs.

Evie has noticed, Arlette seems to have new teeth: artificial teeth resembling her own but shinier, whiter.

Evie notices, with a shock of pity, how wrinkled the backs of Arlette's hands are, and how thin the skin there appears, blue veins visible beneath.

On her thick-booted feet now Evie hovers over Arlette, as if deliberating whether to kiss her mother goodbye. For Evie has decided to leave. Suddenly, she is in a hurry to leave. It is often like that with Evie: her blood begins to pump quickly, it's a sign, a signal to leave. She seems about to kiss the soft-creased cheek. She seems about to draw up the woolen shawl to Arlette's neck to keep her warm, as Arlette would have done when Evie was a baby. Instead, as if impulsively, yet unerringly, Evie's fingers (tasting of grit, salt) grope their way into Arlette's mouth, gently dislodge the dentures, remove the dentures without waking Arlette, and slip them into a pocket; backing away then, in stealth, snatching up the backpack and hurriedly leaving the room.

No one has seen Evie at Pheasant Ridge! Only the receptionist at the front desk who'd taken Evie's name, *E. Hansen,* when she'd arrived, but is nowhere in sight as Evie departs.

Alone in the room Arlette is awakened, confused. Not sure what has happened. Why did the nurse take away her dentures? She is not at the dentist's, she knows. She is in her own room, at Pheasant Ridge. She has not been at the dentist's office in quite a while.

Arlette calls out—"Hello? Hello?" Her mouth feels wrong, her tongue is too big and too loose. She can feel the gums with her tongue. She gropes for the bell cord. She calls, and calls—"Hello? *Hello*"—her voice rising in distress and alarm until at last someone enters the room, switches on the overhead light, a short stout girl in a uniform of white nylon tunic, trousers, asking in a vexed voice:

"Yes, ma'am? What's the problem now?"

2.

THE CALL

At five-twenty A.M. there's a call, a line buzzing with static, S. is awakened from sleep to be informed that her father *passed away* earlier that morning in the hospital at—is it *Yewville?*—S. can't hear the voice clearly, so stunned by the pronouncement she can only stammer there must be some mistake, her father died years ago . . . The voice at the other end of the line repeats S.'s father's name, including even his middle name and his birthdate; S. protests her father died six years ago at the age of seventy-nine at St. Marys Hospital in Rochester; the voice counters by insisting that there has been no *wrong number* called, reciting the number which is indeed S.'s phone number, each digit precisely enunciated, the fact is that S.'s father *passed away* at two-twelve A.M. that very night/morning and S. is needed at home, urgently needed by her mother at home, this is no time to quibble childishly over the phone.

Urgently needed by her mother—words sharp as a knife blade striking stone.

S. draws breath to protest further but the receiver slips from her benumbed fingers to fall to the floor.

Unable to cry as she'd been unable to cry *then.*

Half-awakened, S.'s husband asks what is wrong, quickly S. assures him *Nothing! Nothing is wrong,* urging him to return to sleep for she cannot bear to speak with another person at this time; especially her husband who will have too many questions to ask, and who will dismiss the call as a mistake or a prank. In her jangled state the last thing S. wants is another person to interfere with the rush of emotion she is feeling, a windstorm of emotion leaving her breathless for what a ridiculous phone call, what a ridiculous conversation, a stranger calling her to inform her—*her!*—that her father died just three hours ago and not six years ago; that S.'s father's death has not become a settled part of S.'s life as grasses grow above an ugly gouge in the earth, thinly at first, then more profusely filling in what was mere emptiness.

Still, S. is overcome by a sudden need to be with her mother. Wanting desperately to hold her mother and to be held by her mother.

Frantic, as with hunger. *Urgent!*

In half-light throwing on clothes. Not the overhead bedroom light which would disturb her husband's sleep but a closet light muted as a half-shut eyelid.

Downstairs in the kitchen S. will leave a message for her husband explaining—*Mom called, I'm needed there. Will call you when I can later today. Love, S.*

Tries to think of something more. The man upstairs sleeping *is* her husband from whom she should have no secrets . . .

But nothing more comes to her, she lays aside the plastic pen. Just a girl, a daughter, staring into the abyss of adulthood paralyzed.

It is five forty-three A.M. when she leaves the house. Seeing in the digital clock in the stove, radium-glimmering numerals.

For maybe (maybe!) she will never return.

Breathless in her vehicle driving north. Plunging north through shifting layers of darkness as in a gigantic Rothko canvas.

Consoling herself, *This won't be new, raw; this is old grief, that has grown a scab, and a scar. You can do this.*

This scar, covering S.'s body protective as another layer of skin. Transparent, yet impenetrable.

Driving through early-morning mist. Miles of Thruway, snowy fields, farmland. Deciduous woods leafless in February.

S.'s head is jangling, hearing and rehearing a stranger's words uttered in reproach.

Your father. Passed away. Two-twelve A.M. Urgently needed at home.

Years before, when S. was twelve, her father had almost been killed in a factory accident; he'd been thirty-six at the time. A piece of heavy machinery had fallen, another man had been crushed to death, S.'s father's foot was injured, most of the bones broken, he'd been hospitalized for several days. *But he had not died.*

Recalling the shock of the news, disbelief. Called out of school, seventh-grade social studies class. *Hospitalized, accident at work. Machine-shop press-man killed.*

Yet how faint this memory is, S. has to prod herself to remember. Seeing the stunned-looking twelve-year-old rising from her desk, called into the hallway, as everyone in the room stared at her in silence.

Can't be happening, what is happening?—no. Not possible.

So too the call that morning was obviously a mistake, a misunderstanding. But it is (surely) true that S.'s mother is in need of her; it is (surely) true that S. has been neglecting her mother, living alone since S.'s father's death; perhaps it is her mother's need for S. that is the call, the summons.

For something has happened in the night. Since S. fell asleep shortly after midnight beside her husband and was awakened hours later by a ringing phone.

A soft ring, at least. In the bedroom extension.

But is it in Rochester she is expected, or elsewhere? S.'s parents moved to Rochester after his retirement but before that they'd lived all of their lives in Yewville, where S. was born; if S. thinks of *home* it is Yewville, she has never lived in Rochester.

After her parents' move to what was called a *retirement village* they'd come to regret leaving Yewville. How much of this was the melancholy of advancing age and infirmity, or specific problems with their new quarters, S. was never certain. S.'s father in particular was difficult to fathom, a gregarious man who shunned intimacy.

He'd dropped out of school at sixteen to begin working in the machine shop of an automotive parts factory in Yewville—this, in an era when graduating from high school was not common in upstate rural New York. By twenty he was a married man, by twenty-one a father. Gradually he'd been promoted to safer, higher-paying work in the factory from which he retired after forty years; at S.'s encouragement her parents sold the farmhouse property in Yewville and moved to Rochester where, S. believed, they would have access to better medical care in the years to come.

But in the spiffy new quarters in the *retirement village* S.'s father was mortified that his hard-earned savings melted away so rapidly. Each month there were incidental fees, charges and surcharges, taxes; each year the rent increased. Guiltily S. felt responsible, not that the move to an urban area was a misstep but that her father was made to feel less than adequate, unmanned, at a vulnerable time in his life. S. insisted upon helping to pay her parents' bills, it was the least she could do for them, she had a well-paying job, her income was independent from her husband's, how better to demonstrate her love for her parents, a daughter's generosity, at a distance.

To spare her father further embarrassment S. sent a monthly check directly to the retirement village and after her father's death S. has sent cards, flowers, gifts to her mother frequently, to compensate for not seeing her more often.

There were no other siblings in the family. *She* is the prized child, well into adulthood.

Driving west on the Thruway beside the Chautauqua River out of which mists rise languidly as exhaled breaths. At the roadside, tall grasses stiffened in snow. Overhead cumulus clouds heavy-hanging like udders swollen with milk.

S. has been squinting at the sky, expecting the sun. Instead, a sickle moon at midday.

Traveling upstate is time travel, risky. Mesmerized by the countryside S. will begin to lose her understanding of who she *is*.

For nineteen years S. has been married but S. has never had a truly intimate lover. She has never fully grasped what *intimacy* might mean. For always S. has been protected by the transparent scar like an extra layer of skin covering her body.

Grateful for the husband as she is grateful for her excellent job—director of a foundation that awards fellowships in the arts and humanities to worthy candidates. S. herself was a recipient of one of these coveted fellowships, years ago in her late twenties.

Moving away, leaving home. How proud they'd been of their brilliant daughter . . .

S. had not arrived in time to see her father before he'd died of a brief illness, in the hospital in Rochester. Too late!—lingering at home distracted by the busyness of work and by her father's assurance (on the phone) that he wasn't seriously ill, scoffing for God's sake he was all right, he would be *fine.* Had S. believed her father because she'd wanted to believe him, it was the easiest of all options to believe a dying man, that he was *fine*?

Pneumonia, complicated by congestive heart failure. So it was neatly typed on the death certificate.

In the hospital in Rochester S.'s father had died yet the voice on the phone this morning had murmured what sounded like *Yewville.*

Behind the voice S. had heard muffled sounds. Voices. Labored chuffing breathing that was (possibly) the quick beating of her own blood in her ears.

Urgently needed at home. Needed.

S. is sure, the confusion will be explained once she is with her mother. Once they have touched, embraced.

For it is urgent, S. must *be with* her mother. In person. Her mother dislikes answering the phone, she has been besieged by robo-calls, rarely returns S.'s messages. Email, texting are beyond her.

S. wonders if the unfamiliar voice she'd heard that morning had been a computer-generated voice. A glitch in a hospital computer, a confusion in time. Hopeless, to try to reason with a *robot.*

As the exit sign for Yewville approaches, S. begins to feel unease, excitement.

The conviction has come to her that this is her exit, not Rochester. Her mother is in Yewville, not Rochester. *Home* is Yewville, not Rochester.

Yewville, New York, is the place of S.'s birth. A small city on the Chautauqua River, population twenty-five thousand. Twelve miles south of Lake Ontario, eighteen miles east of Rochester. Farmland, long rolling hills.

What must have happened: S.'s mother has moved back to Yewville, to the old house; S.'s mother is awaiting S. there which is why S. must hurry.

At the Yewville exit, S. feels the steering wheel turning in her fingers.

Exit—*home.*

What will become of us?—most plaintive of cries.

S. steels herself for a rude surprise. Approaching the outskirts of Yewville.

Fast-food restaurants, gas stations, discount stores—eyesores on the highway leading into Yewville but to S.'s relief Main Street appears to be virtually unchanged. S. could close her eyes to summon the familiar downtown, weatherworn façades of red-brick buildings, Klein Brothers, Fehr's Shoes, Holland Furniture, Empire Realty, Rexall Drugs. The post office building, the public library. The wide bridge over the Chautauqua River where as a child S. had leaned over the railing staring at a wraith-like reflection in the water below.

And relief too, the old house on Meridian Road, three miles from Main Street, is still standing.

Formerly a farmhouse, covered in asphalt siding meant to resemble shingleboard. The steep-pitched roof from which small avalanches of snow slid in winter, warmed and loosened by heat rising within the poorly insulated attic.

There is the massive old oak beside the driveway, leafless in winter. Its lower limbs are missing as if crudely amputated.

There, the deteriorating remains of outbuildings—barn,

storage shed. Dark-feathered birds, too small to be crows but noisy, querulous, have gathered on the rotted barn roof shaking their wings.

No vehicle in the driveway. No vehicle visible inside the barn where S.'s father kept his car which became S.'s mother's car after his death and which S.'s mother could never bring herself to drive out of a nervous dread of *having an accident.*

How bright, how *vivid* the February air, now that the mist has lifted. S. steps out of her car feeling slightly dazed, off-balance. Mineral cold to the air, that makes S.'s eyes water.

On the ground, glaring-white skeins of snow looking like artificial snow. Overhead, a sky too suddenly open, raw as bared bone.

S. feels as if a vise were being tightened around her chest. Difficult to breathe!

Pushing open the door at the rear of the house, calling to her mother—no reply, no sound except a thrumming of something electric, the refrigerator in the kitchen. S. is certain, her mother *is* home. S.'s mother is *always* home.

There's a smell of cigarette smoke, S.'s nostrils pinch in dismay.

Each time S. leaves the freshness of the outdoor air and enters the interior of the old house the revelation sweeps over her—*This is your life, your life can be lived only here.*

S. has grown stoic, this is merely a fact. A column of numbers added together yields a simple fact, indisputable.

A life of *use.* Defined by *early, irrevocable loss.*

For S. is rarely gone from this house for long. Virtually never overnight.

Not bitter. Nothing more futile than *bitter.*

The task has fallen to S. out of all persons in the world, indeed out of all persons who have ever lived, to keep the woman who is her mother alive: to lift her mother from the lethargy of despair into which otherwise her mother would sink, drown.

The odor of cigarette smoke is stronger in the kitchen but S.'s mother is not in the kitchen.

Must be upstairs. Lying on her bed beneath a knitted quilt.

S. calls to her mother, keeping her voice light, melodic. A balloon-voice, lifting.

S.'s mother has had difficulty with stairs for years but refuses to sleep on the first floor of the house, insists instead upon climbing, descending, climbing, descending the steep narrow stairs of the old farmhouse despite swollen ankles, arthritic knees, shortness of breath. Outdoors, in public, S. has to help her mother walk even short distances but her mother is often vexed with S., embarrassed, for it is clumsy walking this way, undignified and *hateful.*

About this too, S. is stoic. Telling herself it's the least she can do, her mother has not chosen her life any more than S. has chosen hers.

Upstairs, S. discovers her mother asleep, or rather just waking from sleep, sprawled on her back on the bed beneath a soiled quilt. Blinds at the bedroom windows are drawn. Blinds at these windows are always drawn.

Here too the air is stale, smelling of cigarette smoke. An ashtray on a bedside table, cut glass in the shape of a star which S. has been seeing all of her life, filthy-heaped with butts.

S. has difficulty breathing here. In this room. Blinds drawn at windows never raised.

As if a cloth soaked in ether were being pressed against S.'s nose and mouth which she has not the strength to push away.

Still, S. greets her mother with the airy balloon-voice. S. is *upbeat.*

Bloodshot eyes, groggy with sleep, blinking at S. As if, for a scant moment, S.'s mother withholds from S. the recognition of a daughter by her mother.

You? But who are you?

S. shudders, the vacant gaze. Some day to come, perhaps soon, when S.'s mother will truly not recognize her, who then will S. *be*?

Living alone together, so many years. For one can be *alone* even while *together* with another being.

As usual S.'s mother is reluctant to wake from sleep. Since her life was torn in two, decades ago it is sleep that is S.'s mother's solace. There is something sensual, near-obscene, in the way that S.'s mother sleeps: on her back, arms and legs spread, like an overturned turtle; mouth opened, slack, glistening with saliva; in erratic gusts her wheezing lungs suck in, expel, suck in and expel air like a bellows.

Now seeing who S. is, an expression of sulky resentment, exasperation.

Time for S.'s mother's bath! S. helps her mother to her feet, trying not to note her ankles which seem more swollen than usual. *Edema. Congestive heart failure.*

More than time, indeed. S.'s mother refused a bath that morning as she'd refused a bath the day before.

But now S.'s mother is saying, with a kind of puckish humor, she is *sick of smelling herself.*

With care S. walks her mother across the hall to the bathroom. S. has long since stopped seeing the tarnished faucets edged with grime that no Brillo pad can extricate, the showerhead so clogged with salt-residue that the stream of water has been halved over the years; the deep-stained toilet bowl and bathtub, both impracticably white; the discolored linoleum floor. As S. has stopped seeing her mother at such close range, averts her eyes out of a dread of seeing, out of respect for, the ravaged older woman who resembles S. herself, uncannily. S.'s mother is sallow-skinned, heavyset as if bloated, boneless; her face is a girl's face bizarrely aged, criss-crossed with fine wrinkles like cobwebs, a hungry pike-mouth bracketed by deep creases.

S.'s mother bats away S.'s hands, irritably. But not forcibly. No choice but to allow S. to draw the bath, fill the bathtub with fragrant sudsy hot water, help S.'s mother step into the tub which is a precarious move for one in her condition, fraught with danger.

S. knows, her mother is in terror of slipping, falling. Breaking a hip at her age, cracking her skull, a death-sentence.

As S. knows that, though S.'s mother feigns indifference when S. returns home later than she expects, S.'s mother would succumb to terror, panic, hysteria if S. were really late, or failed to come home at all.

To be *always expected.* To be *never free to surprise.*

S. waits outside the bathroom door as her mother bathes. Trying to breathe, normally. Trying to reason with herself, no one is to blame.

Unless it was *outrageous negligence, unacceptable work-conditions, capitalist exploitation of workers, failure to ensure minimal machine-shop safety standards* as the lawyers charged.

It is not (yet) that time in their lives when S. will have to lean over the bathtub to bathe her mother with a soft sponge, Ivory soap and shampoo, coo and cajole her fretting mother and wrap her in the largest bath towel after the precarious swaying stepping-out from the tub.

Caregiver: one who provides *care.*

That knock at the classroom door. The summons, seventh-grade social studies. Twelve years old, last day of childhood. So long ago. Yet, so vivid in memory. Classmates staring at S.'s stricken face, staring at her back as she left the room. For once your name is called, once you are told to leave the class, to leave school, bring your books with you, it cannot be undone.

Too young at twelve to prepare herself for what was to come. And never could S. have anticipated what the news would be: her father's chest crushed, spinal cord severed, in what the local newspaper would call a *tragic assembly-line accident.*

All of S.'s life, following from this. As if her chest had been crushed with her father's chest, her spinal cord severed with his. It was a co-worker who'd survived the accident with just a shattered foot, not S.'s father, who'd died on the factory floor almost instantaneously.

S.'s father had died at thirty-six. S.'s father had not lived long enough to be transferred to another department in the factory, he had not lived to be trained as a tool and die designer nor had he lived into the year when the factory was unionized, hourly wages for all workers were raised, astonishing medical benefits provided. He had not lived to retire after forty years, he had not lived in a *retirement village* in Rochester that would be partly subsidized by his daughter, he had not lived until the age of seventy-nine in reasonably good health until the final months of his life.

S. had graduated from the Yewville high school with her class and with honors but she'd never enrolled at the University of Rochester or at any other university, never earned a PhD, never taught college, never been hired as an administrator of a foundation in Philadelphia—all that has been a dream, a phantom.

S. took courses at the community college, she is an administrative assistant there, forty minutes away, never far from home. Rarely away past nine P.M. and never overnight for she is her mother's caretaker.

S. has never married, has never been *intimate* with another person. The several men she'd loved had not loved her in return, not enough to marry her. For a while she had wanted children, and then she had ceased wanting children.

She had wanted to give pleasure to another person and to take pleasure from another person but that had not happened. Barely S. can remember, the faces of the men whom she'd loved, and lain awake tormenting herself over, all that has faded with time like newsprint bleached by rain and sun.

Almost it has become a kind of fable, a ballad. How S. was (evidently) picked up from school that day by a relative. (Which relative? S. doesn't remember.) And there in this house on Meridian Road, the shock of her (young) mother weeping. Being held, clutched-at, by relatives, as S. stood staring, repelled, confused, and resentful, not yet grasping what had happened, to her father, and what would happen, to her and her mother, rippling outward through decades. Like a woman on TV made ugly by sobbing *What will become of us! What will become of us!*—as S. stood apart in a cold wash of panic, not willing to be clutched-at, not willing to be yanked down, drowned, gripped in her mother's arms as even now, trying not to hear the sounds of her mother in the bathtub, fleshy sounds, too-intimate sounds, heavy breathing, grunting, S. will take a stoic comfort staring out a window at a raw blank sky, black-feathered birds lifting from the barn roof with graceless jerking wings, trying not to think, no need to think, the throb of the incantation never ceases in her brain—*What will become of us! What will become of us that is not us here, now.*

THE RETURN

My friend was a widow, not really old but already a widow *twice.*

You think of Oscar Wilde's wisecrack—*To lose one husband may be regarded as a misfortune, to lose two looks like carelessness.*

But really, it wasn't funny. Nothing about it was funny. Audra had told (women) friends that Thad, the second husband, had saved her life, virtually—she'd met him within a year of losing her first husband to whom she'd been married for thirty-six years. Which was why I'd been avoiding my widow-friend through the entire pandemic. As if that were the excuse.

Well, Audra had to know that the pandemic wasn't the excuse for my avoiding her. Because Thad had passed away in early 2020, before Covid, he'd died of an unspeakably virulent and swift-acting cancer, the kind of cancer that no sooner do you hear *Have you heard—?* than it's *Oh God. Thad's—gone?*

Like that. Just—*gone.*

So, I'd been avoiding Audra. Even the thought of Audra. Some subjects are just too sad.

But then, the other morning I woke thinking about Audra. How selfish it was of me, to be avoiding her. How cowardly. Felt a sudden need to hear Audra's voice. No idea why, I wanted badly to call her, speak with her.

Not speak *at* her, coolly detached as in an email.

Problem is, no one calls anyone any longer. In our generation, at least. The last friend who called me frequently, as if he took pleasure in hearing my voice, and took pleasure in knowing that I was hearing his voice, was a much-revered poet who'd died three years ago, at seventy-eight; no one in my life has replaced him.

So, I'd lost the habit of using a phone for personal calls. An awkward/adolescent sort of shyness for one who'd used the phone often, decades ago.

Certainly it was awkward to call Audra, after so long. Half-expect a widow to say to you in a pert sarcastic voice *You? Why bother, now? It's too late.*

At the time Thad died, I had called Audra. I'd called, left a message, Audra had never called back, of course she'd been distraught with grief, no one expects a widow to *call back.* I'd sent a sympathy card, I'd sent flowers. I'd seen Audra, in the company of mutual friends. I had certainly meant to see her again, to spend time with her. But soon, as Covid rolled over us like a poison gas, I had not seen Audra again.

So, I called Audra at last, and made arrangements to visit her. Audra was warmly welcoming as if I had not avoided seeing her for two years; which made me wonder, maybe she'd been avoiding *me.*

Several times in the past twenty years, Audra and I had

been on the brink of becoming *best friends.* Yet, it had not happened.

Once you are an adult, you tend to avoid such emotional connections. *Falling in love, loving* an individual of the opposite sex can be risky, arduous, foolish, wonderful; but it is mandated, there are parameters, expectations. But once you are past adolescence, the phenomenon *best friends* is embarrassing, to be avoided.

Or maybe I imagined it, I am likely to imagine things that don't exist for others. *You must guard against that,* I cautioned myself.

"I am so, so sorry to have lost touch . . ."

"I am so, so sorry to have lost contact . . ."

". . . so, so sorry. Forgive me!"

Driving to Audra's house halfway across the state of New Jersey. The first time in two years I had driven such a distance. Feeling gay, giddy. Feeling apprehensive. Covid had kept me indoors and warm like Eliot's *Waste Land* winter keeping us warm, benumbed as root vegetables. If you don't sicken and die, there can be solace in what sociologists call *social isolation.*

It had been years since I'd visited Audra and Thad Klein in their handsome old stone house on a hill above the Delaware River, purchased since Thad's retirement from the university. (Though, as it turned out, Thad had continued to teach graduate courses in the department, and to introduce distinguished speakers. Since everyone who came to the university wanted to meet Thad Klein, one of the university's legendary faculty members, his retirement had been something of a joke.)

As I had recalled, the Kleins' house was set back from the road, only just visible through a stand of tall deciduous trees.

Originally a farmhouse dating from the late 1700s, many times expanded, renovated, refurbished; one of the largest farms in the valley, in recent decades reduced to just three or four uncultivated acres.

A long driveway!—impracticably comprised of gravel.

I discovered that I was reluctant to drive up Audra's driveway. The palms of my hands had grown damp.

My concern was, if I drove up the five-hundred-foot driveway, I would have a difficult time turning around, if I had to leave the house hurriedly.

Out of nowhere such peculiar thoughts come to me in weak moments, like arrows shot at random. I can sense that the veil between myself and something adversarial on the other side has grown perilously thin, that is responsible for these thoughts.

So, I decided to park my car at the end of the driveway, in a grassy area beside the road, and hike up the long drive.

It was a beautiful day in late summer. It was not oppressively humid as usual in New Jersey at this time of year. Cicadas thrummed gaily, fields shimmered with bird and insect life. The gravel drive was rutted and uneven and stippled with weeds, but weeds of an attractive sort, flowering thistles, Queen Anne's lace. Occasional litter, what appeared to be newspaper pages, rain-sodden, rotted, caught in brambles beside the driveway, were a startling eyesore, but minor. Overall the look was shabby-romantic, as in a painting by Edward Hopper.

As I approached the stone house on foot, I thought I saw a movement at a first-floor window, as if a curtain were being pulled aside.

Lifting my hand in greeting. *Hi!*

Wondering then if I should have done this? Indicated that I'd seen Audra at the window? I had the impression that she'd quickly shrunk back out of sight.

She has forgotten you are coming. She has no idea who you are.

The front door was made of old, solid wood, painted a tasteful shade of dark red, that had begun just perceptibly to peel; the knocker was a tarnished brass eagle. I tried not to peer through the vertical windows beside the door as a shadowy figure approached to let me in.

"Why, hello!—wonderful to see you . . ."

"Wonderful to see *you* . . ."

Audra greeted me warmly, tears shone in her eyes. There was a smell in the air of something airy, wonderful as baking bread.

I was astonished I was crying, for I never cry, and how strange that I should cry *now.*

I was light-headed too. My heart was beating rapidly. That fluttery sensation when you realize you are out of control. Another trip of the heart, the heart will be fibrillating. Oxygen won't reach your brain. You will fall in a faint.

For it seemed, I was missing Thad Klein badly. I had not anticipated this, exactly. That I was here in Thad's house, in this particular place, where Thad Klein should have been, but was not; that *I was here,* but *Thad was not*—this seemed to me preposterous.

But there was Audra drawing back, wiping at her eyes, ever sensible, ever in charge—"Well, come inside, Maude! I've made lunch. How was the drive?"

There followed then an interlude of edgy, bright-nervous laughter. The sound of my name in Audra's mouth was a rough sort of caress—*Maude.*

During the pandemic I could go for days in succession not

hearing anyone's voice, in person. Not hearing my name uttered, in a human voice.

Seeing *Maude* on a computer screen, in an email or text message, had no ring of intimacy. Rather, *Maude* seemed like a kind of mockery of intimacy.

No one to call me on the phone. *H'lo, Maude? How are you?*

Audra led me into a living room with a low, beamed ceiling, stone fireplace, well-worn leather sofa, chairs, tables stacked with books, smooth-worn plank floor upon which handwoven carpets were laid; from this, a step down into a screened-in porch overlooking what appeared to be a ruin of a pear orchard, like something in a Tarkovsky film.

Memories of the setting returned, in waves, ripples. As if in recollection of a film, of years before.

Books in stacks, lying horizontally; books in shelves, standing vertically. Rapidly my eye darted about, as our eyes invariably do in such circumstances, seeking out familiar titles, familiar jacket covers—on a coffee table, a short stack of books containing a familiar cover, familiar font, a familiar author's name, my own.

I felt a stab of something like pleasure. But maybe chagrin. For it seemed to me, this book of mine had been in exactly that place, years ago when I'd last visited; if I detached the book from the stack, and opened to the title page, I would discover an inscription in my unmistakable handwriting: *To Audra & Thad with love, Maude.*

Had neither of them read the book, in the interim? Was Audra aware, that my book was on display, sure to attract my eye, as soon as I stepped into the room?

Audra had prepared fruit drinks for us: apricot, banana, yogurt, wheat germ. A circular glass-topped table was set at the farther end of the living room: two citrus-colored place mats facing each other across the table as in a chess game.

Chatter about blending machines, puréed foods, smoothies. Chatter about mutual friends, acquaintances. Colleagues of Thad who had tried to organize a memorial for him, postponed indefinitely because of Covid.

Chatter rapid and pitiless as Ping-Pong. Neither side wishes to let the Ping-Pong ball fly past to clatter onto the floor. The pace quickens, the breath quickens.

As Audra spoke I was nodding brightly. I was still aware of my (unread, unopened) book on the nearby table. I was still aware of the *wrongness* of being in this place, in which Thad Klein was *absent*.

Too much here, to distract me. As I have lived alone for a long time now, I am accustomed to steering my own thoughts along a narrow, fairly straight road. In the company of others, I feel the steering wheel being tugged from me.

And how strange, the blunt *reality* of this room. For *reality* is inevitably *banality*.

Yet, there is nothing *banal* about death. Absence.

The beauty of the setting distracted me for it was, if closely examined, an overabundance of beautiful unrelated things, crowded and colliding. Pale yellow floral wallpaper in the style of William Morris, intricately woven wall hangings that might have been Mexican, a shelf of teapots brought back by Thad from his travels to the Middle East.

Yet, conspicuously, on a rattan table by the front window, what appeared to be a rifle.

"Oh, is that a—gun?"

Gun, not *rifle,* to suggest how foreign to me, how distasteful, such an object was, I didn't even know its truer name.

Audra paused, with a flicker of something like chagrin; glancing at the table as if she'd forgotten the rifle and was annoyed at me for calling our attention to it.

A neighbor had insisted she take the rifle from him, Audra said—"In case I might need it sometime."

"Because you live alone here, and it's isolated?"

"Yes. Because I live alone here, and it's isolated."

Out of a morbid sort of curiosity, because I had rarely seen a rifle close up, because I am a person who abhors and fears guns and would outlaw all guns if I had the power, I went to examine the rifle, without touching it.

"Is this a—.22 rifle?" (I had never heard of any other kind of rifle, this seemed like a plausible query.)

"Yes, it's a .22. Hunters use them for bird hunting, I think. Or maybe—deer. Not that my neighbor is a hunter, he isn't. He's retired like us, he and his wife live the next house over."

"But—do you know how to use it?"

"He's shown me. I've actually fired it." Audra spoke with an air of patience, like one humoring a small child. Adding, embarrassed: "I—I hope never to use it, of course . . ."

A flush came into Audra's face. Clearly, she wanted to change the topic.

A .22 rifle in the Kleins' house! Looking like something a soldier would carry, with a smooth-polished dark wooden stock. Surely it would be heavy to lift, when you dared to pull the trigger there would be a kick to your shoulder like a rebuke.

I would tell no one, when I returned home. I knew that such information would be misinterpreted by mutual friends, it would not be to the widow's credit.

What would Thad think?—a .22 rifle in his house . . .

Oh that is—disturbing. Poor Audra, what has happened to her!

It was touching, that Audra had prepared such an elaborate lunch. Very likely neither of us even ate lunch, most days; it isn't a meal with much appeal, if one lives alone.

Cold carrot curry soup, salad Niçoise, multigrain bread of the hue of rich mahogany which Audra had baked herself just that morning.

"Really! That is amazing, Audra."

I am at a loss what to say about home-baked bread. Usually the loaf is presented as a work of art, a quirky-gnarly artisanal art, often beautiful to the eye, and mouthwateringly aromatic; it is meant to inspire envy, I would guess, beyond simple admiration. When one can so readily purchase novelty breads in local stores and farmer's markets, what is the purpose of such home labor? I felt obliged to ask Audra what sort of bread it was, what sort of ingredients went into it, and where did she purchase them?—with such earnestness, you would think that I intended to take up bread-baking tomorrow; even as a vise seemed to be tightening around my chest, the revelation that came to me another time, more forcibly, that Thad *really wasn't in this house.*

Though I could wait—and wait—and wait—I would not hear the man's footsteps approaching us, feel the vibration of his tread in the old plank floorboards, as he bounded into the room, having heard our voices—*Hey! Hello! Is that Maude? What the hell brings you here, Maudie?*

Audra was explaining how bread-baking had become an integral part of her life since the lockdown. The word *integral* seemed to me particularly poignant, piteous.

Since the lockdown, since my husband died of pancreatic cancer and left me alone in the world, baking bread has become integral to my life.

I was laughing, but then I was coughing, lifting a linen napkin to my mouth, appalled.

"Are you all right, Maude?"—Audra was concerned, staring at me.

Wiping at my eyes. Waiting for the spell to pass.

In a bemused voice Audra was saying how annoying it is, everyone asks a widow if she intends to sell her house, of course it's a reasonable question, and this house in particular is so *remote* . . .

You can gauge a homeowner's pride in property by the degree to which they complain of it. A fretful sort of affection: roof needs repair, furnace needs replacing, termites, carpenter ants, a half-dozen hornets' nests under the eaves; township taxes, ash trees dying and in danger of being blown onto the house in the next windstorm.

"And the driveway!—*that* is a serious nuisance, especially in the winter."

"In the winter, yes—I can imagine. It's so—long."

"It's *long*. And it's gravel. Not practical, like asphalt."

"But gravel is much more attractive."

"It *is*. That's what everyone says. But Thad also thought it was ridiculous, because each winter there's a problem with snow removal, and in the spring thaw half the gravel is washed away in the ditch. Maybe you noticed, the driveway slopes uphill, the house is at the top of an incline, so naturally rain rushes down the driveway . . ."

I wondered why we were talking at such length about the driveway. Gravel! Was there some covert meaning here, which I was not decoding?

It seemed strange to me, that Audra hadn't commented on the fact that I had not driven up the driveway but parked at the road. That I'd hiked up the driveway. That she'd (evidently) seen me, watched me approach the house. Was that not an eccentric gesture, to park out on the road, five hundred feet away? Was that not an eccentric reaction on Audra's part, not to speak of my having done so?

I feared the embarrassment of having to back up and maneuver the car around, as my frowning hostess, standing on the front stoop, watched. Perhaps something like this had happened in the past, at this house. I would be hesitant, for instance, to back over a corner of the lawn, especially if the homeowner was watching.

(Though the Kleins' lawn was overgrown, lush with wildflowers and thistles, hadn't been mowed in weeks, you would not really call it a *lawn* any longer.)

Audra was saying, in a curiously flat, detached voice, as if she were reporting something she supposed might be of interest to me, if but minimally of interest to her:

". . . in the early morning I'm awake before dawn. Usually it's pitch-black outside. I have no idea what time it is. Nothing more depressing than waking so early unless it's raining as well as dark. Can't stand lying in bed so I come downstairs into the kitchen, barefoot, in my nightgown. It's the identical flannel nightgown I owned when Thad and I were first married—just thirteen years ago."

Thirteen years! I would have thought no more than eight, nine years.

The entire lifetime of their marriage, so brief!

But time is accelerated now, like an arrow approaching its target.

". . . I prepare tea, herbal tea. Thad used to laugh at 'herbal tea,' it isn't 'tea,' he said, it's 'herbal infusion.' I come out here, I sit at the table here, I stare out the window and up the driveway. My brain is just blank. I'm waiting for light to return. Colors. How colors emerge out of things, with light. It's fascinating to me. I can't say why. I'm staring at objects that have no color—those tree trunks, that fence post. Deer—there are often deer in the driveway. Not bucks, rarely bucks, usually does with two fawns. Colors emerge, with the sun. You see something dappled moving—it's a fawn. At this time of year the fawns are just a few months old. When we had a cat, I fed the cat of course—Rusty. Rusty has died, I haven't replaced him. People tell me—adopt a kitten! A puppy. But I don't have time. I can't be responsible for another life. I mean—a living thing, that has to be fed. I need to sit alone here staring outside at those trees. I'll see someone in the driveway, or something, and if it isn't deer it turns out to be Thad returning to the house, exactly as he always had. You can see, the way Thad is walking, the clothes he's wearing, the fact that he's carrying *The New York Times*—you can tell, he doesn't seem to *know,* yet.

"Every morning in the years we lived here Thad hiked out to the mailbox to get the newspaper. *The New York Times* is delivered at about six-thirty A.M. here, so he'd get out of bed to retrieve it, it was the crucial start of Thad's day, God help us if the delivery was late or never arrived. He only read the print edition, of course—he'd been reading it, he said, since 1959, at Harvard. All the undergraduates at Harvard read *The New York Times* in those days. Hard to believe, isn't it? Many of them listened to Metropolitan Opera broadcasts, too. Saturday afternoons. Thad said, you'd hear the identical music, voices, wafting through the Yard. From one corner to the other.

"*The New York Times,* you'd have to be careful no one in the residence stole your copy. It was valuable. It was cherished. Some boys read it first thing in the morning, others saved it for the night. Thad saved it for the night, after a day of classes and work. That was his reward. He and his suitemates in Weld Hall actually discussed the news, can you believe it?—1959? Of course, they were smart kids from New York City. Stuyvesant, Erasmus Hall. Competitive kids. So Thad never lost his obsession with *The New York Times,* and it had to be the print edition. The online edition, Thad said, made him slightly sick, nauseated—on a screen, nothing looks *profound.* But the print edition was pure pleasure. He would read through the entire newspaper, or nearly. It would take him an hour or more, at breakfast. That was the point of Thad's breakfast, to provide a frame for *The New York Times.* So intent upon the damned paper, one time he hadn't noticed that Rusty had jumped up on the table and came over to lap milk from his cereal bowl.

"Did I tell you, Rusty died of old age? At least, I think he did. He wandered off into the woods back in the spring, he never returned. Days I searched for him in the woods. Calling his name. Bawling like a baby. Maybe it's better that way, animals wandering off to die alone, not wanting us to distract them with our tears.

"So, I look up and there's Thad walking slowly up the driveway trying to read the newspaper at the same time. Sometimes I'd watch him from this window, he'd be so lost in concentration he didn't know where he was. Once or twice, I tapped at the window—that annoyed him! Not worth it, to risk annoying your husband over a trifle.

"But this time, it's different. He's been gone. He has just been—*absent.* We haven't seen each other in a long time. Longer than any of his trips, when he'd slip off the grid, no way to contact him. And no way to explain this absence. Where has Thad *been*? I'd tried to call him dozens of times. There was never any phone ringing, the call went directly to voice mail. I am stunned, that Thad has been here all along, evidently—at least, somewhere. And now he's walking up the driveway as if he'd never been gone at all!

"It's hurtful, I remember how hurt I'd been, at Thad's thoughtlessness, over the years. Of course, he hadn't always known he was thoughtless. More, he was oblivious. Unaware of how he could injure others.

"Covered in scar tissue, someone said. The price of living with a certain kind of man.

"So—I'm standing there. Staring out the window. In my nightgown, still. I put on a sweater or a jacket, kick my feet into boots, run outside to Thad in the driveway.

"Suddenly, desperate to get to him.

"I'm crying to him, shouting—'Thad! My God—Thad' . . .

"Thad looks up from the newspaper in that way he has, squinting, isn't sure what he has heard, doesn't expect to be seeing me like this, the sight of me is a shock to him, too.

"Whatever is in my face, I can't fathom.

"I should be terrified of seeing him, and of him—but I am not, I am overwhelmed with relief.

"(It's that simple, evidently. When they return, some of them, who can return, like slipping through a crack in a cavern wall, the emotions in their face are plain as a child's, plain as day, nothing subtle or obscure.)

"(We've come to think that the profound truths of our lives are complicated or elliptical as in poetry but in fact they are not. Plain and simple as a hammer striking you on the head.)

"We're together now. Clutching at each other. Thad tries to comfort me, he's stunned and confused but trying to remain level-headed, that was his role in our marriage, *I will be in charge.* You know Thad, any kind of emotional display embarrasses him. He isn't sure where he has been all this time, what has happened, he's watching me to gauge how I am feeling, which will tell him how to feel: It was like that in the hospital, when the oncologist spoke to us, those carefully chosen words. Trying to determine if (somehow) this has been a mistake, but whose mistake. If whatever went wrong was his fault. He'd never been comfortable with anyone criticizing him, however circuitously; he'd listen to unmitigated praise with a strained face, like one waiting for the ax to fall even if it wasn't going to fall. Since his illness he has become hypersensitive, I can see that.

"His hair seems a little thinner on top, silvery-gray, grown a little long on the sides, curling over his ears. I used to comb his hair when it was shoulder-length, no other woman had ever done that, he'd said; he humored me, though possibly he had enjoyed it. He has lost weight, his cheeks are almost gaunt. You know, Thad always boasted that he'd inherited the genes of serfs, peasant stock. His grandparents were from the Pale. Thick wrists and ankles, solid build, if he lost weight with illness it wouldn't show for some time, that was a blessing.

"We are incredulous seeing each other. Our eyes are just staring. Because this can't be, and yet—here we are.

"We understand, we must act quickly. Maybe there has been some mistake, that is why Thad has returned. Sobbing and laughing, tears running down our cheeks.

"Thad is so dazed, part of the newspaper falls from his fingers, he scarcely notices as it blows skittering along the ground.

"Every few feet we stop, out of breath. We're panting! We kiss and hug, kind of crazy behavior, desperate behavior. We're not kids. We are level-headed adults. Both of us, frankly stunned.

"Where the hell, Thad is wondering, has he been?—all these months? Was it years? No contact?

"Where the hell had *I* been, that I hadn't come to pick him up?—Thad wants to know. I had the damned car, all along.

"But Thad isn't accusing me! No. He's just—bamboozled. Just no idea where the hell he has *been.*

"He's wearing his old gray corduroys, that denim jacket that's been hanging in the closet, grimy baseball cap he couldn't bear to part with, a pair of water-stained Nike running shoes. This is exasperating, he has a dozen pairs of running shoes in a jumble on his closet floor, can't bring himself to throw out an old pair when he purchases a new pair, and he has newer shoes than these, I'm sure.

"All this while I'm telling Thad how I've missed him, how terrible it has been without him, how lonely. And no point to the loneliness, no end to it. How anxious I have been for him, wherever he is. How I have tried to call him but he never answers his cell phone. Never returns his messages.

"Trying not to sound reproachful. Or hysterical. Nothing will alienate Thad more.

"Thad seems to know that he has been away. Somewhere. Trying to remember, but it eludes him.

"It wasn't his fault!—unless maybe it was his fault. A man is mortified, in such circumstances. Dying is—*is not*—a manly thing. A man feels weak, emasculated. Thad Klein had been a *mensch,* nothing had flattered him more than hearing himself described as a *mensch.* He'd said to me, in the hospital, on what we didn't know would be the next-to-last day, that is, the last day Thad was clear-minded—*Oh Christ. I failed you by dying. That's what this is, isn't it? Our final days.*

"He'd spoken with reproach—it had been bitter reproach—of himself.

"This was heartbreaking to me, to hear. I protested *No! Don't say such a thing.*

"I told him, he had not failed anyone. He had not *died.*

"All this comes back to me now, I see the opportunity to make things right. We are gripping hands, hurrying to the house. I've forgotten how large his hand is, how warm, such strong fingers. It seems to have taken us a very long time to get to the house. The gravel driveway is much longer than I remember. And it seems to be later now, mid-morning, the sun has risen above the tree line. Maybe the day will be bright-brazen after all. Too hot. There is some urgency, to get Thad safely inside the house.

"But Thad stops dead in his tracks seeing the condition of the driveway near the house, where gravel has been visibly washed away. *God damn!*—all he'd paid for this fancy gravel, still the driveway looks like hell.

"And that ash tree by the house, Thad sees that it's dead. Totally—dead. Skeletal. Not a leaf remaining.

"In fact, Thad discovers several other ash trees, dead or dying. *Since when? Is it the ash borer?—killing ash trees everywhere in New Jersey? Each tree will cost us one thousand dollars to cut down.* God damn.

"I am trying to calm Thad who has become over-excited. Such household expenses always excite him, he isn't accustomed to country life, he'd lived the first eighteen years of his life in Brooklyn, in a crowded immigrant neighborhood. I call his attention to the house, he's squinting at the house. Now tears are streaking his cheeks. He's deeply moved to be home.

"His beard is slightly scruffy, he has not trimmed it in some time with his prim little beard-scissors. This is unusual, in a man of such vanity. He has not showered in some time, he smells of his body. The pupils of his eyes have shrunken as if he's staring into a blinding light.

"Asking if we still have the same lawn crew from Lambertville that mowed the grass, kept the bushes and trees trimmed, where the hell have they been?—Thad is exasperated with me.

"I have no defense, I am to blame. I have *let things go.*

"The one clear sign of depression, despair—*letting things go.*

"Quickly I tell Thad that now that he's back, the lawn will be mowed again, things will return to normal, he can make calls this afternoon when he's rested. He can hire a new lawn crew.

"But now Thad is distrustful of me. *Can* he trust me? He has no idea where I've been all this time.

"Inside the house he's squinting and staring to see if things are as he remembers. Something has changed, he can sense this, but what is it?—he's suspicious.

"*What did you do with my chair, why did you move it?*—this is a hefty, taffy-colored leather chair facing the fireplace, with Thad's stack of (mostly unread) books beside it, of course I haven't touched the chair or the books as I haven't touched most things in Thad's study, his closets. Even Thad's frayed old leather belt hanging from a hook in the upstairs bathroom, I have not had the heart to throw away.

"Thad has many questions to ask about the house, the positioning of things in the rooms and certain artworks on the walls including the numerous photographs he'd taken on his travels but he has no questions about himself, there is a curious reticence about himself, the mysterious things that have happened to him recently, like landscape glimpsed from a speeding vehicle. Each terminal illness is a story beginning slowly but accelerating; you intend to memorize all that happens because it is so extraordinary, because nothing like this has ever happened before, you need to retain each detail in chronological order, each incident has the horrific profundity of a fingernail torn out, never would you forget such a shock; yet soon, there are too many shocks to remember, a blur, a buzzing blur, the landscape is left behind as the vehicle's speed accelerates.

"Naturally Thad wants to see his study, *his things*. Anxious to see if anyone (that would be his wife) has dared to disturb his desk, his enormous console computer (blank dark screen), his folders and files, his books; but I have left everything in Thad's study as it was, anticipating such a return, such a scene, no reason to change anything, though often I come into this large room at the rear of the house, just to sit at the antique desk, marvel at its size, weight; enjoy the springy cushion of the swivel chair, that had cost so much at the time, Thad had laughed at my shock. All of Thad's valuable books remain exactly as he'd left them. Thad's own books, eight books written over a career of more than four decades, over three hundred articles published in prestigious academic journals. Floor-to-ceiling built-in bookshelves, three walls of the study. I have not asked Thad's friends and younger colleagues if they would like to select books from Thad's collection, out of a dread that they would not; but also that, if they did, the precious books might end up on eBay, and if I discovered this, or somehow Thad did, how hurt we would be! Libraries no longer want such special collections, eighteenth- and nineteenth-century first editions, classics of science, the complete works of Darwin, *Life and Letters,* including even volumes on Darwin's rival Wallace. Can't give away scholarly books, the only university libraries that might be interested in such titles already own them, kept under lock and key. The local library is always downsizing, selling books, it's shocking to me to see the books they sell, priced at one dollar in a bin like something at Walgreens.

"Still I am trying to grasp what has happened, what this is: that Thad is returned, at last. Who cares about his books, who cares about anything in this house, the fact is *Thad has returned.*

"Saying, hardly able to speak—*I have missed you so. Where have you been!*—as Thad tries to comfort me saying with a kind of faint jocosity—*Well, I'm back now. I'm here, right?*

"Repeating how we'd missed the other. For what is there to say?—we have stammered our astonishment, our relief. As in life we have been shy to say *Oh I love you! I love you so. Without you, my life is worthless to me.*

"My throat is dry, I am swallowing compulsively. I am frightened that now that Thad is back, he will be disappointed in me, he will be angry with me, for since his departure I have done some things of which he would disapprove.

"His tone can change, in an instant. If I am over-emotional, Thad will draw back. *Well, I missed you too, darling. I hadn't any idea where the hell you were and why—why didn't you call me?*

"Why'd you just abandon me there? In the hospital . . .

"How to stammer, *But I didn't! I didn't abandon you.*

"In the kitchen Thad is sharp-eyed seeing the calendar at once: AUGUST 2022. Looks quickly away, this is a preposterous date, someone is out to trick him, he isn't going to fall for it.

"One of those stupid visual puzzles, neuroscience tests,

how our perceptions are shaped by our expectations, or is it the reverse?—not going to get suckered into trying to figure it out.

"In the cupboard, in the refrigerator, there are foods that puzzle Thad, and the foods that Thad likes best seem to be missing, low-fat milk, for his cereal; no carton of jumbo eggs, for his poached eggs. Where are those Scandinavian crackers he likes, that to the rest of us taste like caramelized sawdust? Where is the jar of peanut butter he'd opened long ago? (With a spoon surreptitiously devouring peanut butter from the jar, mid-afternoons.) There in plain sight is a jar of low-calorie Italian salad dressing, shocking to Thad, this is unacceptable in our kitchen for Thad has nothing but contempt for vulgar diet foods, cheesy processed foods. He'd been in charge of preparing our nightly salad dressing, extra-virgin olive oil, wine vinegar, basil, mustard, what pride Thad has taken in these rituals, established long ago in the verdant days of his first marriage; a latecomer-wife had no grasp of how crucial these (seemingly trivial) rituals were, how offended Thad would become if they were violated.

"I am desperate to hide from Thad how slovenly I have become in grief, how indifferent to my own well-being, feeding myself out of cans, frozen foods, rarely fresh vegetables or green salads, too much energy is required to give a damn about one*self.*

"Next, Thad examines his photographs on the walls, in several rooms and in the hallways. Carefully framed, fastidiously matted in white, starkly beautiful compositions—sand dunes, mountain peaks, sunrises, coastlines shrouded in mist. Too late, I see that two or three of the photographs have loosened inside their frames, of course Thad's sharp eye alights upon these, too. *Damn! Look at this. You need to pay more attention, Audra.*

"Quickly, I apologize. Try to explain, but Thad interrupts. He has never been interested in excuses!

"Only now in this prickly mood does Thad remember to ask about his children, my stepchildren, middle-aged adult sons with whom I am on good terms but whom I scarcely know. With Thad absent between us we're drifting apart like rudderless boats in an affable current, almost too far apart now to wave at one another.

"So far as I know there is no bad news of them, no exceptional news, I suggest that Thad telephone them that evening, they will be thrilled to hear from him.

"Will they! Let's see.

"Thad's face settles into an inevitable scowl when the subject of his sons arises. He is disappointed in them, though both have earned PhDs somehow they have let him down, maybe they've just never lived up to their father's high expectations for them, he's never explained to me.

"As the second wife, I've learned not to ask. When I have Thad says coldly, *That's private.*

"As I knew he would, and had been dreading, Thad asks about our accountant Doug Murphy, another source of irritation to Thad over the years since Doug Murphy often doesn't return calls promptly and there is *just something about him, the twitch in his eyelid* that Thad doesn't trust.

"Not that Thad cares about money. He does not. Keeping our checkbooks up to date has been my responsibility, paying property taxes, mortgage, electricity, though of course if something goes amiss it would be my fault, I would be harshly scolded.

"True, Thad doesn't care about money but he does care about *being cheated.*

"This is a sort of obsession with him. Beginning as an undergraduate at Harvard, a lifetime ago, he'd lie awake at night calculating who had likely cheated him, who was taking advantage of him, his good nature, his naïveté, his willingness to believe the best of people; in recent years working himself into a fury calculating what the total sum might be, of all he'd been cheated of in his lifetime.

"But when I try to explain that Doug Murphy is retiring too, Doug Murphy has had open heart surgery this summer, Thad loses his temper and tells me *Shut up!*—with a look of such hatred, I am rooted to the spot.

"In life, I would flee from Thad when he was in such moods. Such a sudden flaring of hatred for me, his wife, like a struck match in his glistening eyes, but now I stand paralyzed, dry-mouthed, there is nowhere for me to flee, no longer, this is our house, the final house of our lives. This is the life we have been allotted.

"Thad, why do you hate me? You've only come back to me, I am your wife, I have been your widow, how can you hate me?

"These plaintive words, this plea, seizes Thad's attention. Instead of squinting and glaring, he looks at *me.*

"Such frankness is embarrassing to him. Unnerving.

"He's relenting, thank God. Thad Klein isn't an unreasonable man if you can just get through to him. (As his friends have assured me, many times in the early years of our marriage.) In the hospital too Thad hadn't listened to the oncologist, his eyes glazed over in boredom but he'd listened later to the palliative care doctor, a woman, soft wavy hair, soft sympathetic eyes, of course he'd listened to *her.*

"Quickly changes the subject, which is like Thad: *What's for supper tonight?*

"Opening the refrigerator again, perusing the freezer, I am hoping that Thad doesn't see how little remains that might be of interest to him, mainly frozen bread, frozen corn, peas, green beans. No meat, not even chicken. Suddenly he has grown weary of the effort. He says, *I'm tired.*

"The light is draining from his face. His skin had acquired a kind of ruddy vehemence when he was angry but now it is fading, returning to its original pallor. Thad turns to make his way—swaying, reaching out to touch the walls, to maintain his balance—to a back bedroom, where he can lie down.

"Just very—very tired . . .

"At this, I am overcome with fear. It's a familiar fear, panic. The injunction is—*Don't let your husband sleep, he will never wake up again.*

"I'm running after Thad, into the bedroom—I'm pulling at his arm, clutching at him—*No no no you can't lie down, you can't sleep. Wait!*

"Thad throws off my arm. He's disdainful of being touched just now, my desperation means nothing to him, he mutters, *I'm tired. So tired.*

"I try to stop him but he lies down heavily on the bed, with a deep sigh, a sigh to rend the heart, smudging dirt on the comforter, from the water-stained running shoes. In an instant, his eyes are closed."

Audra is silent, suddenly. Hides her face in her hands, in a gesture of misery, shame.

All these minutes she has been speaking in a kind of trance. As I have never heard Audra, or indeed anyone, speak to me before.

I have been staring at Audra, in a trance myself. I stare at her, frightened for her.

In a lowered voice I ask, "Is he—? Did he—? Fall asleep—?"

My heart is beating rapidly. I have a strong compulsion to run to the back bedroom, to peer inside.

Audra doesn't seem to have heard my question. Her flushed face is still mostly hidden from me, behind her hands. Loose skin on the backs of Audra's hands, visible veins. I hate that my friend is breathing so harshly, on the verge of hyperventilating. What will I do, if she begins to hyperventilate? A kind of hysteria, such anguish. There is no remedy, for such anguish.

I am afraid to touch Audra. I think that her skin would be scalding. She would throw off my hand like a snake just as Thad has done.

"I should leave. I—I have a long drive back home . . ."

I am on my feet, my knees are shaking, I must leave this place, I cannot bear this house another minute.

Our lunch has been abandoned. Salad Niçoise remnants on our plates. Half-empty fruit smoothies in tall cut-crystal goblets.

Time to leave! I have stayed too late. I will not embrace Audra in parting, she does not want to be touched, she is shivering convulsively oblivious of me.

I will not look into the back bedroom. *I will not.*

"Audra? Thank you! I will call you . . . I promise."

Eager to be free of the house with its oppressive low ceilings. Eager to escape into the fresh air, where I can breathe.

Half-falling down the stone steps, that are beginning to crumble.

An overgrown lawn, going to seed. Crazy-loud with cicadas in August. Gravel driveway, partly washed away and looking derelict, shameful.

Wildflowers, brambles. Newspaper pages, blown into underbrush.

Hiking hurriedly down the driveway. For the driveway is on an incline—*down.*

In the Delaware Valley, as you approach the river, ever more steeply the land turns *down.*

Resisting the impulse to run to my car. (Barely I can see my car, hidden at the end of the driveway.)

Resisting the impulse for if Audra is watching at the window, she will see, and she will know why I am running. Why I am panting, desperate to get to my car.

Realizing only now, the purpose of the .22 rifle. Whom it is the rifle is intended to protect the widow against.

THE REDWOODS

1.

Needing to get away. Not from other people so much as from himself. Indeed, sick of *self.*

Sixteen-mile trail, Humboldt Redwoods State Park. Hours of solitude, silence. That pristine air. Shafts of dreamy sunshine amid the enormous tree trunks. *Texture* of the redwood bark, a kind of Braille against his fingertips.

Yet voices intruded upon him, a near-inaudible rustling like the soughing of boughs overhead. His elders: parents, professors. But also friends, girls. People he scarcely knew, whose presence in his life was unwanted. A din!

Vann? Where are you?

We miss you.

To friends, he was *Vann.* To family and relatives, he was *Jake.* More formally, *Jacob Vanbrugh, Jr.*

How "voices" haunt us when we are alone. How memories

wash over us in solitude. The only remedy, Vanbrugh thought, was more solitude—more silence.

Tempted to fill his head with music, to drive away the voices. But no, he'd vowed not to give in.

He'd seen redwoods in the past—of course. He'd grown up in Northern California. He'd hiked amid sequoias. But never alone. Never so many gigantic trees in one area. Never such *silence.*

Like stepping into another world contiguous with the human world yet totally different from it. For nothing in the great forest except the (spare) trail markers, and the minimal trail itself, suggested a human presence, still less a human designation—"state park."

The first redwoods predated *Homo sapiens* by millions of years. No doubt, redwoods will outlive *Homo sapiens* by millions of years. In disgust and dismay with humankind Vanbrugh took solace in this thought.

He'd brought a camera with him in his backpack. Not that he was a serious photographer. He hadn't the patience to compose photographs, he acted reflexively, impulsively. Standing staring through the viewfinder for long minutes in a trance . . . In this way swaths of time passed in the redwood forest without his noticing.

A deeper self emerged here, by degrees. He was not so certain he welcomed this for there is comfort in surfaces, in his life he skimmed the surface of all things like a kid on a skateboard. (Indeed, he'd often been a kid on a skateboard.)

Astonishing that, from the ground, you could not see the tops of most of the redwoods, that were shrouded in mist. *Tree-canopy* it was called. Opaque, mysterious. Hundreds of animal species were said to dwell in the tree tops, never descending to the ground through their lifetimes. Many more plants, microorganisms. In some instances, the tops of the redwoods inhabited a microclimate different than the microclimate on the ground.

If you stood at the immense wedge of broken roots that was the base of a fallen redwood, you could not see the top of the tree, on the ground. You could not even see over the trunk, it was so thick. Some of the redwoods were three hundred feet high. Some, as old as two thousand years.

The hiker stood transfixed. The hiker felt awe, yet dread. Privileged to be in this (sacred) place even as he knew himself finite, expendable. It was exposed as laughable, his (petty) (white) (bourgeois) life. Yet, was Vanbrugh's life not noble, too—at least potentially?

I will be a good, brave person. I will be the person I was meant to be.

Without his friends who mirrored him, and whom he mirrored, as in a monkey house of jabbering hilarity, Vanbrugh really was another sort of person. In the redwoods the deeper self emerged, almost shy, guarded.

His soul, that had felt battered and soiled, was being cleansed, scoured. All that he'd required was *aloneness.* An expenditure of energy, effort. A sense that he was putting himself to a test. Not allowing himself to take an easy route: sixteen miles, not six. His heart beat with a strange wild yearning beneath his ribs.

On the trail he encountered few other hikers. The illusion of being alone in the forest was intoxicating. He began to feel invincible, even as he was beginning to tire. Through sheer exertion he'd driven the voices out of his head—even the "good" voices. (Voices claiming to love him were the most insidious.) But as the trail looped back to the trailhead, inevitably he began to hear the voices of actual persons, just audible. He couldn't avoid seeing figures ahead. Hikers who resembled Vanbrugh, equipped as Vanbrugh was equipped, hiking boots, backpacks, nylon parkas. Guys in their twenties, grinning at him as if they should know him—*Hi! How's it going.*

Couples, young families. These he disliked, for they were likely to be talking to one another non-stop. There was even a couple in matching hiking clothes, with hiking sticks, chattering to each other in German.

His *aloneness* was being lacerated, shredded. Mocked by the casual conviviality of others. So rudely, *aloneness* was ending.

Yet it was good, Vanbrugh supposed. To return to the trailhead: restrooms, water fountain, picnic tables. Asphalt parking lot.

His vehicle was where he'd left it, he saw. Amid SUVs and campers, one of the smaller cars.

Hard to return from the redwoods to the ordinary world. Like waking from a dream of such intensity at first you aren't certain where you are, or who.

At the water fountain Vanbrugh waited his turn. He was silent, a penitent. Not unfriendly but not wanting to make eye contact with others. The gravity of the redwoods continued to haunt him. He did not want it dispelled so quickly. Stooping, he splashed water onto his heated face. He felt his whiskers, beaded with water droplets, with an air of surprise. That he had a *face*—how strange this seemed. He stood with his feet apart, slightly dizzy, intent upon regaining his balance.

It was then he found himself observing a hiking couple a short distance away. Something about them, the male hiker's behavior, his curt voice, drew Vanbrugh's attention.

The man, who appeared to be in his early thirties, was addressing the young woman in the assertive tone of one accustomed to giving instructions; the young woman stood silent, contrite and abashed, like one accustomed to being instructed. She was having trouble adjusting her backpack, which weighed heavily on her shoulders. Her companion insisted that she carry her own water bottle—he didn't intend (he said) to share his water with her. Roughly, with a punitive air, he stuffed the bottle into a pocket of her backpack as she winced, in silence. He was the experienced hiker: the woman, the less experienced. He had spiky dark hair, a jutting nose, a spade-shaped beard. She had beautiful dark-blond tight-braided hair arranged about her head like a cap. Wisps of hair on her forehead. Vanbrugh overheard the man address her—*Lise.*

Not *Lisa,* or *Liza.* He was sure he'd heard *Lise.*

Vanbrugh had taken a dislike to the man, immediately. Something arrogant in him. His posture, manner. The neatly trimmed spade-shaped beard, very different from Vanbrugh's soft, wayward whiskers. The way in which he nudged the young woman, as if she required nudging, not merely speech, like a slow-witted child or an animal.

Vanbrugh was standing so that, as the hiking couple moved to the trail, they had to pass by him. Somehow he'd positioned himself here, without knowing what he did. In this way he had a quick, intimate glimpse of the young woman, who seemed to be aware of him, perhaps had been aware of him for several minutes, Vanbrugh observing her and the bearded man, in silence. And it seemed to Vanbrugh that the young woman was smiling at him, or smiling in his direction; a faint, hurt smile that suggested—*Yes. I know. But I deserve to be treated this way and the proof is, I am treated this way.*

Vanbrugh gave no sign that he was noticing the young woman, or at any rate no obvious sign. Though fascinated by the tight-braided hair that looked as if it must be painful, pulling at the young woman's scalp, stretching the skin of her (furrowed) forehead. She was shorter than Vanbrugh, as she was shorter than her companion, by two or three inches. Her face wasn't a beautiful face (Vanbrugh thought) but it was a striking face, with fair, luminous skin, a look of stoic resignation, melancholy. A young face, without makeup. Undefined eyebrows, somber eyes. A thin silver chain around her neck, a small jade cross.

They'd had time only to glance at each other in passing. At once the young woman's gaze slid away from Vanbrugh's face as if she were affrighted by her own boldness.

Clearly the admonition came to Vanbrugh—*Her. You are meant to protect her.*

Meant to love her. Marry her.

A sudden stirring in Vanbrugh, a manic certainty.

Blood beat hard in his face. He was very hungry suddenly, light-headed.

Staring after the young woman and her companion as they disappeared into the forest. A despairing sense of loss gripped him—was he really going to let them go? Let her go?

He was not going to follow the couple—of course.

Ridiculous! He was shaken, disoriented. Slung off his backpack onto a table. God damn!—he was unhappy. So swiftly the spell of the redwoods was diffused, this clamor in his blood at the sight of the girl—woman—a stranger to him yet (somehow: how?) linked to him.

He used a pungent-smelling restroom, nostrils pinched in revulsion. The physical life, *his* life, must continue. After a vision, the eyes readjust. You plod on. Filled his water bottle with (lukewarm) water from the fountain. His muscles ached yet still he was aroused, restless. He ate ravenously—mandarin oranges, date-nut bars. Thinking of the girl with the tight-braided hair, that look of hurt in her face, a stunned sort of hurt, terrible to see.

Calmly he thought: He had no interest in intruding in the private lives of others. He wasn't a hero in an adventure film. He wasn't a figure in a video game. If the girl had been threatened, if the man had been seriously upsetting her, then he'd have intervened. If the man had touched the woman in anger—definitely, Vanbrugh would have intervened.

Hey! I can protect you.

Lise, her name. He would remember—*Lise.*

It had all happened so quickly. He hadn't heard most of what the man had said, he'd seen only the look in the girl's face.

No doubt, he'd had a glimpse of an abusive relationship of some sort. Most likely, an emotionally abusive relationship. No physical violence he'd observed, no measurable cruelty . . .

Still, he'd disliked the male hiker, instinctively. *Him,* in any other setting, Vanbrugh would've liked to pummel.

The girl had glanced at him, blinking and smiling. A hopeful sort of smile. Very young. Yearning.

(What did the jade cross mean? Should he assume that it meant—anything?)

Not too late (Vanbrugh was thinking) to follow the hikers on the trail. He could move swiftly, overtake them within minutes.

His legs were hard with muscle. He was as fit as the bearded man, or more fit. He was six or seven years younger than the man with the spade-shaped beard.

Devouring his third mandarin orange. Sticky juice on his fingers. Eating rapidly, scarcely tasting. Agitated, angry. What was happening to him?

Falling in love—ridiculous. Falling in love with a single glance.

Considering what he knew of *love* close up. His parents' marriage, for instance. If founded upon *love,* not love like a plunge into the unknown but love like a slow steady march on flat terrain in full daylight.

And so, Vanbrugh didn't follow the hikers. Certainly not. Time to leave the redwood park.

Of his hiking that day he would tell his friends very little. No anecdotes to relate, no tales calculated to entertain.

And when he examined the dozens of photographs he'd taken that day he was baffled, disappointed. He'd failed to capture the mysterious soul of the redwoods that had so enthralled him for hours. Tincture of red in the massive tree trunks, a rich, dark, moist maroon-red—nothing like that was visible in the photographs. The achingly beautiful *precision* of the forest—little of that. Vanbrugh knew something of the astonishing fecundity and diversity of life that was sustained by the redwood forest, much of it at the very tops of the trees, where little-known species of creatures—not only insects and birds but small mammals—lived their entire lives without descending to the ground, but nothing in his photographs suggested anything like this. No life was evident in these scenes at all. At their best, Vanbrugh's pictures resembled scenic postcards, and at their worst mere snapshots, banal in composition, not even clearly focused.

But here was a surprise: he'd almost forgotten that he had taken several pictures of the young woman with the tight-braided hair, at a distance of about thirty feet. He'd been cautious taking her picture—risking her companion seeing, and risking her seeing . . .

But these photographs too were disappointing. Barely you could distinguish the young woman through a barrier of sapling trees, splendid tall ferns. The tight-braided hair was not even visible.

Just a blurred figure, sexless and anonymous. Could've been anyone.

But what was the name?—*Lise.*

Nothing magical remained. Nothing out of the ordinary, memorable.

Still, Vanbrugh didn't delete the pictures taken in the redwoods. He would keep them as a record of—what, he didn't know.

A profound experience, somehow. Though he could not have said what this experience was.

After the solo redwood hike in Northern California he'd returned home with resolve, ambition. He'd decided definitely to enter law school. He joined the ACLU as one of his professors had been urging him. As a first-year law student he joined the Innocence Project, which was dedicated to helping wrongly convicted men and women appeal for new trials—but gradually, during his three years in law school, and after passing his bar exam, his resolve faded. He'd never known why.

There! Her.

It was a torment, a curse. Seeing the young woman with the tight-braided hair, always unexpectedly, at an inopportune time.

Hurrying to an airport gate, and the young woman is hurrying in the opposite direction. On an escalator descending as, on an adjacent escalator, the young woman is ascending. In a train station, on a crowded sidewalk, at a crowded mall. Once, in the very hospital in which his father was dying, distracted with anxiety as Vanbrugh stepped into an elevator from which the young woman was exiting . . .

Each time Vanbrugh sees the young woman he is stunned by the sight of her—stops dead in his tracks, staring. She has never changed much—her dark-blond hair is tightly braided and coiled about her head, her skin is still pale, luminous. As Vanbrugh ages, she remains young: in her early twenties perhaps. Or, a youthful thirty.

Sometimes their eyes meet, fleetingly. More often, the

young woman is aloof, oblivious of Vanbrugh. (Is she contemptuous of him? Does she recall his cowardice in the redwood forest?)

He has never seen her with another person. No adult companion, no child or children. *She has never married*—Vanbrugh thinks.

If Vanbrugh makes an effort to pursue her in one of these public places he soon discovers his mistake.

Excuse me! You look like someone I know.

Or—*I'm sorry: is your name Lise? You look exactly like . . .*

Embarrassed, abashed. Stammering an apology.

He has never told anyone about the young woman in the redwoods. Never told anyone about the incident—indeed there was no incident, there is nothing to tell. A young man's shame? Cowardice? Regret? Remorse? And no one to tell. For there would be no one so intimate in Vanbrugh's life as the young woman with the tight-braided hair encountered in the twenty-fourth year of his life.

2.

If a snake could speak it would speak exactly like this female.

"D'you ever think of it? Seriously, I mean."

"Death? No."

Quickly he'd answered. The exchange wasn't conversation but merely dialogue, repartee.

A woman on the periphery of Vanbrugh's social life. A friend, never an intimate. One of those women (there have been many) whom Vanbrugh considered *paths not taken.*

But, well—he had to admit he'd had no premonition. In the matter of death. *His* death. For this random rude remark had come out of nowhere at a cocktail gathering of no significance in his life and went nowhere—breezy, instantly forgotten. Not a glimmer.

Yet, one unexpected day soon afterward: at the age of fifty-two, Vanbrugh died.

At first when it was happening, when the process of *dying* began, Vanbrugh hadn't paid attention. Exactly like Vanbrugh: not paying attention.

On the phone. Concentration elsewhere. (In fact, ignominy of ignominies, he'd been *on hold.*) Couldn't be bothered to take heed of a physical symptom. Or two, or three.

First twinge of headache, nausea, gut-cramps, fever—Vanbrugh's strategy had always been to ignore. Onset of flu, diarrhea—ignore for as long as you can.

Not a hypochondriac. Indeed, the antithesis of a hypochondriac.

Priding himself on being *fit.* For a man of his age, unusually *fit.*

And so, Vanbrugh had no idea it was *dying* that swept through him like a child running through a house switching off lights. Close enough to heartburn, vertigo, malaise he'd experienced in the past with no consequences. And a twinge of pain like a white-hot wire behind the eyes.

Well, the pain was unusual. In an area of his brain that seemed new and of an intensity that was surely new.

Scarcely time to think—*My God what is happening to me?* But already there was no *me.*

Slumped forward limply on his desk, the side of his face on the computer keyboard that exuded an infinitesimal warmth. Must've been an aneurysm, such swiftness. Not what you'd call *dying* for it had not been a volitional act of Vanbrugh's but rather (only just) something that happened to him, like rain.

Sudden pelting rain. Sleet, hail. His eyes lifted, the redwood canopy was being pierced by snow-pellets. His brain was pierced.

Happens so fast by the time you comprehend what is happening, it's over.

At the time not thinking—*Is this a premonition? Of—what?*

Might've made an appointment to see a doctor. Neurologist. If he'd suspected anything. CAT scan, fMRI. Might've saved his life? No?

If his wife had known, she'd have insisted. His mother, if she'd been alive.

Misses her. His mother. Come to think of it, she'd died of a stroke—also. At a much older age.

Cliché: An aneurysm is like a frayed rubber band. When it is going to snap, it snaps.

No omens. No presentiments. Never gave those odd, edgy, mildly disorienting feelings of unease much thought. In the course of a day's consciousness so much rushes at us, debris borne by a river in floodtide, it isn't possible to measure what any of it means or even if it *means* anything.

But this is a fact: a few days before his death Vanbrugh found himself thinking about an episode out of his past.

Something that had happened to him more than thirty years before. An old scar that exerts a tingling sensation, you find yourself stroking unconsciously.

A kind of onanism, of fascinated misery. Totally unlike practical-minded Vanbrugh.

Remembering—he'd been twenty-three, backpacking alone in Northern California. The only time in his life he'd spent so much time alone—almost four weeks.

Something had been decided then. A split in his life: before the redwoods, and after.

He'd married of course. Coming into his maturity, in the world sprawling slovenly and uncharted beyond the redwoods.

The time had come. A kind of peristalsis moved him to the next step: wife, family. Now, his wife is a widow.

His widow. He feels responsible for the woman. An irritable sort of guilt, like a pebble inside a shoe.

There Elise is, alone in the dusk. A shadowy figure, wine glass in hand. As dusk deepens she makes no move to switch on lights. Her life as a new widow has been a nightmare blizzard of tasks, errands, *death duties.* She is angry with Vanbrugh, and will not forgive him for dying so abruptly, with no warning. She is exhausted and yet agitated. Can't sleep. *Excited catatonia,* Vanbrugh thinks. For which he acknowledges he is to blame.

Elise's eyes lift, startled. Is she aware of him? Her bloodshot eyes dart about, unseeing.

Vanbrugh is sick with guilt that his wife has been drinking since the very evening of his death—avoiding family, failing to respond to friends' calls, preferring to drink alone in the empty house. *But this is not like you, Elise! You must let people help you . . .*

Vanbrugh understands, it is his obligation to help his widow. It is his obligation to comfort her, as he'd so rarely had an occasion to comfort her in life. So long as his widow mourns him, he cannot abandon her.

Elise has been talking to herself. Bemused, disgusted. Shaking her head like one gazing into a mirror and not liking what she sees.

". . . hadn't realized I loved you so much. If this is 'love'—feels like an arm ripped off. My God! I hate you."

What can Vanbrugh say to these damning words? In his weakened state they wash over him like warm, dirty water.

Keep your mouth closed, you don't want to swallow befouled water.

Since dying, Vanbrugh has discovered that he is no longer very articulate. Where once he spoke glibly, cleverly, never failed to supply a witty riposte, never backed down from a verbal confrontation, now the eager neurons in his brain are misfiring. Now he finds that he must *think*—but *thinking* is the bane of speech.

". . . if you'd only told me. Been truthful to me. You didn't love *me* . . . or, whatever it was, it wasn't *love*. But—you never did, and I never confronted you. Wouldn't have dared . . ."

Elise laughs plaintively, spilling wine onto her shirt of which, alarmingly, she doesn't seem to be aware.

It is appalling to Vanbrugh, hearing his wife speak like this. The woman's pride shattered at her feet. Deeply unhappy, bitter. Emerging out of the shadows of the large empty house.

"Well! I'd always thought you might be unfaithful to me, or had already been unfaithful, and my heart would be broken—stupidly. Tried to ignore it. But tried to be a wife you would love—if you'd noticed."

Vanbrugh protests, she'd done more than just *try*. She'd been a loving wife, mother. Everyone who knew her loved her, and *he* loved her—he'd always loved her . . . Vanbrugh's voice flattens, fades. He isn't sure that Elise can hear him though she is staring into a corner of the room as if she hears—something . . .

". . . I was a little obsessed, thinking such thoughts. I wondered if all wives were fearful of their husbands being unfaithful to them. I knew—I seemed to know—you were distracted by something, someone else . . ."

The redwoods! Of course, Elise knew.

Vanbrugh wants to protest. Deny.

In life Vanbrugh had managed to avoid such maudlin

scenes. There'd been other women, over a course of so many years, unavoidably. Some were mere flirtations, though enormously exciting, illicit. Some were romantic friendships, several were serious affairs. With all of them, as with Elise, he'd become skilled at avoiding the *female-male scene.* For essentially it is the *female* perceiving the *male* as he is, and the *male* hoping to convince her that she is mistaken.

Though the wish of the female to be (convincingly) deceived is flattering, Vanbrugh concedes. So long as Elise is angry with him, and in despair of her life without him, she is mourning him. *He* is the cause of her misery, the betraying husband.

"Well—then I think, I've been thinking, alone here in the house, what difference does any of this make? To anyone except me? Whether we even existed, let alone whether our marriage was a 'good' one."

The very voice of sorrow, Vanbrugh thinks. Mourning her own life, with his.

"So, what difference does it make if you were faithful to me, or unfaithful? No one cares, no one should care. All so *pointless.*"

Vanbrugh squirms in misery. *Pointless* should not be uttered. Not by a widow. He tries to protest that he'd never deceived her, he'd never ceased loving her and he'd certainly loved Kevin . . . Even in Vanbrugh's ears this protest is weak, unconvincing.

True, Vanbrugh's love for his family had been a certain sort of thing. You could call it *dutiful, prescribed.* His love for Elise had peaked in their early thirties, then mellowed, subsided. This was a *tamed, companionable* sort of love. It was not a love that tore at the heart. Fact is, Vanbrugh had never felt for anyone what he'd felt for the young woman with the tight-braided hair who'd exchanged a single glance with him in the redwoods—so long ago, Vanbrugh scarcely remembers who he'd been at the time.

Those nights, too many to be counted, when, lying beside the sleeping wife, he'd allowed his thoughts to drift, glide, careen, plunge—to enter the redwood forest.

A kind of hush overcame him. A great silence. A chill would come over Vanbrugh, about to enter a sacred space.

Ridiculous! His entire adult life has been in thrall to a phantom. He is damned grateful that no one ever knew—that he didn't weaken and confide in anyone, certainly not his wife.

"Here! Damn you, look."

Elise lifts a scarlet silk pillow from the sofa. Vanbrugh doesn't think he has ever seen this pillow before, though (if pressed to admit it) he'd never paid all that much attention to home furnishings.

A woman friend gave her the pillow, Elise says. The white stitching on it says—*Widowhood is the price you pay for having been a wife.*

Even when Elise laughs, Vanbrugh hears reproach.

Somehow, there is blame between them. Always a sense that one must be to *blame,* if the other is unhappy.

Vanbrugh is anxious to explain to his widow that he hadn't *died.* It wasn't like lifting your arm, it was more like breathing and exhaling—something you didn't actually *do,* not a volitional act of your own. *Dying, death* is a sort of condition that comes over us like a wave of frigid water but we don't initiate it ourselves. We do not perform it ourselves.

Meaning *Please stop blaming me!*

Elise pours the last of the wine into her glass, which trembles in her fingers.

(Can Vanbrugh steady his wife's hand? Very gently, imperceptibly?)

Though she has given up searching for him in the shadowy

living room Elise seems aware of Vanbrugh's presence. Stiffly she sits, refusing to look for him but rather staring at what appears to be her own reflection in a window, as darkness deepens outside. Her face exudes a melancholy irony. *Look what you have done to me! Oh God.* Vanbrugh wonders if he should dare to embrace her; if they might, in their separate alonenesses, commiserate with each other.

Elise begins speaking again, in a low bemused voice, like one deciding to tell an anecdote, out of a loss for words that matter.

Relating how, a few days after his funeral, she'd been lifting a bag of groceries out of a shopping cart, to place in the trunk of the car, in the rain, and the paper bag became soaked through, groceries fell onto the wet pavement. Oranges rolled at her feet . . . She'd stood there in the rain laughing, or maybe crying. All so absurd, futile. Her husband was dead, groceries had fallen at her feet in the rain. How long she'd stood there laughing, or maybe crying, she did not know before someone approached to help her. A man, a kindly man, a man with a familiar face, a neighbor perhaps, though no one she knew by name, carrying an umbrella. *Excuse me, ma'am? Can I help?*

Standing there, she says. Laughing, rain running down her face and groceries at her feet. And somebody calling her *ma'am.*

Elise laughs. Vanbrugh feels hairs stir at the nape of his neck. Why is his wife telling him this story?—is it some sort of riddle? Will this random stranger be her next husband?

Vanbrugh shudders. Not if he can help it.

Dilemma of his life. When he was with others, he'd yearned to be alone as he'd been in the redwood forest on that happiest day of his life; but when he's alone, as he is now, he yearns for companionship.

In fact, he'd lingered at the redwood table. Pushing orange peels into a pile, disposing of them in the trash. Rinsing his sticky fingers in the drinking fountain.

In fact, he'd intervened.

He'd been a brash guy at the age of twenty-three. Sheer rush of adrenaline like a shot to the heart.

The girl with the tight-braided hair stared at him in astonishment. Then, quickly—*Thank you but.*

I am all right—really! Thank you.

Thank you but—no . . .

Breathless, frightened. Glancing over her shoulder to see if the bearded hiker was in sight.

The smell of her—distinct. Sweaty, from the trail. He felt a kick of desire.

Glimpsing on her left hand a ring, possibly a wedding band. Was she a married woman?

You're very kind. But I—I can't . . .

I'm sorry, I—just can't . . .

The bearded hiker was approaching. Quickly the young woman with the tight-braided hair turned from Vanbrugh without a backward glance, hurried to her companion. In her posture something eager to placate, obsequious, piteous.

An abused woman, he was sure. Unmistakable.

Yet Vanbrugh held back. The wedding ring, if that was what it was, had deflected him.

Except: if she was in need of help, how could you be such a coward?

How can you live your life knowing it's your safety you'd fear for, and not hers . . .

Days, weeks pass. Vanbrugh yearns to be free—freed.

If and when, he has reason to believe that his spirit will return to the redwoods.

If indeed, his spirit had ever left the redwoods.

Yet: Vanbrugh seems to be pleased, his wife is still angry with him, and so she is still mourning him. She hasn't (yet) given away his clothes. Not a single item of clothing. Even his tangled socks, underwear in the bureau drawer—untouched by the widow.

Weird to feel a pang of tenderness for his old much-laundered shorts, those dark woolen socks with frayed heels, things pushed to the back of the drawer he hadn't worn in years and would not ever have worn again, surely.

Burberry coat, J. Press camel's hair coat, the pale gray linen sport coat, tailor-made suits—shirts, trousers, sweaters, shoes (including several ragged pairs of jogging shoes)—dozens of shiny silk neckties. So long as Vanbrugh's possessions remain in the house, Vanbrugh's home is here.

Darkness in the house is deepening. In her petulant despair the widow doesn't switch on a light.

Sitting at the rear of the house has become a custom for her. Drinking alone. At such an hour. Nothing Elise had ever done before in her lifetime. In *his* lifetime.

Vanbrugh sees that Elise is deteriorating. She is thinner, her wristwatch slides about her wrist. Her hair is streaked with gray, ashy-gray, and is snarled, disheveled. Her skin is pasty-pale and her eyes are ringed with fatigue. No doubt, she hasn't troubled to shower in days. About her is a smell of resentment, spite. Vanbrugh's wife, always so well-groomed, so *dignified.* The unhappy woman is sabotaging herself, as a way of punishing him.

As soon as she senses his presence Elise says sharply: "You! You have a nerve showing up here! God damn you."

Vanbrugh stammers that he's sorry, he can go away again . . .

"No! For Christ's sake. If you're here you might as well stay here."

Glaring in Vanbrugh's direction with fierce myopic eyes.

Vanbrugh is taken by surprise. He insists that he is truly sorry, he doesn't know what else to say . . .

"Don't know what else to say!"—cruelly Elise mimics Vanbrugh's inane protest. "You must have had some premonition, for Christ's sake. A healthy man just doesn't suddenly *die.*"

Except sometimes, Vanbrugh protests, evidently they do.

"Bullshit. You ignored symptoms—signs. You must have."

Vanbrugh insists, *no.*

"You must have! When was the last time you'd had your blood pressure checked? Your heart? You promised to schedule an appointment with what's-his-name—"

Sobbing in exasperation Elise berates Vanbrugh. Since his death she has become impatient with him, vexed by him, as she'd rarely been, or acknowledged she was, in life. The degree of her hostility is astonishing.

Even her breathing is different. Heavy, husky. Panting. *Her life is effort now. Exhausting.*

Had Elise really loved him so much? Is this what this is—*love*? Raw need like the need of a baby to nurse at its mother's breast? The woman needing sustenance from him, an almost physical sustenance, which Vanbrugh in his disembodied state can't provide.

He is reminded of his father's breathing in the final months of his father's life, which no one had realized were his final months. Out of breath after climbing stairs. Out of breath walking a short distance. No one in the family had wished to acknowledge that there was something wrong with Vanbrugh's father as no one wished to acknowledge that the elderly man should probably—surely—not have been driving his car as long as he had . . .

You don't want to see. Don't want to know. The pride of the afflicted one is such, you can't risk offending him, he will withdraw his love from you.

In his faltering way, in this way that is new to Vanbrugh, he tries to explain to the incensed widow that in fact he'd marked his calendar to remind himself to make an appointment with his doctor. If there'd been any problem, he'd have seen his cardiologist. As if Elise couldn't easily check his calendar (left behind on Vanbrugh's cluttered desk to be discovered after his death annotated with appointments, initials, abbreviations extending into the airy future beyond his death) to determine if he was telling the truth.

In a relationship of longstanding intimacy, *truth* is often a matter of tone. *Truth* is what convinces the loved one that she is loved.

Elise is saying that while she'd had a (living) husband she hadn't known what true *aloneness* is. She'd existed in a sort of dream. A delusion. When she'd been alone in the house she'd assumed it was *aloneness* in which she'd dwelt without realizing that (of course) it was a faint simulacrum of the real thing. For her husband had not then ceased to exist but was simply somewhere else—"Even if you weren't with me you were in the same world with me. And we were at the same time. But now, you are 'out of time.' You are 'gone.' I don't know where you are but I know that you are not here."

But he *is* here!—Vanbrugh tries to explain. He can see her and hear her and—he is haunted by her . . .

(For this is true, perversely. Vanbrugh has become a ghost tethered to the grieving wife and to the darkened house in which she dwells like a spider at the center of a tremulous web.)

Trying to touch her. Caress, comfort her. As he'd done in life. Elise steels herself against him, shuddering.

"Don't be ridiculous! I know you're not here—*no one is here.* You couldn't wait to escape your responsibilities—you never really wanted to be married. I knew, but I pretended otherwise. I thought—*I can love enough for the two of us.*"

Elise laughs. Elise pours another half-glass of dark red wine, drinks, wipes at her mouth with the back of her hand. This very gesture, careless, crude, is so unlike her, Vanbrugh is further dismayed.

"You know, I could never trust you. I think you lied to me continuously. I think there was someone else in your life, who meant more to you than I did. From the start. Before we'd met. I'd always thought it would fade, whatever it was—whoever *she* was. But it never did."

Elise waits for Vanbrugh to protest. But Vanbrugh is stricken with guilt and cannot speak.

"*Was* there? You can tell me now."

But Vanbrugh cannot speak. His (phantom) heart beats with eerie calmness as a mechanical heart might beat unperturbed by the emotions of a mere human.

"Oh fuck. Fuck *love.*"

In exasperation Elise pushes at Vanbrugh. Her flailing hands pass through him as if brushing away flies.

Vanbrugh retreats, alarmed. Frankly astonished to hear his reserved and soft-spoken wife utter such words. Elise who'd so rarely cursed, in fact had never once uttered a common obscenity in his hearing in decades of marriage.

"Go away, and don't come back. I despise you."

Later Vanbrugh would recall: Elise had been wearing an old flannel shirt of his, loose-fitting, cuffs unbuttoned—a shirt that could double as a nightgown. The widow's secret was, she'd been sleeping in her clothes most nights, too lethargic to undress, too tired to shower, shampoo her hair. Unwittingly replicating the postpartum depression she'd endured for months after Kevin's birth, though neither Elise nor Vanbrugh had given a name to her protracted melancholy at the time.

But how Vanbrugh is touched, seeing his widow in one of his old shirts! Which she'd never have worn when Vanbrugh was alive. Hardly.

———

Kevin. Vanbrugh realizes guiltily that he has yet to visit his son.

His excuse is, Kevin (probably) doesn't want to see him.

Not that father and son hadn't loved each other. But they'd parted on strained terms. Vanbrugh can't recall the details. His grievances with his son varied from month to month as (he supposed) Kevin's grievances with him varied from month to month. He'd never felt comfortable with the role—father of a son. A touchy matter, Vanbrugh recalls. The slightest insolence in Kevin's manner, a telltale stiffness about the boy's mouth, a (suppressed) impulse to roll his eyes at a remark of Vanbrugh's—these signs Vanbrugh could detect with the sensitivity of a predator scanning the landscape for prey.

Yeah. My dad. He, like, died . . .

Yeah—it happened fast. Like, I can't talk now. My mom is all broke up. I'll text you.

If the baby had been a girl Vanbrugh would have wanted to call her Lise. He'd have found some reason to convince Elise. (Though possibly Elise would have been flattered? "Lise" would seem to be an obvious echo of "Elise.")

Vanbrugh wonders: had he fallen in love with Elise because her name resembles "Lise"—was that the reason, at least the initial reason, he'd been attracted to her?

Absurd! The names were just a coincidence.

Not wanting to think that his life could be so simply decoded. As if he were a figure in a video game manipulated by an unknown Player. *He,* Vanbrugh, who prided himself on his independence.

For certainly Vanbrugh believes in "free will." At least, in his own capacity for "free will." Though he can easily believe that others less educated than he, less intelligent, from less affluent backgrounds, are likely to be determined by forces they can't comprehend.

Shortly after Vanbrugh's death he'd had a glimpse of Kevin at a distance. His vision was obscured as with mist. A paralyzing chill. Lifting a hand as in life he might have waved at his son, a casual gesture, nothing meant to signify authority, a claim. *Here! Over here for Christ's sake. See who I am.*

But no, not such a claim. Seeing that Kevin was standing apart from the adults, eyes averted from them, his expression more sullen than grieving, a put-upon look, typical of the kid. Though possibly Vanbrugh was judging him harshly, Kevin was just stunned by the loss of his father. In this interlude when everyone who knew Vanbrugh was stunned, at a loss for words. A deep embarrassment as in the aftermath of a misunderstanding. *What the hell? When did it happen? No warning? How is it possible? Where is*—glancing about the room to see who, in this gathering of individuals, was missing.

Vanbrugh wants to call out to them—*But I am here.*

Though actually it wasn't at all clear where Vanbrugh was.

3.

In the picnic area beside the parking lot. Humboldt Redwoods State Park. Waiting.

Excitement glitters in the air about Vanbrugh like silica.

Almost, he is afraid to breathe it in, his lungs will be perforated with minuscule cancerous wounds.

Telling himself—*Whatever happens. Toss the dice.*

Oranges, date-nut bars out of his backpack. Hunger like a flame. At a nearby redwood table a friendly older couple with a tail-thumping dog glances in the young hiker's direction hoping to make conversation but Vanbrugh isn't in the mood.

Yes, these are attractive people, white-haired, in their seventies, could be Vanbrugh's grandparents but no, Vanbrugh isn't in the mood.

Being young, you are naturally aloof, haughty. Not even needing to reason that being elderly is a sort of bog that, if you take care, you will never blunder into. Not *you.*

How long has Vanbrugh been waiting here, and for what is Vanbrugh "waiting"—he isn't sure.

Excited. Anxious. Staring at the trail that disappears into the redwood forest a short distance away.

Well, Vanbrugh relents—pets the older couple's dog, that trots up to him sniffing eagerly at his hands, legs. A friendly dog, thick-bodied, sand-colored, a golden retriever mix with moist brown eyes that lift to Vanbrugh's face as if in recognition.

"Good boy. Now—go away."

Waiting is consumed by studying a much-folded road map of Northern California, spread out on a redwood table. Waiting is a kind of exquisite anguish, a resistance to glancing at the trail more than once each sixty seconds.

Such waiting! No wonder the hikers don't appear.

They'd set out on the four-mile loop trail, Vanbrugh happened to notice. One of the easier trails which confirms his sense that the girl isn't an experienced hiker.

He considers whether he might begin hiking the trail at the end and meet them partway as they approach. (Will the bearded hiker recognize Vanbrugh? He guesses that yes, the girl will recognize him.) If he moves at a brisk pace he could encounter them—how soon? A half-hour? Stares at his digital watch but the numbers are obscured in a patch of bright sunshine.

Go on—go! What are you waiting for.

Through the afternoon other hikers arrive, parking their vehicles. More families with young children. High-school-aged kids. A succession of hikers return to the trailhead from the interior of the forest but the young woman with the tight-braided hair and her bearded companion do not appear.

Vanbrugh considers. What to do?

Just leave. This is stupid.

Don't know. Can't predict.

Whatever happens, that will be it.

He decides to wait. Just a few more minutes.

He uses the men's lavatory that smells fiercely of disinfectant. Wadded tissues on the (puddled) floor, at which Vanbrugh does not wish to glance.

Men, women. He wonders if the women's lavatory (adjoining the men's) can be as dirty as the men's.

Holding his breath against the stink. Peering through a window in the concrete-block wall opaque with grime. On the toes of his hiking boots straining to see—what?

—

In the (finite) universe it is theorized that time must be cyclical. In such a universe you can come to the "end" of time but you would have circled upon yourself, you'd be seeing the back of your own head.

A physicist-friend had told (skeptical) Vanbrugh this. Not sure if the friend was serious or not.

Not sure either how the hell you'd recognize the back of your own head.

Mom? I've been dreaming about him—Dad . . . Kind of a lot, lately.

At least, I think it's Dad.

Asked what does Dad look like, Kevin says, *I don't know, it's hard to see him. Like, he goes in and out of focus. It's his face, sort of, except it's thinner, and his hair is—his hair isn't the way it used to be . . . It's like it has been cut close to his skull.*

His eyes are shadowed. Maybe just eye sockets. He seems to hold himself carefully as if his bones aren't set. His head is wobbly, as if his vertebrae have been broken. He's, like, different than he was in life. He's more human, somehow.

Asked what Dad has been telling him, Kevin says, *It's more of a mood. It's like there's a voice but it's on "mute." I can see his mouth moving, I can almost hear him, but—I guess I can't.*

Kevin begins laughing. No, Kevin is crying.

Kevin's mouth is twisted like a pretzel. Tears shining on his cheeks like radiant light.

Christ! It's so—weird—awful—isn't it?

Assured yes, it is. But no. Only some of it.

Do you think he's trying to—come back?

Vanbrugh is trying to come back. Definitely, Vanbrugh is trying to come back.

Except: he'd had his chance. He knows: that single chance in a lifetime, in the redwoods.

Seeing the young woman's face. The hurt in that face. Widened eyes moving onto Vanbrugh startled and staring as if in recognition.

She'd smiled. Or nearly. A nervous reflex, a surge of hope. Watery light filtered through the high dense branches of the redwood forest illuminating her face.

But it was panic Vanbrugh felt. A rush of alarm. Something he might do, that could not readily be undone.

Turning away, averting his eyes. Adrenaline pumping through his veins left him both highly charged and shaky, weak-kneed.

And so, decades later, Vanbrugh finds himself brooding over the incident. The redwoods.

Can our lives be defined by what has been lost to us, what has never been allowed into our lives? Not the thing itself but the white space that surrounds it.

If he listens closely, overhearing her speaking to her bearded companion, he can detect an accent—nothing he recognizes.

Not Hispanic, not German—these he might recognize. Not Irish. Possibly Eastern European . . .

A young woman in (desperate?) need of Vanbrugh's help whom he'd failed.

With whom he hadn't exchanged a single word. Hadn't so much as shaken hands. Not a single touch, let alone embraced, kissed, made love with . . .

Vanbrugh and the woman's companion/husband had been aware of each other—certainly. But they hadn't exchanged words, let alone blows. Hadn't come close to blows. Vanbrugh had glared at the man, seeing the set of his wiry-whiskered jaws, a ridge of bone above the thick-tufted eyebrows, that look of defiance, arrogance.

Yes? You? Try.

Vanbrugh hadn't wished to *try.* Not out of physical cowardice, he believed. Not out of a wish to protect himself from harm. More, a spiritual timidity. A fatal modesty. That nothing Vanbrugh could do would really make a difference, he'd be deceiving himself if he thought so.

Whatever happens. Doesn't happen. Toss of the dice.

But now he sees, it had been cowardice. The very definition of cowardice.

(In fact) Vanbrugh had been born to confront the bearded hiker. He'd been born to protect that specific woman whose name he would recall as "Lise."

Yet, Vanbrugh had failed. At the crucial moment, Vanbrugh had failed the test of the redwoods.

Casting a tall shadow forward onto his life, of the astonishing height of a redwood. Casting a tall shadow backward over even his earlier life, that became derailed at this juncture.

Vanbrugh feels a sensation of wildness washing over him, such defeat. The encounter had been a rope, a lifeline, tossed to him, specifically to *him.* He had been meant to seize it, to hold on to it for dear life, with both hands. His life, and the life of the woman. This lifeline tossed at him at his young age, as he was about to drift out to sea alone.

Kevin? Hey—it's Dad . . .

Embarrassing, being dead. You have to surrender your authority. Your power over others. The confidence with which you intrude upon the privacy of others. The assumption that attention must be paid unstintingly and ardently to *you.*

But this isn't a good time, it seems. Kevin isn't eager to confront his (deceased) father, in fact Kevin is squirming in alarm, misery.

I—I am sorry that I left without . . .

You know, I loved you—Vanbrugh hesitates, appalled. What has he said? *I l-love you.*

But where is Kevin? Vanbrugh squints and blinks but there appears to be no one there as in a forest endlessly receding.

In the widow's sleep. Gluey dreams, in which Vanbrugh is stuck like a fly on flypaper. Thrashing to be free but lacking sufficient strength.

Poor Elise!—Vanbrugh pleads with her.

Calls her *darling*. Begs her to remember: they'd laughed together in countless beds, in each other's arms, her fingers as nimble and intimate as his.

They'd been happy. As happy as anyone.

Please take care of yourself. Grief is—a dead end.

Painful to Vanbrugh to see that his wife, his widow, has lost so much weight. Shocking to see the prominent vertebrae of her back, the hollow space at the base of her neck above her collarbone; the deep-socketed eyes, ringed with fatigue, despair.

Gaunt is boring, Vanbrugh wants to tell her. Grief is boring.

Vanbrugh is dismayed, Kevin seems to have abandoned Elise. Must've returned to San Francisco, to his one-hundred-hour work-week, as he complains/brags to anyone who will listen . . . Their son has betrayed them both, Vanbrugh thinks. Shallow-souled, ungrieving. Is this his fault, too?—Vanbrugh wonders.

Possibly he hadn't loved Kevin, or Elise—fully. He'd been distracted. A phantom had captured his heart, or worse—his sexual self. That sensation deep in the pit of his being, a kind of pitiless gravity. Pulsing *I am, I want, what I want is what I am.*

Neither Elise nor Kevin had figured in that. No one in Vanbrugh's daylight life.

He'd loved Kevin as a young child but not so much the pubescent/adolescent kid Kevin became. By the age of twelve

Kevin hit a rough passage from which he'd never emerged—like spiky grass growing in some awkward part of the lawn, between a fence and the garage, too narrow a space to be properly mowed, yet too wide a space not to be unsightly.

Vanbrugh wanted Elise not to guess how muted his feelings for her were, how merely *husbandly.* For he'd cared for her and had not wanted to hurt her and took pride in the fact, if it was a fact, that, among people who knew them, they were considered a *happy couple.*

But all happiness has ceased now. All pretense. Vanbrugh runs his hands through his hair as he'd had a habit of doing in life only to discover that—(is it possible?)—his hair has thinned alarmingly after death, cold air wafts against his tender scalp like a taunt.

Let me go, darling! Save yourself.

4.

Vanbrugh recalls: he had accosted the bearded hiker after all.

Not at the trailhead but on the trail itself. For at last, impatient with waiting, he'd set out. The interior of the redwoods drew him like a magnet. Certain that he'd encounter the couple within minutes—and what he would say to them, how he would confront them, he would decide at the time.

And so he had encountered them, in the forest, a few yards off the trail in a copse of fallen redwoods. Here, shafts of steeply vertical sunshine penetrated the forest interior. High overhead small birds flittered among the tree tops—pine siskins, titmice.

Hearing a male voice, crude, jarring. With disgust Vanbrugh saw the bearded hiker straddling one of the redwood logs, carving initials into it with a pocket knife.

Close by, the young woman waited. Vanbrugh understood, she had no choice.

Vanbrugh approaches the bearded hiker. Vanbrugh demands of him what the fuck he is doing—*Cut that out. Jesus!*

Though the tree has fallen, it is still a redwood tree. Though it is a log it is not "dead"—thousands of plants and animals live in its rich fermenting decay.

The two men exchange words. Vanbrugh is incensed, reckless. The bearded hiker is taken by surprise, initially.

Vanbrugh knocks the knife from his hands. *That,* Vanbrugh knows he has to accomplish at once.

One of them shoves at the other, the other shoves back. They are cursing. Pummeling. Within seconds the disagreement escalates, Vanbrugh rushes at the bearded man through a haze of shimmering red. His vision has been narrowed into a tunnel. He is superbly focused, thrilled. The woman stares at them astonished. The men ignore her cries, her pleas. If the woman were to dare touch them, they would knock her aside.

Vanbrugh finds himself falling heavily to the ground. A glancing blow at the side of his head, he'd struck it on a log. Still the shimmering red haze seems to nourish him. He feels little pain, his senses are laser-sharp. He has never felt so—*precise.* Striking his nemesis, scarcely minding that every bone in his fists is aching. The bearded man kicks at him, almost expertly, some sort of judo-kick but he's off-balance, the blow doesn't hurt as it might have.

Sweet acid-hot adrenaline pumps through the (enjoined) arteries of both men. Blindly Vanbrugh gropes for a rock to smash his adversary's skull but seizes instead a tree limb—clubs the adversary with it so hard the rotted wood shatters.

Still, the struggle continues. Both men are bleeding from facial cuts.

Both men have become almost immediately winded, exhausted. Though young, they have little stamina for such a struggle. Vanbrugh hears the other panting like a beast, unless it is himself. His eyes are glaring in his head, with rage. He'd have liked to strangle the bastard with his bare hands, gouge his eyes. In middle school he'd tried out for the wrestling team, but wrestling wasn't his sport. Too sweaty-close, too intimate. Never sure where to direct your gaze. Never comfortable mashing your crotch against the other guy.

Never on rough ground like this, never without a referee. The desperate yearning to seize control of the other, use your weight, overcome. The realization that anything you can do, you will do, to survive. To defeat the other utterly, to ensure that he will never come after you to take revenge.

The woman pleaded with Vanbrugh to stop. Though the woman (surely) understood that Vanbrugh had come to save her yet she screamed for him to stop.

Ramming the other's head against the mutilated log in a frenzy until he heard the *crack!* of the skull and even then Vanbrugh did not—could not—stop.

In fact, he hadn't discovered the couple on the trail. He'd run, panting. Awkward to run in his hiking boots but he'd run, a mile at least. Must've missed them somehow. (Had they stepped off the trail? Had he passed them, without knowing? The redwood forest was dense as a dream in the darkest hour of the night.) On the four-mile trail he'd searched for the couple in vain, he'd turned to run back furious, defeated. Reasoning it would be the quickest route, to return rather than continue. He was frantic not to miss them. He'd worked himself up to thinking that the girl had signaled him with her eyes, had mouthed a plea—*Help me! God please.*

Almost, he could hear this. Silent plea of a girl in fear for her life—and Vanbrugh had failed her.

Cursing himself, he'd made a tactical error. Not wanting to think that the bearded man had led the girl off the trail with him. Where no one would see them. Where he could force her to have sex with him.

For what other possible reason could they have disappeared? Vanbrugh was disgusted, enraged . . . But the fault was his own, he'd let them get out of his sight.

Returning to the trailhead sweating, exhausted. Seeing that the couple's vehicle was still in the parking lot—of course. They were still in the redwoods, he'd failed to find them.

Badly Vanbrugh had to use the lavatory. A crude facility in a small building of concrete blocks. Holding his breath, feeling nauseated. Emptying acid-hot urine out of his body into a tunnel-like hole. His knees shook. Weakness made him stagger. Somehow, he was able to breathe in this place. Made a bargain: in order to live he would have to breathe, and it was this befouled air he must breathe, not the beautiful fresh air of the redwoods.

—

The light of a dull occluded (winter) morning struggles to penetrate the windows of the bedroom. The venetian blind that Vanbrugh accidentally broke months before is sagging badly, like a lewd wink.

Oh, what is Elise doing!

At last, Elise is going through his clothes, laying them on the (unmade) bed, sorting into piles. No, no!

Vanbrugh is appalled. Though he'd begged his wife/widow to let him go, to save herself, he hadn't meant it. He'd assumed that Elise would know, he hadn't meant it.

(And how unlike Elise this was, not to have made their bed. For usually, Elise made up their bed immediately upon getting up; she hated the look, she'd said, of an unmade bed, rumpled sheets. Now, she seems not to have noticed.)

Carrying the husband's clothing from his closet in her

arms, letting it fall onto the bed in a tangle. Already, Vanbrugh sees with a thrill of horror, she has dumped the contents of his bureau drawers onto the bed.

Elise is sobbing. Yet, Elise is angry.

Is it possible—an *angry grief*? Vanbrugh observes from a corner of the room, hesitant to claim Elise's attention.

Elise's cell phone rings. At first, it appears that she isn't going to answer it, out of consideration (Vanbrugh thinks) for him, or rather for the gravity of her task; then, Elise answers the phone, warily.

Staring at the ceiling, as she listens. Vanbrugh has no idea who is speaking to his wife but resents the interruption.

". . . thought it would be impossible, that I could never do it, but—like so much else—it's just another chore. 'Death duties.' I had to make twelve copies of the death certificate . . . D'you think it really happens often, that people try to cheat?—steal? A person dies, someone tries to steal his car? Claims to be an heir? 'Probate court.' " Elise utters the word as if it's an obscenity—*probate court.*

He should have accompanied her, Vanbrugh thinks. He'd had no idea . . . Is this *his fault,* the misery of his widow's life?

But Elise is laughing now, sharply. Her face is lined with fatigue, her eyes exude the yellow light of old ivory. Vanbrugh is frustrated at being unable to identify the voice on the cell phone but he's relatively certain that it isn't a man's voice at least . . . could be Elise's older sister Kate, could be Jenny K., Vanbrugh is jealous of the intimacy between the women, the vehemence with which Elise speaks.

It is touching to see that Elise is barefoot, only partly dressed. She is still wearing Vanbrugh's flannel shirt, which is badly rumpled as if she has been sleeping in it. He feels a stab of tenderness, inside the shirt Elise's breasts appear soft, vulnerable.

Vanbrugh wants to plead—*Are you sure you want to give*

away my clothes? My beautiful clothes. Things you bought for me . . .

Elise is complaining that moths have gotten into her husband's clothes, his camel's hair coat, trousers. He'd been careless storing them away, sprinkling a few moth balls into the garment bags, she should have done it herself, he'd insisted, now half his clothes are ruined, oh God!—the Shetland sweater she'd given him for his fiftieth birthday, everyone had admired—dumped onto the pile for Goodwill.

Wait—Vanbrugh begs.

In a rage Elise gathers up armfuls of Vanbrugh's clothing, stuffs them into several large bags. At least, these are not garbage bags but shopping bags from quality stores like Lord & Taylor.

In a paralysis of chagrin Vanbrugh watches. From somewhere overhead comes a rude thumping noise, a roll of thunder like beer kegs.

Gigantic barrels rolling across the sky. Elise doesn't seem to hear, she has returned to Vanbrugh's closet to fetch the rest of his clothes.

5.

Remarkable!—the intricately braided hair. Vanbrugh wonders what it would be like to undo the braids, to shake loose the tight-fastened hair, let it tumble over the girl's (bare) shoulders.

Running his fingers through it, to loosen the kinks. Burying his face in it. And between her breasts.

The bearded hiker has gone off to use the men's lavatory, the young woman with the tight-braided hair is seated at one of the picnic tables, hunched over, head in her hands. She is very tired. She is trembling, for her companion has spoken harshly to her. The straps of her heavy backpack cut into her shoulders, she has slipped one off. Smiling boldly, seeing his opportunity, Vanbrugh approaches.

He's twenty-three, a brash young guy. Can't imagine a day, an hour, when "his" erection might fail him. Can't imagine the black pit of *malaise* beneath the pettish mood he thinks is *depression.* Hasn't yet witnessed his own son born, is years away from feeling that sick, sinking conviction that, a child of his and his wife's living, vulnerable in the world, no matter how this child matures he will always be an infant with a soft-boned head, a fontanelle at the crown of his head through which life could stick its cruel thumb at any juncture. And so, young, brash, emboldened Vanbrugh dares to approach the young woman with a greeting that sounds almost flippant—*Hey. Hi . . .*

He's been observing the situation, Vanbrugh tells the startled young woman. He's offering her help, she can come with him.

Help?—the girl stares at him. Does he mean—help with her backpack? Or—?

Help. D'you need help. A way out of here—away from him. *That's what I'm saying.*

Vanbrugh is smiling. Baring his teeth. Liking it that the girl sees him close up now. No ambiguity in what he is offering. His ruddy skin, his soft wavy beard. Blood beating heavy in his face, and in the area of his heart, and his groin. Does she need a way out of here?—Vanbrugh repeats, and the girl stares at him blinking and dazed and nods almost imperceptibly—*Yes.*

She is shaking visibly. Her breath smells of something sharp—alcohol? Panic? Vanbrugh guesses, animal panic.

Vanbrugh checks to see that her companion isn't approaching. Isn't in sight. He instructs her to come with him. *Just—do it.*

Grips her upper arm, which is slender, yielding.

She is shorter than Vanbrugh by two or three inches. He can see her pale scalp between the rows of braids, disconcertingly close. In the hollow of her neck, the jade cross gleams. Made of some synthetic material, like plastic.

Passive in his grip, like a woman surprised in a dream.

Is she married? To—*him*? Maybe not. Vanbrugh isn't sure. Guesses he will find out.

Just come with me. My car's right there. We'll just drive away. It will be OK.

Walking swiftly together, to Vanbrugh's car. Somehow, the decision has been made. As, at a particular moment, neither before this moment nor after, a fatally injured redwood bough loosens and breaks free of the living tree, plummets to earth.

Taken by surprise yet the young woman with the tight-braided hair has enough presence of mind to snatch up a handbag, even a bottle of Evian water. Vanbrugh laughs. He is giddy with delight, he is absolutely fearless. He unlocks the car. He helps the breathless young woman into the passenger's seat, removes the heavy backpack from her shoulders, and tosses it into the rear of the car—as if he'd done this, this very gesture, with this backpack, many times before. At once the young woman ducks down instinctively in the passenger's seat, shielding her head. So that no one is likely to see her from outside the vehicle.

Vanbrugh wonders if she is accustomed to hiding like this, making an escape.

I can drive you home. Tell me where. You can get your things. He can't hurt you if he can't find you.

The girl stammers—*He will kill me if—if . . .*

I'll deal with it. I'm not afraid of him. I can protect you.

Backing his vehicle around, gunning the engine, headed up an incline to the highway.

Flooded with certitude, joy. Knowing that at last he is in the right place at precisely the right time.

But no, Vanbrugh is standing transfixed. Hasn't moved in minutes—decades.

The redwoods have captured his soul. Redwood silence has seeped into the very marrow of his bones and a sensation of faintness has swept over him, awe indistinguishable from terror.

Stunned to realize that, standing at the base of the gigantic fallen redwood, on the toes of his hiking boots trying to see past the wedge of gnarled and broken roots, he can't see the sprawling branches at the top of the tree, he can't even see over the width of the trunk. A tree so tall!—so *old.*

No, he can't see the top of the redwood. Can't.

3.

SMALL VEINS

"You have very small veins."

The statement hovers in the air like a moth with a broken wing, fluttering.

The first phlebotomist can't find a usable vein, calls over a second, presumably more experienced phlebotomist who also can't find a usable vein, in a vexed voice calls over a third phlebotomist who must be the most experienced of all, by happenstance the lone male in the bloodwork lab, young for such authority, brusque and super-confident tapping veins in the soft flesh of your inner left arm, and in the soft flesh of your inner right arm, seeking the vein that will be *his.*

"Make a fist, ma'am."

Swipe of alcohol, familiar-sickening smell.

"This will pinch a little, ma'am."

Pinch! Steel yourself.

First try: he's *in.*

This is a surprise. After the flailing of his (female) predecessors, the (young, male) phlebotomist has secured a usable vein on the first try.

Resist thanking him in a rush of relief, gratitude.

Your manner in the blood lab should remain reticent, formal. The focus of your determination is *not-fainting.*

"You can relax your fist, ma'am."

Sitting very stiff, very still in the sturdy utilitarian stool with wide Formica-smooth armrests which you've (mis)remembered includes a restraining bar across the midriff but no, there is no restraining bar.

Very stiff, very still willing yourself to breathe normally, evenly inside the surgical mask you are wearing. Averting your eyes out of a practical wish not to observe your own dark blood siphoning into little plastic vials.

"Ma'am? I said, you can relax your fist."

Of all commands surely this is the most difficult: *relax.*

As best you can, you comply. Your hand goes limp. A peculiar sensation suffuses you, utter cold, detachment.

Must not faint. No!

As in a spell you are fixed in place. The needle siphoning blood from your vein holds you fast.

Dark feathery wing closing over your brain. The phlebotomist stands *so close.*

Very few people have touched you, since the onset of the pandemic. Lockdown, quarantine, "social distance"—you have been conditioned to regard other people as bearers of the (invisible, ubiquitous) virus. Now that the pandemic appears to be diminishing, and some measure of normal life has revived, you have become unaccustomed to anyone, particularly a stranger, standing *so close.*

How strange, these intimacies we experience only with strangers—in medical circumstances, persons whom we have never seen before, whose names we rarely learn.

Though you'd had time to notice from the plastic ID badge affixed to his smock, the phlebotomist's name begins with *M.* Something like *Mateo, Manuel, Miguel.*

The phlebotomist's skin is of the hue of burnt cork, his eyes are very dark, he is wearing a medical-grade white mask over his mouth and nose that contrasts sharply with his skin. On the backs of his hands, swaths of dark hairs. Deep-chested, tight-muscled in green smock and pants, an individual who works out, lifts weights, very possibly an ex-athlete, out of vanity keeps himself fit yet is nonetheless putting on weight. His breath is audible inside the snug-fitting white mask.

"Almost finished, ma'am. Hold on."

Sensing your anxiety. How childlike your need to be reassured.

But M__'s manner is more bemused than critical. Not reproachful like his female co-workers who'd pricked needles into your arms in vain, blamed your *small veins.*

You are ten years older than M__, you estimate. M__ calls you *ma'am,* you are of another generation to him.

Hurtful to you, M__ doesn't see *you.* No one in the oncology blood lab is likely to see *you.*

Like one hopeful of receiving praise, willing to barter some small portion of your dignity in exchange for praise, you volunteer to M__ that you'd remembered to drink several glasses of water that morning before coming to the blood lab, to enlarge your veins, as you'd been instructed to do.

To this, M__ murmurs what sounds like *Good!*

Humoring you. You wonder if, behind the sturdy white mask, M__ is smiling.

How many vials will M__ fill with your blood? He seems to have finished three, and is working on the fourth.

You feel a swirl of faintness, nausea. *No.*

The last time you were in this room, before Covid, before the quarantine, two years ago, or longer, a patient began to faint at the farther end of the room, there was a flurry of activity, a male voice called out, *Hey! I got you.*

Had that been your phlebotomist, whose name begins with *M*?

Thinking dreamily how, if he wished, M__ could continue to siphon blood from your arm by excruciatingly slow degrees, drain your body entirely of blood, pints, quarts, gallons of thick dark blood as you remain captive in the chair, fixed in place, in thrall to him, the phlebotomist: the authority of the needle: your heart, the source of so much pain, agitation, dread gradually slowing, a clock's pendulum gradually slowing, to a stop.

Ceasing upon the midnight, with no pain.

In a haze of light-headedness suffused with relief, exhilaration, joy, you return to the oncology waiting room, take a seat, any seat, weak-kneed, can't keep from smiling inanely in case you are on camera.

See that woman? She is not afraid, she has not fainted from having her blood drained from her, smiling to herself for all is well.

Fear of fainting in the bloodwork lab though (in fact) you've never fainted in the bloodwork lab. Fear of fainting in this waiting room though (in fact) you've never fainted in this waiting room.

Just three times in your entire life you've fainted and these three times, within the span of a single, recent year.

The first time you fainted: a call had come, a stranger's voice, inquiring if you wanted your husband (who'd been hospitalized the previous day for what had been described as a mild case of pneumonia) to be "resuscitated" in the event of an emergency, sudden ringing in your head like the clapper of a bell, deafening, blinding, finding yourself on the cold tile of the kitchen floor, no memory of falling, no memory of striking the side of your head against the floor, above you the plastic wall phone hanging by its cord, turning giddily.

The second time, after your husband's (unexpected) death in that same hospital, in a dead faint falling to the cold tile floor of a women's restroom, waking dry-mouthed, blinking and staring at an unfamiliar ceiling trying to recall where you are, what you must do, what has gone wrong that you are here and not at home, not in bed at this hour of the night with your husband but in this unfamiliar place, smelling of disinfectant, alone, late-night and no other visitors in Telemetry, trying to determine what it is your task to do with the desperation of one climbing a stone wall with just her fingernails to haul herself upward.

The third time was weeks later when tentatively you'd decided that you were *all right,* determined to convince friends that you were *all right,* no need to worry about you any longer, with friends you were in a restaurant, opened a menu, had difficulty reading the menu in the dim light, realized that your husband wasn't at the table with you, wasn't opening a menu, you had lost him somehow, not sure how, not sure where, or why, it was a wrong thing, his not being at the table with you and your friends, no chair was empty for him, no place at the table for him, how unnatural that was, how obscene that was, no one except you seemed to notice that your husband wasn't with you, nowhere in the restaurant, this realization sweeping over you like an undertow, sweeping you away, extinguishing the feeble flame of your brain as a candle's flame is extinguished by a random gust of wind.

Someone called an ambulance, you'd refused to go with them. *No no no no no* you were not going with them.

Terror of being away from your home in the night. Overnight. For if *he* is to return to you, it will only be in that place.

Each time you've fainted, that feathery sensation of lightness, airy as milkweed seed borne on the air. No pain, no fear, not even alarm, for there is no anticipation. As if air were shunted into your brain, there is a shrinking, vision narrowing as in a tunnel, disappearing into a tiny dot.

So that when you recovered you'd dared to think—*Will death be so painless? So merciful?*

—

Forty minutes in the waiting room. Grating on your nerves.

Usually the waiting room is a subdued place where no one speaks to anyone else. No one looks at anyone else out of a dread of knowing them, and being known.

Why it's a relief, to be wearing a mask.

Some sort of renovation is underway in the waiting room. Carpeting has been removed from the floor, parts of the ceiling are missing. Voices echo over-loud, jarring; a receptionist, speaking on a phone, has a voice like fingers scratched on a blackboard. The magazine display is entirely missing as if it had never existed. You are disappointed for where otherwise would you encounter *Women's Health, Healthy Living, Heart Health, Family Health, Healthy Foods, Health Habits, Hospice Care, Yoga for Cancer Patients.*

At last your name is called by Dr. G__'s nurse. Behind her mask, she appears to be friendly—smiling. Perhaps she remembers you or perhaps she is confusing you with another woman of your age, height, general appearance, who has vanished from Oncology never to return.

Briskly she leads you into the labyrinthine interior of Oncology where in one of the examination rooms she records your weight, height. Takes your blood pressure which (you gather) is unusually high.

Dr. G__ will be in shortly, you are told.

Another interlude of waiting. You have learned to be patient, stoic.

Three years ago you'd been diagnosed with a "rare blood disorder" related to anemia which was described as a chronic, incurable, but slow-growing leukemia—unless it begins to accelerate, in which case it can be fatal within weeks.

Slow—unless suddenly fast.

Who knew, there are more than one hundred types of leukemia! You'd had no idea.

A poet-friend diagnosed with the identical blood disorder had been assured by his oncologist—*You will never be cured but you will most likely die of something else.*

Such things doctors tell their patients, meaning to be kind.

In fact your friend died of the blood disorder after all, or from the ravaging chemotherapy prescribed to treat it, within a few years. Waking from the torpor of remission like a great beast rousing itself to gallop to the precipice, and over.

Initially, the acceleration is said to be scarcely discernible. A matter of a decimal point, a fraction of a number in the bloodwork. *Asymptomatic.*

You are different, you believe. You know, or believe that you know, that the "chronic"—"incurable"—condition has begun to accelerate.

And so, that morning waking in the darkness before dawn. Waking to a sensation of apprehension, dread. As birds began to waken, isolated cries at first, sounding tentative, uncertain.

Yet, you dress very carefully for that morning's appointment. Plum-colored cashmere, a skirt to mid-calf, Ferragamo shoes with a medium heel. Somber, subdued.

You have not seen Dr. G__ for eighteen months and scarcely recognize him, in the sturdy white surgical mask that covers half his face. He is Indian American, of youthful middle age; slightly built, with kindly eyes, thin cheeks; the pandemic seems to have diminished him. A shy person who smiles in situations of unease, Dr. G__ is disadvantaged by having to wear a mask; you see his eyes crinkle energetically at their corners.

Dr. G__ greets you with his usual courteous warmth, asks how you've been feeling?—even as his eyes expertly scan the laptop screen, the only authentic measure of your being.

Observe what you can see of Dr. G__'s face. Is the news good, or not-so-good? Is it disastrous? *Has there been no change?*

In the matter of a chronic and incurable blood cancer, the most that can be reasonably desired is *no change.*

English is not Dr. G__'s first language and so he speaks with particular care, choosing words that tend toward the abstract, the non-specific. You have difficulty understanding him through the sturdy white mask that fits his slender face awkwardly and through a buzzing in your ears but you gather that, in some respects, your condition has improved—yet, in other respects, it seems to have worsened. Is it a matter of *red blood cells, white blood cells*?—the production of one is good, the other not-so-good.

Whatever Dr. G__ has told you, he now assures you that treatment isn't required at the present time.

You don't ask Dr. G__ what the treatment is.

Nor do you ask him if the remission is ending—has ended? Your mouth is too dry. Your throat has shut up tight.

Particularly, you are not going to ask Dr. G__ a maudlin question about how long you can expect to live.

You can guess what Dr. G__ will say: *That is not predictable.*

Should you begin to make plans?—plans to end your life?

Like smoke curling upward in the air, and of scarcely more substance than smoke, the thought of taking your own life comes to you, not for the first time, as a solace, consolation.

Almost, news that the remission may be ending is a relief.

A fearful sort of happiness, like opening a window, a window that swings open horizontally, and a violent wind seizes the window and crashes it open, jubilantly, out of your control . . .

Seeing that you are sitting very still, that you have uttered not a word, Dr. G__ assures you another time, there is no need to begin treatment just yet.

To this you stammer an inane reply—*Thank you, Doctor.*

The consultation isn't over. At this point, Dr. G__ asks you to lie down on the examination table. He listens to your heartbeat with his stethoscope, he asks you to cough. He checks your lymph nodes, your ankles. He taps at your abdomen. There is an absurd solace in this—a physician setting aside his laptop, taking time to touch his patient with deft practiced hands.

Politely Dr. G__ asks if he might take your blood pressure again? For he has noted it is exceptionally high.

This time, it is lower. A relief of course.

But when you try to sit up, you are very dizzy. Your head feels as if it's filling with helium, it will detach itself from your shoulders and float away.

Your mask has become crooked. You adjust it, with trembling fingers.

You will be all right, Dr. G__ assures you. Things will be robust again, not soon but sometime soon.

Robust? An odd word, a quaint word no native speaker of English would choose, in this context.

You realize that Dr. G__ is talking now about the loss of your husband, he'd seen the prominent obituary in the local newspaper. He had never met your husband but he offers condolences.

It seems like the ending of everything now, Dr. G__ says. But it is not. You will see.

The end of your life, the end of the meaning of your life. It will seem so. But it is not *so*.

You laugh, nervously. What is Dr. G__ saying? As if pushing something at you, a party balloon, a candied apple.

You are sitting up now, the wave of faintness has subsided. Is the examination not over? Dr. G__ has something more to tell you, in a lowered voice alarming to you.

He would like to share something with you, he says.

Not many know. No one in this office.

His daughter has died, Dr. G__ says. Before she was to return home from college, at Harvard.

Just weeks ago, the news came to him and his wife, Dr. G__ says. She was just nineteen, she was a violinist, she was to major in molecular biology. But then the news came, not good news of a kind they were accustomed to receive from her and about her, not good news but very bad, a call from a dean's office, a summons to come to Cambridge at once.

An overdose of medications. She had been very unhappy—hard to stay still in one place, concentrate on her work, practice her violin. She had not wanted to disappoint.

They had been going to a family therapist, Dr. G__ says. When she'd been living here at home.

But it had been thought, she was strong enough to return to college. She had insisted so, she had regained much weight she'd lost. She had stopped playing the violin but had taken it up again so they had been hopeful . . .

You have wakened from your trance of self-absorption. You tell Dr. G__ how very sorry you are to hear this. Only nineteen! What a tragedy!

You hear yourself stammering. You are dangerously close to bursting into tears. You recall having seen small framed photographs of Dr. G__'s family in his office, on previous visits. Smiling girl, smiling boy. Beautiful faces, radiant smiles. You'd felt a stab of something like envy.

No idea why Dr. G__ has singled you out in this way. Speaking to you so earnestly, as he has never spoken to you before.

You are touched, you feel yourself privileged. Though you are still light-headed you resist the impulse to lean against a doorway. You don't want Dr. G__ to notice. You must be stoic, calm for Dr. G__'s sake. A worthy repository of a father's tragic story.

Dr. G__ leads you to his receptionist, he will see you again, he says, in three months.

Three months, not six as usual?

Three, Dr. G__ says. It is better.

Shake hands as usual, in parting with Dr. G__. Make your way unaccompanied along the labyrinthine corridor, back to the waiting room with its grimly bare floor and over-loud voices, through that exit and to the parking lot where your vehicle is parked amid rows of similar vehicles. Remove your mask, you can breathe again!—draw in a deep breath that swells your ribs with a sensation like helium.

You will be halfway home before you understand why Dr. G__ told you his story.

REFUGE

Three bridges she will have to cross. Ninety-six miles to the Buddhist monastery in Bucks County, Pennsylvania, where the *estranged husband* has taken refuge.

The first of the bridges is the small plank bridge over Stony Brook Creek, near the rented house in which, for the past five weeks, Lorene has been living alone since her husband departed without warning, or an explanatory note; the second is a slightly larger plank bridge over the Delaware-Raritan Canal at Griggstown, that has become icy-slick overnight; the third is the largest, and the most daunting, a six-span steel truss bridge built more than a century ago over the Delaware River at Lambertville.

It's a raw wet-windy day in late winter. Shafts of sunshine make Lorene's eyes ache. She can feel the car, a Nissan compact, shake in the wind, ascending the ramp to the bridge at

Lambertville. Drafts of cold air from one of the rear windows, cold-caress at the nape of her neck.

His touch, at the nape of her neck.

The Delaware River is much wider than Lorene recalls. The bridge is much longer than Lorene recalls. Built in 1904, the bridge is too narrow now for oversized vehicles that pass oncoming traffic with excruciating slowness; Lorene feels the first, fluttery symptoms of panic, trapped on the bridge with no way to turn back like a cervical exam that, even as the doctor (invisible behind the patient's raised knees) murmurs cheerfully *Almost over!*, goes on and *on.*

Fact is, it's rare for Lorene, though she is no longer a naïve girl, nor even an especially young woman, in whom such inexperience might be excusable, to be driving alone on a lengthy trip; nearly always it has been Lorene in the passenger's seat, and an adult male driving.

Until she'd left home at eighteen, her father, who'd have never let anyone else drive if he was in the vehicle. In the seven years of her marriage, her husband Marcus Coyne.

Where have you been, Lorene! I've been trying to reach you.

I love you, I need you.

Whatever you did, I forgive you.

It's almost that Marcus is in the car with her. She can hear his voice. Chiding, affectionate. Exasperating. *Forgiving.*

Despite oncoming traffic Lorene can't stop from glancing nervously beyond the bridge railing at the Delaware River—the vast shimmering river, steely-gray, beautiful, yet frightening, for it *is* wider than she can easily see, disappearing into the distance at the horizon like a funnel.

Deceptively placid, slow-moving. Of the hue of molten metal, that could not possibly move swiftly, treacherously. But it does.

Thirty-seven days, nights. The *estranged husband* has been missing.

How many times Lorene has called the husband's cell phone, left anxious messages, plaintive messages, pleading messages, never any answer until at last a smug little (female) machine voice informed her *this mailbox is full.*

Friends of Marcus's, few of whom Lorene knew, she might have called, but finally dared not, for Marcus would be furious with her if he knew; more practicably, Lorene guesses that they wouldn't know where Marcus was any more than she does. And if he was staying with any one of them, or with a woman friend, they wouldn't betray him by telling her anyway.

(There was general disapproval of Lorene, among Marcus's friends. Not at all intellectual. Not an artist, writer. Not Marcus's equal, or anything near. But yes, *young.*)

Nor did Lorene dare call any of the individuals or businesses for whom Marcus did intermittent computer consulting. For such a betrayal Marcus would never forgive her.

Yet, Lorene has considered calling the help desk at the university computer center where Marcus sometimes works. Not to ask if Marcus Coyne was there (never!) but on the off-chance that, if Marcus were there, and happened to pick up the phone, Lorene would recognize his voice at once and be assured that he was alive . . .

Or, Marcus would recognize Lorene's soft pleading voice and in that instant realize how he loved her and how he needed to return to her, at once.

Calling a *help desk*! Lorene has to laugh, is this desperation?

Never show your desperation. Never show your hand.

This was Marcus's advice, whether flippant or serious Lorene didn't know. Marcus so often spoke in riddles.

As a left-behind wife Lorene is grateful now that she'd

never given in to the temptation to boast of her husband to co-workers at the Blue Bird Day-Care in Millstone, New Jersey, where she has worked for several years: for Marcus has an MD from a prestigious medical school, and Marcus is locally valued as an *expert computer consultant.*

She'd marveled at her husband, who knew so much about computers and electrical devices of all kinds yet scorned such knowledge as mere *techne*. (And what was *techne*?—a Greek word that means *craft, technique.* Lorene herself would have liked to master some valuable *techne*!) A life for the two of them *off the grid* was Marcus's plan: somewhere outside the United States, possibly Cape Breton, or Prince Edward Island, Canada; but maybe Indonesia, Bali. (Marrying a not-much-educated girl with no career plans, no specialized training to exercise, was a way of ensuring mobility when it came time.) It was possible that Marcus had thrown his cell phone away in a gesture of disgust. Of repudiation. Longingly he spoke of being *unattached:* to persons, to possessions, to the pride of accomplishment, to primitive appetites, above all to idiotic devices like cell phones. As he'd quit a coveted residency at New York-Presbyterian Hospital in New York City in his mid-twenties so he'd declined full-time employment as a computer programmer even if such employment included medical benefits. He spoke of himself as a sixties-style hippie, a pilgrim set upon a lonesome path, born in the wrong century, into the wrong demographic. He was drawn to *the abstract, the impersonal.* The perennial search for *enlightenment.* Which most persons mistake as a search for God.

Marcus spoke of such matters with a sort of radiant intensity. His dark eyes shone, his eyelids quivered with excitement. His skin was pale but exuded an aura of heat. Lorene was just nineteen when they met, Marcus Coyne was eleven years older. Lorene could have swooned in girlish adoration of so ardent a man, like no one she'd known.

Soon after they met, they became lovers. And soon after this, they were living together in Marcus's rented place on Stony Brook Road.

After just a few months, they were married.

Lorene would not remember afterward having said *yes* to any of Marcus's requests, it was as if he'd sucked her breath from her, she'd had no voice.

Yes yes yes—she adored him. She did!

A restless search for *enlightenment* drew Marcus to the Ramapo Mountains in northeastern New Jersey, formerly inhabited by natives of the Ramapough Lenape Nation, for this seemed to Marcus a sacred space, ideal for fasting, meditation. *Cleansing the soul, self-purification.*

In the early idyllic days and weeks of their life together Marcus took Lorene hiking with him on steep mountain trails in the Ramapos, in rocky terrain for which Lorene, inexperienced in hiking, with weak ankles, wasn't suited; but Lorene was determined never to express discomfort. Whatever Marcus wanted in a wife, Lorene was determined to be that wife. But soon Marcus took pity on Lorene, or lost patience with her, and ceased inviting her.

After the mountains Marcus would spend several days *in retreat* at a Buddhist meditation center/monastery at Upper Black Eddy, across the Delaware River in Bucks County, Pennsylvania. This was a small community of Mahāyāna Buddhist monks, nuns, novices, and lay persons, who managed the center. Here, Marcus had been a novice at one time, but had dropped out; the Tibetan-born abbot of the monastery was Marcus's teacher, the *most spiritual, most silent* person Marcus had ever met.

Marcus was welcome to stay at the monastery whenever he wished, he'd claimed.

A place of silence, and respect for silence. A place of celibacy.

Hard for Lorene not to consider the monastery—*silence, celibacy*—a rebuke of her. A rebuke of Marcus's marriage.

It is also possible that Marcus isn't at the monastery. That Marcus is staying with friends sworn not to tell Lorene where he is. Someone came to pick him up on the day he'd left, Lorene had never known who. He'd had a "complicated" life before Lorene, she knew, and that life had not ended with Lorene.

One of Marcus's women friends is a potter named Miriam, who advertises her boldly colored pottery on a website Marcus designed for her, several years older than Marcus, who'd been his lover before he'd met Lorene . . .

Or: Marcus isn't with friends, or at the monastery, but somewhere else. Injured on a hiking trail, alone, helpless. Even if he had his cell phone it would have gone dead by now.

Experienced hikers never hike alone—Marcus said often.

Soon after they were living together he'd taken Lorene to a hiking supply store to outfit her with hiking boots so heavy, Lorene became tired just lifting her feet; their laces had to be double-knotted, yet were always coming loose. Marcus would hike behind her to oversee her, calling out in exasperated affection—*Your laces! Jesus.*

Ever more lately Marcus seemed to relish danger, he'd spoken of his life as dice being tossed. Either you toss the dice yourself, or someone else does. Or fate.

It was like lovemaking, that should be spontaneous and unprotected. For, in love, no one should wish to be *protected.*

Marcus spoke in this way, in riddles. Lorene thought that *unprotected sex* and *protected sex* were very different for women than for men but she did not say this to Marcus who would have been displeased, for Marcus did not like to be questioned.

You could never be sure if Marcus was serious, in any case. Or joking.

Or, serious and joking simultaneously.

"Lorene, darling—you must learn to decipher the signs that surround you. That's enlightenment. The pathway to enlightenment. Don't look to others, not even to me. Look *within.*"

Tenderly he'd smiled, framing her face in both his hands and kissing her forehead as you might kiss the forehead of a child, as a kind of blessing, a kind of forgiveness.

Lorene wanted to protest—*I look to you, my husband. You are within me.*

She had a face like a sunflower, Marcus told her. So open, trusting.

Other women, girls—their faces were sly, circumspect. Multifoliate roses, petals folded over petals, you could not trust them. *His wife* was different.

He'd left Lorene in the past, but always returned within a day or two. Or three.

Estranged. The word came to Lorene as if in a dream. She was sure, Marcus himself had never uttered it.

Estranged: with *strange* embedded. It was true, Marcus did feel strange to her, so often distracted, gazing bemusedly at her as if he couldn't quite place her, or comprehend why they were together. She'd wanted to implore him—*Why did you marry me, if you don't love me?*

But he did love her, he would insist. The girl with the sunflower face! But there were times when he needed to be alone, Lorene must respect that.

It wasn't *her.* It was his own life, his identity that choked him. Walls closing in, always the same walls, a man's spiritual worth reduced to the work he does for others, and that work of little value in itself. He needed to seek refuge elsewhere, he hoped she would understand.

In February, something happened between them, Lorene hadn't fully understood at the time. Except to know that she had provoked him, unwittingly.

Not good to think of it. Not now.

But—thirty-seven days, nights! Lorene recalled a friend whose husband moved out of their house without any explanation; served his wife divorce papers with no warning; no counseling, no compromise. No chance for the left-behind wife to ask what had gone wrong, how was she to blame, how could she become a better wife, stunned to realize that the marriage was *over.*

What a shock! Like death. How could anyone who'd once loved behave in such a way to the one he'd loved? Marcus wouldn't do that to her, Lorene was sure.

Waiting for his call, the call that would forgive. How many nights sleepless in the bed from which the *estranged husband* had departed.

When do you accept that you've been *left*? *Rejected, abandoned?*

Lorene could not inquire among friends, relatives. Coworkers at the day-care. Too shameful but maybe (as she wanted to think) premature: Marcus would return, surely?

Still, Lorene must make a decision soon, what to do if Marcus doesn't return. If he never returns. How to *move on.*

She was only twenty-seven! More than merely a long miserable life must lie before her.

Practical matters like moving to a smaller place, a rental in East Millstone. Returning to the university night school, getting a degree in education. Adopting a dog from the Millstone Animal Rescue to replace the beloved dog lost . . .

Jolted awake, a phone ringing in another part of the house.

It was the landline, in the kitchen. A phone rarely used any longer but a necessity in this semi-rural house in which cell phone reception was unreliable.

Barefoot in the dark Lorene hurried to the phone, frantic to get there before the caller hung up.

Where have you been, Lorene! God damn, I've been trying to reach you.

I love you, I need you.

Whatever you did, I forgive you.

His voice, unmistakable. Lorene could barely hear over a sound like crackling flames, the connection was so poor.

Lorene tried to reply, to explain, she'd been at work, much of the day at work, she'd tried to call *him,* many times she'd tried to call him desperate to know where he was but Marcus seemed not to hear her, talking past her in a rapid lowered voice as if he were in fear of being overheard.

Where was he, what had happened to him?—Lorene couldn't comprehend.

Fumbling in the dim-lighted kitchen for a notepad, a pen, to write down directions, an address, but the connection was continually breaking. She would come for Marcus, of course she would come for him, but—where was he? Lorene could hear only snatches of words as if the phone line were alive with crackling flames.

It seemed that Marcus was agitated, impatient with Lorene, blaming her, as if the poor connection was Lorene's fault, another of her failings. A grate was shutting in her brain leaving her adrift amid a rushing sound like wind, like distance, like time, as if the man who'd come miraculously into her life were already lost to her, gone from her, the *estranged husband* who would never return to her for of course she had failed him, she was a failed wife, failed at love, failed at keeping love alive, clutching a phone receiver pressed hard against her ear in frantic need like one listening to words in a foreign language.

Was Marcus in some sort of danger? In his lowered voice claiming that calls were not allowed here, cell phones forbidden, no visitors, barred windows and locks on the doors, no heat, they were starving him, threatening him, he'd sought refuge but there was no refuge, baring his soul he'd sought the *awakened one* but his pilgrimage led him to Hell.

Lorene wondered if Marcus was in a medical facility. Had he injured himself hiking, had he fasted too severely, had someone found him, brought him to a hospital? But where was this hospital? Had he checked himself into a psychiatric treatment center? Had he been taken into police custody, and involuntarily committed? Lorene recalled Marcus speaking of a psychiatric facility in New Brunswick where a friend of his had been a patient, a woman who'd slashed her wrists, Marcus had visited her but Lorene didn't remember the name of the facility, at the time she'd taken little interest in Marcus's friends, or former friends—they didn't factor in Lorene's life, Marcus had dropped most of them when he'd married her.

The line had gone dead. The crackling noise abruptly ceased.

Quickly Lorene replaced the receiver. Waited for the phone to ring again but it did not.

Where are you! Why have you done this to me!

You say that you love me . . .

Like a hook in the upper lip, a flailing fish trapped by a hook, writhing suffocating in air because hooked: *love.*

In the freezing kitchen in weak light trying to decipher the words she'd scrawled on a notepad. The handwriting was the handwriting of a stranger, frantic, feverish: *yeddy, delwar, refug, river, buud, uder blek. Skane, nyaard, weir, yeddy, delwar, buud mons, refuge.*

Despite the late hour Lorene searched online for hospitals, medical facilities, psychiatric treatment centers, Buddhist meditation centers within a range of fifty miles . . .

In the morning after a few hours of exhausted sleep, when she examined the scrawled words more calmly Lorene saw that the nonsense words made a kind of sense, like a poem, or a puzzle:

Delaware River Upper Black Eddy
Buddhist monastery refuge

Refuge!—Lorene recalled, Marcus had told her once of going to the Buddha for *refuge.*

In a state of despair, having given up, humbling yourself utterly, not a shred of pride remaining, you go to the Awakened One seeking *refuge.*

North on River Road, into rural Bucks County. Glimpsed through trees on her right, the wide shimmering Delaware River.

So that is where the *estranged husband* has fled: the Mahāyāna Buddhist monastery in Upper Black Eddy. Retreating from the world, applying for *refuge,* as a political refugee might apply for asylum. If only Marcus had let Lorene know, weeks ago!

This new day, mid-March, still cold, gusty, but suffused with hope, and the anxiety that attends hope.

There is no question of forgiving Marcus, Lorene is grateful that he is alive. In her worst imaginings he has been dead, lost in the Ramapo Mountains and his body never discovered.

Or, with another woman. The potter-woman, what was her name . . .

Would you rather know that your husband was dead, or had betrayed you with another woman? Lorene smiles grimly, best not to think like this.

Grateful that he has called her finally. That he forgives *her.*

Can you love, if love is not returned? Not returned equally?

The most profound of questions because it is a question about how to live one's life. For it is rare that love is fully reciprocal.

Lorene can love Marcus more than Marcus can love her, she will impress Marcus with the depth of her love. Sunflower lover, rawly open, vulnerable. *Take me, I am yours.* Marcus will realize.

Perhaps Lorene will become a Buddhist, to join him. She has given religion little thought, that has been part of her immaturity. But she is a mature woman, now.

For this (first) (crucial) visit to a Buddhist center/monastery Lorene has dressed with care. Beneath her slightly worn red fleece jacket she is wearing black: a long-sleeved silk-wool tunic purchased in a consignment shop, high-quality cashmere flawed by a scattering of minuscule moth holes no one is likely to notice; an ankle-length black skirt in a shiny quilted fabric, also an upscale consignment shop purchase; stylish black boots in faux-leather. This is not the young woman in well-worn jeans, T-shirts adorned with kittens and puppies and jingly bracelets on both wrists who works three days a week at the Blue Bird Day-Care—the young woman who *chatters* to entertain, and disarm—but rather a calm reasonable dignified unanxious ungroveling undesperate young woman with a face like a beacon, bright, open, warm-smiling, frank amber-brown gaze, no makeup.

Well, just a light daub of vermilion on her lips, that otherwise resemble the drained-purple lips of the drowned.

Do Buddhist women cover their hair? Their heads? Lorene isn't sure but she is wearing a black wool slouch-brimmed hat with a whimsical little pheasant feather, just in case.

Her hair! Since Marcus's departure Lorene has been neglecting her hair which has become snarled and matted; at the day-care she wears gaily colored headbands, her smiles are quick and guileless as the smiles of children who adore her because they know nothing of her, have no need to feel sorry for her.

Reading stories to small children is pure pleasure, never do they question the logic of a story, the improbability of so many happy endings.

Animals who think, speak. Animals as respected as human beings.

Happy endings. Possible?

Lorene recalls how, when they were newly lovers, Marcus admired her shoulder-length hair. Running his fingers through the dense wavy chestnut-brown hair, spreading it about her head like a sunburst. When he made love to Lorene tenderly, reverently by candlelight, she'd thought her heart would burst. That this man might love *her.*

Later she would wonder if the lovemaking—Lorene's hair spread out on the pillow around her head—had been in mimicry of the famous/infamous photograph of John Lennon and Yoko Ono lying together . . .

Lighted candles beside their bed disappeared gradually. One night Lorene would realize that there'd been no candle on the bedside table for some time.

One night Lorene would realize that there'd been no lovemaking for some time.

An hour's drive north to Upper Black Eddy. Not all of last night's snow has melted here, ice glitters on tree limbs, twigs. Sunshine is bright, blinding. Razor-sharp slivers of light in the river. The beauty of the world overwhelms Lorene, in an instant she feels weak, enfeebled. How unlikely is it, Marcus is waiting for her somewhere ahead!

Desperate words she'd scribbled onto a notepad, barely legible by daylight—*yeddy, delwar, refug, river, buud, uder blek.*

Telling herself that she could be happier without him.

Telling herself that it would strengthen her, to live alone. And none of this remotely true.

Marcus was drawn to Buddhism, he said, because it is the most godless of religions—not really a religion but a way of being. It has no theology, it is a *practice.* It has no commandments, only revelations. That all ephemeral longings are futile, all attachments come to nothing. Raw appetite burns itself out and becomes ashes.

How earnest Marcus was! Lorene was impressed with the severity of his principles until she realized that *longing, appetite, futility* were identified with weakness of the flesh: *sex, erotic love.* The surge of hot blood which the (male) brain cannot control.

Did he blame her, Lorene wondered, for his sexual need for her? For any woman? Or—just *her*?

Love you, need you.

Whatever you did, I forgive you.

Lorene's mistake—(she would realize belatedly)—was enrolling in an introductory computer course at the university, in the night school, without telling Marcus.

She'd mentioned taking a course but not what the course was and Marcus hadn't been listening, or might have assumed that whatever Lorene was taking was an arts or crafts course—painting, ceramics, art education for elementary school teachers.

Lorene had assured Marcus, she was paying the six-hundred-dollar tuition out of her day-care salary.

He hadn't liked her being away at night, away from him, when *he* was home. Just Tuesdays and Thursdays but these were lengthy classes, six P.M. to seven-twenty P.M. Dinner was delayed, or there was no dinner per se. Walking Little Bear, their rescue pup, fell to Marcus by default.

Nor did Marcus like it, that Lorene was taking a course in computing, *techne.*

Lorene had assumed that Marcus would approve. Marcus would be impressed. Since he was himself a computer technician, one of those entrusted to help university faculty and administrators with their computer problems, which were of every imaginable sort, inexhaustible. As a technician Marcus was unfailingly professional: he never displayed the impatience he felt for the university staff, he simply considered them computer-illiterate. He was flattered by their gratitude, he made it a point to decline private payment from them, for he was paid by the university computer center; still he couldn't help but boast to Lorene of how he'd come to the rescue of distinguished professors brought to the brink of tears by the intransigence of their computers.

No one so accomplished that he isn't humbled by another. How vulnerable, how foolish we all make ourselves.

One evening early in the semester, in February, when Lorene returned home from the university it was to discover that Little Bear was missing. A terrier-spaniel mix still young enough to quiver and thrum with excitement each time Lorene, or less frequently Marcus, took him for a walk; clumsy, eager, with oversized paws, moist brown hopeful eyes shiny as plastic buttons.

But how did Little Bear get outside the house, Lorene asked Marcus tearfully, and Marcus claimed to have no idea, he too had been away most of the day, he guessed that Little Bear missed Lorene, might have thought that she was abandoning him, or maybe he'd gone to look for *her.*

Into the early hours of the morning Lorene called for Little Bear, searched for him outside with a flashlight, along the road, trying not to despair. Neighbors claimed to know nothing. Marcus helped Lorene for a while calling Little Bear's name with a forced (or was it ironic) urgency, professed concern and sympathy but did not appear to be as agitated as Lorene was, nor was he patient with Lorene's distress beyond a day or two.

Repeatedly Lorene asked how had Little Bear gotten outside, where could Little Bear have gone, why would Little Bear run away?—he would not have run away. Behind the house was an uncultivated field, trees in abundance, underbrush, marshy land which he was allowed to explore daily, off-leash. He never ran out of earshot, he was exuberant but rarely disobeyed. Not a willful or troublesome dog.

Lorene thought, *Of course, he has punished me. He has punished Little Bear.*

A part of her mind did not believe this, entirely. Did not want to believe.

She did not dare accuse Marcus of taking the dog away. In their marriage Lorene was inclined to chatter while Marcus half-listened as if charmed by her—but only to a degree. Of serious matters in contention with him, Lorene did not speak. She had not the words, the vocabulary. Marcus had all the words, Marcus had the authority. Of serious matters, *he* spoke. Lorene could only hope that he'd brought Little Bear to some place where the little dog might be discovered and taken in, find a new home. Or taken to a shelter.

Lorene recalled how Marcus had borrowed a .22 rifle from a neighbor, to shoot at groundhogs. Lorene did not want to think that he'd shot Little Bear and dragged his body back into the woods.

He could not have done such a thing—could he? Not Marcus, who'd been so amused by Little Bear.

Sitting in the car weeping. Trying not to imagine Little Bear's disbelief, and mounting terror, that one of the humans who'd given him a home would harm him . . .

Lorene would say nothing to Marcus but he sensed how she distrusted him, shrank from him. How hurt she was, that he'd taken Little Bear from her. Punishing an innocent creature in order to punish *her.*

And now Marcus was frequently irritable with her, the

slightest thing set him off. A dropped fork, a vacant look in Lorene's face. Her habit of shrinking from him, just perceptibly. He spoke harshly to her, coldly. He quizzed her on the computer course. He came late to bed, or didn't come at all; in bed, he turned his back to her, or seized her roughly, as in a parody of lovemaking.

Without telling Marcus, Lorene contacted animal rescue shelters within a distance of ten, twelve miles. She emailed photographs of Little Bear, missing *in the vicinity of Stony Brook Road*. She spoke on the phone describing Little Bear, yes he was microchipped, yes he had his rabies and distemper shots, yes he was (reasonably well) trained, no he would probably not come if called by name by a stranger, no she had no idea (beginning now to cry, helplessly) how he'd managed to get a (locked) door open, slip outside, and run away during the day with no one seeing him . . .

None of this Marcus knew. But surely Marcus suspected.

One day Marcus lost his temper, pushed Lorene against a wall. Unthinking Lorene pushed him back as a child might do. He shouted into her face, pushed her down onto a sofa, closed his fingers around her throat.

So swiftly this happened, Lorene would have difficulty recalling afterward. Her hands—her affrighted fingers—flailed, pushed at his hands, she tried to draw breath to scream, to plead with Marcus; in the next moment he released her, stepped away.

He had not squeezed her throat, he'd only just pushed her down. It was over immediately. *He had not strangled her.*

She'd provoked Marcus's anger and made him into something he was not—a brute.

That night Marcus was away, didn't return until Lorene was in bed. Next day when Lorene returned from work he was gone with just a suitcase missing, his laptop and electronic devices, a few clothes and shoes including hiking boots.

He'd left her the car, he must have made arrangements for a friend to pick him up. It was kind of Marcus, decent—leaving Lorene the car which was his car, in his name; this decency at the core of Marcus Coyne, inviolable. He would leave her, he might repudiate her, but he would not harm her. She was sure.

Leaving no note, no explanation. But there was no need, Lorene understood.

Though telling herself, *This didn't happen. He didn't mean it.*

Examining her neck in a mirror. There were no bruises that she could see. Not a trace. Possibly, just a shadowy indentation in the skin.

At the Blue Bird Day-Care she wore rainbow scarfs casually knotted about her neck. None of the staff suspected, she was sure.

Yet, when Lorene stood at the sink in the upstairs bathroom, a shadow fell upon the underside of her jaw resembling a bruise. Weeks later it still does.

At Upper Black Eddy Lorene turns left onto narrow Harbinger Road, away from the Delaware River, steeply uphill beside the Bucks County Land Preserve. A handmade wooden sign so unobtrusive it might be overlooked indicates that the Buddhist meditation house and monastery is two miles ahead.

The air feels thinner here, colder. No one seems to live on Harbinger Road.

Lorene noticed, on River Road, a number of beautiful old fieldstone houses overlooking the river. Most were set far back from the road, like country estates. Bucks County is an affluent county, within commuting distance of Philadelphia; on the Pennsylvania side of the river, properties are large, lavish, while on the New Jersey side most houses are small and undistinguished.

It is something of an anomaly, that a Buddhist monastery is located here in Upper Black Eddy, at the top of a small mountain, in a weatherworn old Bucks County fieldstone farmhouse with outbuildings at the rear. A well-to-do landowner, presumably a Buddhist, must have left this expensive property to the monastery.

Lorene drives up a gravel drive, to the main building. Her heart has begun to beat hard in anticipation of Marcus, whom she expects to see at any moment, awaiting her.

Thank God! I love you, I am so sorry.

Take me home, I am so sorry.

But no one is awaiting Lorene, no one is in sight. Except for vehicles parked at the side of the main building, one of them a new-looking Land Rover, the place might be deserted.

On a walkway to the building is a weathered wooden bench—no one sitting there, awaiting Lorene.

Close by, a statue of the Buddha, squat, stolid, about five feet in height, in a rough material that might be sandstone. Lorene is mesmerized, she has never seen a Buddha of this size.

Broad flat Asian face of peace, enlightenment. Unusually large, elongated eyelids lightly shut over protuberant eyes. Long straight slender nose. Lips firmly closed as a flower that has not (yet) opened. The Awakened One in his meditative state, consciousness turned inward like a fierce flame. The Buddha is not a teacher, he exudes no "wisdom." Words are irrelevant. Words are mere static. Words are deceptive. Human speech is created to deceive, divide. Before the Buddha Lorene knows herself petty, insignificant. Her grief for the ruin of her marriage—the *failure* of her marriage—for the loss of Little Bear—is ephemeral desiccated leaves blown in a swirl on the walkway.

Yet, as Marcus has explained, there is no god Buddha: *Buddha* means *enlightened one.*

You are yourself the Buddha, in your purest state.

But how does one acquire a *pure state*?—that is the dilemma.

Marcus had tried to teach her. He'd been patient with her, even affectionate at first.

So awkward!—trying to fit her body, her fleshy thighs, into what is called the *lotus position.* Trying to sit as Marcus did with a ramrod-straight spine that her mind might become empty—a vessel to be filled. The ideal was a cleared mind, distracting thoughts repelled as you might brush away annoying insects. But a force like gravity tugged at her. Thoughts came in swarms, stinging.

How do you do it, detach yourself from *time*? For all of her adult life Lorene has dwelt in time. She is keenly aware of time passing too swiftly, not having enough time, she wears time in a watch on her wrist, in any room in which there is a clock she is likely to check it compulsively. Each day she falls farther behind, fails to accomplish what she should. Soon the sun will begin (again) to slant in the sky, dusk will arrive. Soon, another day gone.

Marcus claimed to be able to meditate without intrusive thoughts for as long as an hour—for Lorene, just a few minutes would have been a triumph. How much more Marcus would have loved her if she'd succeeded. Beyond love, he might have admired her.

Sitting in meditation Lorene had been uncomfortably aware of her body. The region of her lower abdomen, her groin, that exuded heat and was over-sensitive to pressure. In memory of the affably smiling Buddha she'd placed her hands before her, palms up, resting lightly on her knees. Shut her eyes. Shut her ears to all sounds but could not not hear Little Bear fretting on his leash, softly whining, whimpering on the farther side of the house where, when Lorene and Marcus were meditating on the back porch, Marcus had secured him.

There was something too *precise* about meditation. Lorene was forced to experience her body too intimately. It was all that she *had,* or *was;* this was humbling. A beating heart, a brain, stomach, intestines, the hidden interior labyrinth of uterus, ovaries, cervix. A sensation of cold swept over her, a terror of life reduced to flesh: was that all that she was? And a woman's body, so vulnerable. Men had pinched her nipples, that had seemed to them beautiful but also in some way annoying, crying to be hurt. Tongues had been poked into her reluctant mouth. A boy had once spat upon her, after he'd mashed his mouth against hers. More than one boy had deliberately hurt her pushing his penis into her, ignoring her whimpers of pain. Even her adoring husband had seemed to wish to hurt her at times, in some way exasperated with her, the very flesh of the woman, soft and unresisting, passive and yielding and yet beyond his control.

For weeks she'd tried, tried hard. Emulating Marcus. Willed her mind to purity, emptiness: except, Lorene was a vessel stuffed tight as a sausage with guts, blood, ungovernable thoughts, that could not be emptied.

That's all right, Lorene. You tried.

Meditating isn't for everyone, don't force yourself.

Marcus had been disappointed with Lorene yet (possibly) vindicated, too. For Lorene was the girl he'd selected to marry, not an intellectual equal but in awe of him, docile and unquestioning.

He'd had what he called difficult relationships with women closer in age to him who expected more, always *more.* The girl with the sunflower face was not one of these.

These long minutes Lorene has been staring at the sandstone Buddha. Feeling an uneasy tingling sensation, almost dread, she'd felt as a child staring at mannequins in clothing stores she couldn't help but feel were somehow sentient, aware of her.

Marcus has spoken of the *uncanny valley.* Our unease in the presence of objects or creatures that resemble human beings but are not human beings.

Something you think is human but is not.

Lorene wonders if anyone has been watching her through a window—in bright sunshine she can't see inside, doesn't want to appear to be looking. Still she is half-awaiting Marcus, expecting to hear him call warmly to her—*Lorene! You came . . .*

Except Marcus's voice so often has expressed impatience, exasperation in recent months.

Lorene! Where have you been . . .

In a small interior courtyard crowded with a wheelbarrow and stacked debris Lorene knocks on a heavy oaken door. There is no doorbell, no knocker. No sign of life within.

Against the fieldstone façade are desiccated vines, untrimmed bushes, lilac, wisteria; forsythia on the brink of bursting into bloom in the next warm spell. All of nature poised as in a long-withheld breath.

Lorene realizes that her teeth are chattering. Her life, the remainder of her life, may be decided in the next several minutes.

She wants to think that there is something consoling here, in the unkempt courtyard. In the general derelict feel of the place. And the sandstone Buddha dreaming close by, such a look of peace on his face . . . Safety here, no judgment. Refuge.

At last the door is opened, a woman stands in the doorway squinting at Lorene as if expecting to recognize her but does not; smiling nonetheless, her eyes remarkably warm, softly dark. "Hello! Welcome! Come in."

Possibly Lorene *is* expected?

Lorene steps inside, smiling hopefully. So hard, the lower half of her face hurts.

"Have you come alone? Have you visited us before?"

"I—I am alone. I have not visited you before . . ."

Lorene glances about the room, which is a kind of anteroom or foyer, sparely furnished, not perceptibly warmer than outdoors, and not well-lit. Windows are small, set in thick walls, surprisingly unclean. Underfoot is a bare plank floor, somewhat at a slant, with just a few scattered carpets thin as towels. White walls that need cleaning, or repainting. On a stone table, another likeness of the Buddha, with more finely chiseled features, about eighteen inches high.

No Marcus! Lorene has expected to see him inside, waiting for her. Her heart is thudding hard in disappointment.

The smiling-squinting woman introduces herself to Lorene—a breathy name Lorene can't quite hear, like Martha, Agatha, yet neither of these names. The woman is perhaps fifty years old, but girlish in her manner; in eccentric clothing that resembles jodhpurs, a mismatched jacket, a coarse-knitted sweater over a white shirt with a creased collar; on her feet gray woolen socks, open-toed leather sandals. Her graying hair is cropped short.

The woman clasps Lorene's hands in hers in a friendly greeting but stiffens when Lorene explains that she has come to bring her husband home—"Marcus called me last night."

"'Marcus'—?"

"Marcus Coyne. You must know him, he's here on a retreat—*refuge*. He has been here many times . . ."

Lorene expects the woman's face to light up in recognition but instead her face seems to have shut up like a fist, as if Lorene has said something offensive.

Explaining stiffly to Lorene that the staff is not authorized to give out information regarding anyone in residence at the monastery. Or anyone who *has been* in residence.

"This is a private place for meditation and instruction, a sanctuary. You have to understand."

"But—Marcus is my husband . . ."

"I'm sorry, Mrs. Coyne. I am not authorized to say if your husband is here or not."

Lorene recalls now, Marcus has a Buddhist name. Of course!

Lorene tells the Buddhist woman that Marcus has a *dharma* name, she thinks that's the word—*dharma.* He'd told her, a few years ago, she can't remember clearly, no idea how to pronounce the name, something like *dai-kan chis-ho* . . .

Lorene is embarrassed to be speaking in this way, mangling words. She has no idea even which language these words are—Tibetan? Chinese? Thai?

The Buddhist woman fails to respond as Lorene expects. With studied politeness she listens to Lorene stumble with the *dharma name* as one might listen to a child struggling to enunciate an unfamiliar word.

Politely the Buddhist woman repeats that, when an individual seeks refuge in a monastery or a temple, his privacy is sacred, inviolable.

"But—my husband called me. Last night, late. He sounded upset, agitated . . ."

Lorene too is beginning to be upset. She is smiling at the woman, smiling hard, as if her mouth is fixed into a smile; a smile of desperation, a smile of pleading, a smile of mounting anger.

Yet: wondering if this is all an error, the long drive to Upper Black Eddy along the river, the interpretation of the scrawled words that morning; the frantic telephone exchange of the previous night. Just possibly, Marcus hadn't uttered the words *Upper Black Eddy,* or even *Buddhist,* or *monastery.* In her frantic need to make sense of his words she'd heard wrongly.

Just possibly, Marcus is nowhere near Upper Black Eddy, Pennsylvania.

The *estranged husband* is miles away. The *estranged husband* will never return.

Lorene glances about, uncertain what to do next. Her heart is a silly little bird thrashing inside her rib cage. Patiently, kindly, the Buddhist woman stands before her waiting for Lorene to leave—waiting for Lorene to understand, without being rudely told, *it is time for you to leave.*

But Lorene can't leave!—she stands rooted to the spot.

Seeing, through an arched doorway, what appears to be a meditation room, empty.

Tall waxy-white candles, unlighted. Yet, Lorene thinks she hears chanting in the near distance.

Vehicles at the side of the building, as many as ten, twelve. People are here, somewhere in the compound of buildings, meditating, chanting, is it *mantras*?—and Marcus among them, surely.

Lorene has expected to see monks in robes, nuns. With shaved heads. Is the Buddhist woman a *nun*?

If so, an American nun. A secular sort of nun. Celibate, sexless as a root vegetable.

On the soiled white walls are poster-sized paintings of mandalas, that might have been finger-painted by children. Larger photographs of what appears to be a Buddhist temple with a large squat placidly smiling Buddha positioned at the top of moss-covered stone steps.

"Is that a sacred temple—China? Tibet?" Lorene asks the Buddhist woman, as if there is no strain between them, no unresolved issue; it has always been Lorene's strategy to deploy her earnestness as a shield. Words tumble out, Lorene so wants to be liked.

"Tibet. Jokhang Temple."

Lorene inclines her head. *Jokhang Temple.*

No idea where this might be. She will ask Marcus when she sees him. If she can remember—*Jokhang Temple.*

"You know—I could volunteer here. Marcus has said, volunteers are welcome at Buddhist centers. I could help clean these walls, I'm good at repainting. The bushes outside, I could trim with shears."

Feeling a sudden urgency to volunteer, offering services. Offering *herself.*

I will join you here, I will help you. I will stay with Marcus, here.

You will see, I am one of you in my heart.

The Buddhist woman smiles awkwardly as if unsure how to reply. Lorene perseveres, suggesting, as if she's just now thought of it, that she could look for Marcus herself, call his name outdoors, at the rear of the building, but the woman cuts her off gently—"No, I am sorry."

Lorene wipes tears from her eyes. She has come too far to be turned back now.

Asking, trying not to plead, is there someone else to whom she might speak? A director here?—supervisor? A *monk*?

Looking relieved the Buddhist woman hurries away and shortly then a younger man appears, shaved head, ascetic-looking, yet with unnervingly blue eyes. This is—is it *Colson*? *Conrad*?—the *interim director* of the center who greets Lorene with the merest glimmer of a smile, and it is a wary smile, a smile like a creature peeking out of a burrow with no intention of pushing farther out of the burrow, and asks what he can do for her.

Colson, or Conrad, is wearing loose-fitting clothing, woolen socks with sandals. His young-old face is glazed like crockery. He has the ascetic's look of detachment, irony. When Lorene undertakes to explain why she is here, how her husband Marcus called her, asked her to bring him home, he shakes his shaved head politely, yet curtly, so sorry, he is unable to give out information of this sort unless he has permission to do so, and he doesn't have permission, and so—"I'm afraid I can't help you, Mrs. Coyne."

"You know my husband's name—'Coyne'?"

"I was told the name. Just now."

Of course, he knows. They all know Marcus.

There is something steely, even disdainful in the blue-eyed Buddhist, who regards Lorene with an icy sort of compassion.

Yet, like one who has no choice but to follow a prepared script Lorene says that she is sure that Marcus is here—somewhere.

"His *dharma name* is . . ."

Lorene attempts the name, the blue-eyed Buddhist listens politely but doesn't help her pronounce the unfamiliar words.

". . . he has a mentor here. Your abbot . . ."

Abbot. Lorene isn't sure if that is the correct term, isn't an *abbot* a Christian?

Colson, or Conrad, is not encouraging yet still Lorene persists, no choice but to blunder forward, like the driver of an unwieldy vehicle who has no space to turn around, trying to smile, to smile disarmingly, as an attractive young woman might smile haphazardly at a man, any man, no idea what she is saying but she cannot give up so easily, "I—I know—I mean, I can realize—it's painful for a person like Marcus to live in the secular world. He's very spiritual. That's why he came here, for *refuge.* He might have been in the mountains first—in New Jersey—and then came here. But I think that something must have happened, something went wrong—here . . ." Lorene's voice trails off. The director of the center is failing to provide for her even minimal social cues of the kind sympathetic persons provide for others, a fleet nod of the head, a semblance of a smile, as one might encourage, at least out of pity, an individual stumbling, trying to walk. How like the serene indifference of the sandstone Buddha, the shaved-head man's stony composure!

"I realize—of course—you have to protect the privacy of people who come here. But Marcus called me, last night after midnight. He sounded agitated. He said he was trapped, there were bars on the windows, he was being starved . . ."

These words tumble out, Lorene has gone too far. She sees, she has strained the patience of the blue-eyed Buddhist whose composure has finally cracked. He is frowning now, severely.

"No. That's enough. No one is confined here, no one is 'starved.' Your husband is not here, Mrs. Coyne. You should look for him elsewhere."

"But—*was* he here? Did something happen to him?"

Now the director's face is shut up too, tight as a fist.

"What have you done with my husband? *Where is he?*"

Grimly the director opens the door, indicating that Lorene should leave. In another moment she will be screaming.

The Buddhists will have to expel her bodily, Lorene thinks. Nothing would enrage Marcus more than his wife *causing a scene* in this sacred place.

"I—I am leaving. I will leave."

In the courtyard Lorene sees again the wheelbarrow, piles of debris, bushes in need of trimming. Even in her dazed state, in a flush of racing pulses, Lorene is thinking that she could offer to help with spring cleanup at the monastery, she is not eager to return home to the empty house, she is eager to be *of use,* but doesn't dare to offer, no longer, too late, she has ruined any future for herself at the Upper Black Eddy Buddhist monastery.

In silence the blue-eyed Buddhist escorts Lorene to the walkway at the front. He is unnervingly tall—at least six feet six. He is probably not so much older than Marcus. Beside him Lorene feels like a child, intimidated and yet grateful, the man has decided to be kind to her, in his impersonal way; he is shielding her from a harsh truth.

"Marcus was here—is that it? Something went wrong, he left? Had to leave?"

Lorene speaks hurriedly, breathlessly. This is her final chance.

"Please tell me: did you ask Marcus to leave?"

"There's no one here by that name, Mrs. Coyne."

"Yes, but—there *was*?"

With a shrugging gesture, an almost-imperceptible nod *yes,* the director turns away.

Lorene stares after him, stunned. So it is—*yes.*

For this parting kindness, Lorene is grateful. As a starving dog is grateful for the bone negligently tossed to it.

Yes, your husband was here. And yes, your husband was asked to leave.

So grateful! Lorene wipes tears from her eyes. Calling after the director as he walks swiftly away—"Thank you! Thank you so much. I—I love you . . ."

So meekly murmured, *I love you* is heard by no one.

It *is* a kindness, Lorene is truly grateful.

For now, she knows. Without exactly knowing what she knows.

Look for your husband elsewhere.

Your husband is not here.

Taking care to maneuver the Nissan compact out of the parking area. Not a time to collide with another vehicle! For surely this is a Buddhist principle—*attentiveness.*

Assuming that (probably) the Buddhists inside the center are observing her closely, waiting for her to leave.

At least, Lorene has been allowed to know: Marcus has

been here, and Marcus is not here now. But Marcus is alive, and he has been *here.*

Lorene should be relieved, Marcus hasn't moved in with Miriam, the potter, or with another woman. He has not perished in the Ramapo Mountains, his ravaged remains undiscovered until spring.

Forlorn hope like last year's leaves, swirling in the wind: Marcus will be home when she returns. Waiting for *her.*

Driving with care, caution out of the Buddhist compound, the gravel drive is narrow, rutted. It feels to Lorene as if she has been in this secluded place a long time, an unfathomably long time, shocking to see it has been less than a half-hour.

And again on Harbinger Road descending to the Delaware River.

Glittering ice droplets on the branches of trees overhead, dripping onto the hood, windshield, roof of the car like coarse tears.

Your punishment is, you will never see your husband again pierces Lorene's heart like an arrow even as she sees, approximately thirty feet ahead, by a curve in the road, a man's figure in a familiar windbreaker, a backpack at his feet—*Marcus?*

The man steps into the road, waving his arms at her. In his face—it *is* Marcus's unshaven face, gaunter than Lorene has ever seen it—an expression of exaltation, joy.

Lorene brakes the car. Marcus is at the car door, opening it, pulling Lorene out in a rough embrace.

"You *came.* You're *here.* My darling wife!"

Marcus is laughing, in delight. Marcus is kissing Lorene's face, quick wet kisses like the kisses of a frantic pup, hugging her hard, squeezing the breath out of her.

"God, I'd forgotten. You are *beautiful.*"

Marcus's rough unshaven face, against hers. For a moment Lorene is stunned, light-headed as if about to faint.

Jubilant Marcus tosses his backpack into the rear of the car, insists upon driving. He isn't tired, he is feeling fine. He is wearing hiking boots, he is feeling God-damned *restless.*

Takes Lorene's place behind the wheel *of course.*

How swiftly this has happened, Lorene's life restored to her, she hasn't had time to comprehend . . . In the passenger's seat beside her husband.

"Thank God. *You* are here. My wife."

Marcus speaks jubilantly, his face is flushed with excitement, gratification. He drives the Nissan much faster on curving Harbinger Road than Lorene would have dared.

He is speaking rapidly, in a tone of exaltation, then of indignation, vexation. Jesus what a fool he'd been!—allowing himself to be *misled, betrayed.*

Also he's hungry. Fucking *starving.*

Lorene is shocked, Marcus so rarely speaks vulgarly, profanely. Lorene is sure that she recalls Marcus describing profane/obscene speech as a symptom of weakness in both men and women.

Weakness, insecurity. A reversion to the juvenile. Too-explicit anger.

There's a place in Lumberville, that sells sandwiches, Marcus recalls. They can get something to eat there.

"Then, we're going to Black Rock Point. There's a trail there, hiking trail. Atop a hill there's a *vision.*"

Hiking trail. Vision. Lorene is trying to absorb what all this means.

Her life restored to her—in an instant. Seeing the *estranged husband* waiting for her at the side of the road as naturally as if the meeting were planned.

Life restored not as she'd imagined it would be restored but in a way totally unimagined, totally in Marcus's control.

And this reminder, which she has nearly forgotten: When you are married, your life is determined by another. He holds your heart in his hand, a raw beating heart entrusted to the fingers of another.

As if Marcus can read Lorene's thoughts he gropes for her hand, which he squeezes hard, in reassurance. Gropes for her knee, squeezing harder. Not taking his eyes off the road, to Lorene's relief. Telling her he loves her, she has saved his life, she has not let him down as others have, fucking others he'd *trusted like a fool.*

"My wife. *My* wife. 'Love of my life.'"

Lorene has rarely seen Marcus in such a heightened state. Usually he is impassive, rueful, detached as the Buddha.

And he has become so thin! Even his wrists, knobby-white inside the frayed cuffs of the nylon jacket.

Lean, lithe as a greyhound Marcus has always been but now his cheekbones are sharply defined against his tight skin. His forehead is oddly creased, in vertical striations like small cuts. His beard has grown out unevenly, threaded with mica-gray. His shoulder-length hair which he'd sometimes worn in a ponytail is gone, shockingly—quill-like hairs sprout from his shaved head, darker and thinner than the beard; he looks like a man newly released from prison, staring and blinking in the sun. Above his left eye is a scabby half-moon that looks fresh, not yet hardened into a scar.

Has Marcus been in a fight? Not with Buddhists, surely?

Lorene sees, Marcus's knuckles too look scraped. *He has been in some sort of physical struggle!*

Lorene tries to recall if Colson, or Conrad, the director of the center, had had scraped knuckles too.

"One thing feels damned good," Marcus says, grimly, "—being *off the grid.*"

Lorene wonders if, for Marcus, marriage is a part of the *grid.*

Lorene has been waiting for Marcus to apologize for having

been away so long. For having been out of contact with her. Even as she realizes that Marcus has no thought of her, as an individual apart from himself. And, he has been *off the grid: in refuge.*

Thirty-eight days, a lifetime. Yet, to Marcus apparently of little consequence.

His eyes appear to be faintly yellow, as if with jaundice. There are visible veins, broken capillaries, in his nose. Even at the wheel of the car he is restless, breathing through his mouth. A smell as of something damply earthy exudes from the nylon jacket, which has become soiled. Has Marcus been outside all night, expelled from the Buddhist center, sleeping on the ground? That smell of soft-rotted leaves, late winter chill, bodily chagrin.

Hesitantly Lorene asks if Marcus is *all right?*

(For Marcus certainly does not seem *all right* to her.)

Marcus laughs airily, of course he is *all right.*

Lorene tells Marcus that she'd been very worried about him. Frantic, at times. Unable to eat, sleep, concentrate. And with no one in whom to confide. For thirty-eight days she'd had no idea where he was . . .

Quietly and evenly Lorene speaks for these are words she has rehearsed. She is not accusing the *estranged husband,* nor is she reproaching him; this is a mere statement of fact. For he has returned to her, after all. As if nothing is wrong between them.

And if nothing seems to be wrong between them, perhaps it was all just a misunderstanding on Lorene's part . . .

Marcus was never *estranged* from her, that has been Lorene's interpretation. From Marcus's perspective he'd simply left his familiar life to go on a spiritual retreat, to seek *refuge* in a Buddhist monastery.

"'Thirty-eight days'"—Marcus utters these words as a

scientist might hold a peculiar species of animal at a distance from him with an instrument, merely observing, not assessing or passing judgment.

"I—I think it was, yes," Lorene says, weakly.

"Well, I doubt it. 'Thirty-eight'—have you been *counting*?"

Marcus laughs, how ridiculous Lorene is. Or maybe it's the situation that is ridiculous.

"Darling, time is an illusion. A delusion. A wife of mine should know better than to throw statistics at me, statistics have no inherent meaning."

Lorene protests, she'd been worried about him. Not knowing if he was alive or—whether she would ever see him again.

Marcus laughs, he is losing patience with this exchange.

Turning onto River Road, which is just slightly wider than Harbinger Road, pressing down hard on the gas pedal. Gusts of wind from the river rock the compact car.

"If it had happened that way, that we'd never have seen each other again, then—*that would have happened.* It's the roll of the dice, all that *is.*"

Marcus's tone is more sympathetic now. But matter-of-fact, bemused.

"If I were dead you'd know it, Lorene. You would have been contacted. Fact is, I was never far away. My trip to the East won't be for a while. When one 'disappears' from one place it's to 'appear' in another. I did try to call you, you were never home."

Flat-out, Marcus is lying. Lorene knows. Presenting this unlikelihood as if challenging her to disbelieve him, or to believe: it's all the same to him.

Lorene would like to protest but cannot find the words. It is always the case, in Marcus's presence, that Marcus lays claim to all the words.

And isn't it wisest to be grateful, the *estranged husband* is returned? The left-behind wife has not been publicly humiliated, shamed. She is not an object of pity. No one at the Blue Bird Day-Care has even suspected that Lorene's husband was gone for—has it been *five weeks*?

Marcus tells Lorene that he is bursting with energy, feels like a balloon that has been *released.* The last forty-eight hours of his life have been quite a kick in the gut but—*transformative.* Like Saul on the road to Damascus, struck by lightning into *Paul.*

And now, reunited with his dear wife, hoping to re-consecrate their marriage—he is *very very happy.*

Lorene has no idea what this means—*re-consecrate their marriage?* The thought is uplifting, promising. Renewing vows? Remarriage, in a religious ceremony?

(Possibly, in a Buddhist ceremony? Seven years before, they were married in a perfunctory civil ceremony by a municipal official to which no one from either of their families had been invited.)

Marcus recounts how in the Ramapo Mountains he'd gone backpacking to clear his head of spiritual toxins—*materialist, techne.* How long, he'd lost track.

Then, like a pilgrim he'd gone—on foot, crossing the river at Lumberville, over the bridge at Bulls Island—to the monastery at Upper Black Eddy where in the past he'd been made to feel welcome; but the elderly abbot who'd been his teacher wasn't so welcoming this time. None of the staff seemed to be welcoming this time. Something was wrong, he'd never discovered what was wrong. In a dream he'd been summoned to the monastery by the Buddha himself, the Buddha in disguise as an ordinary man—which is why you dare not turn any stranger away, for that person might be the Buddha.

Must've hiked forty miles over several days. In his face they could see the raw yearning but—the very persons who could have saved him, failed him.

Marcus is speaking bluntly, flatly. His ebullient air has

faded. In sympathy Lorene reaches out to touch his bony wrist. It is the first time that Lorene has touched any person in such a way, to give solace, in so long, she is unprepared for the emotion that rushes through her leaving her faint.

"But now you'll be home again, Marcus. Home can be your 'refuge.'"

Marcus laughs sharply, baring damp teeth that look larger, more uneven than Lorene recalls.

In Lumberville they stop at a small store where Marcus is forced to purchase cellophane-wrapped sandwiches for himself and Lorene. He sits in the Nissan, in the driver's seat, eating hungrily: processed turkey, processed cheese, doughy white-bread roll thick as a man's fist. He is ravenously hungry, Lorene observes. It is rare for Marcus to eat meat, especially meat as synthetic as turkey roll, he is indifferent now, in the throes of raw hunger.

Marcus interrogates Lorene at length about the Buddhist center. Who spoke to her, what did they say about him, what lies, what subterfuge even as Lorene insists that no one had said anything critical about him at all. They hadn't even acknowledged that "Marcus Coyne" had been in residence there until just as Lorene was leaving when the director indicated to her—"not in words but with a nod of his head, an expression in his face"—that Marcus had been there, but wasn't there any longer.

Marcus scoffs, disbelieving. He has more questions for Lorene, who denies that the Buddhists had said anything negative about him, anything critical, it was just at the very last minute that the director had seemed to feel sorry for her . . .

"The director? 'Colson'—that liar? What did *he* say?"—Marcus is losing patience.

"He said, 'You should look for your husband elsewhere.'"

Marcus sucks at his lips, considering this. How like a Zen koan this remark sounds, repeated now.

Marcus tells Lorene that his mistake was seeking *refuge* in a place where *refuge* is no longer possible. A time-honored Buddhist custom, taking in a suffering soul, mired in despair, saving a life. But the Buddhists at Upper Black Eddy have sold out, allied themselves with rich benefactors. Accepting large sums of money, properties—like the property at Upper Black Eddy—thirty acres, millions of dollars of Bucks County real estate—is corrosive to the soul. No spiritual person can accept material goods without being debased, contaminated. The Awakened One teaches: You must unburden yourself of possessions. Attachments.

But it was *his* mistake, Marcus acknowledges. *He* had been the one to prostrate himself before them, like a fool.

It's true he'd come to the monastery without being invited, without contacting anyone on the staff first, but he *was* desperate, the abbot who'd been his mentor in the past didn't seem to have time for him, he'd been given something like an (unheated) storage room in which to stay, just a futon on the floor, not clean. He'd been assigned the worst of kitchen duties, cleanup. And there was a woman—allegedly a *nun,* an *initiate*—the claim was that she'd spent several years in a monastery in Thailand but the flat nasal vowels of the woman's speech betrayed her as a native New Jerseyan, what a fraud, what an imposter, her *dharma name* was something like "Myō"—"Meimei"—Marcus had seen through her in an instant, she possessed no spiritual depths, you could see in her flat glassy eyes. She'd recognized Marcus as a rival for the attention of the abbot.

Determined then to sabotage Marcus, destroy his concentration. The anguish of his desire for *awakening.*

Intruding upon his privacy, his vow of celibacy, putting

herself in his way but when he'd responded to her as she had clearly invited him to respond she changed her mind, accused *him*, and the others chose to believe her, and not Marcus.

Trying to explain but they'd misinterpreted his words. Distorted his words and transformed them into something ugly, obscene.

Threatened to call the Bucks County police.

Or—(Lorene isn't sure what Marcus is saying, he is speaking rapidly and angrily)—*Called the Bucks County police . . .*

Lorene listens in astonishment. Had Marcus harassed a woman? Not the middle-aged woman who'd spoken with Lorene, surely—but a younger woman? A *nun*?

Marcus has finished his sandwich, doughy white roll and all, and licked mustard from his fingers. He is still hungry so Lorene passes him her sandwich, which she has hardly touched. Spittle has gathered at the corners of Marcus's fine-chiseled lips. Lorene is reminded of Little Bear lowering his head to his bowl to eat, turning his head to one side in a gesture both brute and delicate as his eyes softened in the sensuous pleasure of eating.

Little Bear! Lorene knows she will wait in vain for Marcus to speak of the little lost dog.

Marcus sends Lorene back into the store to purchase two cans of (refrigerated) beer and two bottles of Evian water. It is dismaying to Lorene to see Marcus drinking, especially during the day; occasionally he might have a glass of wine with a meal, no more. Dismaying too that Marcus has requested Evian water for this means that Marcus is serious about a hike on the way home.

Quickly Marcus drinks one of the cans of beer. The other he grips in his left hand as he resumes driving south on River Road close beside the glittering river, at a speed twenty miles above the limit.

Should he be driving so fast?—Lorene asks, quietly.

And should he be drinking, so openly? What if . . .

Marcus laughs, shrugs. Clearly Lorene's concern for Bucks County law enforcement is of little significance to him.

" 'Falling into the Pit of the Void'—that is the subject."

A translation from Sanskrit, Marcus explains. The phenomenon of meditating too long, too intensely. *Burn-out.*

He had meditated too much. He'd fallen into "the Pit of the Void."

He'd come relatively late to Buddhism, lost in the material world, stumbling and staggering in the mud and mire all around him, medical school, computer technology, a season of video games, drugs, numbing the brain, he'd come to Buddhism in his late twenties, almost too late. So you always feel hurried, desperate to catch up. Such hunger, to scour the soul. Like scouring a filthy toilet with a brush. Sitting in meditation for hours each day until his legs went numb, barely he could get to his feet. His vertebrae were out of line. His brain was drunk with too much oxygen. He'd become a vessel that overflows with abundance. Chokes on its own virtue like you'd choke on your own vomit.

Marcus confides in Lorene, as if he has returned from the dead to enlighten her.

"In *the Pit of the Void* you can be so happy you forget to breathe. Start to lose your animal nature. Meditation is a matter of the lungs. Control of the lungs. Control of the heartbeat. But once you take control you can lose control. You can lose the old, mechanical way of breathing, thinking. When the Buddha enters you, you have no literal need any longer to sleep, eat. No need for other people. Because you cease to exist like a small stream emptying into a river. *You are all other people, in one.*"

Lorene listens in both wonder and dread. Thinking that, to be *all,* to be *one,* is to be *no one, nothing.*

As Marcus is both Lorene's husband, whom she loves with

a love that leaves her breathless, and another person, gaunt-cheeked, flush-faced, unshaven, with bright bloodshot eyes, whom she scarcely knows.

In boxes still unpacked after years, in the rented house on Stony Brook Road, Lorene has discovered manila folders containing old papers, documents, receipts belonging to Marcus, even yellowed clippings from a Montclair, New Jersey, newspaper—*Marvin Howard Coyne has been named valedictorian of Montclair High School Class of 2006.* Transcripts of (uniformly high) grades in high school and college, belonging to *Marvin Howard Coyne.*

Marcus must have renamed himself, Lorene supposed. Not officially, not legally but informally, identifying himself to people he met as not Marvin but *Marcus.* When letters came addressed to *Marvin Coyne* she'd assumed that these were just simple errors, typos.

Never has Lorene mentioned this discovery to Marcus. Never will she.

Saying, as if she has only just now thought of it, that Little Bear did turn up about twelve days ago—"In a rescue shelter in Montgomery. So far away—I can't imagine how he got there . . ."

Beside her at the wheel of the car Marcus is stunned into silence by this seemingly casual pronouncement. Lorene does not look at Marcus.

With Marcus away, so much time alone, she'd continued to search for the lost dog, made calls, written emails, sent photos, finally there was a match in the shelter in Montgomery on the very day that someone was going to adopt him. There must have been a slip-up with the microchip, Lorene had never been notified.

"I burst into tears when I saw Little Bear in his cage. He looked older, rougher. He wasn't a puppy any longer. I didn't let him see me, I didn't want to interfere with his new life. Is that what is meant by *karma*—what is deserved? He'd left us, maybe he'd sensed that something was wrong between us but now there were new people in his life, who can love him. That felt right to me."

Lorene's voice quavers. None of this is true and yet, Lorene is shaken by the vision of the little lost dog in a cage in a rescue shelter.

Marcus has stiffened, intent upon his driving. His expression is tight, taut; his jaw appears clenched. He seems to have no idea how to respond to what Lorene has told him, trying not to react in surprise, shock, chagrin, guilt even as the Buddha would not react to such a revelation but would remain impassive, obdurate as a sandstone statue.

Finally Marcus says, "So—it turned out well. Little Bear escaped—he didn't want confinement with us. He'd learned not to trust us—even you. Remember, you'd stayed away late that day, when he went missing . . ."

Lorene does not reply. Her heart is beating hard with the enormity of what she has said, like one in a card game who has risked everything on the turn of a card.

"Not all the time in the world remains."

At the trailhead at Black Rock Point there are a two-mile hike, a four-mile hike, and a seven-mile hike. Of these, Marcus insists upon the four-mile hike to a watchtower on a high hill.

Lorene tells Marcus that she doesn't think she can hike that far—it would be eight miles, in all. The trails are strewn with winter debris, there are fallen limbs everywhere. She hasn't slept well lately, she is feeling exhausted . . . Also, she is wearing sneakers, not hiking boots of the kind Marcus is wearing.

Marcus insists, frowning: This day is a special occasion. *This* day.

He has been on a lengthy journey, he says. A pilgrimage.

A husband would have the right to expect that his wife would respect this journey. And now, his return. It is time for a *re-consecration* of their marriage.

After sitting in meditation for hours each day in that unheated place, his muscles were knotted, gnarled but now—strengthened. Like his determination to be detached finally from earthly snares.

"We need to share this vision. We *will* share this vision."

A tawny light has come up in Marcus's eyes, as in a cat's eyes, glistening in half-light.

"I—I don't think . . ."

"*Don't* think. Just act."

Marcus hands Lorene one of the Evian bottles to bring with her on the trail. It is crucial, Marcus says, to always hike with a bottle of water. Dehydration can strike suddenly, fatally.

Saying again, with emphasis—"Not all the time in the world remains."

Nervously Lorene glances about. No other hikers in sight, no vehicles parked at the trailhead. The trails have not been cleared for months. The sky is shrouded in thin tattered clouds like strands of cobweb. The sun has disappeared, there is a sudden draining of color, a sudden chill, as in an eclipse.

No idea what Marcus means: *Not all the time in the world remains.*

Trying to recall, not so long ago, Lorene would have been thrilled if Marcus invited her to hike with him, in one of his special places. Hiking to an elevated place, promising *a view, a vision in all directions.*

"Let's get started! You go first."

At the trailhead, a crude stone marker, Marcus pushes Lorene before him.

Insisting that Lorene hike in the lead so that he can watch over her—if she has an accident, turns an ankle. If she hikes behind him she will hike too slowly to keep pace with him, lose sight of him, might wander off the trail, become lost.

Saying, in the tone of a father warning a child, with just a hint of humor—*Yes, there are black bears in rural Bucks County.* All the more reason for Marcus to hike in the rear, to oversee.

Lorene sets out, Marcus follows close behind. Lorene's thin-soled sneakers are already wet.

It is as Lorene has feared, the four-mile trail to the watchtower is cluttered with storm debris. Hikers must make their way slowly, carefully. Bramble bushes, wild rose, sharp thorns that catch in Lorene's clothing, scratch her bare hands; branches that whip back, stinging. There are stretches of the trail that are fairly open, one can walk at a fast pace, but stretches that are soaked with rain, muddy, rocky. Marcus nudges Lorene to *look down, watch out for flat rocks*—never step on a wet rock, you can slip, fall.

The trail is so steep suddenly, Marcus finds broken tree limbs for Lorene and himself, to use as walking sticks. Marcus *insists.*

Lorene is determined not to disappoint Marcus. This hike is a sort of test, perhaps.

A test she'd failed as a young wife, when Marcus had ceased inviting her to accompany him on hikes into the Ramapo Mountains.

Thinking—*Play out this scene. You can!*

Then, the return home. Of which she has been dreaming for the past five weeks.

Resuming that life. The life she'd been in terror she had lost.

She will prepare an early supper, Marcus's favorite food. A loaf of Marcus's favorite multigrain bread she can possibly pick up at a bakery in Lambertville, on the way home.

Marcus will be exhausted, fall into bed early. And Lorene beside him.

Except now, at midday, Marcus is energized, exuberant. As they hike up the increasingly hilly trail, addressing Lorene in his low, hypnotic voice.

". . . merely personal life, lives like ours, we have to know are not worth living. The strife. Banal comfortable life—*strife.* Meeting 'the love of your life'—mating with that individual—reproducing your DNA—(though it's absurd to claim ownership: *your* DNA)—succumbing to time—dying. Salmon swimming upstream, the most beautiful of fish, literally wearing themselves out, dying in the effort, symbols of something noble—but nothing could be farther from the truth. Ask the salmon if they would rather live another season. No creature cares about reproducing the species. Spinoza said—*All that lives yearns to persist in its being.* Substituting the life of the individual being for the life of the species is obscene. The Awakened One would insist: *strive for being, and beyond.*"

The sky has grown fainter, light and color are draining away from the trail. Lorene recalls an eclipse when she was a girl, a class of (frightened, giggling) seventh graders herded outside the school building, instructed to peer at the sun through "smoked" lenses . . . A sudden sliver of light had seemed to penetrate her vision, Lorene had dropped the glass with a little cry, hidden her face.

But had it been *too late*? For weeks afterward she'd been terrified that she would go blind.

". . . remember Schopenhauer? I'd read to you, when we were first together? The world is 'will and idea.' But the 'idea' is greater than the 'will' which is brute unreflective existence, mere sex-desire. In the throes of sex-desire we might as well be sea slugs, cockroaches."

Lorene winces, it is like Marcus to say such blunt things.

But there is a perspective, Lorene supposes, from which Marcus, like Schopenhauer, is not wrong.

Lorene has never been able to resist Marcus's *certainty.* Never has Lorene been close to, intimate with, or even acquainted with anyone so suffused with life, purpose as Marcus. Everyone else whom she has known—family, relatives, classmates, friends—has seemed adrift, oblivious; unreflective; acted upon rather than acting, making few conscious choices. Marcus Coyne is one of the map-makers, others have not even maps to guide their way.

When they'd first met Marcus had predicted that the love of God would one day pierce Lorene's heart, she would not survive as herself.

When Marcus had seemed to believe in God. Or what he'd meant by God.

In those days Marcus's lovemaking had been gentle. He'd seemed to encourage Lorene to make the first move, to touch *him.* As if he were holding back his strength, in proportion to Lorene's weakness.

Nights when Marcus drifted into sleep, his back to her as Lorene lay against him, the side of her face pressed against his back, which had seemed, not heated, but cool; and Marcus would take Lorene's hand, and clasp it against his chest, and Lorene too would gradually fall asleep in utter bliss, secure, protected.

Later in the marriage Marcus began to linger in his study past midnight. Dazed with exhaustion Lorene usually went to bed by eleven P.M., couldn't keep her eyes open. Trying not to think that, for no reason she could comprehend, her husband was intent upon outwaiting her: she would be asleep by the time he came to bed.

Trying not to think—*Does Marcus no longer love me?*

On the trail, a few feet behind Lorene, Marcus is speaking

animatedly, expansively, recollecting his years in medical school, before he'd met Lorene, about which he's spoken to her only in patches, always in a tone of self-reproach, irony.

His term as an intern at New York-Presbyterian—a coveted position. He'd been wanting to be a surgeon and was at the time assisting a much-respected surgeon whose specialty was gynecological oncology, the surgery was an emergency hysterectomy, removal of uterus, cervix, ovaries but there was only a body, an anesthetized female body, horrific to see, the *unconsciousness of the body,* no longer a person, an individual, a sentient being, one moment twenty-five-year-old Marcus had been fully conscious, masked and gowned, keenly awake, alert, focused upon the surgeon's glittering instrument, incisions in the abdomen spurting bright blood, nothing that should have been surprising in the slightest but the next moment Marcus was on the floor, he'd lost all sense of himself and fallen, like a dead weight fallen, an astonishment to the others, an irritant to the surgeon, he'd had to be carried out of the room, revived by nurses but of course in those swift minutes his life was changed, the trajectory of his life was changed, a railway car derailed, fallen into a chasm, the punchline to a crude joke, no going back.

Cleared out his locker, walked out of the hospital, never returned, never looked back.

Saying now, the only *sure path* is to disappear. Leave no craven note behind, no apology or explanation.

Saying now, to Lorene's back, the more sure it is, the path is to erase yourself. The *self.*

"Erase all memory when you erase yourself. Not just shameful memories but all memories. Tying you to the world. The purpose of disappearing is not to leave confusion in your wake, for others to clean up; the purpose is to take yourself into an entirely new place."

On one side of the trail suddenly is private land—*No Trespassing No Hunting* signs are posted.

Marcus is infuriated to discover these, tears them off tree trunks.

"No land is fucking *private.* All land is *public.*"

In an instant, Marcus is in a rage. The ruminative hypnotic voice has vanished, Marcus is speaking vehemently, disgustedly now.

And suddenly too, Lorene is weak-kneed. Has to sit, half-falling onto the remains of a rotted log. A pulse of pain has been throbbing behind her eyes that she has tried to ignore. Her sneakers are soaked through. To add to the discord, close overhead are scolding birds, angrily flapping dark-feathered wings.

"Lorene, what the *hell*? Why are you *sitting down*?"

Lorene tries to explain, she is very tired. Her legs are tired, her head aches. She'd tried to explain to Marcus, before they'd started out . . .

Marcus is furious, what is wrong with her *now*? They have hardly hiked a mile, not two miles, why is she so *weak*?

Doesn't Lorene understand, this is a special day? Today they will *re-consecrate* their marriage, that is the plan.

Marcus speaks so harshly, Lorene shrinks from him. This is a mistake: lifting her hands to shield her face in a childish gesture that is maddening to him.

Shrink from an angry man, you will make the man angrier.

Invite retaliation, punishment. The female draws harm to herself, for which the man will be blamed.

Marcus pulls at Lorene, tugging at her wrists. Up! Up on her fucking feet!

Time is running out for her, for him. Shifting, sifting sand. He'd known, no doubt about it, when she'd lied to him, brazenly lied to him about the God-damned dog.

The dog! *The dog!*

That had decided it. No going back.

Marcus stoops over Lorene, pulling her up by her wrists into an awkward half-crouch, pressing his (grim-smiling) mouth to hers, hard; his teeth strike hers; Lorene will not open her mouth to his prodding tongue, she is paralyzed with fear.

Marcus laughs at her, the expression in her face. But it is infuriating to him, not funny at all.

"What are you afraid of! Afraid of *me*—your husband?"

Lorene sees no love for her, in Marcus's eyes that are threaded with broken capillaries. No recognition of *her.*

Trying to push him away but Marcus is too strong for her, wicked-strong despite his thinness. The strength, Lorene thinks, of a sinewy-muscled snake, strength coursing through its entire body.

"Afraid to fucking *die.*"

Roughly Marcus shakes Lorene by the shoulders, pushes her onto the wet ground. He curses her, tears at her clothing as she resists him like a panicked child, blindly flailing, kicking.

No time to think—*This can't be happening, what is this that is happening to me!*

Marcus's fist strikes Lorene on the side of her head—a stunning blow. A second blow to her eye, another to her nose, that leaks blood. Grunting, Marcus stoops over Lorene and closes his hands around her neck low, at the collarbones, squeezing.

Lorene is writhing, clawing at his hands, choking on her own blood. She is terrified of Marcus, of being strangled.

Marcus shouts into her face: If she would just *stop struggling.* If she would just *cease resisting.*

They will die together, Marcus promises. Lorene will not die alone.

Lorene continues to resist, struggling for her life. A black mist has passed over her brain, still she is fighting, clawing at Marcus's hands. Marcus turns her over, pushes her face into the ground, his knee at the small of her back. At least, he has released his hands from her neck, Lorene is able to breathe in panicked gasps.

Marcus is tugging at the red fleece jacket, yanks up the quilted black skirt with which Lorene had hoped to impress the Buddhists as well as the *estranged husband,* is Marcus going to rape her? In a way to injure her, punish her? Humiliate her? Leaning heavily onto Lorene, using his weight to his advantage, knee at the base of her spine. Again closing his hands around her neck, harder. Furious, cursing—*What you deserve for betraying your husband.*

Somehow, Lorene will never comprehend how, she manages, by sheer desperation, to squirm loose from Marcus's grip. Wildly she strikes at him, his head, his face. Kicks, claws at him. It is sheer animal instinct, she is unable to think. Her fingers grope about for something to close upon, anything, anything of substance, the broken tree limb she'd been using as a walking stick, with this she strikes at Marcus's head and shoulders until the limb shatters in her hand.

Rotted through, crawling with tiny black ants. But hard enough to stun Marcus, to send him onto his knees.

Panting now, able to breathe just enough to keep from fainting, breath thin as if sucked through a broken straw yet Lorene is able to remain on her feet, weakness passes in and out of her leg muscles yet she remains on her feet, if she falls her assailant will murder her, no choice but to summon all the strength of which she is capable *to remain on her feet, not to fall,* seizing a rock from the ground, small enough to fit into her hand but sharp-edged, large enough to do damage to the assailant's scalp, face. At once the sickle-moon scab above the assailant's eye begins to bleed.

The assailant has no name, he has become a dream-figure, a nightmare, *the other, the other who means to take her life,* no longer her husband, no longer anyone she knows—*the other, who means to take her life if she does not prevent it.*

Wherever the rock can strike, quickened with its own furious life. And so, Lorene stumbles free. Her assailant has fallen to his knees, fallen to the ground, shielding his head with his hands. Finally she releases the rock slick with blood, lets it fall.

Running limping along the trail like a wounded animal. Knowing to breathe shallowly for her ribs throb with pain, each breath is an inhalation of flame. Making her way back downhill, falling and heaving herself to her feet. Her nose is dripping blood.

Running for her life. *Her* life.

Time has passed, it is later in the day, the sky has darkened with thunder clouds, an icy rain has begun.

Thinking, there is a place to which she can go, seek refuge, vaguely she recalls—the Buddhist monastery at Upper Black Eddy . . .

In confusion thinking that the monastery is close by then realizing that Upper Black Eddy is miles away. Lorene can never get there on foot, she would collapse before she reached Harbinger Road.

Exhausted, skidding downhill on her heels. Wet grass, slippery rocks, rain pelting her face, icy-cold but bracing, keeping her awake, alert.

Faintly the man is calling after her—*Lorene! Don't leave me.*

Yet more faintly—*I love you . . .*

Where is Lorene?—through skeins of rain, she can see the Delaware River, on the farther side of River Road.

That look of molten lava, too thick to run swiftly—you'd think. Raindrops like bullets on the rough surface of the water, like life quickening beneath the surface . . .

At the trailhead, at last. At River Road. Behind her the voice has faded, there is only a sound of pelting rain, wind in the trees. A rapid panting like a dog's, that is Lorene's own breath as she has never heard it before.

The concrete marker at the trailhead, darkened with rain. The compact Nissan, to which Lorene doesn't have the key.

On River Road she will wave her arms when a vehicle approaches. For soon, within minutes, a vehicle is sure to approach.

She will not shrink back on the shoulder of the road, she will stand defiantly in the road. Bleeding from a head wound, from her nose. Front of the fleece jacket darkened with blood. Wet hair matted against her skull, clothing torn. Headlights in the murky wintry light will fall upon her, a vehicle will brake to a stop, a motorist will lower her window, call out alarmed—*Hello? Are you hurt? D'you need help? Were you in an accident? D'you need me to drive you to a garage?*

Jesus, your face!

Get in, for God's sake!—it's freezing.

NIGHT FISHING AT ANTIBES

The two women, seen often together, sometimes even mistaken for each other, had both become widows within the year, and neither had adjusted well. Their friendship, initially social, casual, had become crucial to each of them. Meghan called Zahira, or Zahira called Meghan, at least once a day, often twice. If they were not seeing each other that day, they might speak on the phone three times. If there was a crisis—well, if there was a crisis, Meghan would probably be at Zahira's house within minutes.

With exasperated affection Zahira joked—*Meghan can get here faster than any ambulance.*

It was so, if Meghan tried to contact Zahira by phone, email, text and did not receive a reply within thirty minutes Meghan would hurry to her car and drive to Zahira's house in a state of anxiety. The women lived less than one mile apart in a residential neighborhood of custom-designed houses bordering the wooded grounds of the Institute for Advanced Study at Millstone yet Meghan always took her car for she anticipated the worst: having to drive Zahira to the ER on the farther side of Millstone.

(Meghan was prepared for this, for Meghan was prepared for disaster: she'd driven her husband to that very ER at the start of his swift-acting illness two years before and she'd expected to be her husband's caretaker in their home when he was discharged from the hospital but this had not happened because her husband had died without being discharged from the hospital and so Meghan had been cheated of the role of caretaker for which she'd believed she had been destined. And telling herself that she would not make that same mistake again. Rehearsing how she would explain to friends how she'd saved Zahira, brought her to the ER just in time—*I knew something was wrong, I had a premonition, Zahira didn't answer her phone, she didn't call back, thank God I drove to her house when I did.*)

(For there was the fear, voiced principally by Meghan Dunne, but shared, in varying degrees, by others in the Institute community, that Zahira Kruk, devastated by her husband's death, had become *clinically depressed, suicidal.*)

(So far, Zahira had not required Meghan's anxious scrutiny. But by degrees, Zahira was growing to depend upon it.)

When their husbands were alive the women saw each other only occasionally—always with others, at dinner parties or Institute functions, never had they spent time alone together. Zahira, who was far less social than Meghan Dunne, could not remember a conversation she'd had with Meghan of any substance, in that time *before;* barely could she remember Meghan Dunne, whom she'd never taken very seriously. (Very few wives of her husband's colleagues did Zahira take seriously.) Nor had their husbands been more than friendly colleagues at the Institute, in different departments; of the two,

Zahira's (molecular biologist) husband had had the more distinguished career, as a perennial candidate for a Nobel Prize, while Meghan's (social scientist) husband had acquired a reputation as a public intellectual, publishing articles in *The New Yorker* and *The New York Review of Books* on the role of ethics in a world rapidly changing through genetic engineering, artificial intelligence, and the Internet.

It was approximately six weeks after Zahira Kruk's husband Herman died that Zahira and Meghan began to be seen together walking in the early morning in the Institute Woods or on a three-mile hiking trail at Watershed. Less frequently, they were seen at Institute events—chamber music concerts, films, lectures; they shopped together at the organic food co-op, they volunteered at the Millstone Animal Rescue. For a while there was a rumor that one of the women, more likely Meghan, was going to sell her house and share the other's house with her; for both widows had inherited impracticably large houses overlooking the Institute grounds, expensive to maintain. There was a rumor—(in fact, it was not merely a rumor)—that the widows planned to travel together in the fall, to Italy; they hoped to rent a villa for the month of October on the Amalfi coast.

It soon became evident that if you invited Zahira to an event, you should invite Meghan as well, for Zahira was not likely to come without Meghan, as Meghan was less likely to come without Zahira. (Though Meghan would more likely come to an event without Zahira than Zahira without Meghan.)

Don't try to drive a wedge between us! Can't be done.

It was puzzling to both women, that they were being mistaken for each other not only by acquaintances who knew them only slightly but by longtime friends, neighbors. Zahira didn't know whether to be amused or offended for surely she was the more beautiful of the two, as well as several years younger than Meghan; Meghan was flattered to be mistaken for Zahira and quickly cleared up any confusion: "Oh no, I think you mean Zahira Kruk. That wasn't me, that wasn't anything I would be likely to say."

Or: "Definitely *no.* That's the Kruk house you're thinking of—Zahira's house—on Gödel Lane. Designed by Michael Graves. My house is just an old colonial on Plymouth Road."

Nervously deflecting attention away from herself. For now, in the aftermath of her husband's death, Meghan had become a *half-self,* a widow. It pained her to glance into a mirror without steeling herself for what she saw there: stark staring glassy eyes depthless as reflectors.

Like a tick it was, burrowed into her skin, minuscule, yet toxic: the awareness of the husband's death of which she was determined not to think.

Meghan had long admired Zahira Kruk, from a little distance: for Zahira was somewhat aloof, and could be cuttingly sarcastic; her dark brows, striking dark eyes, and glossy black hair suggested an exotic and aristocratic parentage, said to be Egyptian, or half-Egyptian. Zahira dressed in dark silk clothing, designer clothing, wore gold necklaces, bracelets, earrings; her shoes were elegant, high-heeled; on social occasions she was known to rebuff ritual courtesies of the kind practiced by Americans—cheery reiterations of *How are you? How was your summer? Do you have any trips planned?* In Zahira's presence these clichéd exchanges fell to the floor like hollow coins, clearly counterfeit.

Yet Zahira enjoyed confounding expectations by revealing, if probed about her background, that her birthplace wasn't exotic at all but Michigan (Ann Arbor) and her birth name had been "Sarah"—"Too many Sarahs at my school, had to change it."

(*Was* this true, about Zahira's name? Meghan doubted it.)

Meghan had to laugh at Zahira's odd remarks, that were

met with baffled silence at social gatherings; where everyone tried to please, Zahira did not try at all.

What pleasure, to not care if people dislike you!—Meghan, who since childhood had wanted only to be liked, *loved* by the entire world, was moved to envy.

Darkly glamorous as a Modigliani female, with that look of maddening abstraction, in public, at social gatherings, Zahira seemed detached, lost in thought; roused only if her husband was speaking, and then intensely interested, as if, whatever Herman said, it must have a particular meaning for *her.* A woman indifferent to most people but deeply in love with her husband and that was Zahira's weakness, Meghan thought: vulnerable as the fontanelle in a newborn's skull.

It was a matter of (secret) chagrin to Meghan that the Kruks had not once accepted an invitation to her house, nor had they invited Meghan and her husband to their house; but she would make up for this, she was sure, now that Zahira was a widow.

At a small private memorial for Herman Kruk at the Institute, a few days after his death, Meghan dared to approach Zahira Kruk as she would not have dared previously. Seeing how ashy-pale Zahira had become, how shaken, how *mute, abashed, broken,* Meghan came quietly to stand near her; and, when the opportunity presented itself, as a string quartet played a Schubert piece said to be Herman Kruk's favorite, Meghan took hold of Zahira's limp, icy hand, as if she were a relative unacknowledged until now. At first, it seemed that Zahira might shrink away from Meghan, in surprise and dislike, but she did not—the hand remained in Meghan's like a small creature captured.

Startling to Meghan, and exciting, so close to Zahira, to see that Zahira's usually clear beautiful dark eyes were threaded with broken capillaries, and to smell Zahira's unmistakably sweaty body inside swaths of dark-purple velvet falling to her ankles. On Zahira's feet, not her usual elegant shoes but well-worn ballerina flats she'd forgotten to change.

Leaning close to Zahira to murmur in her ear, *It's all right, you will be all right, one breath at a time.*

Only another widow, a woman, could understand.

On all sides, unfamiliar faces. People they'd known for years. But now unreal. None of this real. Nightmare. No more depth than paper cutouts.

In the dark a flashlight beam moved jerkily about a shadowy-grassy space not immediately identifiable as a *lawn.* Must have wandered here, off the roadway.

Too late! *Trespasser.*

The beam leapt blindingly onto the trespasser's face. With outspread fingers the trespasser shielded her eyes that were already aching, furtive.

A terrace door had slid stealthily open, an alarmed voice was calling, *Hello? Is someone there? What do you want?*—even as the trespasser spoke calmly, with an air of apology, explaining that she hadn't realized that this was private property, she was just looking for a lost cat, a long-haired gray cat, name of Minx, wearing a blue collar, missing since earlier that day from 19 Gödel Lane.

Finding herself, a nighttime insomniac-prowler, in a neighbor's grassy rear lawn, having lost track of her surroundings beneath a sullen half-moon.

There followed then: a flurry of words, mutual apologies, sympathy for the seeker of the lost cat, and concern for poor Minx (defined as a "shy indoor cat, not young" who never went outdoors and would find the outdoors terrifying, not to mention the Institute Woods, with its foxes, raccoons, and coyotes, dangerous if not lethal), an exchange of phone numbers, a promise to keep an eye out for Minx.

Good night!

Good night.

Turning away, briskly walking away. Half-running away.

Wiping tears from her eyes. So tired of *tears*!

For these brief minutes recalling, beyond the abyss of the death of the husband, the mystery of their beloved cat Minx who'd wandered off, they'd theorized, into the Institute Woods seven years before, no trace, not even a small cat-skeleton discovered in the woods after months of searching.

Telling herself—*It's all right, you will be all right.*

One breath at a time.

A sleepwalker by day and by night, a trespasser of dark places.

Interminable days during which Zahira passed in and out of oblivion like splotches of sunlight and shadow driven by wind along the ground.

It was like an abyss, a sudden deep sinkhole in the earth. Raw and gaping. On the farther side, her life *before*. On this side, her life *after*.

No bridge between. No walkway across which she could even crawl.

Since the death Zahira rarely slept at normal times and in normal places. She dreaded lying awake for hours—(it was hell to hear the first birdcalls, cardinals, signaling dawn)—and so avoided trying to sleep for as long as she could. Exhausted herself walking for miles each day in the Institute Woods and beyond. Her solace was a promise of night, sleep if she could fall into bed sufficiently exhausted. For there is a definable point at which physical exhaustion melts into the bliss of collapse, sleep. Whatever is meant by *sleep*. But she'd lost the knack, it seemed. She'd lost the beat. Possibly, it was related to *heartbeat.* She could no longer depend upon night, sleep. For there had been the panicked fear, for weeks, that if she slept, in that interim her husband would die, and indeed something like that had happened though she'd been in the hospital at the time, but not at the bedside, unforgivably. And so, she remained upright, vertical, for as long as she could each day. Sheer exhaustion held the key to collapse which is the most dependable kind of sleep. Losing, shunting aside, what is called *consciousness.*

He'd said, We don't really know what *consciousness* is. But we know when *consciousness* is absent.

It was a time of perpetual motion. Sitting, not-sitting, standing, walking, upstairs, downstairs, in a loop. The house was large, too large even for two people of whom one had amassed beyond thirty thousand books, still the walls were confining, the ceiling pressed low, a kind of forehead pressing low, if you did not keep your eyes open, alert.

Zahira has work to do, she is a translator. She has translated poetry into English from Arabic, French. At the time of Herman's hospitalization she'd brought work with her to the hospital, so much quiet time she'd envisioned, yet somehow there had been no quiet time, no time for reflection or concentration, and when in the interstices of medical emergencies she'd glanced at her work on her laptop it had seemed to her of no consequence, totally useless, worthless, why was she deceiving herself?—*none of this matters.*

Herman had used to ask her about her work, he'd taken time to read drafts of her translations, in the early years of their marriage he'd been particularly interested in Zahira's work but not recently, Zahira has to admit. *None of it.*

Yet certainly she *did not* take sleeping pills. She *would not* take sleeping pills. Understanding that the yearning to join the deceased husband was so strong, she must not take even the first step.

Yearning for oblivion, so powerful, as powerful as any physical desire, once she began to rely upon medication she would soon require a higher dosage; she would be dissatisfied with the thin gruel of medicated sleep lacking dreams; lacking the wracking depths of dreams; she would seek ever longer periods of sleep, a deep well, deep well of a pit opening into nothingness, into oblivion, Zahira dared not peer into it, she dared not lean over to see the pale wraith-face awaiting her below.

And so, in dark clothing, dark jacket with a hood to cover her head like a penitent, self-punisher, aching with tiredness and yet impatient with herself in thrall to such futility prowling by night in the residential neighborhood surrounding the Institute that, lacking sidewalks, lacking street lamps, with tall trees and dense funereal shrubbery, resembled a nocturnal countryside in a Nordic painting. Prowling, thinking—*He may be somewhere out here. He may be lost, too.*

An unreasonable statement by day but by night, reasonable.

All things are reasonable in darkness.

Words drifting through the widow's brain like neutrinos through (seemingly) solid matter.

Gusty emotions on wet roads on autumn nights.

Oh Life, begun in fluent Blood,

And consummated dull!

Stumbling in daylight as if it were darkness. Breaking off a call from a concerned neighbor, wife of one of her husband's colleagues. Suddenly very tired of another human voice. *His* voice is silenced, there is no other voice she wants to hear.

Moonlight bright as day but the landscape is drained of light. A sleepwalker must not be wakened but Zahira is not sure if she is awake or asleep.

Nighttime walking is like swimming in dark water, invisibly. A half-mile inside the woods is a narrow stream, a makeshift bridge over the stream, primitive in structure, wide enough for a single person at a time, with ropes to grip as you cross; you must pull yourself along these ropes for the bridge sways and lurches as if about to collapse and fall into the water below.

Zahira has crossed this little bridge many times by day. She knows to grip the ropes, for balance. Drunken sense of being released from gravity. Almost, there is a feeling of gaiety here, giddiness.

Not that Zahira is in danger of drowning in the shallow stream—she is not. Too sure-footed to lose her balance and probably the water is less than two feet deep. Nor are there rocks against which she might strike her head if she falls.

Cease upon the midnight with no pain.

Not often but sometimes they would walk together in the woods. Not often but sometimes Zahira's husband took time to spend with her that was unplanned, spontaneous. It would only be at Zahira's behest, Herman would never think of so frivolous an excursion himself. His life was his work, he had warned her before their marriage. Only a thin sliver of emotional life would have to satisfy a wife of Herman Kruk, this Zahira understood. Like a sickle moon in the night sky, narrow, yet radiant, mesmerizing.

Out of this sickle moon she'd expected a child at least.

Yet, it had not happened. Why, *why* had she had such an expectation.

It is another time now. Now, it is *after.*

Zahira is alone, there is no one beside her whose hand she

might (shyly) clutch. No one beside her whose silence is so intense, she would never wish to interrupt.

The most profound love, not words but being.

Being near, being present. Love, silence.

Never had Zahira's husband crossed this makeshift bridge with her. Never had they walked so far into the woods together for invariably Herman would want to turn back, the placidity of nature did not engage him, bored him; for the molecular biologist it is the *molecular* that fascinates, not mere biology. For Zahira, the fact of a walk together with her elusive husband would have to matter more than the length of the walk.

Returning from each walk Zahira would think—*I will remember this!*

But really, Zahira does not remember individual walks. Virtually all of what they'd said to each other, thirty-two years of marriage, mostly forgotten, water swirling down a drain.

Crossing the pedestrian bridge Zahira is lulled by the sensation of swaying, lurching. Standing very still gripping the ropes to steady herself. Leaning over to peer into the dark water below. There, a slight current, just-visible rippling like the skin of an animal rousing itself from sleep.

Staring down as her eyes adjust to the darkness. Feeling light-headed, adrift. A smell of wet earth. Rich, rotted leaves. For a scant moment freed from the malaise the widow has yet to give the name *grief*—(for naming the sensation that suffuses her waking and sleeping would be both too facile and inadequate)—as if the darkness has lightened.

Seeing reflected in the water a figure beside her own; a motionless figure, yet companionable; standing very close to Zahira as if murmuring into her ear.

Such fear, Zahira feels that she might faint. Her tongue has gone cold. Her heart has jolted as if about to go into fibrillation.

No one beside her on the bridge—of course . . .

Zahira turns away, eager to get off the bridge. The spell is broken, she has no wish to gaze down into the slow-rippling water.

Following the leaf-strewn path out of the Institute Woods. Half-running, short of breath. Burrs are sticking to her dark clothing, the soles of her canvas shoes are spongy-damp. Out on the roadway behind the Institute buildings making her way back to the house on Gödel Lane which she'd left with lights burning in most of the rooms to suggest an air of activity, even festivity to any observers driving past.

Not a residence—obviously!—in which a lone person, a widow, is cowering.

Zahira is still shaken but has begun to forget why, *why* is she out of breath from running, there is no reason for her to hurry back to the house which awaits her exactly as she'd left it: empty.

In all the rooms: no one.

No one expecting her. No one awaiting her.

It is surprisingly late—or early: four-fifteen A.M.

For a confused moment not sure where she has been. Looking for their lost cat Minx?—but Minx has been gone for years.

(Herman had seemed barely aware of the cat but missed her, when she'd vanished.)

(Zahira had observed him glancing about, frowning. Missing the long-haired gray cat without seeming to realize what it was he was missing.)

(Just—*something is missing.*)

(Something is wrong.)

Halfway up the stairs when a sensation of dread sweeps over Zahira, she realizes it will be a mistake to try to sleep in her bedroom. A safer idea to sleep downstairs.

Extinguishing lights one by one. Falling onto the bed in the guest room, sinking almost at once into a dazed dreamless sleep as into the blackest of muck. So exhausted!—Zahira feels as if her brain is dissolving, into oblivion; in such a state she would forsake ever having to wake up.

The figure on the bridge beside her. In dark-rippling water reflected.

I did love you, you know.

Now, my mouth is filled with ashes.

Zahira?—her name is being called, at a distance.

Wakened abruptly, rudely. It is seven-twenty A.M.—Zahira has been sleeping for three hours . . .

Not sure where she is, why in this room downstairs, sheets damp with sweat and heart pounding like a trapped bird inside her rib cage—why, someone at the door, at this hour. A shrill doorbell, knocking, her name called urgently—*Zahira? Hello?*

Waking her, when she so badly needs sleep. Zahira could cry, scream.

Leave me alone! Go away.

Still the voice persists. Unbelievably, the doorbell is rung another time.

Panicked, Zahira wraps herself in a soiled silky robe. It is cruel to expel her from such a deep dreamless sleep, barely can she keep her balance, leaning against walls as she makes her unsteady way barefoot to the front door. Hair disheveled about her pale puffy face, mouth dry as if lined with sand.

Zahira? Hello . . .

Through a narrow vertical window beside the door seeing, on the stoop, that woman—Meghan: Meghan Dunne. *That* woman.

The woman who'd dared to take Zahira's hand at the memorial the other evening. The woman who'd dared to lean close to Zahira as if they were sisters.

No choice, Zahira has to open the door. Owes it to her

husband (she thinks) to behave civilly, sanely in this community in which everyone knows everyone else and will spread tales of her if she fails to behave appropriately.

In the intruder's face a look of relief at the sight of Zahira awake, on her feet. And chagrin, that Zahira is so clearly not pleased to see her.

Awkwardly Meghan explains that she walks every morning at this time, thought she'd check to see if Zahira is all right . . .

"Why would I not be 'all right'? Are *you* all right?"

Zahira's voice is hoarse as if she hasn't spoken in some time. Meghan Dunne smiles inanely.

"I—I'm sorry, I'd thought . . ."

"Did you think that I'd killed myself? 'Overdose' of something?"

"No, no—of course not . . ."

"Well, I didn't. As you can see. You can report. Thank you for your solicitude."

Even as Meghan's mouth is moving, some sort of banal apology, Zahira shuts the door rudely, turns away.

Is Zahira Kruk suicidal? She is not.

Later that morning, Zahira will find a small gift-bag on the front stoop. Inside, several bottles of fruit smoothies (strawberry-banana, vanilla-peach, blueberry) and a card—*Sorry to disturb you. Did not mean to alarm you. I am up early most days. Join me if you'd like to walk. Can't presume to know (exactly) what you are going through but would guess you are eating properly. Your friend Meghan.*

Zahira laughs in derision. Meghan Dunne scribbled this note for her so quickly, she'd left out a crucial word—*not.*

Would guess you are not eating properly.

Signing—*Your friend Meghan.*

What a fool! Intruding where she isn't wanted.

Tempted to throw away the smoothies, a cloying drink Zahira dislikes for its sweetness, and the card—especially the card.

Instead, light-headed with hunger, Zahira devours the strawberry-banana smoothie sitting at the kitchen table. Famished, she drinks most of a second bottle.

Very tired suddenly. Cannot keep her eyes open.

Stumbles somewhere to fall onto a sofa, within seconds deeply asleep and not waking until mid-afternoon.

Death duties require all of the widow's (daytime) energies. No time for anything else.

Making telephone calls in an era in which it is rare, it is virtually impossible, to reach a living person. Filling out (online) forms. Speaking with a bank officer—finally. Speaking with their lawyer. Filing documents: Probate court. Arranging for titles of property (house, vehicle) to be reassigned to *Zahira Kruk, Wife.*

But nights, too restless to remain in the house. Excited, in no mood to sleep. In dread of lying sleepless. Can't read, can't work, can't watch TV. Can't sit still. Scarcely listens to messages on her answering machine, kindly invitations from friends. Rarely checks her email except to see that the number of unread messages in her inbox has risen to four figures.

For *why*? No one will contact Zahira for whom she has the slightest feeling.

Discovers that the password she has been using for Herman's computer has become *invalid.*

Must be remembering it incorrectly. Typing the word incorrectly.

Still: *invalid.*

At dusk venturing out. Like a nocturnal creature. When no one is likely to see her.

In dark clothing, with a flashlight—filmy clouds are being blown across the face of the moon . . .

In dread of losing her way. Even by day it is easy to get lost in the Institute Woods where trails are notoriously poorly marked.

How she'd searched in these woods for the long-haired gray Minx, weeks and months after knowing the search would be futile. On the lookout for furry remains, or a skeleton . . . For somehow it seemed worse to Zahira, more painful, the little cat wandering lost and desperate searching for her home but never finding it.

Shining the flashlight ahead. Drawing swarms of gnats, moths. Waiting for the moon to reappear. It is midnight, or later than midnight. Zahira has lost her way, already her feet are soaked. *Weeks later, the body is discovered.*

Eventually Zahira finds her way to the stream, the makeshift bridge in the interior of the woods. Farther from the trailhead than she remembers.

Stepping out onto the bridge carefully. Grasping the ropes. And there again reflected in the slow-rippling dark water below (not clearly but dimly like a faded Polaroid) is the figure beside her. *A man. A man's figure. No face, all is shadow.*

If Zahira holds herself very still, if she stares long enough, hard enough.

If she doesn't turn to see that, beside her, on the bridge, there is no one.

"You are absurd. Disgusting."

Shocking to the widow, deeply disturbing. Like the bouts of ravenous eating, falling asleep as into a coma for nine hours at a time.

Discovering in herself in a region of her soul she'd believed to be numb, deadened as a nerve might be deadened against pain, an emotion crude as *envy, jealousy.*

"Not possible. You *fool.*"

Though Zahira has avoided seeing people, women friends, acquaintances, Institute people, solitary men (divorced, widowed) who have called her or emailed her or attempted even to approach her in public places like the grocery store (impossible to avoid, though Zahira shops in the unpopular hour before closing), still she finds herself brooding upon the good fortune of women of her acquaintance who still have their husbands; women who are not (yet) widows.

Their husbands, Zahira does not really covet. Their *marriages,* Zahira covets.

Walking out at night too restless to stay indoors. Passing the warm-lighted houses of neighbors set back in two- and three-acre lots behind scrims of trees, shrubbery.

Will you want to sell your house? If so, I can put you in touch with . . .

Though Zahira can see lighted rooms in some of these houses, even the movement of persons inside, the glow of a TV screen, it is evident that Zahira's neighbors are indifferent to the prospect of being seen. For this is a tranquil neighborhood in which there are few pedestrians at any time.

Dog-walkers, joggers, an occasional cyclist. Early-morning walkers, like Meghan Dunne.

Curving roadways, lanes. No sidewalks.

Feeling an ache of something like resentment, anger. That she, Zahira Kruk, is now one of those *excluded,* where for all of her adult life she has been *included.*

Marriage protective as a densely woven nest. One of those nests—crows, magpies—so tightly, lovingly constructed they are virtually waterproof.

Of all houses in the neighborhood it is the Greb house that

draws Zahira, a half-mile away on Feynman Drive. Of all marriages, it is the Grebs' marriage that fills her with envy.

Not that Zahira would wish to be Hester Greb, she does not. Nor even Ilya Greb's wife, not really.

It is just—the Grebs' *marriage* . . .

Ilya Greb, a biologist colleague of Zahira's husband. Several years older than Herman, and more lauded—at the age of fifty-one he'd been awarded, with one or two others, a Nobel Prize for his work in immunology; of fellow biologists, it was Ilya whom Herman most admired. Not an attractive man, not obviously, with a craggy simian face, a low forehead, an uncomfortably intense stare, a startlingly warm smile—when he smiled . . .

Years ago, Zahira is embarrassed to recall now, Ilya Greb had behaved somewhat foolishly, imagining himself in love with her, the (much-younger) wife of his colleague; but nothing had come of it—of course . . .

Like a movie seen long ago, recalled only in fragments. Herman had never known, no one would have told him. Hester might have known, for women sense such things.

If ever you have a change of heart, I am always here.

Passing the Greb house which is one of the older houses in the neighborhood. Stolid, squat, dark brick and stucco. Rotting slate roof. Untidy hydrangea bushes, overgrown hedges. Houses at the Institute were originally built in the early twentieth century, households had staffs of servants in those years, no one could afford such staffs now.

No lights downstairs in the Grebs' house. A single light upstairs, very likely in the Grebs' bedroom.

Zahira feels a stab of hurt, loss. The intimacy of a bedroom, bed: sharing a bed with a husband.

Even a husband so remote from her. Nonetheless in her arms, *hers*.

All that has been taken from Zahira, now.

Since her husband's death Zahira has not seen or heard from Ilya Greb, who is known to have had surgery recently; to be recovering, but slowly, rarely leaving the house, with Hester caring for him. Hester, herself harried-looking, had come to the memorial for Herman, and has left messages for Zahira expressing sympathy, has sent a card. No doubt, Hester signed both her and Ilya's names on the card; probably, Hester has sent flowers as well. Distracted by grief, Zahira has barely noticed. She has no intention of preserving cards, dutifully writing thank-you cards in return.

Recalling now that peculiar phase in her life, more than twenty years ago.

A nerve long believed to be dead, suddenly quivering with life.

That season when Ilya Greb, long-married, with adult children, a caring wife, began to approach Zahira Kruk at Institute gatherings to speak shyly with her, yet persistently; most awkwardly, he'd gazed at Zahira with adoring eyes. He'd pronounced her name with a touching sort of reverence: *Za-hir-a.*

Always he seemed about to blurt out something absurd—*But I think I know you! I've met you—somewhere . . .*

In Institute circles, Ilya Greb was already renowned. A molecular biologist who'd been awarded a Nobel Prize in physiology. He'd won other distinctions, young. None of this acclaim turned his head, his humility was genuine. Reacting with embarrassment when he was congratulated, murmuring that the work for which he'd been given a Nobel Prize had been done years before, in his thirties; his younger colleagues were really responsible for the new vaccines, not him.

He was shy in Herman Kruk's company as well. Covertly watching the younger man, as if measuring himself against him: not nearly so attractive, not so self-confident, something of a *klutz,* he called himself.

Shy, yet like many shy persons Ilya could be funny. Making

others laugh was a way of appropriating them. He loved the films of Charles Chaplin, the Marx Brothers, Buster Keaton. He'd cultivated a *Keatonesque* manner—droll but deadpan, puppet-like.

Seeing that Zahira was uneasy in his presence Ilya tried to make her laugh, awkwardly. He *was* funny, in his maladroit way.

Not unfamiliar with male attention since early adolescence, Zahira had cultivated ways of deflecting such interest without risking insult: taking care to smile, but not to smile too readily; acknowledging unfunny jokes without bursting into laughter; never seeming to be acknowledging complicity, *rapport*. It was a challenge for Zahira, she might have said jokingly, to maintain an intimate *rapport* with her husband, she could not squander her emotional energy on other women's husbands.

Zahira had no interest in sexual adventure, she had work of her own, difficult translation projects, a penchant for severe self-criticism, self-censoring. It was true, her birth name had been "Sarah"—a mask of convention, blandness; "Zahira" was the more appropriate mask, an ideal name for a translator from Arabic. (Zahira's languages were Arabic, French, Italian, as well as English; her specialty was literary Arabic.) She had no time for romantic fantasies nor would she encourage another woman's husband to court her out of sheer vanity as some women did; to have admirers among their friends' husbands of a kind not unusual in communities like the Institute community; not serious romances, not affairs, no sexual expectations or obligations, just platonic relationships of a public nature. But Zahira resisted even these, that seemed hypocritical to her.

Still, Zahira stopped by Ilya Greb's office at the Institute, just once since he'd persisted in inviting her. He was a renowned scientist, Zahira was genuinely interested in his work as it involved public health, epidemiology. She was always searching for subjects about which she could speak knowledgeably with her husband. And Ilya was a genuinely kindly man, a gentleman.

Listening to Ilya speak with such enthusiasm, wishing that Herman could share such thoughts with her. Her husband was intensely private, Zahira felt often as if a scrim of thought shielded him from others, including even his wife. His gaze veiled when he listened to Zahira speak, as if his thoughts were elsewhere.

But Ilya Greb addressed Zahira directly, fixing her with his intense gaze, the flattery of such a gaze. That Ilya would speak to Zahira as if—almost—they were equals, that Zahira could understand the complexities of which he spoke—was touching to her, flattering.

Disease, contagion. History of epidemics, pandemics. The earliest forms of medical care. The (fortuitous) development of inoculations, vaccinations. Zahira was thrilled to think, with Ilya, as with Herman, that scientific research was a way of life that is impersonal, "selfless"—beyond the (mere) self. A kind of secular religion, far more reliable than the sacred. Like Herman, Ilya truly did believe in the accumulation of objectifiable knowledge, through painstaking experiments; a selfless enterprise in which one stood on the shoulders of countless others. No one was isolated, no "solitary genius." Zahira was moved to think of a line in one of Flaubert's letters—*Nous devons nous aimer dans notre art comme les mystiques s'aiment en Dieu.*

We must love one another in our art, as the mystics loved one another in God.

In Ilya's office was a framed print of Picasso's *Night Fishing at Antibes* taking up much of the wall. Ilya saw Zahira studying it intently and told her that it was the first work of art he'd ever really noticed, at the age of ten; he'd come across it reproduced in a book, with no idea who Picasso was, or that the picture was of a large oil painting. He'd been fascinated by the strangeness of the artwork, that resembled a dream, of unusual colors, subdued, unnatural-seeming, and flattened cartoon-like figures that particularly struck him—"I had no idea why, they made me anxious, they seemed very lifelike. Yet they were not lifelike at all."

Years later as an adult Ilya discovered the oil painting in MoMA and was astonished by its size, and the visible brushstrokes, an air of tension and anguish in the canvas that wasn't suggested in the reproduction. Several times he'd returned to look at *Night Fishing at Antibes,* it was like a riddle to him, an irritant. He ended up purchasing a high-quality print from the museum, had it framed.

"My wife hates it, she hates Picasso on principle. But I'm happy to keep it here, close by my lab. *Here* is where I spend most of my waking hours."

Ilya told Zahira that Picasso had painted *Night Fishing at Antibes* two years after *Guernica,* the painting for which he was most famous. It shared similar themes—of war, violence—with *Guernica.* One of the cartoon-figures represented Picasso himself, Ilya would have thought that the artist was young at the time but he'd been fifty-seven.

"The artist 'fishing' in dark waters. Surrounded by danger, death. The 'fishing' is the unknown adventure."

Ilya spoke with unusual warmth as if he were confiding a secret. Zahira was slightly embarrassed by the man's intensity but moved by his words, for it was true: We are all fishing in dark waters, at night. Each in our own groping way.

Surrounded by unnatural subaqueous shapes, colors—muted greens, purples. Human faces flattened as masks.

Ilya spoke at length about his earlier life, his work, to which he'd come by accident, having been accepted at medical school but deciding to defer for a year, and that altered the course of his life.

"I would have been a frantic clinician. I would have worn myself out treating patients. No one would ever have heard of 'Ilya Greb,' I wouldn't be *here.*"

Pronouncing "Ilya Greb" with an air of bemused irony. As if it were something that had happened to him, a destiny.

And now, meeting her, Zahira—"I feel as if my life is poised to move in another direction, again."

To this, Zahira could think of no reply. It was preposterous, absurd—for Ilya Greb to think that, for even a moment, Zahira might consider him as a lover, or—whatever he was imagining her role might be in his life . . .

Not a second wife, surely? A woman in her mid-thirties, divorcing her husband to marry a man nearing sixty, however youthful he appeared?

And that man with a wife of decades, children and grandchildren.

Zahira tried to smile, faintly. She was embarrassed: for having blundered into such a situation.

Of all decent people Ilya Greb did not deserve to be trifled with. Zahira knew.

Not by words but by her manner allowing Ilya Greb to know—*Yes, I am attracted to you too; but no, nothing will happen between us.*

Just a fringe of hair on the high dome of Ilya's head, a soft spreading belly, narrow shoulders, and pale spindly legs—(she'd seen Ilya in shorts). He wore Birkenstock sandals, with socks; he perspired with excitement when he spoke of his work, standing too near Zahira who told herself wryly that, even if she were not happily married, she could never make love with a man who wore sandals with socks. Ilya was too kindly, *avuncular.*

Ilya had the (mistaken) impression that they were having lunch together, Zahira explained that she had to be elsewhere.

The expression of childlike hurt, disappointment in the simian face!—Zahira pretended not to notice.

Really he never had lunch at the Institute, or anywhere, Ilya said, usually he ate a sandwich in his lab, a working lunch, but today he'd made an exception, for Zahira he'd made an exception. There was a reservation for them in the Institute dining room . . .

Firmly Zahira shook her head. *No thank you, Ilya.*

Ilya tried to turn the rebuff into a comic routine. Shuffling about like Buster Keaton, stymied, yet still persisting—*No? Not? Nothing? Not—a THING?*

Zahira laughed, unable to resist.

"Another day, then?"

"I don't think so. I'm sorry."

"Really?"

"Yes. I mean—*no.*"

Knowing that, to appear with Ilya Greb, in public, in the Institute dining room, would be a conspicuous gesture in the eyes of the community. Even if there were nothing between them, as there (almost) was not, the mere appearance in that dining room, a kind of theatrical display of their being, however improbably, *lovers*—would be in poor taste, vulgar.

And word would get back to Hester, and to Herman, surely.

(Though Herman wouldn't have seen them, since, like Ilya Greb, Herman never had a formal lunch, worked through most afternoons without leaving his lab.)

"Goodbye, Ilya. I have to leave . . ."

Like a crestfallen Buster Keaton, Ilya followed Zahira to the door. Bungling, clumsy, clownish, heartbroken. Deadpan.

Touching Zahira's wrist with his forefinger, lightly, saying in a lowered voice, "Well, dear! If ever you have a change of heart, I am here."

If ever you have a change of heart, I am here.

It has been a fitful night. Zahira has circled the Institute grounds, a loop of three miles. She has not felt strong enough to hike into the woods. She has felt drawn to more familiar places, like a lost dog, a lost cat seeking its home.

But dreading being seen, identified. Early hours of the morning, a lone figure, making her way along Feynman Drive, onto Gödel Lane.

At last returning to the house, entering by a side door. Thinking, as she usually thinks when entering the house, that if Herman is here, upstairs, he will be asleep; he will not hear her enter surreptitiously. He will not call out to her in a frightened voice as he had in the hospital—*Zahira? Where are you? Why have you left me alone here?*

Stumbling into the guest room, to sleep in the unmade bed. Disturbed sleep in which Herman is seeking her but (as Zahira can see) the face isn't Herman's but the face of Ilya Greb.

Not the face of the man now, a man in his late seventies. The face of decades ago, youthful, animated.

If ever you have a change of heart . . .

And now, is Zahira to be further humiliated? Falling in love, with the memory of a (married) man who'd once touched her wrist?—gazed at her adoringly?—whom she has not seen in any intimate way, spoken with in private, in years.

Nor has Ilya contacted Zahira, since Herman's death.

Later that morning Zahira will discover an unfamiliar vehicle in her driveway.

Behind the wheel, apparently asleep, that woman—Meghan Dunne.

Zahira laughs. How ridiculous! How *silly.*

She is beyond the age for emotional connections, friendships. A rapport between widows.

The time for *best friends* has passed. Through her adult life, after leaving a tight-knit immigrant family in Ann Arbor, Zahira has avoided emotional intimacies, really she has wanted no close relationships. Deliberately she'd married a man like herself, who'd cherished his privacy. Between her and Herman there had been subjects about which neither would have been comfortable speaking.

Especially, such emotional relationships with other women never turn out well. Zahira is sure.

"You make yourself ridiculous. *You.*"

Not sure if she is addressing Meghan Dunne, or herself.

Still, Zahira supposes it would be a friendly gesture, a neighborly gesture, to at least acknowledge the woman sleeping in her vehicle, so boldly in Zahira's driveway.

(Zahira isn't surprised, on the passenger's seat beside Meghan is a bag from an expensive food store in Millstone. Croissants, fruit tarts. Multigrain bread. Cheeses.)

Tap at the window of the Mercedes, at least. No need to invite Meghan Dunne inside her house though that is what Zahira does.

A widow's life is *tragic,* there is no place for *banal.*

Yet somehow, without Zahira's consent, no decision at all, nothing conscious, purposeful, it began to happen that Meghan Dunne called Zahira frequently and that, if Meghan failed to call, Zahira awaited a call from her; it was a kind of tic, a twitchy nerve, the phenomenon of *waiting for a call* she didn't especially want, half-dreaded to receive for the voice of the other woman was an irritant to Zahira: a high-pitched voice, a breathy voice, a voice exuding both aggression and apology.

Am I calling at a bad time? I can call back . . .

It was never not a *bad time*. But, Zahira knew, Meghan knew this.

Soon then, somehow it happened that Zahira found herself walking, in the early morning, with Meghan Dunne.

Yes, it *is* exhilarating, to walk early in the morning. Not to lie in bed groggy, leaden.

Walking briskly, a three-mile loop. Lightening sky, amazing cloud formations, Meghan's voice bright, relentless.

Not so often wandering alone at night, as before.

The nocturnal life, fading. That melancholy nocturnal life, her heart in tatters. Wanting to die. Swoon into death, as into the dark-rippling stream in the Institute Woods.

A daylight life coarse and lacking in subtlety as a sunflower emerging.

How like a sunflower: Meghan Dunne. Pushing up through cracks in concrete. Unstoppable.

Weeks of avoiding people with the grim certitude that she has no wish ever to see anyone again, certainly not to speak with anyone again, yet Zahira finds herself meeting Meghan in front of her house on Gödel Lane to walk with her at seven A.M.

Accepting an invitation from Meghan, who has an extra ticket—(the deceased husband's ticket)—for a play, concert. Joining Meghan at lunch with another woman friend, dinner at a neighbor's house, not recalling when she'd said *yes*.

Meghan insists, Zahira should join her volunteering at the Millstone Animal Rescue one or two afternoons a week.

It is Zahira's idea, however: to drive out to Hart's Nursery to purchase (young, hardy) trees to replace the half-dozen ash trees that have died and been removed from her and Meghan Dunne's properties.

And it is Zahira's idea, warmly supported by Meghan, to donate trees to the Institute in memory of their husbands; and establish endowments at the Institute in their husbands' names.

Tragic, banal.

How much more dignified for a widow who'd loved her husband to have taken her own life by now, Zahira thinks, instead of walking companionably with Meghan Dunne in the Institute Woods. Constant chatter of the other woman bright and inconsequent as fake gold coins.

Confiding in Zahira, who must promise never to tell anyone, that she'd been desperate for the past several years that her husband was going to ask for a divorce, dreading the possibility, trying to win back her husband's love which (she believed) had drained away gradually like water in a sink, no one to blame, well—*she* was to blame, for not being able to prevent it.

Confiding in Zahira, it wasn't Zahira she'd worried might kill herself, actually it was Meghan herself, on the worst nights.

Confiding in Zahira, she'd done something very foolish a few days ago.

Very embarrassing but comical, too. Yes.

With the enigmatic murmur that is characteristic of her, Zahira seems to express curiosity, sympathy. Though dreading what sort of intimate confidence Meghan is going to utter.

In an abashed voice Meghan narrates how she'd arranged to meet a man whom she hadn't seen in forty years, since they were undergraduates together at Middlebury; when he'd first contacted her (on Facebook) after seeing her husband's obituary she hadn't answered him but the other night impulsively she did, no idea why, they'd exchanged a few emails, suddenly she wanted to see him very badly, he was eager to see her, they made arrangements to meet for dinner in New Brunswick—(forty-minute drive for Meghan, two-hour drive for her friend)—but when Meghan arrived she saw her friend—"Lawrence"—before he saw her, waiting for her, in a booth in the restaurant; she saw him, and fled . . .

"I just couldn't go through with it. I am so *ashamed.*"

"Well. I wouldn't be *ashamed.*"

Zahira is never sure what response Meghan expects from her, in these exchanges.

Sympathy, or—laughter? Most of what Meghan tells Zahira has a comical cast as if, since becoming a widow, Meghan has lost an essential *gravitas;* you begin to feel, she has told Zahira, like litter blown along the ground.

"It wasn't that he'd aged so much—though he has, of course. He looked like a hippie-granddaddy. Or that I didn't know what to say to him. I was just—I felt—that I might make a complete fool of myself, breaking down, bursting into tears. Just—so *needy.*"

"'Needy'—of what?"

"Having a husband. Being married. Again."

"Is that how you feel?"—Zahira is surprised, her friend has seemed so much more assured than she; so much more adjusted to being a widow.

"Not that I would want to 'get married.' But to *be married.*"

Zahira agrees, amused. To *be married,* in (maybe) the tenth year of the marriage, or the twentieth year. Not to have to begin anew.

Both women agree, they are envious of women their age who still have their husbands.

"Suddenly they have the advantage, they have something to live for. Not just living but—living *for.*"

Zahira has confessed to a desperate thought. In the isolation of the insomniac night such an insight is profound, jarring; on this early-morning walk with her friend, in this familiar setting, her woman friend attired in a stylish beige-pink jogging suit with a redundant hood, it seems to her merely diminished, pathetic.

Envy, jealousy. How petty she has become.

Yet there is a kind of comfort in it, pettiness. Something sisterly.

"Hester Greb. I envy *her.*"

"Oh, Zahira, really? *I* envy Hester."

It is rare for Zahira to speak so impulsively. Suddenly the women are laughing together like schoolgirls.

Of course in the Institute community, among surviving husbands of that generation of brilliant research scientists, gentlemanly, sweetly-funny Ilya Greb with his Nobel Prize is the ideal.

Confessing to *envy, jealousy* of Hester Greb, of all people. How surprised Hester would be.

"She doesn't deserve him," Meghan says, seriously, "—I mean, she's so plain, earnest—always going on about her grandchildren. I don't think she has any idea of the person she's married to. *He* has such a sense of humor . . ."

Zahira thinks—*And he loves me.*

That is—*Loved me. Once.*

It has been so long, Ilya misses you.

Ilya very much appreciates visitors.

Ilya is improving every day!

Seven weeks after Zahira's husband's death when Hester Greb invites Zahira and Meghan for lunch at their house.

Zahira politely declines, Meghan insists *yes.*

In fact, as Zahira vaguely recalls, Hester Greb has invited her to visit them several times. She has *reached out* to Zahira, since Herman's death. But Zahira declined the invitations, or ignored them.

"This isn't because you're a widow, or because I'm a widow," Meghan says, "—it's because Hester hopes that people will visit Ilya. He's such a nice person, it won't be a strain. It's said that he is recovering from surgery, or he has 'long Covid'—or both. He misses his laboratory terribly. He misses the Institute. We have to say *yes,* it's the friendly thing to do."

Zahira hesitates. It is very hard for her, her throat shuts up, at the prospect of *yes.*

Of course, Zahira has been thinking a good deal about Ilya Greb. Her obsession with the (lost) husband has shifted into an obsession with the (lost) "lover."

Fearing that she will see in Ilya's face the expression of his old feeling for her—that look of adoration; and Ilya now in his seventies, in a wheelchair . . .

But I do love you, I have always loved you. Za-hir-a.

Fearing how she will respond, in this ravaged state of her own. Like an amputee, hobbling about on one leg and a crutch and people are trying to be kind pretending that she has both legs.

How brave Zahira is! But we see through the imposture.

Explaining to Meghan that she feels such jealousy of Hester Greb, she's afraid that she will be overcome with emotion in the Grebs' house, will have to excuse herself and leave.

"Don't be ridiculous, Zahira. It's just *lunch.*"

"Not the lunch, the *marriage.*"

"We should be happy for Hester. We shouldn't feel like rivals."

Zahira sucks in her breath, resentful. Hester Greb *is* a rival.

"Hester is Ilya's primary caretaker, it must be a strain. Of course they would like visitors. You must have noticed, Zahira—Ilya always seemed so fond of *you.* We don't need to stay long."

Always seemed so fond of you. Had others noticed? Zahira has wanted to think that Ilya's feeling for her was entirely secret, private.

"We'll go! We're all neighbors."

Weakly Zahira tries to resist but Meghan prevails, of course Meghan is right. Ethically right. It *is* the neighborly thing to do.

Though the Grebs live a half-mile from Zahira's house Meghan insists upon picking up Zahira to drive her there. Zahira pleads: "We can walk, Meghan! Please."

"We are not going to *walk.* If something goes wrong, if anyone needs to be driven to the ER, I will have my car. Plus, we need to wear nice shoes, not running shoes. This is an occasion."

So, Zahira allows herself to be driven in Meghan's car. She feels weightless, fated—a figure in a movie.

It is true, Zahira is too vain to wear flat shoes to see Ilya Greb, she will wear a sleek silk Peruvian dress in an exquisite print, long sleeves, summer shoes with a medium heel. Bare legs, pearly-pale. A necklace of antique-looking Greek medallions, conch-sized earrings.

Zahira feels a wave of faintness, approaching the Grebs' house by day. So often she has drifted by this house in the middle of the night, staring at dimly lighted windows as if hypnotized; feeling that the occupants of the house must be aware of her, a wraith haunting their household.

Reasoning how, with a just-slightly-different shake of the dice, Zahira could be the wife with a (living) husband, and not Hester Greb; in an alternate universe, Zahira *is* Ilya Greb's wife.

That moment when your doctor checks your bloodwork on his computer screen: will he say *Nothing has changed* or will he say, after a moment's hesitation, in a quiet voice *It looks as if something has changed.*

It's that, that enrages Zahira. Mere chance!

As, in her dreams, Zahira is plagued by cruel dreams of *before.* She is in a place in which, in a provisional way, she is "happy" as a child might be happy; there is some question, or instability, or risk to this happiness, but she doesn't know what it is, for Herman is with her, or in another room, or actually he is nowhere but there is an intense *awareness* of the husband until the dream breaks off—abruptly.

Stunned minutes are required for Zahira to realize that she has been dreaming. She has been deceived, taunted.

There is no *before,* there is only *after.*

Exiled from *before,* from any hope of happiness. Waking to suffocating anguish, the knowledge that the husband is gone, the husband has died, the husband will not return.

How many times, the identical dream! Trapped in the coils that crushed Laocoön.

Meghan glances at Zahira staring with vacant eyes—"Zahira! Watch where you're walking."

On the cracked walkway leading to the Grebs' front door is a rake Zahira narrowly avoids stepping on in her stylish cork-soled shoes.

The women see: Someone has been toiling in overgrown flower beds, must be Hester Greb. Ragged hydrangea bushes, anemic-looking roses, tiger lilies past their prime, flattened and desiccated. Weeds have choked most of an ambitious garden, a few lone rows of tomato plants, green beans, peppers remain amid fresh-tilled and watered soil.

Meghan stoops to pick up the rake, set it safely aside. Zahira sees filthy gardening gloves abandoned in the grass, she doesn't touch them.

The Grebs' house is a large sturdy brick and stucco house more than a century old. Like several other older houses in the Institute neighborhood it is no longer in prime condition. Its owners are retired, their children have long since moved away. The Grebs have not their former interest in home maintenance, possibly they are not aware that weeds have pushed their way through cracks in the driveway, tiny saplings are growing in rain gutters, parts of the (slate) roof need replacing. Zahira takes in all this, this vision, Zahira is filled with apprehension. *Her* house is not nearly as old as the Grebs' house, it is one of several local houses designed by Michael Graves in the 1970s, an architectural gem it has been called, now the widow's burden to maintain.

"We all remember when Ilya insisted on mowing his own lawn," Meghan says. "After he'd won a Nobel Prize! Now it looks like no one is mowing it regularly."

Zahira does recall. Ilya had shoveled snow from his driveway, sidewalks. How many years.

She'd waved at him, she remembers. Ilya Greb in a red wool cap, fleece jacket, breath steaming about his face. Waving back at *her*.

Hester Greb opens the door to the women, looking startled as if for a moment she has forgotten that guests are invited. A small woman, her hair is frothy-white, her plain-earnest face is creased with something like wonderment. When Meghan asks uneasily if something is wrong Hester laughs, "You are both looking so *young*."

Zahira recalls, Ilya's wife had been a serious musician at one time. She'd played harpsichord, brightly brittle Bach compositions, at the Institute's Thursday concert evenings long ago.

Hester Greb does appear stunned by the sight of Zahira whose composed face looks unlined, if you don't look closely; and Meghan with blond-streaked hair, shapely hips and bustline enhanced in a tight-fitting jersey top.

Hester is wearing very casual clothes—rumpled shirt, cotton slacks with soiled knees. Her fingernails are darkened and broken, obviously she has been working in the garden.

"We didn't come on the wrong day, did we, Hester? Or—the wrong time?" Meghan asks, concerned; but Hester regains her poise quickly, "Oh no. Of course not. Ilya has made a salad, you know that's Ilya's specialty."

Hester hugs the women, each in turn; she is looking frail, has lost height in recent years. Zahira holds her breath, fearful of breathing in an odor that will repel her sensitive nostrils, even as Hester says apologetically, "If you don't mind—Zara, Meghan—we always remove our shoes here."

"Oh. Yes." Meghan speaks flatly, annoyed.

"Oh—that's no trouble," Zahira says quickly.

With a glance at Meghan, amused.

You see? We didn't have to wear dressy shoes after all.

On a mat beside the door are paper slippers, as well as the Grebs' shoes.

Both guests are obliged to put on the paper slippers, not very cheerily. Zahira can't resist inquiring, "Are these paper slippers like the ones you get in hospitals? I hope you won't make us remove our clothes, Hester, and wear those white paper gowns with ties that open in back or open in front."

"Oh—oh no . . ."

Blank-faced Hester seems not to grasp that Zahira's remark is meant to be funny unless it is meant (as Meghan seems to be thinking, disapprovingly) to be sarcastic.

Chattering nervously Hester leads the women through the downstairs of the stolid old house in the direction of the kitchen. In her wake Zahira shuffles in the paper slippers in a way that might be called *ironic,* hoping that Meghan will smile.

A cluttered household of the era of Zahira's grandparents in Dearborn, Michigan. Surprisingly small rooms for a house of this size, high ceilings, discolored moldings, well-worn sofas and cushioned chairs crowded with small shiny pillows.

Crowded bookcases, many books shelved horizontally. On the walls amateur-looking oil paintings, on a fireplace mantel framed family photographs. Depressing, Zahira thinks: no sign that a world-renowned scientist has lived here most of his life.

A smell of baking bread—very aromatic. But a sinister smell beneath, Zahira's nostrils detect, something medicinal, familiar.

Zahira is feeling nervous, apprehensive. Half-listening to their hostess's chatter: How Ilya had his first surgery in December at Sloan Kettering; had to return again in March; the second surgery was seven hours; it took him many days to recover from the anesthesia; then, in bed for three weeks his leg muscles atrophied, and there were risks of blood clots; there *were* blood clots, but they've been treated with medication . . . A physical therapist comes to the house several times a week, Ilya has been making progress. Of course, being Ilya, he is impatient with himself, he has always hated weakness in himself.

He can forgive others, but not himself. He is embarrassed needing a walker or a wheelchair. That's why they haven't seen much of him, or of Hester too, he's reluctant to appear in public, people will feel sorry for him, his friends, his lab assistants, Ilya has a dread of people feeling sorry for him or feeling *sad.*

"But he misses you all, too. He misses his laboratory, all those young people, like a family to him. It's been seven years since he retired but—in a research scientist's life, research is the meaning of his life. *That* can never be replaced."

Hester speaks primly, as if expecting her guests to object.

"Of course, his family is special to him, too. But not so real to him, sometimes—as the other."

"Yes! That's so." Meghan so quickly agrees, it's likely that she hasn't been listening to Hester.

This prevailing odor, Zahira is trying not to notice. Mixed with the smell of fresh-baked bread, it may prove nauseating.

Is it—isopropyl alcohol? Sharp-smelling disinfectant used to sterilize IV lines, ports. Hospitals, infusion rooms. Hand sanitizers.

Hester tells Zahira and Meghan that Ilya has been excited about their visit and has been awake since six A.M. He has prepared a green salad with tomatoes and basil from Hester's garden, and his own special Italian dressing. Ilya is *almost his old self,* he spends mornings on the terrace, he has his laptop, cell phone. His former colleagues are always conferring with him, asking his advice . . .

In a haze of expectation Zahira follows Hester and Meghan down a short aluminum ramp from the kitchen door to the terrace. It is brightly sunny here, a relief after the torpor of the old house. Zahira's heart is pounding giddily, she is wondering—*Is he still in love with me?*

Fearing that, if she sees that look in Ilya Greb's face, a look of urgency and yearning which she has not seen in years, in that instant she will weaken; she will feel a rush of emotion, painful as blood rushing into a frostbitten limb.

"Ilya! Your visitors are here!"—Hester calls out gaily.

Ilya in a wheelchair, smaller than Zahira recalls, but seated calmly, erect. He is squinting in their direction, broadly smiling, lifts a liver-spotted arm in greeting.

Ilya's face hasn't aged much, Zahira thinks, relieved. Craggy-simian, sharp creases around his eyes, not an unattractive older man, really. For a man of his age.

Hester has chosen for Ilya an oddly boxy white cotton shirt with short sleeves that seem to billow, to his elbows; his jaws look freshly shaven, there are tiny bleeding nicks on the underside of his jaw.

His face seems longer, gaunter. His hair has nearly vanished, just a few tufts on the (regal) dome of his head. He has removed his bifocals, not wanting to be seen wearing glasses. His eyes are damply alert, squinting fixed upon Zahira's face, excitedly he calls out, *Hello.*

Pronouncing Zahira's name as if it were music: *Za-hir-a!*

More difficulty with Meghan's name: *Marg-hem?*

Ilya makes a show of kissing both his visitors' hands, Continental style; except, it isn't a merely airy gesture, he actually kisses the backs of their hands, first Zahira's, then Meghan's, wetly.

"Dear ladies! Dear beautiful ladies! Thank you so much for coming here."

Ilya's lips are curiously cold, rubbery. Though his manner is exuberant. Zahira wonders if Hester helps Ilya shave now, as she'd helped Herman shave, tenderly steadying his hand. She sees how intently Ilya is looking at her, a blue pulse beating in his temple.

Zahira Kruk, glossy-dark hair to her shoulders, lithe in a beautiful silky dress, absurd paper slippers on her feet.

Between Zahira and this elderly man in a wheelchair, faint glimmer of their old *rapport* like a light in the distance.

Out of her oversized tote bag Meghan presents Hester and Ilya with a bottle of white wine which Hester receives hesitantly even as Ilya thanks Meghan profusely.

"Ilya is on a new medication . . ."

A look of caution has come into Hester's fine-wrinkled face. Unheeding Meghan jokes she hopes the new medication isn't *steroids.* "Steroids drive me *crazy.*"

Hester explains that Ilya can't have wine right now and Ilya speaks over her insisting he *certainly can.*

Zahira intervenes, to be helpful: "Some medications are not compatible with alcohol, you know."

Incomprehensibly, Meghan laughs. As if mocking Zahira she says, "Oh. Is that so, Doctor."

Brusquely Meghan takes the wine bottle back from Hester,

says she will put it in the refrigerator. Zahira wonders if Meghan has realized her blunder, taking the wine away so that Ilya will forget it.

But Ilya is looking sulky, glaring at Hester.

When Meghan returns from the house she is laughing boldly—her shoes, and Zahira's shoes, in her hands. "Since we're outdoors, Hester, surely we can wear our shoes! Hoping you don't mind."

Hester stares blankly at Meghan, as a mother might stare at a mutinous child, then smiles weakly as if to say *Of course.*

Minutes pass now in a flurry of chatter. Talk of the Institute, a new acting director of whom Ilya has "nothing good to say"; talk of the weather, how difficult it is to find reliable handymen in Millstone. And carpenters. And plumbers!

Zahira, relieved to have her shoes back, is only half-listening. Her shoes are open-toed; her toenails have been polished magenta, to match her lipstick and nail polish.

What a charade, lipstick! Nail polish! First time in six, eight months.

Upstairs in her bedroom, lipstick in hand, gazing at herself incredulously in a mirror. *You can't be serious.*

While the other women chatter Zahira puts on her shoes. Elegant cork shoes with criss-crossing black straps, slender white feet. Aware of Ilya observing.

No wish to see poor Ilya's feet or atrophied legs, mercifully hidden by the glass-topped table to which the wheelchair is pulled close.

Hester has urged her guests to sit at the table, which is set for lunch with cloth napkins neatly folded beside colorful ceramic plates. A pitcher of iced tea is on the table. Fresh-baked bread, banana bread. In a wheedling voice Ilya is calling for the wine to be returned to the table, Hester pretends not to hear.

Still more chatter about household maintenance. You would

think the subject might lend itself to lighthearted anecdotes but Hester appears to be seriously distressed. Meghan inclines her head to the older woman, as if listening closely. The toilet in the downstairs bathroom!—after you flush it it just keeps making this leaking trickling sound, it never stops, all day all night, so much water is being wasted, Hester is at her wit's end trying to get a plumber to look at it, at which Meghan leaps to her feet, *she* will look at the toilet, maybe she can fix it; re-entering the house with Hester close behind, weakly protesting.

Zahira is left alone with Ilya at the table. For a moment neither can think of anything to say.

Zahira wonders if Ilya recalls, her husband has died? Herman Kruk, whom he'd known well.

In a wifely way Zahira pours iced tea into Ilya's glass. Ilya thanks her but reverts to the subject of the white wine. "Like a child she treats me. Like a bum."

Bum is not a word Zahira has expected to hear. Ilya has more to say, he is in a complaining mood, clearly unhappy with his wife, the way she treats him, as if he has a leash around his neck, there's a surprise for her in store, Ilya laughs quietly. Just maybe, this very day.

"This is a special day. You know."

"Is it!"

Zahira feels light-headed, just slightly nauseated. Ilya's breath is stale-smelling, coppery-metallic, foul. Zahira recognizes the smell: chemotherapy. Unmistakable.

Hester, the wife, has ceased noticing. No choice, you cease noticing. Your olfactory sense is benumbed. You sleep with them, you hold them in your arms.

Ilya compliments Zahira on the Greek-medallion necklace. Gravely Ilya thanks her for wearing it as if (Zahira is thinking) it is a necklace Ilya once gave her, or imagines he'd once given her; in fact, a gift of long ago from Herman, when they'd traveled in the Greek islands soon after they were married.

"It suits you. Yes—*thank you.*"

In triumph Meghan and Hester return to the table, carrying bowls and platters of food. There's a glow about Meghan, Hester is marveling at Meghan, for within seconds Meghan repaired the leaking toilet that had so stymied the Greb household for days, baffling even the Nobel Prize–winning Ilya Greb. Just lift the lid, back of the toilet, Meghan says, very easy to adjust the rubber stopper which had failed to close securely over the drain—no mystery to it, and no need to pay a plumber.

Hester thanks Meghan effusively. Hester is very impressed by Meghan.

Just like that, Hester says wide-eyed. Like magic, the trickling *stopped.*

Did they all know, in Millstone it's one hundred seventy-five dollars for a plumber to just *visit*? Whether they repair anything or not?

Zahira gives Meghan a slantwise smile. Proud of her brazen friend at such times.

You don't always want Edith Piaf, sometimes you want Ethel Merman. Need Ethel Merman.

Lunch is served, with Meghan's assistance. Zahira makes a feeble gesture to help but Hester insists no more help is needed.

Cold cucumber soup with fresh dill, Greek yogurt. Fresh-baked bread. A salad of fresh greens, romaine, arugula, tomatoes from Hester's garden, basil, something chewy, tarry like figs. Ilya's (secret) salad dressing, extra virgin olive oil and wine vinegar, herbs (basil, mustard), sea salt, Sichuan pepper. Zahira is grateful for the cold soup, its very blandness is reassuring. Ilya's salad too is good, though spicy. Trying not to cough, flecks of coarse-ground Sichuan pepper at the back of her throat.

Herman had always favored pepper. Fresh-ground pepper. Impervious to the eye-watering fit of coughing on Zahira's part.

Conversation has shifted to Hester's garden which is, Zahira wearily gathers, one of the passions of Hester's life but a "terrible disappointment" this year. Of several tomato plants only one has thrived, after Hester was reduced to picking aphids from it, one by one. Red leaf lettuce, planted early in the spring, was soon devastated by the sun. All these greens—except the basil—are from the Millstone Market. Hester's green peppers have failed to thrive, green beans are doing poorly. Too much heat, too many slugs, Japanese beetles, rabbits, a resident groundhog; too much rain, not enough rain. Once, Hester had grown asparagus in her garden!—but no longer, she has given up.

Almost, there is a sob in Hester's throat. Zahira stirs herself to say that Hester might just have to buy most of her groceries at the Millstone Market like everyone else, a lighthearted remark she thinks, not meant to be sarcastic, but Hester says grimly, "Yes. And how expensive groceries are."

Meghan sends Zahira a bemused/warning glance—*Girl! No irony please.*

To involve Ilya in the conversation Meghan says flirtatiously, he's a biologist, he understands that "garden pests" have to eat like everyone else, every kind of "parasite" and "predator" has a place in "the great scheme of things"—yes?—but Ilya merely grimaces, isn't going to be humored even by an attractive younger woman with blond-streaked hair and an exuberant bust.

Zahira has been thinking about the Picasso painting—*Night Fishing at Antibes.* Led through the Grebs' house by Hester she'd glanced about in anticipation of seeing something she couldn't have named, realizing now it was the painting, the framed print in Ilya's office, of which she has not thought in years; though possibly, in the Institute Woods in the night, staring down into the dark-rippling stream below the bridge, a dim memory of *night fishing* had beckoned to her, not fully within her range of vision.

Night fishing! Gripping the rope railing tight.

Casually Zahira inquires if the print—*Night Fishing at Antibes*—the Picasso painting—is still in Ilya's office at the Institute?—even as she speaks realizing that of course Ilya has retired, he no longer has an office at the Institute.

Ilya leans closer to Zahira as if straining to hear. Staring at Zahira's moving mouth.

Hester says, "The ugly poster! I made Ilya throw it out when he moved his office back home."

"It's a reproduction of a painting, a print—a high-quality MoMA print. It isn't a poster."

Zahira speaks carefully, politely. Zahira is not going to be rude to Ilya Greb's philistine wife in her own house.

"I hate Picasso. Those leering centaurs."

"Satyrs . . ."

"I *hate* him."

Hester's frothy-white hair resembles a cocoon, quivering with indignation about her wrinkled-prune little face.

Meghan glances at Zahira, baffled, bemused. No idea why this sudden outburst, what on earth did Zahira say to unleash it?

Zahira signals to Meghan, *she* has no idea.

Ilya seems confused, he hasn't heard Zahira's query clearly but doesn't want to ask her to repeat it.

Hester has warned her guests that Ilya tires easily, he'd been awake at six that morning excited about seeing them, he will need his afternoon nap early today, so maybe—(both women are thinking)—they should prepare to leave?

But Ilya seems energized. He does not want his attractive young(er) guests to leave just yet.

Ilya has pushed aside his bowl of cold cucumber soup, he has taken only a bite or two of a slice of banana bread. He has eaten most of the salad he'd prepared himself. Iced tea seems to have stimulated him, he brings up the subject of a new appointment at the Institute, the Greb Professorship (as it is called), in his honor; he'd had no part in choosing this person, he tells his listeners, and he is deeply unhappy about it as (it seems) he is deeply unhappy about the recent election to the National Academy of Sciences of several biologists whose work is "over-rated."

"Too much 'diversity.' Not enough 'merit.'"

Zahira murmurs something vague in response. Tells Ilya that she's sure Herman would feel the same way.

Meghan says, in a harsher flirtatious tone, "Well! It took the Institute thirty-two years from its founding to appoint its first woman scholar, and she had to be the most brilliant person in her field."

"All that has been exaggerated," Hester says, "—please do not bring up *that.*"

"A biblical scholar, wasn't she? I don't remember her name . . ."

"Ilya was not of that generation! Ilya had nothing to do with appointments, he never has."

"That is true, I know. I do know that, Ilya."

Meghan, seeing that Ilya seems to have become agitated, quickly defers to him.

In his wheelchair, sitting very straight, Ilya tells them that speculating about the past, as people do, continually, as they have been doing, is a kind of *time travel*—"And time travel is junk science."

Zahira knows that if there is one thing one must not discuss with a scientist it is *time travel;* yet, Meghan makes an effort to engage with Ilya on the subject, asking the kinds of questions a bright middle-school student might ask to impress her teacher.

Ilya, usually so polite, interrupts Meghan to speak of Einstein, the famous pronouncement, the nonsensical pronouncement, that *time does not exist;* when Einstein certainly knew that *in fact there is only time: the hourglass that runs in one direction only.*

Excitedly Ilya says: "We would trade all our prizes for the simplest thing—more years in the laboratory. If we could return to our 'young selves.' If we could return to the beginning. When we were working so hard, it was all that mattered—the work; by the time the prizes come, it is already too late."

Zahira is feeling somewhat hurt, sidelined; Ilya Greb seems to have forgotten that he is in love with her, or ever was. It is *working so hard* of which he speaks wistfully.

If ever you have a change of heart, I am here.

Hester has been clearing the table, seemingly not listening. Or, Hester has heard this lament before and has no intention of taking it seriously.

Meghan leaps up to help Hester, unforgivably abandoning Zahira who dreads being left alone with Ilya Greb.

"There's a secret here," Ilya says, leaning conspiratorially forward, fixing Zahira with his damp myopic gaze, "—*she* will not respect."

"What—what is the secret, Ilya?"

"An open secret."

Ilya opens his hands, holds the palms out before him; both his hands are shaking.

"What I really—really—want is to die."

Zahira isn't sure that she has heard clearly. She has been smiling inanely.

"You could help me, you know. Today." He clutches at her hand. "Dear Za-hir-a."

Fortunately, Hester and Meghan are returning with a bowl of fresh-cut fruit—(pineapple, strawberries, bananas, kiwi fruit)—small bowls, and cutlery. The strong sharp smell of pineapple makes Zahira's nostrils pinch. As the women chatter brightly, Zahira quickly withdraws her hand from Ilya's. Sending a signal of great need to Meghan, that they might leave soon, but gaily smiling, Meghan doesn't seem to notice.

Ilya has rammed his wheelchair as close to the glass-topped table as he can. He is baring his teeth in a mirthless smile, he might be Buster Keaton in a pantomime of silent anguish.

"My secret is—(I know that you ladies like to ferret out secrets among your friends)—that I really *really* want to die, and *she won't let me.*"

Hester laughs, startled. Her mouth moves convulsively.

"Oh—that again. What has he been telling you?"

Hester ignores Ilya, briskly spooning fruit salad into bowls. Meghan steadies the large bowl for her, Zahira is looking fixedly at their deft hands. A large beautiful engraved silver spoon, just slightly tarnished, from a set of old silverware.

Hester asks if Ilya has been complaining to them, the children don't come to visit? The grandchildren?

"How can anyone blame them, if he criticizes them? Quizzes them? What does it matter to anyone if the grandchildren have no idea how many 'light-years' it is to the sun, or how many billions of years is the age of the earth, or trillions of years the age of the galaxy, or what *is* the galaxy?"

Ilya says that *is not* the subject.

Ilya tells Hester why doesn't she go back into the kitchen and rinse the damn dishes, that's all she really wants to do, put them in the dishwasher, clean up the mess, it's what she really wants to do. *He* is talking seriously.

"Seriously?—*you*?"

Ilya laughs. In his wheelchair sitting straight, erect. His

head is quivering just perceptibly, there is a tremor in his neck.

"Yes! Because I really *really* want to bring this charade to an end and I *really* want more than just an audience of gaping ladies, I want *participants.*"

Ilya is speaking almost gaily, as with the expectation that his small audience will laugh in appreciation of his humor as they have often in the past; a droll dry silent-movie humor redolent of Eastern Europe between the wars.

Hester says, a catch in her throat like a rasping hinge, "You are not funny, Ilya," and Ilya says, with a wink at the stunned women guests, "No—but you *are*?" raising his eyebrows like Buster Keaton.

"You say such hateful things, how can you say such hateful things in front of visitors, this is not like you, Ilya," Hester says, more urgently, beginning to cry, "—you say such wounding things which you don't mean," and Ilya says in a bright puckish voice, "If I don't mean them where's the harm? *You* are the one who isn't funny."

It is so shocking, that Ilya Greb of all people would humiliate his caretaker-wife, Zahira is moved to touch Hester's arm to comfort her; but Hester pushes Zahira's hand away—"*You!* Daring to come here of all places."

As if Zahira were somehow to blame for Ilya's strange behavior, and not rather as disturbed as Hester herself.

"Ladies! It is not an accident that you have been invited here. It is the eve of my birthday—my seventy-ninth. You have been invited here for a purpose. I do not want to die alone, it is very lonely to die alone but a ritual, a ceremony, a benediction, is a solace, so, ladies, beautiful ladies, I have poisoned you all—*us.*"

As the women listen speechless, Ilya continues with gusto, quivering in his wheelchair as if he were about to spring out of it, explaining that he'd prepared the salad with special care, mixing into the dressing several *Gastropoda,* infected with the parasite *Angiostrongylus,* whipped in the blender—"A fatal parasite. No cure."

What is *Gastropoda*?—common garden slug. *Angiostrongyliasis*?—parasitic infection of the brain.

"Already you are beginning to feel a giddy sense of—weightlessness? Neurons are breaking like bubbles. Zahira dear—*you* are feeling it, yes?"

Still the women sit stunned not knowing if Ilya is joking, or serious; or, imagining himself serious, yet mistaken. Hester plucks at Ilya's gesticulating hands, to hold them still. Zahira is feeling faint, sick; Meghan's jaw has dropped.

"Why, Ilya—what are you saying?"

"Haven't you been listening? Why are you gaping at me like that?"

Zahira tries to rise, she is feeling weak, panicked. Her brain does feel as if it is swelling—about to burst. Pressure of brain matter against the obdurate skull reminding her of a ghastly interlude in her young married life, altitude sickness in Ecuador, in the more than nine-thousand-feet-high city of Quito, how suddenly a violent headache had felled her, how alarmed Herman had been, but also *annoyed;* for he'd planned for them a trip farther into the Andes, to visit the Incan sites at Machu Picchu, and instead Zahira had to be airlifted to the coast.

Meghan, looking very pale, stammers that she will drive them to the ER, they will need their stomachs pumped . . .

Yet, Ilya is bouncing in his wheelchair, laughing boyishly. He *is* laughing, evidently it is all a joke.

"He isn't serious," Hester cries, "—he's trying to terrify you. He does this. He—he has begun doing this . . ."

Ilya lays a finger along his nose like a sage.

"Ladies! Of course I'm joking. Can't you ladies take a joke! I thought you were *liberated.*"

Zahira is reeling with nausea. On the verge of gagging, vomiting. She manages to get to her feet, pulling at Meghan.

Must leave! Must escape! They are already outdoors, they are wearing their shoes, thank God. They have only to leave the terrace, make their way around the house, through the overgrown grass, to Meghan's car parked at the curb.

Hester calls frantically after them, Ilya is *just joking*.

Hand in hand like frightened schoolgirls the women run. Hearing behind them a faint-repentant cry—*Ladies! Beautiful ladies! Can't take a joke . . .*

At Meghan's car Hester catches up with them, short of breath, pleading—"Please! I am so sorry. Ilya doesn't really mean it—of course. It's just this new medication, it *is* some kind of steroid, to control fibrillation, but it is making him worse. He can't sleep, it's like he's dreaming while he's awake, he sees things that aren't there, he makes these terrible jokes . . ."

Effusively Meghan and Zahira assure the distraught woman that of course they understand, Ilya obviously isn't himself. Hester begs them not to tell anyone and they promise, of course they will not tell anyone, they have always loved Ilya, everyone loves Ilya, it is no one's business, Ilya will be all right.

Hester begs them to return, please will they come back, but both Zahira and Meghan shudder at the possibility, thank you *no*! Hester clutches at them, each in turn. A short woman but *strong,* hugging them hard. It seems to Zahira that Hester has shrunk in just the past hour, child-sized, with protruding collarbones, wrist bones.

"Please—just return for five minutes, to say goodbye. Ilya wants to apologize . . ."

"No, really—we have to leave. Thank you, Hester—"

"—goodbye!"

In Meghan's car they make their desperate escape not

looking back at poor Hester Greb standing forlorn by the roadway.

A block away Meghan brakes the car to a jolting stop. Too agitated to drive! Beside her Zahira is choked with laughter, not a normal laughter but high-pitched, like a small dog's barking; can't catch her breath; Meghan gives Zahira a shake, hard—"Zahira! Stop it! You're being hysterical"—but begins to laugh herself, fit of crazed laughing, drunken women clutching at each other in full view of anyone passing on Feynman Drive.

Can't go home just yet, when the fit passes Zahira asks Meghan to drive out to Hart's Nursery where they select saplings, young lilac and wisteria bushes, rose bushes, flats of coleus, petunias, zinnias, begonias, and dahlias to be delivered and planted around their houses. Zahira insists upon paying the bill. Zahira will not hear of Meghan sharing the bill.

Whenever Meghan's birthday is, Zahira says, this is Meghan's present she is giving her, has to be this very day.

ACKNOWLEDGMENTS

Thanks are due to the editors of the publications in which these stories originally appeared, sometimes in slightly different forms.

"The Frenzy" originally appeared in *The New Yorker*.

"The Fear" originally appeared in *Michigan Quarterly Review.*

"The Bicycle Accident" originally appeared at NewYorker.com.

"The Call" originally appeared in *Fiction.*

"The Return" originally appeared in *Harper's Magazine.*

"The Redwoods" originally appeared in *American Short Fiction.*

"Small Veins" originally appeared in *Fictionable* (UK).

"Refuge" originally appeared in *Zyzzyva.*

ABOUT THE AUTHOR

Joyce Carol Oates is a recipient of a National Humanities Medal awarded by President Barack Obama, the National Book Critics Circle's Ivan Sandrof Lifetime Achievement Award, the National Book Award in Fiction, the Jerusalem Prize, the Prix Femina étranger, and the Cino Del Duca World Prize, and has been a finalist for the Pulitzer Prize multiple times. She has written some of the most enduring fiction of our time, including the bestsellers *Blonde* and *We Were the Mulvaneys.* She is the Roger S. Berlind '52 Distinguished Professor of the Humanities Emerita at Princeton University and a member of the American Academy of Arts and Letters. In 2024 she received the Prix Fitzgerald and the Raymond Chandler Award for lifetime achievement given to a "master of the thriller and noir literary genre."

X: @joycecaroloates

ABOUT THE TYPE

This book was set in Caslon, a typeface first designed in 1722 by William Caslon (1692–1766). Its widespread use by most English printers in the early eighteenth century soon supplanted the Dutch typefaces that had formerly prevailed. The roman is considered a "workhorse" typeface due to its pleasant, open appearance, while the italic is exceedingly decorative.